BLACK ABSINTHE

a novel by

Ted Dewberry

THE IMMERSED WORLD

The first word of Gaslight came when construction crews from the entire eastern seaboard were unavailable for most of that year. Charter planes flew day and night to a mysterious private island in the Caribbean. Barges packed with construction equipment left Florida nearly every day. A cruise ship was rented at a premium to house the workers of a mysterious excavation and construction project. It was through these construction workers that the word came of the creation of a huge underground world that looked like a massive Charles Dickens set.

There was talk of an underground world-class hotel and even more mysterious rooms beneath it all. Who funded this giant project and why they were building an underground Victorian-era London in the Caribbean were mysteries that would remain unsolved for years.

Finally, the construction crews returned home and a similar drain began in the hospitality sector and surprisingly, the theater community. There were no advertisements. No news stories. The entire Gaslight project relied on word of mouth. Customers, it was said, heard that it was an immersive experience like no other on the planet. At this point, immersive theater, with just a handful of projects in New York City, London and a scattering in other theater centers, was a relatively obscure theatrical format. The concept was riding a wave of modest success as patrons entered environments that were unlike any others before. Entire buildings were "sets" with several stories unfolding simultaneously, opening limitless possibilities for exploration. These experiences were limited to an hour or two, but allowed the audience the thrill (or terror) of walking amongst the actors as the play was unfolding. Most of the time, there was a bar waiting at the end of the experience for the audience to decompress. It was a great time for immersive theater because it was so new. The first audiences felt that it was their discovery.

Gaslight changed all that. With a capacity of three thousand audience members and a nine-week span, this experience was expensive both in cash and the commitment of time. A mysterious website sold a ticket, hotel, flight package that could only be paid in cryptocurrency. The confirmation scroll came to the door of each customer by a hooded courier, stamped with a wax seal. The first year of Gaslight was sold out in just one week. Three thousand tickets at one-hundred-and-thirty-thousand dollars in Bitcoin or Ethereum each.

No one outside of the Gaslight audience, actors or creative inner circle knew with certainty how things went during that first performance. Everyone entering the stage had to sign a non-disclosure agreement. The people that dared to reveal anything were sued into oblivion by a cabal of powerful lawyers that somehow proved to the court that the defendants had caused over a billion dollars in damages. After they were through, the leakers were living in cardboard boxes under freeway overpasses. This was a very effective warning to the others and no more leaks emerged.

The mystery this created sparked an unmatched frenzy for the following year's tickets. This time, only five hours passed before it was sold out. These tickets were only sold to individuals and were not transferable, much to the chagrin of scalpers.

By every measure the second year was an even bigger smash, and the same pattern of mass talent hiring came to the actor concentrations of Broadway, LA, and Chicago. New for year two, Gaslight created grants for low-income people to purchase a ticket for two thousand dollars. This was also the year that they instituted the "Master" program. The standout actor from the previous year was crowned THE MASTER, and was effectively the king of the actors, a person that could advocate for every thespian on the island.

Year two was when the famous, but aging movie star Franco Valor accepted the pittance of a paycheck for the chance to take the first Master title as an actor. The man had won awards and could've had almost any movie he wanted, at least as a supporting actor. Instead, he chose to enter the unknown of a new and gigantic immersive theater experience.

It was rumored that Valor entered the first year under a false name and disguise. His natural talent propelled him straight to the coveted role of The Elephant Man. This was the performance that won him the title of The Master. It was only then that he revealed his true identity.

The cult of the Valor personality is what led to the tragic events of year two. Citing his desire to make an actor's utopia out of the production, The Master briefly seized control of Gaslight, using his cult-like followers to murder the stage manager and Playwright before he and his followers were overwhelmed by actors trying to protect the audience. They chased The Master and his followers to the surface where the usurpers vanished in a network of caves. It is rumored that they survive in those caves to this day, worshiping The Master and plotting another coup attempt. After the dust was cleared, three members of the creative team and two audience members were dead. It was a disaster, but everyone agreed that if regular actors didn't stand up to Valor, it would've been a scene straight out of Jonestown.

Those that knew Valor since the old days sensed that he had changed in recent years, becoming self-radicalized to make his dream of an actor's paradise a reality. The problem was that he had no problem using violence to achieve his goal and felt no empathy for those that he victimized and discarded like trash.

The creative team at Gaslight moved fast to repair their image. Part of that process was finding the right actor to play The Elephant Man.

THE RIGHT ACTOR

"Artists, thank you for joining year three of Gaslight!" The Concierge announced through the plane's intercom.
Applause and cheers almost made The Concierge smile.
"Please." The Concierge gestured for the actors to return to order. His olive complexion and piercing eyes commanded Joseph's attention.

Just a few hours before, Joseph sat in a greasy spoon, an out-of-work actor with an oxycodone addiction that was just barely defeated three months before. When he woke from the grip of his problem, he found all of the doors closed to him, his reputation as an actor destroyed by his thirst for pills on the heels of a chronic painful injury sustained in the second Iraq war.

Without work, Joseph's addiction started to telegraph through his despair. He passed by the places where he could score pills, like an asteroid getting closer and closer to the orbit that would burn him up.
It was in this bottom that The Concierge introduced himself, offering the chance of a lifetime. An acting job on Gaslight with a role that was yet to be determined.

Joseph initially turned the job down, skeptical of the man's story;

sure that it was a scam. By the time he changed his mind, the plane was fueled and sitting standby on the tarmac. He made it in, but only just barely. He couldn't believe how fast his life was changing, at last not for the worse.

"There is much to discuss and little time." The Concierge cleared his throat to speak, but was interrupted by the DING of an announcement.

"Ladies and Gentlemen, this is your pilot speaking. Please prepare for immediate departure."

The Concierge reluctantly paused.

"We'll go through everything once we touch down." The Concierge grudgingly took his seat and whispered something to one of his assistants.

To Joseph, The Concierge seemed like more of a drill sergeant than someone tasked with providing comfort.

It seemed that his role was most like a liaison between management and the actors. It also seemed that there were many dressed like him, in refined formal clothes, but he carried himself like he was in charge. The others nodded and bowed to him, like one of those samurai movies where they genuflected incessantly to their shogunate masters.

It was already apparent that the culture of this place was like an International zone. A place with no culture other than the one it made. Measurements were metric, American English was the preferred language, and many of the actors referenced Russian theater. Currency was, except for the mysterious Glass Paris bar, strictly crypto. The Glass Paris was, for reasons that were unclear to Joseph, operated under different rules.

Takeoff was unlike anything Joseph had experienced. They shot up at a speed and angle that seemed more like a fighter jet than a passenger plane.

"Woah!" A woman from behind Joseph screeched as she gripped the back of his seat. This was a military-style takeoff to get to cruising altitude as fast as safely possible.

"Shit man." An actor with "Eddie" on his nametag said through clenched teeth. At that, Joseph felt his ears pop hard.

The jet started to level off to the relief of the more sensitive stomachs in the room. The sound of retching into barf bags was widespread through the cabin.

"Ladies and Gentlemen, we are ascending to a height of 41,000 feet where we will cruise at approximately nine-hundred and fifty kilometers an hour. Our travel time to the island is approximately four hours. Your junior concierges will arrange for drinks and food. Please remain in your seats until I turn off the seatbelt light. We may encounter some turbulence." The Concierge returned the microphone to its cradle and took his seat. A flight attendant had a martini waiting for him.

On cue, the plane became momentarily weightless.

"Whoa." Several passengers called out as if riding a roller coaster. "Ugh." Eddie held his gut, the barf bag clutched in his hand.

Then, as quickly as it started, the roller coaster ride smoothed out into a calm climb.

"Let's continue…" The Concierge stood and displayed a vacuum-sealed bag filled with passports.

"When you signed your contract you waive your right to come home before the season is complete. You give up the right to communicate with the outside world except through a concierge like me. If you break these rules, you will be responsible for the cost of your fare home as well as forfeiture of pay. In return for all these concessions, you'll have an acting experience that will compare to no other on the planet. You will inhabit your part for nine full weeks in total immersion. You will have at your disposal, a brick by brick recreation of ten square kilometers of Victorian London. It is a stage like none other. You are lucky to be here and conversely we are lucky to have you. We will have a weekend of social events, culminating in a soirée at the Tower of London. If you have any questions or concerns see me or one my junior concierges. So, in behalf of the production team of Gaslight…welcome."

A swell of applause from across the plane, then another round of drinks. The Concierge gathered his junior officers together for a whispered conference. Another round came and Joseph politely waved it away. He thought about the previous year and all the traps he had fallen into. In the balance, he was just glad to be alive and still working at the craft that he loved

GASLIGHT AIRFIELD

The wheels thudded against the tarmac shaking Joseph hard. He opened his eyes and saw nothing outside. It was completely black, save for three blinking lights in a shack that appeared to be what passed for an airport on this island.

"That's it?" Eddie asked.

"I think so." Joseph replied, straining his eyes for any details.

Joseph turned and saw something distinctly out of place in a tropical island.

Two ancient gas lamps, about ten feet high burned warmly, illuminating a huge metal etched sign that simply read "GASLIGHT".

"Oh my." Joseph whispered to himself. There was a wide entryway with rows of empty booths, presumably where staff would greet the paying customers. Joseph tried to imagine the luxurious scene as millionaires were gently whisked to the underground city.

Joseph felt the man's hand fall on his shoulder. A chill ran through him.

"Don't worry. Everything will happen as it should." The Concierge gave Joseph a hard squeeze on a shoulder as he nudged him forward. The words stayed with Joseph as he exited the plane, feeling the hot tropical air.

"Happen as it should...for whom?" He wondered as he followed the Concierge down the pit-like entrance surrounded by a steel gate. It took several minutes for the actors to fill the giant elevator floor space. The gaslight lamps threw warm flickering light in every direction, creating an ominous glow that Joseph found menacing.

"Artists, please fill the gated space completely." The last stragglers stepped across the threshold and one of the assistants gave the Concierge a thumbs up.
The Concierge hit a button on a controller and all of the actors let out a collective gasp as the enormous platform pulsated and began to descend.

As they cleared the concrete ceiling leading to the stage below, all they could see was the flickering gaslight lanterns. Tiny as if planted on a gigantic layout for a model train set. Joseph knew that each of those gaslight posts were about two meters high, putting into perspective the enormous scale of this underground stage.

The next sensation that penetrated the darkness was the smell. Dirt, grime, human and animal waste all brought together to enhance the illusion. To further stimulate the senses, the feeling of moisture and the sound of water just below them, presumably the Thames River. Some of the actors gasped as the London Bridge became visible through a thick fog. It seemed so real to the untrained eye. Joseph recognized through wafts of fog that some of the illusion was facilitated by forced perspective. As the bridge stretched across the Thames, it shrank into the size of a garden shed as it reached the other side of the river. There, toward the center of London was the Tower. As the platform finally settled at ground level with a vibrating thud, the Concierge held up his hand for silence.

"The nerve center of the backstage…The London Tower. The Concierge pointed to the ominous edifice. It reminded Joseph of a secret interrogation site he saw in Mosul. "The show is run twenty-four hours a day right there. If you get into trouble, any kind of trouble, that's where you want to go. My office is there. As you leave the platform, my assistants will hand you your curriculum and directions to your living quarters. Stop and see where you will be spending the next nine weeks of your lives. Tonight, and for the next few days, you will be staying at the hotel hidden under Whitechapel. Enjoy your last taste of electric lights and flushing toilets. Enjoy your last taste of the modern world. Tomorrow we will assign your roles. We'll do a small run through to get your juices flowing and then of course our famous welcome soirée. Sleep well, artists. We look forward to seeing what you can do.

The Concierge walked the actors to the well-concealed entrance to the hotel.

"Just note artists, this is the Whitechapel District, home of the Ripper murders." He said in passing.

The cobblestone streets didn't look clean and processed. They were smelly, dirty and the place had a weight to the air that made Joseph sure that the Victorian residents were just about to step into the streets. The irony was that the "residents" of Whitechapel were some of the actors that looked as if they stepped out of an LA tanning salon, far from the pasty skin characteristic of London.

"If you are impressed now…" The Concierge continued. "Just wait until you activate the space."

"Activate the space?" Joseph thought to himself. Butterflies filled his gut as he felt the weight of his responsibility. The set was simply perfection, but it couldn't "activate" without the actors. Without him.

The Concierge stopped in front of a giant wooden gate. He pressed a button on a remote and a great whirring sound reverberated beneath them. It revealed a gas lit brick tunnel that continued on for about fifty meters before making a hard left turn. The Concierge waved the actors forward. As they progressed closer to the left turn, Joseph felt wind buffeting him from every angle. He realized that the smell of Victorian London had instantly evaporated, replaced by a cool neutral smell with a faint trace of lavender.

It was as if he had passed through a force field that separated the past from the present. As the actors passed this barrier there were plenty of raised eyebrows and confused murmurs.

The real change happened at the left turn where a short tunnel led to a massive mahogany lobby with a towering art nouveau statue of a toga-wearing girl. The nouveau design of the lobby was clever in its short time-jump ahead of the Victorian era.

The check-in desk was designed to handle the massive influx of people that would arrive en masse from chartered flights. A peculiar feature near the desk was a circular structure wrapped with iron letters that read "*TELEGRAPH*". In it, several desks with telegraph machines stacked in rows.

"Is that?" Joseph asked Eddie.

"Telegraph office. Yes. No phones here. No Wi-Fi. Just dots and dashes."

"Dots and dashes. Wow." Joseph thought about rich millennials living one day without social media. How would they deal with nine weeks of their connection to the world brought down to a trickle of Morse code?

There was just five desk staff handling the massive line of actors. As they waited to check in, smartly dressed servers emerged with glasses of champagne and hors d'oeuvres. After two glasses of the stuff, the long wait to access the front desk became more tolerable.

"Joseph?" The elegant young lady at the desk asked with a smooth voice.

"That's me."

"Room 332. Enjoy your stay." She handed Joseph a card key and a map to his room. Parting from Eddie, he followed the map to the ornate open frame elevator that only led down. In this hotel, indeed, floors were measured in depth, not in height.

Joseph tried to imagine the lowest floor lying deep below sea level. He wondered how such a thing was constructed on such a remote island. There were rumors about those deep rooms. It was supposedly where sex workers met the guests away from the grit of the active play area. Joseph tried to imagine it, but couldn't.

The tinkle of a bell sounded, indicating that the elevator had descended to the third floor below. The door opened to an elegant hallway with beautiful dragon wallpaper in emerald and gold leaf. A numeric map with arrows guided Joseph to his room. He slid the key in and was greeted by the smell of lavender and fresh linin. There was a four-post bed with a canopy waiting for him at the center of the room. Sheer fabric was draped over the top, adding to the elegance. There was a writing desk, a loveseat and a small mini-bar with nuts chips and drinks. The items in the mini-bar were contained in glass bottles and tins, the contents identified with handwritten labels on ribbons or oval tin tags. "Even the snacks are in character." Joseph mused to himself. There wasn't a single object in the room that was cheap or tacky. Not a single piece of plastic.

As a poor actor, Joseph stuck to motels. Cheap, bug infested rooms with dirty carpets and broken mirrors.

This kind of room was something he had only seen in movies. The lighting system somehow sensed how heavy his eyelids were. The dimmed ever so gradually, lulling him to sleep.

It gradually diminished until there was only a low-purple glow.

Joseph woke to a stream of hot light right into his eyes. Wanting to get more sleep, Joseph turned away from the light, but the illumination never left his face. He opened his eyes and saw the offending light. It was a system of mirrors that moved across the walls. It functioned as an alarm clock, imitating the sunrise. As his blurry eyes refocused, he saw an 8x10 envelope sitting in front of the door.

"I'm up. Please turn off the light." With that, the mirrors flipped over, revealing a black non-reflective surface.

He opened the envelope, careful not to tear it too forcefully.

"Welcome, Artist! Breakfast will be served at 0800 hours at the Queen Victoria Dining Room. Please be prompt, as you will receive your assignment information today.

Sincerely, The Concierge."

The Queen Victoria dining room was a themed four-star restaurant set in the late 1800's London. In contrast to themed restraints at other resorts, the food here was reputed to be world class. Breakfast was a buffet that very serviceable considering the skeleton crew in the kitchen.

There were lots of fresh pastries, eggs and good coffee served out of giant French presses. Sliced papaya was the fruit of choice, probably grown on the surface of the island.

"Sleep well?" Eddie sat across from Joseph who had almost finished eating.

"Yeah. Almost too well. The alarm clock was interesting."

"Well, there's no real sun down here. Some creativity is required to keep your circadian rhythm." Eddie said, smirking.

The overhead lights flashed several times, prompting dozens of actors to abandon their plates and follow a line of concierges directing them to an auditorium across the hall.

"Well." Eddie said, wiping his mouth. "Shall we go see whose skin we'll inhabit for nine weeks?" They left their food, though Joseph refused to leave his half-finished mug of amazing coffee.

"French press." He made a mental note to buy some when they rotated back to the world.

At the auditorium, the Concierge waited for the actors. A projector illuminated the logo of "Gaslight" on the screen behind him.

"Welcome, artists. Let's begin."

The image of a Victorian-era detective, presumably an actor from the previous year, appeared with a name dissolving on screen.

"Inspector Alcott. Role number 231"

The Concierge opened an envelope, revealing a list of names.

"Jeremy Quinn will place Role 231. Please stand and follow one of my assistants."

Actors noted him with polite applause. Joseph thought that Jeremy, early twenties at best, seemed a bit young to play the middle-aged inspector.

Jeremy left the room with the skinny junior concierge.

In an instant, The Concierge returned to the screen. A new part appeared, this time; the illustration was a drawing of what appeared to be a doctor. The name "Doctor Frederick Treves. Role 111" dissolved onscreen.

"Role 111 will go to Eddie Boyle." More polite applause. Joseph slapped Eddie on the back and watched him leave. Joseph was sure he wouldn't see much of his new friend again. They probably would be in the opposite side of the stage, especially if Joseph played someone poor like a garbage man.

"Next role, number three hundred. Joseph Merrick, The Elephant Man."

Gasps from the audience and real applause this time.

On the screen, a drawing of the hooded Elephant Man appeared.

"This role will go to Joseph Bickle." Joseph heard his name and felt the blood rush to his face. He could hardly believe it. He was expecting a minor role, a chimney sweep. Instead, he got possibly the best role in Gaslight, the Elephant Man himself. Someone reached over and shook his hand.

"Get up. They're waiting for you." Someone else said as they gave him a gentle push.

A junior concierge was waiting for him at the hallway door.

"Joseph, please come this way." The man turned and led Joseph to a room that contained a body scanner similar to those in airport security.

"Please go behind the curtain and put your gown on. The gown was a standard hospital gown, open in the back.

"Take off everything." The Concierge noted.'

Walking into the body scanner, Joseph grabbed the back of his robe to keep his ass cheeks from hanging out.

"Mr. Bickle, please come forward." The slight young man waved him over.

"We're going to fit the costume to you. Please don't move during this process.

"OK."

The costume team clipped and fastened the wardrobe. A separate team took on the fitting of the elaborate mask.

Most of it went on with magnets and straps, but part of Joseph's face was a thin layer of silicone with an adhesive. This application would require an elaborate fitting every day. The costumers explained that they tried to keep the materials simple enough for actors to do it themselves. Rarely, a story-specific costume demanded a visit from the wardrobe and makeup team due to its complexity. Obviously, the Elephant Man costume and makeup was one of the more intense packages in the play, leaving the total prep time at around sixty minutes.

They applied the partial face appliance with a spray adhesive to his left eye, cheek and jaw. Joseph felt the remaining mask sections snap in place and then had his first chance to see the result. What he saw in the mirror was an astonishing transformation, especially considering the expedited process. He saw the seams only because he saw the make up being applied. A patron, in an activated environment, would never notice it.

"What do you think?" The Team Lead asked.

"It's amazing. Seriously." Joseph could barely contain his excitement.

"Your cane." The Team Lead handed him a cane that appeared wooden, but was actually cold metal.

"This cane will work with your leg prosthetic to help you walk like Merrick. The Team Lead said.

"Why not use something cheaper?" Joseph said in a puzzled tone.

"Like what?" The Team Lead seemed puzzled.

"Like acting. All that hardware has to be expensive." Joseph said, confused at the need for such expenditure.

"We take some things out of your hands so you can concentrate on the interaction with the audience." The Team Lead said as he slapped Joseph on the back.

"Go ahead. Try it out. Let the others see you."

Joseph took a few steps and, as promised, he had a lurching gait that was completely automated. The normal movement of walking was reigned in by hidden mechanisms in the costume. Joseph was impressed. This contraption, he realized, would help him inhabit the character rather than get in his way.

"Here. Take the cane and go meet your fellow actors." The Team Lead placed it in Joseph's hand. "Right down the hall. Introduce yourself by name. You're lucky enough to have the same first name as your character. That's the only exception to the no-names rule."

The Team Lead gestured to a long dark hallway leading to a distant red velvet room. As Joseph approached it, he felt butterflies as he inhabited the role of the Elephant Man. Joseph saw the outline of his fellow actors, barely visible though the spotlight trained on him.

"Joseph!" The Concierge called out from the dark.

Joseph lumbered onto the stage and was faced with thunderous applause that went on for so long that Joseph felt obligated to bow.

"I am, Joseph Merrick, the Elephant Man." Joseph said in Merrick's impaired voice. No one told him to say it this way. It just seemed the right thing to do.

The applause intensified as they heard Joseph speak in character for the first time.

He felt a hand on his elbow that led him to the back of the stage where Eddie stood as Treves. Joseph thought he looked like something out of a Victorian painting with his formal breasted suit and doctor's briefcase. He was that part.

"I guess we'll be working a lot with each other." Eddie noted, his eyes never leaving the crowd.

"I suppose so." Joseph considered the story of Joseph Merrick and how much Frederick Treves was involved in the last years of his life. He hadn't seen the script yet, but he assumed that he would have the lion's share of his time with this character.

"You going to the party by the London Bridge?" Eddie nudged Joseph whose vision was obscured by his facial appliance.

"Not in this." Joseph gestured to the bulky costume. Thirty minutes in this costume and I'm tired already."

"You know the acting day is twelve-hours long?"

"I'll never make it." Joseph said in all seriousness.

"You'll make it." The Concierge's hard velvet voice made the hair on the back of his neck stand on end.

"You won't believe…how strong you are Joseph." The Concierge put his hand on Joseph's shoulder before vanishing through one of the heavy curtains.

"He's got his eye on you, Joseph Merrick." Eddie noted.

"Is that a good thing or a bad thing?" Joseph asked.

"Remains to be seen." Eddie warned.

In the end, only thirty actors came on the stage. The only costumed actor that received more applause than Joseph was the actor playing Jack the Ripper wearing a luxuriously ominous black and purple overcoat and top hat. This was the de-facto Master. The faded star from Broadway hired after Valor went berserk. Eddie told him that the man wouldn't even talk to the other actors whom he regarded with contempt. Joseph, however, didn't trust the gossip. He wanted to meet the man and make up his own mind.

"You know why they won't let us talk to him?" A rough-looking man of about thirty asked Joseph with a nudge. It's so no one discovers what a shitty actor he's become from all the pills and vino." Joseph got a look at the man and recognized him as The Street Sweeper.

"Get off that stage, Sweep!" The Concierge screamed.

"Blimey. No place up here for a bit player like me." The Street Sweeper joked as he retreated from the stage.

"Lead actors take a bow!" The audience applauded as the actors took their bows. Everyone except for Joseph.

"Joseph, you are a lead actor now. Please bow and acknowledge your position." The Concierge said with a hint of irritation. Joseph followed suit and bowed as far as his suit would allow. During the embarrassing few seconds of praise, Joseph realized that he was now an essential part of Gaslight. It was hard to conceptualize. As a lead, he was guaranteed a sixty-thousand dollar payday at the end of nine weeks. In his entire acting career, he made only about five-thousand dollars in a year, supplementing this pittance with a slew of soul-killing side hustles, like cleaning out toilets. With this one gig, he would be out of debt when he circled back to the world. He hadn't been out of debt for his whole adult life.

Joseph thought of his father who had condemned his pursuit of acting and had eventually cut him off when Joseph refused to change his college major. Desperate to return to theater school, Joseph joined the military for the GI bill and was sent to Iraq. Returning with PTSD, he never did finish school, but he had proven something to his father. Achieving that, Joseph thought it was worth the burden of carrying his battlefield ghosts with him.

In the end, he managed to get a few paying roles and by the time he clawed to a juicy role in a Tennessee Williams play, he rode his second wave of redemption. A redemption that eventually collapsed around him as those ghosts relentlessly hunted for his sanity.

THE WHITECHAPEL SOIRÉE

The Whitechapel soirée began three hours later, giving the lead actors a chance to change and freshen up.

Joseph and Eddie stood in the men's room and checked each other's new suits.

"Here." Eddie shifted Joseph's collar and nodded. "Looks good, man."

Joseph glanced in the mirror and had doubts.

"I look like an idiot."

"Well, let's be idiots together, then." Eddie opened the curtain, leading to the dance floor. He noticed something on Joseph's face and pointed to it.

"Piece of makeup there." Eddie said as he applied some spit to his handkerchief and rubbed off a bit of latex. "Now, you don't have elephant on you." Eddie smiled as gestured for Joseph to follow.

All eyes were on Joseph as he moved across the room, heading towards the bar.

A security guard stopped them, mid-way across the floor.

"Come with me." As Joseph followed the security guard, another man appeared from the darkness and stopped Eddie in his tracks.

"Not you." The man said, his hand grasping Eddie's shoulder.

Joseph was ferried through the crowd where there was an empty seat waiting for him at The Concierge's booth.

The man held court with several of his junior assistants.

"Joseph please, I have a drink I'd like you to try."
The black-robed waiter shuffled to the table with a drink in a highball glass. It was purple with a garnish of lime.
Joseph slid into the booth and was immediately bookended by the Concierge's assistant.
"Try it."
Dutifully, Joseph took a sip. The drink tasted like black licorice that was left out in the sun too long.
"Disgusting." Joseph said, struggling to swallow the concoction.
"Like it?"
"No. Not really." Joseph confessed. The Concierge laughed at his reaction.
"I like you Joseph; you tell it like it is. Please take another sip. It gets better the more you drink it."
"What's in it?" Joseph said as he drank a little more. In fact it DID taste better.
"Absinthe. Real Absinthe. It even has that wormwood that they say will make you crazy." The Concierge said with pride.
"Well. It's certainly interesting."
"Joseph, do you have anything you want to ask me…about your predecessor?" The Concierge leaned in, expecting the questions to come.
"I don't have any questions. Furthermore, I don't care. What happened last year isn't my concern." Joseph said.

"Glad to hear that." The Concierge took a sip of his drink, a green absinthe and handed it to Joseph.

"Try this. The purple stuff is too much for some people."

Joseph took a tiny sip and realized that the Concierge was correct. The green stuff was much more to his liking.

"We studied your file." The Concierge admitted.

"I didn't know I had a file." Joseph said, not enjoying the J. Edgar Hoover quality of the conversation.

"You do. You saw a lot in Iraq, didn't you?"

"I saw a lot in New York City too. So what? You just want to know if I can keep my eye on the donut and not the hole." As Joseph said this, the Concierge started to chuckle.

"Yes, but you said it in a more clever way than I could. I'm just trying to see, now that you have a lead role, where things are. Right here." The Concierge touched his chest.

"Things are…just where they need to be." Joseph said without hesitation.

"I hope you're right." The Concierge responded as an assistant slid out of the booth and gestured for Joseph to leave.

"Don't forget your drink." The Concierge said dismissively as if Joseph was already gone.

Joseph wandered past the dance floor, feeling warmer, partaking of his drink as he made his way to the cobblestone street outside. Only a few actors were there.

"Hey." A woman's voice called out to him.

Joseph turned to find a slight young woman, maybe twenty-five. She waved at Joseph nervously.

"You're the guy playing the Elephant Man?" She asked.

"Yeah." Joseph responded with a voice slurred by absinthe.

"Look up there." The girl gestured to a small rise leading to a foggy alley.

"That's your real home. You should go take a look."

"OK." Joseph turned and started toward the alley.

"I play a Flower Girl." The girl said meekly as she approached Joseph. "Can I hug you?" She said with a cracking voice.

"OK." Joseph said, feeling a bit confused as the girl wrapped her thin arms around his neck. She rubbed his back and her necklace got caught on his shirt. Neither of them noticed that the pendant had broken off when she embraced him.

The Flower Girl retreated, wiping tears from her eyes as she ran back to the party.

Joseph knew that people had visceral reactions to Joseph Merrick's story. The Flower Girl's need for a hug was just a preview of the emotional intensity he was likely to experience from the audiences to come. At least that's how Joseph explained away the strange encounter with the girl selling roses.

Joseph glanced up the hill and stared at the gas streetlights muted within the fog. He started up the incline glancing at the shuttered butcher shops and shoe store waiting to be activated in the coming days.

At the crest of the hill, he saw the carnival nestled in a vacant lot. Gaslight lit the exterior of a large tent as well as several small game booths. Venturing further into the carnival, he saw it. The freak show set inside another tent; The Reptile Boy, the Mutant Queen, the Pygmy Bride, and The Elephant Man.

The painting on the canvas was an almost comical drawing of an elephant's head. Inside the dim tent, the stall that was the stage for Joseph Merrick looked like a pen for an animal. Joseph touched the steel bar that would separate him from the audience.

"Something on your mind?" A woman's voice asked softly.

He thought he was alone.

A woman stood at the open flap of the tent, the gaslight illuminating her fiery red hair.

"I'm Rose, the 'Mutant Queen'. I'll be in the next cubicle." Rose said, pointing to a tiny stage with a thick wooden armchair and an end table with the candelabra. She started to light the candles with box of hand-made matches.

"Do you know how you'll play him?" She asked, approaching Joseph.

"Right now, I'm not sure. It feels so overwhelming."

"There's not much time to get your ducks in a row." The Mutant Queen said as she approached Joseph. "You want some help?"

"I'm not sure yet. Maybe." Joseph didn't know what to make of the MQ and it made him uneasy.

"You think I'm a spy for "The Concierge?" She said sarcastically.

"It doesn't matter what I think. I'm here for the gig. If you're a spy, you're gonna be pretty bored with me."

"You're hiding something." She said, not reacting to Joseph's accusatory expression.

"What makes you say that?" Joseph asked his distrust of the MQ growing.

"I can feel it. You're hiding quite a bit, Joseph. The Playwright doesn't choose just anyone for a lead role. There was something he saw in you."

"I think you're projecting your worries onto me." Joseph said and the Mutant Queen's smile deflated. "You ARE hiding something, baby. Don't worry, your secrets are safe with me. I'm going back to the party in a minute." She nudged Joseph. "Join me for a drink and we'll swap some…secrets."

"OK." Joseph said, fully intending to not return to the stupid party.

The MQ passed the candelabra to Joseph.

"You may want to see where you sleep. Right through that door." She pointed at the ragged door behind the stage, and then left him there alone.

With the Queen gone, there was eerie silence as he approached the door. It creaked as if it was talking.

The flickering candles threw haunting shadows across a dismal living space no larger than a walk-in closet. The bed was matted hay. There was a bucket to urinate and defecate in and a crude hook where the Elephant Man's hood was placed. Joseph put down the candelabra and took the hood down. He pulled it over his head and felt immediately claustrophobic. The small rectangular eye slit was almost impossible to see through. He wondered how he could possibly act in it.

To his surprise, a tiny screen appeared superimposed on the eye slit. He could see a crude thermal image of everything around him. It would take some getting used to, but he felt grateful that the technical team had thought enough of him to give him a tool like this. Lost in thought, he almost missed the thermal signature warning. Someone was standing right behind him.

"Enjoying the set?" The Concierge purred. Joseph pulled the hood off and clutched his chest.

"Please don't do that!"

"Oh. Very sorry Joseph, but you can't blame me for being curious when you leave one of the best soirées in the western hemisphere."

"I felt like wandering around…and being alone."

"Alone for quite a while. It must be something that you're used to, Joseph."

"Your file tell you that?" Joseph snapped. Joseph felt a wave of resentment, yet The Concierge continued pushing.

"Your mother was a single parent to you. She died young. Drug overdose?"

"You know everything. Why ask me?" Joseph said bitterly.

"The Elephant Man lost his parents. I need an actor that can feel that pain. Our casting process is unusual, but we cast based of life similarities, not just talent. It's nine weeks of immersion. Nine weeks! The toll on the human mind can be devastating as your predecessor could tell you."

"You mean, Franco Valor." Joseph asked.

"We prefer simply, 'The Master of Year Two'. Our best actor…" The Concierge said sullenly. "…and our biggest mistake."

"That man was my hero. The most solid actor I ever saw on a stage. If he couldn't pull off this part, how the hell am I supposed to?" Joseph said, remembering seeing Valor playing Mark Antony on Broadway. A performance that was his swan song before he retired, though some say pushed out, from Broadway.

The Concierge pondered this.

"I think because you…Joseph don't have the need for praise built into your acting. Praise was an essential ingredient, and weakness, in his formula. You don't have that weakness. I can see it in you. As the Tibetans say, 'The need for praise is a trap'." As The Concierge said this, Joseph became silent. It was a correct observation. Praise indeed made Joseph uncomfortable. It made him feel dirty.

"The power lust of The Master and his followers nearly brought Gaslight to its knees last year. Despite everything, they don't want to leave. Turns out they're better underground dwellers than the Viet Cong and are dug in…waiting for their moment." The Concierge said with finality that Joseph found unnerving.

"Moment for what?"

"We hope not to find out. We just keep them contained. Quarantined." The Concierge said with a tone of doom.

"Like a virus." Joseph noted.

"Or a wildfire." The Concierge countered as he lifted the curtain to Joseph's entrance, revealing a view straight into the Mutant Queen's tent. She was naked from the waist up, revealing her large firm breasts. She searched through her party clothes.

"She's an interesting woman." The Concierge said with a sarcastic tone.

"Put the curtain down." Joseph admonished him.

"Can we talk another time, Joseph? I'm going out with her for a drink." The Concierge said, telegraphing that there was only one man in this conversation that was getting laid tonight.

"I wasn't the one that needed to talk." Joseph said dismissively as he felt something pinch on his chest. "Hold on." Joseph dug into his shirt pocket and found a gold pendant. He studied it, mutely until The Concierge snatched it out of his hands.

"Eros. The Greek god of love. Why Joseph, I had no idea you partook. The Concierge smiled.

"It's not mine. I didn't partake of anything."

"Then you won't mind if I put it in lost and found." The Concierge slipped it in his trousers as he left Joseph for the Queen's tent.

Joseph was having a tough time containing his dislike for The Concierge. Still, the purposeful antagonizing felt like the man was trying too hard.

What was it all for? Did he want Joseph to abdicate to a lesser role? It's not like he hadn't considered that move just to relieve the immense and increasing pressures brought about by the part of The Elephant Man. The thought of downgrading to a bit part was an attractive thought. The womb of mediocrity was many things, but at least it was warm and predictable.

"Come back to the party. That's not a request." The Concierge said to Joseph before vanishing into the Mutant Queen's tent. Joseph thought about what to say, thought about having an outburst and confronting The Concierge. Instead, he said nothing and made the long walk back to the party.

Back at the soirée, there was already a crowd around the new Master. Joseph thought it resembled one of those forced and uncomfortable meet and greets during press junkets. The actress playing Queen Victoria was there, but Joseph couldn't see her through the crush of bodies.

Soon, a crowd was gathered around Joseph. There were already preprinted photos of Joseph as The Elephant Man, complete with a short biography of Joseph on the back. His fellow actors approached him as if he were a rock star.

"Please, can you make the autograph out to Sarah?" A peppy young actress probably just out of high school bounced nervously as she approached Joseph.

She thrust the photo and silver pen into his hand, a black and white image of Joseph as the Elephant Man taken during the wardrobe fitting. He signed the photo and handed it back to Sarah. She gave him her card. On it, her name "Cat, the barkeep' (at the 12 Bells)". "Come and find me at work. I'll buy you a drink." She said, batting her eyes.

The Twelve Bells was rumored to be a rowdy place both in history and in its incarnation at "Gaslight". What followed were several such invitations by both men and women and two couples. He was certain that one or two of his admirers were sex workers. Under normal circumstances, these people were all out of his league. These were not normal circumstances.

"Why do they find the Elephant Man so attractive?" The Concierge said as he slid into Joseph's personal space. "…He is a misshapen freak, but everyone that plays him gets more ass than a toilet seat." The Concierge jibed again with a tone that rang of fake antagonism.
"Ahh…endless distractions. I'm sure that'll help me be the best I can be?" Joseph muttered.
"Ah, chastity, I should've known that about you." The Concierge said with a wicked grin.
"It's called discipline. Commitment. I just want to do him justice." Joseph said, showing the Concierge the photo.
"That I am sure about, Joseph. That I am sure about." The Concierge said in a gentle voice that marked a shift in tone. This

gave Joseph hope that the man would trust him a little and stop busting his balls.

"Good night. We expect great things from you." The Concierge said as he started to leave.

Joseph continued to sign autographs, slightly confused at the behavior of The Concierge. Finally a waiter came by his table with an aquavit cocktail that he knocked back too quickly.

"You're so brave…" They said again and again. "…After what happened last year….blah…blah…blah."

He heard variations on that all night. He tried to be gracious, but found the only relief from the stupid questions was more aquavit cocktails.

The next morning, Joseph woke in his suite and was not alone. The strong hand of a tall and muscular butler shook him with restraint.

"Sir, it is time to get up. Would you like coffee before your shower?" The butler asked with real concern.

"What do you think I should do?" Joseph asked.

"Coffee then shower." The butler replied.

"OK."

The coffee was remarkable. There was a baguette with butter and fig jam.

It was an amazing breakfast. The shower treatment was equally impressive. The butler helped wash his hair. Dried him off. Helped his get dressed in his street clothes.

"Please, can I ask your name?" Joseph asked the butler.

"Tif is my name. My only name. I am here to serve the actors." Tif said in a regal tone that added weight to his presence. "I'm here to serve you." Tif reassured.

"With everything that has happened, I've forgotten the itinerary." Joseph mentioned, hoping Tif would enlighten him.

"You meet with the Playwright and work out your scenes. I can't say more because I am simply not in the loop, sir."

"I understand." Joseph said, wondering what stories Tif could share with him.

The actors at Gaslight were outnumbered three-to-one by support staff. People like Tif, people like the bartenders, the electricians, the medics, the hotel staff and the hidden sex workers in the sub-basement.

"Time to go, sir." Tif said in a gentle voice.

In the lobby it was easy to find the ballroom where the all-cast meeting was about to start. Actors rallied around the entryway and most of the seats were filled. The mood was that of hung-over joviality.

Joseph saw Eddie who stood and waved to him, pointing to a chair that he saved. As he stepped down the row, Joseph felt hands patting his shoulders and a couple of pinches on his ass.
"Sit down before they start tearing your clothes off." Eddie laughed.

The Concierge took the stage and was greeted with polite applause. "Thank you for coming so early. I know the Twelve Bells' drinks pack quite a punch." A smattering of laughter followed this comment. "Let's get on with the show here. For those of you wondering who wrote your scripts, he is a true genius who has literally had to create dozens of storylines that all combine to make the Gaslight experience. Hundreds and hundreds of script pages created by The Playwright. If it were possible to replay the nine weeks of this production over and over, it would take ten years to experience all of the storylines. This is a work of love, talent and endurance. Ladies and gentlemen…the Playwright." The Concierge gestured backstage and quickly moved into the shadows.

The Playwright was a tall, pudgy man of perhaps thirty. He wore a Goth robe that covered his overweight frame like a mumu. The audience was more generous than they were with The Concierge, giving the man a standing ovation that The Playwright tolerated for a few seconds before waving everyone back to their seats.

"Please. There's a lot to discuss." He said, chiding with a knowing smile.

The applause petered out and everyone took their seats as The Playwright waited patiently for them to settle.

"Welcome to year three of Gaslight!" The Playwright said like a proclamation. Cheers and whoops slipped out from the audience. "For those of you returning, welcome home. For those of you who are new here…I can only say that I envy you. You see I cannot experience Gaslight the way you will. The creative team has directed every cobblestone in this place, every sound effect, every whiff of fog so that you, the actors can do your jobs in an immersive environment unlike any other on planet Earth. Now it's your turn to complete to circle, as you inhabit your role. Coming around to you is your character packet. I want you to take the rest of the day and study it.

Men and women wearing dark-hooded robes drove carts filled with packets down the aisle. Joseph watched the hooded figure pass a huge pile to the actor at the end of his row. There were dozens of thin packets, one thick one and one that resembled a goddam unabridged dictionary. It wasn't hard to guess which one was his.

"Veteran actors will help you if you have any questions. The Concierge and his team will be consulting with each of you to make sure you have all the information you need to get started with your character. Don't worry if you don't get everything right away. The more complex characters especially will take time." The Playwright's face grew sullen and the audience felt it coming. He was about to talk about year two, a dark subject that permeated everything at Gaslight with a sense of a wound just barely closed. "I cannot fill the original Playwright's shoes, but I will do my best. A moment of silence everyone." The Playwright bowed his head and all conversations stopped. The only sounds were the noises of imitated factories and the humming sound of electric pumps sending water throughout Gaslight.

"Thank you." The Playwright concluded. "Enjoy your day. I will see you bright and early right here tomorrow." With that, the Playwright exited the stage to more applause. Many of the actors left immediately, clutching their packet under their arm. Others stayed in their seats and ripped them open.

Joseph's packet detailed the life of Joseph Merrick from the time of his birth until his death at age 27. One of the most complete documentations of the life of The Elephant Man was the memoir of Frederick Treves. There were differing accounts about how TEM ended up working at a freak show. Most concluded that his mother who could no longer care for him abandoned him at a London workhouse. Another account detailed his mother's death, leaving Joseph Merrick at the mercy of a stepmother who took the first opportunity to be rid of the deformed boy. The best that The Playwright and Joseph could do was to digest all of this information and make a choice that would serve the story. From the start, Gaslight never pretended to be historically accurate. That would be best left to a living history society. Ironically, the inaccuracies needed to heighten the drama made the story seem more realistic.

"Joseph. We've been reading for hours. Let's go home." Eddie said, nudging him.

"I've got a short run-through before bed. Freaks only." Joseph smiled.

"Now? Everybody's going out tonight." Eddie said, recognizing the extra work heaped on Joseph.'

"Is that all you think about. This isn't a frat house we're in, good doctor. It's fucking Gaslight." Joseph was joking, but there was a hint of truth to his jibe.

"Go on. You're screwing up the bell curve for everyone. Go on." Eddie waved Joseph away with a twisted grin before he hit the trail to the Twelve Bells.

On the walk to the freak show, Joseph came across the Chimney Sweep studying his packet that amounted to one page. He imagined that the man would probably have a much better time than he. The Sweep could loaf most of the day, only interacting with the audience when he had to. He probably had a hovel he could return to with a fifth of whiskey and drink himself into oblivion until the morning bell. Repeat that for nine weeks and come home with ten thousand dollars. Not a bad gig.

"Hey mate." The Chimney Sweep slurred in a boozy Aussie accent.

"Take a look at my homework." Joseph displayed the heavy stack of papers and the Sweep laughed.

"Put it all in the bin and come to the Twelve Bells. None of that shit will matter once we're under way." The Sweep noted, lighting a fresh cigarette. "All that goes out the window."

"I'm sorry, but this is a school night." Joseph waved his promising suggestion away.

"They all say a variation of that on their first year…you'll learn mate, you'll learn." The Chimney Sweep said as he slid his one-page packet into a barrel fire, and then tapped his skull with his thick finger.

"Committed to memory." He noted.

When Joseph got to the freak show, each freak was already in place along with their managers. The Bearded Lady, The Lizard Man, the creatures with partially formed twins growing out of their buttocks. No Mutant Queen. Interestingly, her marquee had been removed and replaced with Siamese Twins Chu and Au.

"Allo" A thirty-something man greeted Joseph as his manager, The Carny.

"Hello, I'm…" Joseph started.

"I know who you are. Get behind that curtain, mate and do as I tell ya, when I tell ya. Yer late!" The Carny snapped. Joseph glanced at him in disbelief at his rudeness, but went behind the curtain anyway.

Moments after this, projections of audience members (presumably from previous years) appeared in a freak show tent.

"The Elephant Man!" The Carny called for Joseph who rushed to put his cloak on so he wouldn't emerge in street clothes. Joseph flung the tent flap open and limped to the stage.

"Show them, lad." The Carny commanded him.

Somehow, when Joseph removed his cloak, the entirety of the illusion took hold. The layers of misshapen flesh were projected onto his skin seamlessly.

"The monstrous Elephant Man!" The Carny presented Joseph's disturbing visage to an audience of terrified holograms. They winced at seeing Joseph for the first time. One woman even vomited at his sight.

"Bloody disgusting!" The hologram of the woman screamed as she threw a cabbage that seemed so realistic that Joseph flinched when it went through him harmlessly.

The hologram faded to darkness. The scene was over.

"Ah, it's time for a pint, mate." The Carny noted as a purple light flashed in the sky noting the end of the rehearsal. "Sorry I was so choppy to ya. I just needed to be in character a bit."

"I understand." Joseph said, shrugging it off. "I've never rehearsed against a hologram before, never had holographic makeup before."

"It's pretty lifelike, ain't it?" The Carny said.

"Yeah."

"It helps me to see the faces and the reactions, even if it were fakery."

The three bars at Gaslight were the hotel bar, the Twelve Bells and a rarely mentioned place called The Glass Paris. Joseph was already tiring of the rowdy Twelve Bells and dreaded the prospect of drinking at the modern and unnamed hotel bar.

"Should we get a drink at The Glass Paris?" Joseph asked and it was as if he had farted at the dinner table.

"You nuts? We get free drinks at Twelve Bells. Good drinks. Glass Paris charges US dollars and only has Absinthe." It was obvious that The Carny didn't like or didn't understand Absinthe. It was, historically, the drink of choice for French artists and writers of the Victorian era.

"Why do they charge when the others are free?"

"To keep the riff raff out, I guess. Let's hit the Bells." The Carny said.

They got their pints and started drinking. Before long, The Carny started talking about his life in Australia.

"Retired from the Aussie military ten years ago...Third Batallion, RAR. Got bored. Tried acting on a whim. Here I am."

"Third Battalion? I ran into a few of you boys in Mosul." The beer had loosened Joseph's lips. He usually never shared information about his tours in Iraq, not even to other veterans.

"I was in Mosul, mate." Vicker's voice got sullen and quiet. Obviously uncomfortable. "It's where I got this."

The Carny removed the majority of his forearm and let it plop onto the table. This left Joseph speechless as he didn't even notice that The Carny had prosthesis.

After a long pause and a few more sips of beer, Joseph forced a smile.

"You know what they say...'Good soldier, bad civilian'." The Carny said, triggering something in himself. He became figitey, like a tweaker.

"Let's talk about something else, OK?" Joseph said, trying to calm an agitated Carny.

"Yeah mate, excellent suggestion. Get another pint, will ya?" The Carny said in the low and sad tone that Joseph recognized instantly as the "I just don't want to talk about it" voice common to battle-hardened veterans. He went and fetched two pints. When he returned, The Carny was gone.

Joseph took a seat and went to work on the pint. As he finished it and started on the one intended for The Carny, he started feeling good again.

"Hello, Joseph." A voice purred. It belonged to an older woman wearing a violet dress and a black fur. She took a seat.

"I don't want…" Joseph started to say that he didn't want company, but the woman interrupted."

"My name is Missy and I have an opportunity for you."

"You mean like a multi-level marketing opportunity?" Joseph replied sarcastically.

"Just listen and stop being difficult. I'm trying to give you an opportunity to make money." The purring voice was replaced by the shrill tone of a school marm.

"Did anyone tell you that some characters are…coveted by a certain clientele? The Elephant Man is one of those characters." She said.

"Are you suggesting what I think you're suggesting?"

"You want to make double? Come and see me. Customers will pay handsomely." Missy slid her card to Joseph. It only had her name and her address just above the butcher shop.

"Send me a telegram any time." Missy's voice purred again as she slinked away into the darkness. Joseph pocketed the card and hailed down a waiter for another beer.

A few of the actors rose from their seats and started for outside. Joseph didn't think much of it until he heard the distinct smacks that only came from a fist hitting against flesh. With his new pint in hand, Joseph followed the crowd where it was circled around two men fighting. One of them was The Carny. The other was the

Chimney Sweep.

They pounded each other to the applause of the audience of peers.
Joseph knew that The Carny was playing with the Chimney Sweep
who fought sloppy. Carny was just waiting for his chance to
knock his block off.

Sure enough, the opportunity came. Carny hit the Chimney Sweep
with a brutal punch that made an audible POP as he fractured his
opponent's jaw. Teeth rattled on the cobblestone and the Chimney
Sweep went down.

At that moment, two members of the security force broke through
the crowd and prevented The Carny from kicking his opponent
who was already unconscious when he hit the ground.

"Stop! Stop!" They screamed at Carny who almost escaped their
grip. Joseph was sure that if he got loose, he would kill the
Chimney Sweep dead.

They sprayed his eyes with pepper spray. This did nothing to calm
Carny, but it blinded him long enough for them to taze him clean.

There was a collective sigh of disappointment that the fight had
ended. He took one look at the Chimney Sweep's shattered jaw
and realized that one more hit from Carny might've killed the man.
Without structure, the jawmeat hung limply, revealing the teeth at
an impossible angle.

"Call a medic!" One of the guards cried to a nearby junior
concierge.

Word trickled in later that both men had been taken back to the states in an emergency flight. The Chimney Sweep had his jaw rebuilt with one of his ribs.

Neither man was allowed to return. Joseph was sad as he liked both of them.

The following day, Joseph had an abbreviated makeup session before the Playwright arrived with his entourage that included the Lighting Director, the Assistant to the Playwright, the Stage Manager and the Concierge.

He snapped his fingers and an assistant arrived with a folding chair placed directly in front of Joseph's stage.

Until then, Joseph had been acting to holograms. Those were unceremoniously paused and gradually went dark.

Joseph watched The Playwright nervously from behind his hood. They made eye contact and it was too late to hide.

"Please, go on, Joseph. Just do what you were doing with the hologram." The Playwright said, gesturing to Joseph.

A new actor had already replaced Carny. The new man was doughy and smiled a lot.

"Hello mate." The doughy man said to Joseph.

"I'm waiting on you." Joseph replied, wondering why they hadn't started already.

The Carny began...

"Ladies and Gentlemen, ten years ago, I saw something on the street that looked like a lump of meat lying in the gutter. When that lump moved and stretched its hand out to me, begging for a coin, I knew that I had to share it with the world. Abandoned by his mother, who was rumored to be impregnated by a witch's secret bestiality ritual. This poor wretch paid the price for his mother's dark pleasures. The innocent child, now a man...THE ELEPHANT MAN."

An assistant yanked off Joseph's hood unceremoniously. Joseph couldn't see himself, but the reaction of the entourage said it all. The Playwright sat stone-faced, but some of the entourage gasped, some applauded, some cried, and some walked away, unable to watch as the Carny whipped Joseph with a razor strop to motivate him to walk in circles on the stage.

Though it looked brutal, the padding in Joseph's suit absorbed all of the impact. The beating continued, culminating in the Carny pushing Joseph to the edge of the stage.

"Come and shake hands with the Elephant Man. Come!" The Carny called to the audience. He grasped Joseph's deformed right hand and hung it over the stage. Thrown out like that, it looked like a flipper from a gruesome deep-sea fish.

"Say 'allo to the gentleman!" The Carny spat to Joseph.

The Playwright rose from his chair and took the paddle-like

appendage in his hand.

"Well done." The Playwright said as he released Joseph's hand. As the Playwright turned, the Carny's club came down on the flipper with a cracking sound. This actually hurt, even through the padding.

Looking at the Playwright's entourage, several of them had covered their eyes, unable to watch the cruelty onstage.

The Playwright moved on to the other freak show acts as Joseph felt hands underneath him lifting him to his feet.

"Sorry about that mate." The boss said apologetically.

"Yeah, you may want to tone that down a little." Joseph replied, showing him the broken prosthetic.

"I was in the moment, you know man." The Carny smirked.

Once backstage, Joseph peeled off his arm piece to reveal a green bruise forming under the skin of his wrist.

"Someone need first aid?" A medic, a tiny girl about twenty-five appeared from the backstage door. She had a small kit on her.

"Joseph's wrist, The Carny got a little crazy with the stick." A junior concierge noted.

"I thought he was padded better than that." The Carny called from the stage.

"It's fine." Joseph waved the medic off. She took hold of his hand, inspecting a broken blood vessel.

She crushed a small bag of what appeared to be blue sand. It instantly turned frosty. She took Joseph's free hand and directed him to press the cold pack on his bruise.

"I'll put in an urgent report. The suit is designed to absorb that blow. We'll have wardrobe look at it. In the meantime, keep a cold pack on it and omit the hit from the performance, understood?" The medic ordered.

Joseph nodded as the Carny emerged from his dressing room wearing sweats and a t-shirt.

"See. Not my fault." He muttered.

The medic lingered, watching Joseph's bruised arm in motion as he talked to the Carny. There was something about the bruise she didn't like.

"I'm going to take you back to medical for an x-ray." She advised Joseph.

"Is that really...?"

"...Yes. Sometimes it looks fine on the surface, but it could be cracked. As she snapped her fingers, two stagehands appeared and started to remove the heavy costume. The makeup unhooked at the magnet points, leaving a few patches of applied cosmetics in the transition spots. A stagehand gave Joseph a wet cloth to remove the residual.

"Can I get a transport from freak show to medical please? Code green." The medic spoke into her headpiece.

"Transport sent. ETA five minutes." A woman's voice crackled through the small speaker.

"I could just walk." Joseph told the medic who was already ignoring him.

The medical facility was hidden inside what appeared to be a blacksmith shop. There was a small advertisement pasted on the window. "Overflow Medical Services" in woodblock letters. Joseph supposed it was a backup clinic there to handle a mass trauma event or a disease outbreak. The front third of the building opened up like a garage door, revealing an ER style triage that any small hospital would be envious of.

"Sit in the waiting room and we'll take you back in a minute." The medic told Joseph before leaving to consult a nurse, who glanced at Joseph several times, nodding. Surprisingly, Joseph was not alone in the waiting room. The Master, dressed in Jack the Ripper garb, was there his hand supporting a bloody gauze bandage against his forehead.

"Hey. Joseph." The Ripper called from across the waiting room. Joseph was startled that this man, an actor in a stratum even above the leads, would address him. Joseph assumed he would have an entourage or something, even in the ER.

"When you're done playing with the nurses, let's you and me go up top and see actors in their natural habitat."
"Thanks, but I don't think I'm allowed." Joseph said, trying to

hint as his discomfort.

"Bullshit." The Ripper said. "You're allowed if I say you're allowed."

As Joseph started to rise, the Ripper laughed.

"Curiosity will get the better of you eventually. You know where to find me. I love the Twelve Bells. The VIP lounge. I'll get you a day pass." The Ripper said haughtily.

"Ah. A hairline fracture across the ulna." The nurse said, glancing at a digital 3d image of the injury."

Joseph could see the break that ran lengthwise down the bone.

"As break's go, it's not too bad, but you'll need to wear a brace. No more direct hits on the arm. The stage master will get on the costume issue right away. Will you be able to continue?"

"It's fine. I broke my foot during Hamlet and I finished the run. I'll live."

A doctor entered the room, nodded at the nurse's assessment and left the room without looking at Joseph.

A few minutes later, a technician emerged with a cast that seemed to be 3-D printed. He slid the cast over Joseph's arm and snapped it in place. It fit perfectly.

"Amazing." Joseph noted.

"This kinda cast is illegal in the US." The technician noted. "Silly, huh?"

"Yeah, silly." Joseph said, his thoughts turned back to the next day's work.

"Look. We're not supposed to socialize with the actors, but…"
The nurse wrote a hotel number on his cast.
Go to that address tomorrow night. The civilian crew…firefighters, medical, etcetera are having a party."
"I'm pretty busy with rehearsals. I'll just have to see."
"OK." The nurse realized that he probably wasn't coming. That knowledge aside, the nurse still watched Joseph longingly as he disappeared into the streets of Whitechapel.

With Joseph's accident, he had the whole night off, even though he wanted to continue working.
"Go rest up." The stage manager ordered. "Be fresh tomorrow."

Joseph roamed the streets, feeling the extra weight each time he swung his arm. He felt the printed cast and smiled. Gaslight was like a country that made its own rules. There was no need for FDA approval and years of study. If they wanted to do something, they just did it. It occurred to him that that was a knife that could cut both ways.

The imitation sun was setting and the golden hour bathed Gaslight with in orange. As he walked another block, the sun dipped below the horizon and the gaslight lanterns clicked rhythmically as the automated systems turned the streetlights on. The gas flames lit with little "whooshes" here and there, then several at once. As the last of them lit, Joseph realized that he had walked straight to The Glass Paris.

It was just ahead through a thin, dark alley that was too thin to accommodate a taxi. There were no customers sitting on the patio outside, though the candles on the five wrought iron tables were lit and ready for the customers.

Joseph approached the bar and saw two signs in the window. One read

"US Dollars ONLY". The other read "REHEARSAL WEEK HOURS 6pm-10pm".

Joseph entered and wondered if it was really open. Behind the bar were several jars filled with absinthe. While most were green, there were some blue and purple selections. At the top, accessible only by a ladder was a carafe of black absinthe.

Joseph sat at a tiny table, set up for two. A waiter dressed in the French style of that period emerged from behind the curtain and whispered something to the barkeep before approaching Joseph.

"We open in ten minutes, but you are welcome to wait." The waiter said with a soft voice.

"I've never been to a bar like this."

"We hear that a lot, sir." The waiter said confidently. "I'm sorry to mention this, but are you prepared to pay in US dollars?"

Joseph dug in his pocket and produced a small wad of twenties that he got at the ATM at Kennedy airport.

"Loaded for bear." Joseph said, grinning.

"Each drink is twenty dollars. May I suggest the standard absinthe cocktail?"

"You may. Let's do that." Joseph nodded.

"Very well, sir. A wise choice."

The waiter returned to the bar and leaned over to the wizard-like character making the drinks. The man glanced at Joseph and nodded wordlessly. He took an absinthe glass and a slotted spoon, pouring the emerald beverage from an ornate bottle.

He placed the half-completed drink under a crystal water decanter. He placed a slotted spoon with a rectangular cube of sugar on the lip of the glass and set the water to a slow drip. Slowly, hypnotically, the drink began to change into a glowing aquamarine color.

Joseph was so fascinated by this alchemy that he didn't notice that he was no longer the only customer. Two women in street clothes were emptying their pockets, separated their American dollars from a red currency that Joseph didn't recognize.

The waiter brought the finished drink to Joseph.

"I hope you like it sir."

Joseph smiled and the waiter left him to attend to the two ladies outside.

He took a deep breath and had his first ever sip of the drink nicknamed "The Green Farie".

It was unlike anything he had ever tasted, different from the drink given to him by The Concierge in the same way a packet of powdered soup was different from the home made equivalent. His taste buds struggled to place the flavors. The overwhelming taste was anise of course, but there were other notes that he couldn't identify. He still couldn't figure out if he liked it.

As Joseph got halfway through the drink, he decided not to order another one. It wasn't really needed as it was so strong.

"Will you be having another?" The waiter said, holding a tray with two purple drinks on it.

"Not tonight."

"Very well." The waiter left to serve the women who seemed overjoyed. Joseph guessed that they frequented the bar last year and had craved the drinks since the end of last season. They clinked their glasses and cheered for the moment before they took a sip.

"I'll just leave this here, sir. Please come again."

"Thank you." Joseph replied, glancing at the bill that had some scribbled French word and a circled "$20". There was no tax here of course. There was no real government to impose tax. Joseph left an extra five for a tip and closed the leather server book. He finished the rest of his drink and brushed past the two ladies who recognized him instantly.

"Good night, Joseph." The brunette said, already slurring from half a drink.

"Good night ladies." He didn't recognize them.

Walking home, he passed the Twelve Bells and thought about going in. He watched it for a while and decided that he'd rather avoid a hangover on the first full rehearsal day. He had that huge packet of material to finish reading. He decided to head back to his straw bed.

Joseph sat alone in the freak show studying his packet. There was a photograph of The Elephant Man as a child of five. The bulbous masses on his head were much smaller, mere lumps. It was probably the last time that he appeared somewhat normal. Joseph imagined what he would've looked like if his diseases had not progressed. He could've had a relatively normal life. Maybe had a family of his own.

The tragedy of The Elephant Man's downward spiral made Joseph think about his addiction issues. Joseph's pill addiction had brought him to a rock bottom where his body had turned against him. He had a choice to get help and return to a relatively normal life. Mr. Merrick had no such option. His body turned against him from the very start.

"Thought I'd find you in here." The Team Lead of the makeup department peeked into Joseph's tent and gestured to the row of empty hovels next door.

"You're the only one staying here. The others found more comfortable accommodations."

"I want to be here." Joseph said trying his best to sound patient.

"Well that's what it takes to be a lead actor, I suppose." The Team Lead replied.

"What can I do for you?" Joseph said with a forced smile.

"A full body cast. We have to do it for a scene. Do you have a couple of hours tomorrow?

"I'm pretty busy all day.

"Good. Shall we say four thirty?" The Team Lead took out a tablet from his pocket.

"Right before dinner then?" Joseph nodded.

No, four-thirty in the morning". The Team Lead smirked.

"Well, I'll try to make it as painless as possible." The Team lead entered the appointment into his tablet and slipped it into his jacket.

Joseph's mind flashed back to a field hospital in Mosul. He sat looking down at his left hand fully split in two by shrapnel, exposing the tendons and muscle all the way down to his wrist. A young medic injected him with Dilaudid and studied the wound.

"We'll try to make this as painless as possible." The medic told him as Joseph felt the Dilauded made its warm path through his veins.

Joseph opened his eyes and saw his left hand lying palm up in front of his face. Aside from the zigzag of the pink scar, the hand looked and functioned normally. "That stupid kid did a great job." Joseph thought to himself.

"Are you OK Joe?" The Team Lead watched Joseph with concern. "I'm just tired. Look, I'll see you tomorrow, OK?"

"OK." The Team Lead left Joseph alone with his pile of homework. Indeed no one came back to sleep in the freak show that night. Joseph had it all to himself until an ALARM woke him up at three AM according to his wind-up Big Ben.

"Joseph, are you hurt?" A voice cried out to him as lights blinded him from three different directions.

"Who? What happened?" Joseph groaned as he rolled out of bed. "Proximity alarm! We have an intruder." The room rustled with shadowy figures. Joseph made out at least three.

The flashlights turned to the far wall in Joseph's bedroom. Several stair treads jutted from the wall. Part of the ceiling was torn off and the stair treads continued far into the darkness.

"The Tread Setter." One of the security guards whispered to the other.

They turned the overhead lights on and Joseph saw a set of tiny footprints leading to and from the stair treads, leading right to the edge of his bed.

"What's going on?" Joseph felt a rush of real fear.

"The Surface Dwellers. Sometimes they break into Gaslight. It looks like one of them took enough interest in you to do a recon mission." The security guard said. This chilled Joseph. The idea of someone standing over him in his sleep was completely unnerving.

Suddenly something fell from a hole in the ceiling, something about 3x5 inches. It tumbled end over end, finally landing flat on the floor. One of the guards picked up the paper and turned it over. It was an instant photo of Joseph sleeping.

"Well, I'm definitely not going to sleep now." Joseph stood up and put his street clothes on.

"We'll find where they broke in and seal it up tight. By the time you head home tonight, it should all be done." The Concierge said over the intercom.

"They could've cut my throat if they wanted."

"But they didn't. They just wanted a look at you, Joseph. We'll make sure we keep a closer eye on you. If you want to stay in the hotel, I can set you up with a room."

"No. Just fix the roof please."

"No problem. Why don't you freshen up and have some breakfast and we'll get you going with your day." With this, the Concierge clicked off the intercom.

"OK. Good luck with this mess." Joseph gathered his shower

supplies and slipped on his sandals to make the early walk to the communal shower.

"Sorry for the inconvenience." One guard said while the other called the emergency maintenance department.

Joseph's early morning walk through the streets of Gaslight was peaceful. Even the drunk actors passed out in the gutter seemed to add to the ambiance.

Two girls passed him, holding one of their friends who had thrown up all over her shirt. They staggered a few steps, stopped, took a few more steps, stopped.

Joseph, by contrast felt great, despite his interrupted sleep.

There was a crude, hand-written sign pointed to the makeup department where the communal shower was. He followed it and found the building closed. With nothing open, he just decided to stand at the door and wait.

He closed his eyes and listened to the sounds of Whitechapel. Crickets, an owl, the horn of a distant boat. It was amazing to him that all of these sounds were set on a digital timer in a machine in the Tower of London.

He opened his eyes and saw someone approaching him pushing a cart through the cobblestone streets. Finally, he got close enough for Joseph to see his face. It was Tif, the butler.

"Good Morning, sir." Tif said cordially.

"Hello, Mr. Tif. What are you doing here?"

"Why, I'm bringing you breakfast, sir." With that, Tif lifted a
dome off the plate, a plume of steam rose so vividly that Joseph
had to take a step back.

As it cleared, Joseph saw a plate with sausage, beans and a couple
of eggs. There was a pot of coffee and some cream and sugar
along with some orange juice.

"Irish breakfast, sir."

"You are going to spoil me, Tif."

"I hope so sir." Tif said with a grin as he poured the coffee. When
he had the breakfast fully presented, Tif pulled something flat from
the bottom shelf of the cart. With one movement, he pulled it
apart, revealing a stool. He placed it there in front of the breakfast
cart so Joseph could eat in comfort.

"Please, sit sir."

"You got style, Tif. You really do." Joseph felt overwhelmed and
a bit emotional. He couldn't believe how good they were to him.
"Eventually...I will have to swallow the semen." Joseph thought,
suspicious of the kindness. "Not today, but it's just a matter of
when."

Joseph dug into the blood sausage and eggs and French Press
coffee. He asked Tif a few questions about his life as he ate.
Turned out that Tif was from a long line of butlers, dating back to
the real Victorian times.

He told the family yarn that he was most proud of that his
grandfather was a guest butler for Winston Churchill for two

weeks. He recounted Churchill's drinking routine that included scotch in the morning with breakfast.

Just as Joseph finished eating, the entire makeup team was headed to open the facility.

As he stood and prepared to greet the team, Tif stealthily packed up the cart and was already heading back to the commissary. He felt bad at not saying "good-bye".

"Joseph. You're here early!"

"They're doing some work at my condo and I can't get my beauty sleep." Joseph joked.

"Yeah, that really sucks. I'd complain to your HOA." The Team Lead replied with a deadpan that Joseph found amusing.

The antique doors flung open to the makeup studio. The Elephant Man prosthetics and mask hung in a corner, taking up twice as much real estate as any other character.

"I saw that you got breakfast." The Team Lead noted with a hint of jealousy in his voice.

"I did. It was amazing."

"I had a piece of dry toast. Not all of us can have Tif at our service." The Team Lead said, joking, but not joking. "Take off your clothes and stand on this platform. You'll be here a while."

"Everything?" Joseph asked with slight irritation.

"I'm afraid so. No other way to get your full body cast." The Team Lead gestured for an assistant to bring the plaster. "You don't have a Prince Albert, do you?"

"A what?" Joseph had no idea what the Team Lead was talking

about.

"Genital piercings. You don't have any of those, right?"

"Ummm. No." Joseph wondered why a piercing like that would be called a Prince Albert.

 "Sorry we don't have privacy curtains, but you might as well get used to people staring at your junk. It's about the only part of the Elephant Man that wasn't deformed." The Team Lead said as he applied cold plaster on Joseph's leg. An assistant brought a metal appliance filled with goo.

"Open for me." The young woman shoved the foul tasting junk into Joseph's mouth and held his jaw shut.

"That's a sport!" She said before pulling it out with a hallow sucking sound.

"That was horrible!" He said as the woman chuckled.

"Let's hope this dental mold is good or we'll have to do it again. The mouth prosthetic needs to be perfect to work right." She said, holding the goo like a laboratory specimen.

"Let's hope." Joseph said, spitting flecks of the grey plastery goo on the floor.

The platform supported Joseph with two pads under his armpits that were strapped to him with a belt. He found the standing restraint so comfortable that his eyelids got very heavy.

"Go ahead and take a nap.." The Team Lead said in a jealous tone. "You're not going anywhere anyway."

"OK…sounds good to me." Joseph was already nodding off. For some reason the rhythmic brushing of plaster against his body worked better than any sleeping pill.

"Glad someone gets to sleep." The Team Lead muttered to his assistant.

As Joseph was resting, a crowd had gathered to watch the makeup process. As the body cast dried, Joseph's face was painstakingly applied, dwarfing the temporary makeup package that he wore the previous day. This headpiece and makeup combination looked real, even close up right down to the moles and necrosis on the skin.

"Joseph...Joseph!" The Team lead nudged Joseph awake. "I have to get you up. We have to take the cast off. That'd be a rude awakening, especially below the southern border if you know what I mean.

"Oh shit." Joseph muttered as the entire makeup team took hold of the body cast as the Team Lead tapped the outer rim of it with a hammer and chisel.

After covering the entire rim of the cast with hits, the Team Lead cracked the cast open like an egg. As they separated Joseph from the cast, he began to feel an uncomfortable tugging that quickly became sudden jolts of pain.

"My balls!" Joseph screamed out, panicked. The crowd gasped and winced as the Team Lead kneeled down to study the situation. Indeed, Joseph's balls were stretched out dramatically as if they were trying to make a rapid escape from the rest of his body.

"Ohhhhh." The Team Lead said as the crowd gathered to see and wince at Joseph's situation.

"What the hell?" Joseph screamed out.

"Hold on. I'll fix it!" The Team Lead took a ball peen hammer from his tool kit and reached into the mold, carefully pointing the tool away from Joseph's stretched out balls.

"Be careful!" Joseph screamed

"Just don't move." The Team Lead said.

"Yeah, trust me, don't move!" Eddie said from somewhere in the crowd. Joseph was too panicked to be angry at being watched by thirty people.

The Team Lead brought the hammer down once. It came so close that Joseph could feel the wind from the hammer strike on his ball hair. Immediately there was relief as the plaster that held him prisoner was broken free, leaving a softball-sized hole in the cast.

"Thank God!" Joseph cried, feeling a dull ache between his legs.

"We'll make a patch on the broken part. Worst part's over, mate." The Team Lead grinned.

"I'm glad you're happy." Joseph said with more than a hint of irritation.

Tif entered the room with a robe that he draped over Joseph as he was pulled free of the body cast.

"Sir. We have a room set up for you to relax in while they complete the mold."

As Tif led Joseph away, audience of peers burst out in applause. Joseph kept his head down, embarrassed at the attention.

Tif brought Joseph to a gold elevator with a placard for the spa.

He pushed the lower button on the panel and the doors closed gently.

"Hungry, sir?"

"That breakfast filled me up. I'll be fine." Tif nodded politely at this. "Tif, what are we doing in the spa?"

"The isolation chamber. It'll help you relax before the next session."

Joseph knew what an isolation chamber was from an article he read. It was a dark pool filled with salt water. A person basically floats in the darkness with total lack of stimuli. Sometimes one can reach a state of complete relaxation. Once in a while though, someone can hallucinate as the brain searches for stimuli that it can't find.

"Couldn't I just get a massage?"

"Just try it once. I think you'll like it." Tif said with a confident air. "Everyone does it here."

Tif didn't bring a bathing suit for Joseph as he would have the chamber to himself.

He asked Joseph to shower then he opened the chamber door. Glancing inside, it was not what Joseph expected. The dim LED lights illuminated a pool much larger that Joseph imagined. It seemed to stretch on forever.

"Why is it this big?" Joseph said, stepping into the warm salt water.

"Usually people isolate socially." Tiff winked. I'll come back in two hours. Call on the intercom if you need anything. Relax and enjoy your session."

Tif closed the hatch behind Joseph and the lights dimmed further. The landing that Joseph stood on was about a meter deep. He took a step further and immediately slipped into a much deeper section. He sank for a moment, and then bobbed up like a buoy in the salt water.

As he floated there, the only sound he heard was a distant "drip drip drip" of condensation falling back into the pool. He only felt sensation when he touched his own skin. His vision was slowly being choked off by the steadily dimming light until it was completely black in the chamber.

His eyes seemed so desperate for stimuli that they made their own light flashes that sparked in his peripheral vision. His ears sounded like the inside of a seashell.

Joseph tried to relax and let his body float. For the first few minutes, he completely surrendered to the experience. After a while though, he began to realize that he had floated away from the chamber door. This of course was where the intercom was if he needed to get out early. He reached around him, hoping to find a wall so he could make his way back, but it was hopeless. He had probably drifted toward the center of the tank.

Just as he realized that he was away from the edges and disoriented, Joseph began to feel movement in the water. A disturbance that could be someone or something getting into the chamber with him.

"Hello?" He said, hearing his own voice come back to him in an echo. A few more drips fell from the ceiling as his voice reverberated.

"Hello?!" Joseph yelled as he felt more tiny seismic waves coming from beneath the water. For a moment, he thought he felt something brush against his feet. Not the edge of the pool, but something alive in the form of three finger-like objects that brushed up against his ankle.

Joseph screamed. He panicked, hyperventilating. If there was someone in the chamber with him, he was helpless. He thought of the stair treads in his room. He wondered if, when finally they did come, they would find another set of those stairs leading through another hole in the ceiling of the salty chamber.

"Joseph." A voice echoed through the chamber. Joseph's heart pounded and he could see the pulses of blood in his eyes. Suddenly a rude light blinded him, forcing Joseph to cover his blinded retinas.

"Are you all right? I heard the scream over the intercom." It was Tif, much to Joseph's relief. "No, I'm not. Get me out!" Joseph screamed. As the lights turned on, Joseph realized that he was just mere feet from the southern wall of the chamber. He grabbed onto its edge and shimmied back to the door.

"Next time, just book a fucking massage, OK." Joseph said."

"Very well, sir." Tif reached out his hand and helped Joseph from the chamber. "They should be ready for you soon, sir." Tif handed Joseph a shower kit bag and a fresh towel. Joseph glanced down at his body and saw a thick layer of salt crystals drying on his skin that resembled psoriasis.

"I can't wait to get this off me. Disgusting."

Joseph sighed as he stepped into the hot shower. He lathered and rinsed three times before he felt free of the sensation of tiny crystalline rocks in every crevasse of his skin.

Tif gave Joseph a snack of cheese and watercress sandwiches that he gobbled down like a starving man.

When Joseph entered the makeup department, they were waiting for him.

"Good timing. The full body makeup is ready." The Team Lead held up the skin of The Elephant Man. It had been carefully painted, the tumors looked especially realistic.

"Damn. That's amazing." Joseph felt the skin's texture and shook his head. It feels so real.

"A special formula that we made. It radiates heat from your skin to the surface of the appliance. If someone touches you, they can feel your body heat. "

"That's just tits." Joseph smiled, the memories of the isolation chamber fading.

"You ready to try it on?" The Team Lead grinned.

When the makeup department was done fitting the skin and dental prosthesis on Joseph, he glanced down at the skin and was grotesquely fascinated by the hundreds of cysts that riddled the

Elephant Man's skin. Folds upon folds of excess flesh trapped putrid odors. He tried to imagine the real man, Joseph Merrick, trapped in the hell of his own body. It was hard to conceptualize that kind of suffering day in and day out.

"Dental appliance." The Team Lead picked up the device with gloved hands.

"I don't want it." Joseph protested.

"I get it. OK, open up." The Team Lead slid in the appliance that simulated the bony growths inside the Elephant Man's mouth. Joseph likened the feeling to having a tennis ball glued to the inside his palate. Speaking was extremely restricted, but with some effort, he could make himself understood.

"My friend, I think we're done." The Team Lead turned a full-length mirror to Joseph.

The sight was jaw dropping. Joseph was transformed completely, head to toe.

He stared at his unclothed body in disbelief.

Polite applause broke the silence. The actors and makeup artists clapped and some of them cried at the enormity of the metamorphosis. A couple of the makeup crew came up to The Team Lead and shook his hand.

The Flower Girl stood from her makeup chair and approached Joseph. She took his hand, causing Joseph to flinch. With the makeup narrowing his field of vision, he didn't see her coming. It was a strange moment with Joseph standing on a two-foot platform. Her head was nearly level to his exposed genitals. He did his best to put his mind somewhere, anywhere other than where he was. He realized that he was breathing harder as the thought of her there excited him. He thought of puppies and flowers. Apple pies and hot tea on a cold day. Anything to avoid getting an erection.

"I'm so proud of you Joseph." The Flower Girl said with total sincerity.

"Thank you." She kissed his hand and returned to her chair.

"She likes you, man." The Team Lead stated the obvious.

"Can I get a robe or something?" Joseph glanced around the room for something, anything to cover himself. Luckily, the Team Lead passed him a beautiful terry cloth robe from the Biltmore Hotel.

"That's better." Joseph instantly felt twenty degrees warmer.

"Hi mate." Eddie slid up to Joseph, looking very much like a Victorian doctor in his vested suit, complete with pocket watch.

"I just read my script." He unfolded a partial script with about five pages stapled together.

"It's medical gibberish. I don't think it even means anything." Eddie said, waving the pages in front of Joseph's eyes.

"You don't have to understand everything. Just enough to convince the audience." Joseph repeated the words of one of his old teachers.

A bell rang.

"Clear the makeup. Take your places." The Stage Manager's voice called over the intercom.

Eddie helped Joseph through the hallway and into the classroom at the London Hospital. Joseph took the platform and Eddie secured his place by the chalkboard.

The classroom was not set up with seats, but rather with rows that only encouraged brief observation before shuttling out to the hospital wards.

"Let me see your script." Joseph reached for Eddie's script and scanned it.

"Sometimes, nonsense is the only thing that makes sense." Eddie noted.

"Stand by." The announcement came over hidden speakers. Joseph glanced around the set and was deeply impressed. The classroom seemed to be lifted from old drawings and photographs. There wasn't a flaw in the set, only the adaptation to "walk-through" observation rather than the bench seats that would've been in the real room of that period.

Joseph slid in his dental appliance. It was a bitch to get in, but he felt it slide into the slot custom made for his molars.

"Thirty seconds." At that announcement, the hologram of audience at the classroom door appeared frozen and dim.

"And...action."

The hologram started to play. The audience filed in to the observation deck.

"This unfortunate creature was working at a freak show in Whitechapel when I found him. He says that his name is Joseph Merrick." Eddie circled Joseph with a wooden pointer. He touched it to Joseph's forehead. "The especially virile growth on his right forehead has sealed his right eye shut and has extended to his mouth to render his speech almost impossible to understand. Will you say your full name, Joseph?" This was off script and took Joseph by surprise.

"My name…is Joseph Merrick." He said through his dental appliance. He sounded like he was speaking through a wad of cotton.

Some of the audience members in the projection had presumably not seen the freak show and perhaps didn't even know who the Elephant Man was. They shielded their eyes, some cried, some pointed at Joseph's exposed groin and laughed. Joseph realized that this was probably the video from the previous year. He wondered if the video was taken of the previous Master, Franco Valor.

"Notice the flaps of excess skin all across his body, especially in his torso."

Once of the audience holograms fainted as Eddie lifted one of the flaps to reveal a ghastly yeast infection. A reaction from a year ago.

"With the poor hygiene of the carnival, the skin is susceptible to infections and putrid odor if Mr. Merrick isn't bathed on a regular basis which he unfortunately he is not."

A few of the audience members covered their faces, presumably at the smell that the olfactory team would pump through the classroom. The smell must have been horrific as most of the audience headed for the exit. One person threw up on the floor, prompting an even more rushed exodus.

"Hold." The Stage Manager came over the speaker and the projection froze.

"You boys want a sample of what they're smelling?"

"No. Not really." Eddie replied.

A hiss was followed by an odor that could only be described as garbage, covering vomit, covering feces turned by a blender. Eddie immediately gagged, righted himself, and then leaned over to throw up the entire contents of his stomach.

"We'll need to get you acclimated to the smell." The Stage Manager said flatly.

"No one could get used to that." Eddie said as he spit out residual vomit.

"You'd be surprised what you can get used to here." The Stage Manager chuckled. "That smell is great to clear the room as you can tell."

"I saw that." Eddie noted.

"OK. Shake it off and we'll start again. Joseph, you doing OK?" Joseph gave the unseen Stage Manager a thumbs up rather than trying to speak.

This room was very clever, Joseph thought to himself. It sets up the Elephant Man story after the initial freak show scenes with this shocking examination of the fully nude EM, rancid smells and all. This got people in and out quickly as a new group would be waiting in the lobby. This was one of the few scenes that stressed a time limit because so many people wanted to see it. Nothing else but immersive theater could do this.

"That was the LOWEST setting, my friends."

"How high does it go?" Eddie asked.

"We crank it until everyone leaves the room. One year this guy wouldn't leave and we found out he had no sense of smell at all because of a brain injury. The two actors had to go to the infirmary."

"That's dedication." Joseph commented.

"We added that question to the audience screening process. That can't happen again."

Eddie grinned sarcastically.

"They thought of everything, didn't they?" Eddie noted.

"Treves and Merrick, report to the second floor infirmary." A new voice commanded.

"Where?" Joseph asked through his dental appliance.

"Second floor. Come on and see where you'll sleep for eight of the nine weeks."

The voice responded.

Eddie led the way up a steep staircase. Getting to the second floor with the movement restriction of the costume was quite a chore and Joseph found himself winded and grasping the side rail as he negotiated the last few stairs. The LED work lights were still on, thank goodness. In less than a week, they would have to use gaslight and imitation candles.

Eddie pointed to a cluttered office just off from the stairwell. On it were dozens of charts and Merrick's chart was the only one open.

"The audience can come in my office and look at the charts when I'm not here? A real violation of HIPAA if I do say." Eddie joked. They passed some large rooms with barrack style facilities, typical of a Victorian-era hospital. Finally, they stopped at a closed gate with a sign that read "No Admittance without permission from Dr. Frederick Treves."

Eddie opened the gate leading to a flight of stairs. There, past a final door, a plain wood-paneled room with a single bed, a small nightstand and a chamber pot.

"Well, this is it." Eddie said, gesturing at the humble room.

"Are people really going to be barging in my room in the middle of the night?" Joseph said, noting that there was no lock on his door.

"There's a guard that's supposed to shoo night visitors away, but…someone always gets through."

This alarmed Joseph. How could he sleep not knowing when he would have nocturnal visitation? They didn't really expect him to sleep in full makeup, did they?

"What do they want, the night audience?" Joseph asked, dreading the answer.

"Hard to say. Some just want to watch you sleep. Some want more." Eddie's dour tone indicated that some might come with their freak fetishes. It made Joseph feel ill.

"My God." Joseph said, his voice filled with dread.

"They have a simplified costume for sleeping. It's so dark in your room, the audience would never know the difference."

"I'm never gonna be able to sleep now." Joseph said, trying to estimate all the nightly interruptions.

"Come on. They're waiting for us to start." Eddie gestured to the stairway leading downstairs.

Downstairs in the bathing room, Joseph glanced at his script. There were no lines for him, just general actions.

"TEM (The Elephant Man) is examined by Treves and two nurses to attempt to address his filthy condition. The doctor and nurses were waiting for him in the bathing room." The text explained.

"Merrick, take off the robe and lie on the exam table." The Stage Manager barked through a hidden speaker.

"I'm naked a lot in this." Joseph said, half-protesting.

"Cry me a river. Get ready." The Stage Manager yelled.

The nurses purposely avoided looking at the naked Joseph. The hologram started with the nearest audience member being far down the hallway.

"And...begin." The SM commanded.

As the rehearsal began, that awful necrosis smell was pumped into the room just as it was in the classroom. Joseph felt his head spin.

"Nurse, I want you to prepare a bath for this man." Eddie started.

"Doctor." The nurse said as she finally turned to look at Joseph.

"Dr. Treves, you ask the impossible. He is not only horribly deformed, but absolutely filthy."

"I can't treat any patient who is this dirty. Nurses, are you willing to bathe him?"

With that, the younger nurse clasped her hand over her face and vomited right through her fingers. She fled the room.

At this moment, the hologram of the first audience members appeared. They seemed instantly revolted, but stayed in the room anyway, covering their faces in a vain attempt to mask the smell.

"Well. It's up to you. Will you help me?" Eddie asked the remaining nurse.

"Yes. If you do it with me." The nurse replied.

Eddie sighed at this. "Nurse, I have patients."

"You want me to bathe him alone? I'm afraid not, doctor." The nurse turned to Joseph, holding a handkerchief over her face.

"What a horrible creature. Could he possibly know how wretched he is?"

"Yes…in fact I do." Joseph said bitterly through his dental appliance.

The nurse took a step back, horrified and embarrassed.

"He can understand me?"

"Yes…I can." Joseph said as best he could.

"I thought he was a vegetable." The nurse seethed.

"Will you help him, nurse? He needs you." Treves said, imploring.

"Very well." The nurse left the room to get supplies.

"Are you angry at her? Eddie asked.

"Her reaction. Nothing new to me." Joseph said in a barely understandable voice.

"Can you walk to the bath with me?" Treves pointed toward the bathing area.

Joseph held out his left hand to Eddie who helped him for the first few steps.

As Joseph walked in his lumbering gait, he saw that the hologram audience had grown drastically to fifty or so audience members

"Thank you." The stage manager said, ending the scene and turning off the hologram. "You have five minutes until the bath scene."

One of the stage assistants emerged from a hidden door and drew the bath water, carefully checking the temperature.

"How do you think it's going?" Eddie asked Joseph.

"It's one thing to read about this process, quite another to do it." Joseph admitted.

"Just wait until we have a real audience."

"Elephant Man, get in." The Stage Assistant motioned Joseph into the tub. Joseph wondered about the makeup and how it would fare in the warm water. He realized that it wasn't his place to worry about someone else's job. He had his hands full pulling this role together. He got into the tub and the makeup and prosthetics held firm. He realized that the Gaslight crew had indeed thought of everything.

"Three minutes to audience." The Stage Manager said over the speaker.

"I fucked up that line." Eddie said with a frown.

"Like it said in the manual, just keep acting. Don't break character." Joseph reminded Eddie. "Don't overthink it."

"Story of my life. I overthink everything." Eddie admitted.

"And...GO!"

The scene began with the nurse scrubbing Joseph's back. The scaly psoriasis came off like onion skin. This was intentional to imitate the Elephant Man's skin disorders, but as with the smell, the effect was sickening as flakes of skin floated on the bath water. The audience filed in and their reactions of disgust were immediate as they saw the soup that Merrick had made in the bathtub.

"Mr. Merrick, do you have any living family?" Eddie asked as he took notes.

"I don't know where they are…or if they're alive." Joseph said.

"I see." Eddie noted this.

"Dr. Treves, do I have to go back to the freak show?" Joseph asked with a hint of dread in his voice.

"Do you want to go back?"

With that, Joseph was supposed to cry, but he could only manage a whimpering howl.

"We'll get you healthy, Mr. Merrick. We can talk about it then." Eddie glanced at the nurse and mouthed the words "thank you". The audience faded away and the projector whirred down into standby mode.

"Very Good!" The Stage Manager said over the intercom. "Thank you for a good rehearsal. Special thanks to the makeup team. The playwright is very pleased. We will reconvene tomorrow morning. At 0800 hours."

"What are you doing for the rest of the night, Joseph?" The older nurse asked.

"I'm not sure. I think I might go for a drink."

"You want some company?" The nurse smiled coyly.

"I've had a long day." Joseph said, not wanting to hurt her feelings.

"OK. Another time then." The nurse said, trying to hide her disappointment.

"I'm sorry." Joseph realized that he HAD offended her.

"Whatever." The nurse said as she stormed off, leaving Joseph alone. He looked for his walking stick.

"Eddie?!" He called out, hoping that his friend was still in earshot. Eddie leaned through the door with Joseph's walking stick in his hand.

"Looking for this?" Eddie smiled.

Joseph smiled. "You know I can't walk without that fucking thing. The prosthetics. I'm so sore from them."

Joseph followed Eddie back to the makeup department where the team quickly disassembled TEM headpiece. A young female assistant reached into Joseph's mouth and took the dental appliance. It felt like half of his mouth had been pulled away.

"Oh thank God." Joseph gasped with relief.

"Not your favorite?" She said nodding, cleaning it off with a denture brush.

"It's the worst." Joseph said, still slurring as if he still had the appliance in his mouth.

"I'm going to be in this gear sixteen hours a day?" He asked with dread.

"Pretty much." The assistant admitted.

Another assistant, a young man, brought Joseph a box.

"What's this?"

"A little gift from the Team Lead. Wear it when you go out tonight. He picked it out for you."

"We're still in rehearsals. Why would he give me clothes."

"Because Gaslight is special, mate." The assistant said with pride.

"Even in rehearsals. We can't have our Elephant Man performer running about in jeans and a t-shirt." She said.

"OK." Joseph opened the box. White pants and a purple shirt. A white scarf. White leather shoes with black socks. Finally, there was a black slinky thing that looked like a bikini bottom."

"It's good underwear. Flaunt what you got." The assistant said with a wink.

"Go shower and change. We all want to see you in it." Eddie laughed.

Joseph followed the handwritten signs for the "Communal Shower".

The room was a long hall of showerheads. He took the one in the middle and waited as the hot water took its long journey from the downstairs boiler. When it finally arrived, it instantly filled the narrow corridor with steam. Joseph stepped underneath the water and let out a moan of relief. The hot water felt so good. The adhesive from the appliances washed away with a little scrubbing.

Seldom-used muscles from his previous sedentary life were

screaming from the hard work of ambulating the Elephant Man costume. Joseph could only hope that things would get better as the days progressed. He felt completely out of shape. Physically inadequate for this part. A far cry from his days in the military.

Drying off, he laid out his new clothes. Glancing at the label on the shirt it read "Gaslight Made: Gaslight Island, The Caribbean". He slipped the shirt on and it indeed fit perfectly. The underwear gripped his genitals into a knot that looked impressive but was pretty uncomfortable. The pants were custom tailored and fit like skin on his body.

There was even a small vial of cologne in the box. He sprayed himself twice with a pleasant fruit-like fragrance.

He glanced at himself in the mirror and smiled. He really looked great. It was such a rare moment, for him to feel confident.

"Thank you." Joseph whispered as if the Team Lead could hear him.

When Joseph made his way out to the waiting room, he forgot that Eddie and the others were waiting for him. They greeted him with whistles and catcalls.

"Oh, mate, you are smoking hot!" The Team Lead exclaimed.

One of the makeup assistants couldn't help herself and rushed to adjust Joseph's shirt and scarf placement. She noticed the cologne in his hand and took it to apply more behind his ear.

"You need more of this, sexy animal." She said.

Eddie slapped him on the back. "If you don't get laid tonight, there is something wrong with the world."

He didn't like Eddie's comment. He was thinking of the Flower Girl and would just enjoy having a drink with her. Joseph wondered where she was tonight. He really didn't care about anyone else.

It was seven pm and already dark. As he stepped out of London Hospital, he could see the chaos forming at the Twelve Bells that would no doubt go on until closing time at two am and beyond. He avoided proximity to the bar by cutting through an alley. Somewhere at the edge of the set.

A young boy somehow found Joseph as he was making his shortcut.

"Telegram for you, sir." The boy said, holding out a yellow slip of paper.

"What's this?" Joseph didn't know what to make of it.

"It's a telegram sir. Please read it." The boy thrust the message into Joseph's hand and ran down the street, vanishing around a corner.

"They're watching you…" Is all the telegram said. The sender's name was left blank.

Joseph pocketed the message and headed to Glass Paris anyway.

The tables were mostly empty except for the patio where three actors, ironically bartenders from Twelve Bells, sat smoking cigars and drinking blue Absinthe.

"Slow night. Sit where you want." The server said. Joseph picked the seat and ordered a standard green drink. In a few minutes, the server brought it over.

"Good to see you again, sir." The server said politely.

"In about twenty minutes, please bring another." Joseph asked.

"Certainly, sir. Will you be trying a purple Absinthe for your second drink?"

"No, I'm playing it safe with the training-wheel drinks."

"Very good, sir." The server smiled and returned behind the bar, whispering Joseph's request to the bartender.

In the dark, private table, Joseph sipped his aquamarine drink and waited. To his right, there was a bookshelf just a few inches from him. One of the books, *Alice in Wonderland*, was inching out of its home like a caterpillar. Joseph glanced around. No one was watching him, no one that he could see anyway. He pulled the book from the shelf. Peering at the wall behind the book he saw a small hole drilled into it, about the size of a silver dollar.

"Hello, Joseph." A craggy voice whispered.

"OK." Joseph whispered back.

"Don't talk, just nod yes or no. Understand?"

Joseph nodded.

"HE wants to meet you. The real Elephant Man wants to meet you." The voice promised. "Open the book to page ninety-three.

There you will find it. You will be safely escorted to the surface."
Joseph opened *Alice in Wonderland* to the page and found a hand
drawn map bookmarked between the pages. He pocketed it, took a
sip of Absinthe, then firmly shook his head.

"You will want to talk with him. This is your only chance.
Tomorrow. Be there. Goodbye Joseph." The voice trailed off as
if it were crawling through the walls.

"Do you feel like you've slipped down the rabbit hole?" The
waiter's voice broke the spell. He had the second Absinthe in his
hand.

"What?" Joseph asked, half-stoned from the first drink.

"Do you feel trapped in wonderland?"

Joseph glanced at the book still in his hands.

"I don't know if 'trapped' is the right word." The server studied
Joseph for a moment and nodded.

"I understand." He took the empty glass and replaced it with the
new one that seemed to glow with its own light source.

"Enjoy." With that, the waiter left him. There were no more
stirrings from inside the wall. Joseph drank slowly and quietly,
nursing his Absinthe for another hour. Before leaving, he
discreetly stuck the map down his shirt.

When he staggered out of Glass Paris, Joseph found the edge of the
building where just a few inches separated the Glass Paris from a
non-descript storage building.

He squeezed into the tiny space and found a breach knocked into the brick. Glancing inside, he found the tiny hole where someone had whispered dark offerings. He could see the exact spot where *Alice in Wonderland* was pushed from the bookcase on the other side of the wall. Then, as he almost slipped into the breach he saw them. A row of stair treads affixed to the wall, leading down through a hole in the floor. It was the person that did reconnaissance in his room that night, the ones that the security guards called "The Tread Setter".

"Are you Joseph?" Someone called at him from the street. He peeked from the breach in the building. It was a black-cloaked elderly man that had the garb of a taxi driver.

"Yes?" Joseph emerged from the breach and slithered sideways through the gap between the buildings to get closer to the man.

"I was sent for you. Why don't you come out of there and I'll give you a ride." The taxi-driver opened the coach door and helped the drunken Joseph into the cab. He was so relieved to get a ride home, he didn't question who had sent the cab. When he tried to pay with his credit voucher, the taxi driver refused to accept it.

"Compliments of The Concierge, sir."

"Of course." Joseph said, realizing that it might not have been the greatest idea to take this ride.

"They're watching you." The telegram had said.

At Joseph's hotel room, The Concierge was waiting for him.

"I had Absinthe added to the menu at the hotel bar. You can enjoy it there. Please don't go to the Glass Paris again."

"OK." Joseph said, knowing it would probably be shitty Absinthe without the wormwood.

"That's all you have to say?" The Concierge pressed him.

"Yes." Joseph replied blankly.

"Joseph, I won't lose my Elephant Man just a week before showtime. Last year almost destroyed my career here. I won't let that happen again. That place is...ill omened."

"The Master went to the Glass Paris?" Joseph asked as if completing a prophecy riddle.

"I think you know the answer." The Concierge said grimly.

"How could having a drink or two there make someone incite mutiny? I think the mutiny was already in them." Joseph noted.

"I brought you some dinner. You'll need your strength for tomorrow." The Concierge rose to leave.

"No more surprises from you, Joseph." He said with his back turned.

Joseph said nothing as he watched The Concierge leave.

Rather than dissuading him, The Concierge had compounded his curiosity. What really happened last year? People continued to drop hints, but they were probably too scared to tell the whole story except with cryptic puzzle pieces. The only one with the answers had just invited him to the surface to unlock the mystery. Joseph uncovered the meal brought by The Concierge, a prime rib dinner with mashed potato and root vegetables. By the end of the meal, he had made his decision.

Joseph showered and got ready for his day. He would be back at the London Hospital and would be there for the duration of rehearsals according to the schedule.

In the hotel lobby, there was a huge white board that stretched twenty feet across the entrance to the hotel.

"Reminder: The hotel will close to actors in 4 days. Prepare your living quarters on the stage. You are responsible for this."

Joseph could sense the anxiety in the lobby of the hotel. They had it so good here. Food, parties, comfortable beds. Now the actors would sleep wherever their characters slept. There would be little in the way of creature comforts for the run of the show.

"EM, please report to suite 111." The Stage Manager called out over the speaker system. Joseph wasn't certain he heard the room number correctly and was waiting for the message to repeat. It never did.

"Did anyone hear the room number?" Joseph called out to his fellow actors.

"111" A female voice called out over the distance.

"Thank you."

Suite 111 was on the lobby level. A Junior Concierge, boy fresh out of high school, appeared in the lobby to escort Joseph.

"The Playwright wants you." Was all he said.

Suite 111 was not in the actual hotel, but inside The Tower of London, connected to the hotel by a hidden tunnel. Waiting for them was what appeared to be a sports car. It was an automated shuttle, narrower than a street vehicle, but fast enough to push Joseph back in his seat. At the end of the three-minute white-knuckle ride, the shuttle came to a halt in front of a palatial double door that seemed completely out of place in the tunnel. It was suite 111.

As Joseph entered the suite, he saw the "nerve center", a huge monitor propped up in the living room. As he approached, he saw the name of every character in Gaslight depicted by a colored line that zig-zagged like a volatile tech stock on the board. The chart was marked by time and location as well as the character. It showed where every character was at any moment in the show. Hundreds of characters, including Joseph, were represented by dots in a kaleidoscope of different colors.

"What do you think?" The Playwright slapped Joseph on the back. "How do you read it?"

"Oh, you get used to it." Indeed, the Playwright ran his finger along the list of characters to the Elephant Man. He then ran his hand horizontally along the line.

"You start off at the Freak show and then…to the London Hospital where you stay for the rest of the play. Two locations. I can also see where you are right now. " The Playwright clicked a button on his remote and Joseph was the only actor on the screen, sitting dead center in the Tower of London. The Playwright returned the screen to the "Daily History" of all actors and that's where he saw her. Joseph saw the Flower Girl's history. Her line was all over the place.

"Weekly history." He clicked the remote again and Joseph could see seven days of her movements. It seemed like she slept in a different place every night.

"I called you here because I wanted to make a change and I wondered how you would feel about it."

"You want to know how I feel?" Joseph assumed that he would just order him to change a scene. Why did he need to know how he "felt"?

"Yes. I have a new idea for the Elephant Man. A new storyline that takes you out of the London Hospital at least at night."

Joseph was at once scared and excited. What could The Playwright have in mind?

"Look at the nerve center at Whitechapel. Who do you see nearby?"

Joseph stared at the mess and shrugged in confusion

"I'm not sure. Help me out."

The Playwright took Joseph's finger and helped him follow the timeline. There was a character that always was nearby, within two or three blocks of the hospital. That character was Jack the Ripper.

"Oh my." Joseph was surprised that he didn't catch this before.

"At night, Joseph Merrick searches for Jack the Ripper. Why does he search for the Ripper?"

"I have no idea." Joseph said.

The Playwright snapped his fingers. A middle aged woman appeared on the screen with short red hair and button like eyes approached Joseph in full costume. She was a streetwalker. "Who did the Ripper target?"

"Prostitutes." Joseph responded automatically. It was the Ripper's only target according to all the documentaries he had ever seen.

"Correct. It was all over the newspapers. Now what would bring the Elephant Man out of the comfort of his hospital bed to search for the most dangerous man in London?"

"If someone he loved was being target…" Joseph stopped, mid-sentence, realizing where this was going.

"Elephant Man, meet your mother, Emma, a well-known lady of the night in Whitechapel." The Playwright took a step back and studied Joseph's reaction.

Joseph didn't see this coming. This was not a minor plot point, but a huge detour in the story. Of course, it was a factually false narrative. The Playwright didn't seem to care.

"Joseph, you look like a deer in the headlights."

"I need a drink."

"Waiter, could you get this man bourbon, please?" The Playwright said, snapping his fingers.

"Right away, sir." A waiter replied from across the room.

"Why…such a big change? Why now?" Joseph asked.

"We don't try to be historically perfect. Our job is to pose the 'what if's'. You and the Ripper indeed shared the same space and time historically. That gives us enough flexibility to expand those possibilities."

"Well…"

"What do you think, Joseph? In addition, you would be upgraded from lead actor to Primary actor. In addition to the prestige, you get a pay upgrade…One-hundred and fifty-thousand dollars." Joseph's drink arrived and he took a gulp of it, trying not to lose control of his bowels in front of The Playwright.

"OK. I'm in." Joseph exclaimed. The Playwright slapped Joseph on the back.

"Good deal. Go on to your rehearsal. I'll send the pages along by courier."

Joseph nodded, finished the drink and planted it in the waiter's hand.

Returning back to the hotel, Joseph walked past the dormant telegraph office and the very full hotel bar. No one noticed him until The Playwright began to speak over the intercom.

"I have an announcement. It's quite exciting." The Stage Manager's voice called out over the speaker system.

"The Elephant Man's role has upgraded to PRIMARY." Actors in the lobby gasped and clapped and cheered. The closest comparison Joseph could make to it was a college football game.

"Let's congratulate Joseph on his achievement!" The Stage Manager cried from the club.

People streamed out of the bar, rushing to Joseph. Someone very tall and strong picked Joseph up and threw him on their shoulders. It was mayhem. Almost idolatry. Joseph might have understood this reaction better if he fully understood how high he had risen at Gaslight. Primary actors currently could be counted on one hand. There was Queen Victoria, the Ripper, and now The Elephant Man. That's it.

When they finally set him down, the Flower Girl was there waiting for him. She was crying tears of joy for him and hugged Joseph as he passed, kissing him on the cheek.

Joseph looked into her big eyes and realized that she was doing something to him that he considered impossible after what happened in Iraq. He was falling in love. She had pierced through the concrete layer around his emotional core. He then realized how cold and desolate his life had been as if the veil had been ripped off the mountain of pain he had hidden so well. His vision went blurry and he realized that he had started to cry. He embraced The Flower Girl and in his mind, they were alone in the crush of people.

Above the stage, in a cave of exiled actors, the former Elephant Man, the former Master, heard the news and knew that Joseph would not meet him today. He thought about taking Joseph by force, but decided to wait instead. Joseph's curiosity was quashed for now, but he wouldn't be able to help himself. He would have to know what the Master knew. There were too many gaps in the official story.

The remainder of the day, Joseph was heaped with adoration. Random actors mobbed him, begging him to put in a good word to the Playwright about them. Some asked for autographs. Someone tore a piece of his clothing. A special area in Twelve Bells was roped off for the Primary Actors with its own special entrance. The Concierge encouraged him to spend some time there to be seen by the others. Joseph wasn't excited about going to the Twelve Bells. He had grown a palate for Absinthe and had been itching to try the blue variety.

The Flower Girl didn't stay with him long.
"They need me at rehearsal. I can't wait to tell them about you, Joseph." She said as she hugged him goodbye. She laughed as she pulled out the notes for her character.
"You got that huge stack of homework. Look what they gave me." The Flower Girl laughed. It was probably five pages long.

Joseph walked back to the freak show as the sun went down. The gas streetlights hissed as he passed them on the incline.
He sat at his stage reading pages from the Joseph Merrick file. Joseph didn't know what he was looking for, but hoped he would find some insight into the man he was playing. From all indications, Merrick was far too weak to pose a threat to anyone.

The concept that he could plot revenge felt wrong to Joseph. Aside from his physical infirmary, from all accounts he was intelligent and kind, Leaving Joseph unsure about how to sell the concept of a revenge-driven Merrick to an audience.

The Playwright could write the words, but it was the actor's job to make the audience believe. Joseph wondered if he could pull it off when the time came. The doubts ate at him as they always seemed to.

"TEM, please report to the VIP section at the Twelve Bells right away. TEM, report to the Twelve Bells. Thank you."

Joseph sighed and tucked the papers back into his file. He had hoped to make more of a dent in the Elephant Man file tonight. He didn't want to be paraded around or interrogated by anyone. That said, he didn't want to appear like a prima donna so he sucked it up and changed into his purple shirt, slathered on some of his cologne and started out for the Twelve Bells.

At the bar, a junior concierge saw Joseph and lit up, opening the special entrance that was well camouflaged behind a panel.

"We worried that you weren't gonna make it." The junior said as he led Joseph down a dark corridor to a closed-off area with velvet Victorian furniture. There was a waiter and a bartender serving just three people, Jack the Ripper, the Playwright and Queen Victoria. When the Playwright saw Joseph enter, he stood to greet him. Victoria and the Ripper didn't stand.

"Welcome, Joseph, welcome." The Playwright shook Joseph's hand and led him to the puffy purple fainting couch.

"I'm very excited at the new direction for your character, Joseph. We all are." The Playwright said. Victoria and the Ripper didn't seem nearly as thrilled. The Ripper and defacto Master yawned widely, not even looking at Joseph.

A small crowd of production staff gathered at the entrance to the VIP area, trying to get the Playwright's attention, but would go no further. The Playwright saw this and excused himself, leaving his drink.

"Another life threatening emergency. I'll catch up with you all later." He said in a snarky tone. As he entered the hallway, the Playwright was surrounded and whisked away by his team.

"Hurry up and wait. That's all this place is." Victoria groaned.

Joseph glanced at Victoria who ignored him until she saw that he was about to speak.

"You don't belong here, Thomas." Victoria said coldly.

"Joseph."

"Whatever your name is…" Victoria said, slurring. "…I didn't spend twenty-five years on Broadway to be thrown in with an amateur like you. Go to the common drinking hole down there. Those…those are your people."

Joseph searched for a reaction from the Ripper, but got none. His face was deep in his drink.

"I heard someone wanted to see you tonight." The Ripper said, not looking at him.

Joseph felt a momentary panic, wondering how The Ripper knew about the message and invitation from the real Master. He wondered how The Ripper knew this, then tried to calm himself, realizing that the man was probably talking about The Flower Girl. In any case, he had had enough of the VIP lounge and its odious elitism.

"I think I will drink with the peasants down there." Joseph noted with satisfaction.

"They will appreciate you and shower you with praise." Victoria commented as she gestured to the bartender for another martini.

With that, Joseph made his exit, met at the door by the Junior Concierge.

"Going so soon?" The junior concierge said in an almost panicked tone.

"The air is stale in here." Joseph glanced at Victoria, who was gobbling down another drink.

"But.." The JC asked in a pleading voice.

"I'm going back to the hotel to drink, not to The Glass Paris. Follow if you don't believe me.

The junior silently watched Joseph leave.

Back at the hotel, Joseph perused the liquor store attached to the gift shop. He picked out a nice bottle of wine and gave the clerk his voucher card.

"No charge for Primary Actors, sir."

"What do you mean?"

"Actors at your level can have anything they want, courtesy of the production."

"You mean I can get anything here. Anything I want?"

"One bottle at a time. That is the only rule."

"Joseph slid the bottle back on the shelf and scanned the substantial selection. His eyes perked up as he found the California selections.

"Andrew Murray Syrah 2010...not too shabby. I'll take that one."

"Good choice, sir. It's an excellent wine in its category."

"And a corkscrew, please."

"Of course, sir. Also on the house."

Joseph foresaw a sweet night of solo drinking ahead of him at the freak show.

The clerk wrapped both items and put them in a canvas bag.

Joseph nodded thanks and headed toward the exit when someone approached him. A young man with a yellow hat.

"Telegram for you, sir."

"Telegram?"

"Yes, sir!" The boy smiled, handed the yellow card to Joseph and returned to the kiosk.

"I'm in room 353 waiting for you. -FG" The card said, opening a new range of possibilities for the evening.

With his heart pounding, Joseph clutched the wine bottle as the elevator descended to the third floor.

He opened the door and found The Flower Girl sitting on the bed in silky pajamas. Joseph smiled.

"I brought wine." He said.

Joseph opened the bottle and poured himself a taste. He smelled the cork, then took a sip. It was a beautiful Syrah. He wasn't a regular wine drinker so he couldn't explain why it was so good. It just was.

"Oh. California." The Flower Girl studied the bottle. "I've never been there."

"It's a jewel." Joseph reflected to a trip he took to San Simeon while on leave. It seemed like a lifetime ago.

"Pour me a glass or do I have to beg?" The Flower Girl asked with soft indignation. He poured quickly and handed it to her.

She drank her wine in three gulps, holding the glass out for Joseph to pour her another.

Joseph poured it to the rim and she laughed.

"I'm a skinny girl, you're going to get me hammered." She said in an admonishing tone. "It's OK Joseph, I want to get hammered as long as it's with you."

As she got drunker, Joseph detected a vaguely eastern accent that intrigued him.

"Where did you say you were born?" Joseph asked as The Flower

Girl finished off her glass.

"I didn't…and I won't. I'm going to change now."

"OK." Joseph was puzzled at her secrecy, but decided not to push her for answers, at least yet.

The Flower Girl emerged wearing black lingerie and a fur boa.

"What do you think?" She grinned, her bedroom dimples on full display.

Joseph realized that his mouth was open and he was gawking over her.

He brought his glass to his maw, doing his best to recover his cool.

He sat on the chair and watched her. She seemed to be running down a mental checklist, perhaps something she read in a book.

"What do you want me to do?" The Flower Girl's smile faded. She seemed like a virgin, in love with the idea of the act of love with no idea how to act upon it.

Joseph sipped his wine and watched her silently. This seemed to confuse her more than anything.

"Now that we're here, I'm not sure what to do next." The Flower Girl said, looking embarrassed.

"Don't overthink it. Just do what you want to do." Joseph said, trying to relax her.

As he said this, Joseph saw a thin trickle run down the Flower Girl's leg.

"You see what you do to me? I never get that wet." She exhaled.
She lunged at him, pulling him to his feet with strength that he
didn't expect . She tore down his pants, followed by his designer
underwear, then plunged his half-erect cock in her mouth before
putting two of her fingers in Joseph's ass.

The fingers were a shock, but it turned her on in a way that he
couldn't refute. She gave him head as if her life depended on it.
Joseph, sensing her almost desperate desire to please him, verbally
talked her down.
"Slower…slower. If you go too fast, it hurts."
She pulled back and looked up at him, his cock firmly in her hand,
her grip tight.
"You like it slower?" She said as she held his erection inches from
her face.
"Slower, yeah." Was all Joseph could manage.
She concentrated just on the head with two fingers still in his ass.
She broke from his cock for a moment and stared at him like a wild
cat.
"I've thought about you so much. When I'm out there on the
street, all alone, I think of you. Do you think of me once in a
while?"
"Yeah. All the time."
She plunged his cock into her mouth and kept going, her long thin
fingers entering and exiting until she felt the tell-tale spasms of his
impeding orgasm.

She pressed hard against his prostate as he came. The sensation was insane. A hundred times harder than any orgasm he'd experienced before.

Joseph fell against the chair, totally spent.

"Did I do OK?" The Flower Girl asked coyly.

Joseph had never come so hard. He was literally breathless and helpless where he fell against the chair. He wondered how such a meek girl uncovered such secrets.

"I read a lot about sex." She explained later as they cuddled in bed.

"Time well spent." Joseph advised her.

He got up to shower and his head was spinning. The steam shower clouded the room until all Joseph could see was the water hitting his face. He washed his body and realized that he would be very sore in certain places tomorrow.

"Wow." He mumbled to himself, hoping the Flower Girl would come into the shower with him.

Coming out of the steam-filled bathroom, all he found was an empty bed with a note on his pillow.

"I love you…" Three little words that almost made up for her leaving.

"Yes." He whispered to himself as he climbed back into an empty bed. He could still smell her everywhere. Even when he finished the bottle of wine and finally went to sleep, The Flower Girl's smell was still inside him, permeating his dreams.

In the morning, Joseph glanced in the bathroom, hoping that she'd be there, but all he found were a clean set of towels.

"Hello, Joseph." The smooth voice of The Concierge made the hair on Joseph's neck stand up. It was an intercom announcement. Joseph felt an immediate sense of relief that the Concierge wasn't in his room. He felt hung-over and dizzy.

"Ready for your day. I'm glad you took my advice and stayed in a room."

"OK." Joseph croaked.

You got new pages from the Playwright." The Concierge said, almost in a warning tone.

"I'm very excited." Joseph said, not meaning it.

"Meet me in the lobby in one hour. We have paperwork for you to sign."

"OK." Joseph said as the intercom clicked off.

Before entering the command center in the Tower of London, Joseph stopped at the "One Pager's Guild". A meeting place for bit players who literally had a one-page description of their role handed to them at the opening meeting.

This is where the Flower Girl would relax until they called her for rehearsal. A rehearsal that amounted to repetitive tasks that made them eerily similar to AI characters in a video game.

As Joseph walked through the busy social center, a woman followed him. When Joseph turned, he initially thought it was the

Flower Girl. It was her costume, but another actress was wearing it. Someone he didn't recognize.

"Hi, you're the guy playing The Elephant Man, aren't you?"

"Yes."

"Can I help you with something? You seem to be lost here."

"I'm looking for the Flower Girl. I saw her yesterday."

The woman looked confused.

"I'm the Flower Girl." The actress said.

"Is there another one?" Joseph felt a dark pang go through him.

"No. There is only one and I've played her since opening day."

Joseph smiled, but inside he thought of the possible reasons why this was happening. All of them involved being tricked. He could only hope the sinister scenarios playing out in his mind were a case of him catastrophizing as he often did.

"Thank you. I'm sorry I bothered you."

The second Flower Girl smiled. "No bother. Come by anytime."

Leaving the One Pager's Guild, he felt for the note from The Flower Girl, but the paper was gone. The only proof that she existed had vanished. This was a problem he would have to deal with later. The Concierge was waiting for him.

They sat at the restaurant; the concierge had a stack of forms for Joseph to sign. A waitress came with French press coffee and Danish for The Concierge. Joseph had an omelet.

"Please read these over and sign at the "X". Your new contract and commitment letter to us. Congratulations, you are at the top of the pay scale. You make more money than I do." The Concierge said, sounding softer than before.

"Really?" Joseph grinned.

"Your rise here has been swift, but I think you've taken it all in stride. Not let it get to your head." The Concierge noted as he chewed his Danish. "I'm impressed, I really am." The Concierge pushed down the plunger on his French press and poured the jet-black coffee.

"You have a list of new perks at your disposal. I saw that you already found the bottle service perk."

"I did, thank you." Joseph said, stirring his coffee.

The Concierge dug in his satchel and produced script pages, a stack about an inch deep.

"I highlighted your part. Feel free to take the morning. Read some of it. I'll arrange for a stand-in to take your place until two pm. Sound good?"

"Sounds great." It really did sound great to Joseph. He appreciated that they were giving him a little time to go over the new pages. Most projects didn't afford actors that luxury.

As he scanned it, he was struck by the active role the Elephant Man was taking in the revised story. The desire to find his mother and his disappointment at finding her prostituting herself. The grief turning to obsessive rage after his mother falls victim to the Ripper. For the rest of the play, the Ripper and Merrick hunt each other. The physicality of the enhanced role frightened Joseph.

The Elephant Man suit was built to constrict movement. Some of the scenes in the new pages required running, jumping and fighting. They would have to make adjustments. Joseph was sure that they already knew they would do this and chose not to worry about it.

The one concern he had still centered on Joseph Merrick himself. As he made progress with his background file, Joseph found him to be uniquely empathetic toward the suffering of others. How would he be able to correlate the real man with a violent revenge plot that the Playwright was set to introduce?

As an actor, he saw the potential for problems. If he were a fictional character, there would be no moral dilemma. Joseph Merrick was not fictional. Such flagrant alteration of the arc of his life felt distasteful to Joseph.

Finishing his breakfast, Joseph took a blank slip of paper from his pocket. He re-wrote the note from the Flower Girl, trying his best to replicate her handwriting. Something had happened last night and into the morning. It was like she had been erased, but not in his memory.

Why did she leave? Why did she feel the necessity to play someone else's part in an environment void of real identity? It was puzzling.

Joseph was approached by the Team Lead, rushed to get him fitted for a new flexible suit that would allow more action in his movements.

"Can I study while you do whatever you do?" Joseph asked.

"I promise. Study away. We won't bother you. We just need your body." The Team Lead smiled. "I'm sure you've never heard that kind of deal before, mate."

"No. Not really." Joseph smiled.

They sat Joseph in the same chair they used to cast his body. There was a central trunk that he had to pull around his midsections and they added sections to the suit, starting with his thighs and working down to his feet.

Joseph read the script and was touched with dread. The scenes of revenge were cut from the same cloth as revenge movies, making The Elephant Man into a character tormented by the murder of his mother, turning this in course to a twisted obsession to seek payback. It was extreme and very much out of sync with the real man, at least in the circumstances of his life.

What if, however, the Ripper DID murder Merrick's mother? Could his gentle demeanor become overtaken by rage? This is the question that gave Joseph an "in" to the possibility of the new storyline. If you put anyone in such an extreme emotional situation, a certain percentage is bound to break. Certainly, he had seen it up close in Iraq.

FALLUJAH 2003

Joseph, a sergeant in the 82nd Airborne had just finished a patrol
with his buddy Darkman, a thin corporal from a hick town in
Kentucky and Bonner, a staff sergeant from Madison, Minnesota.
At the temporary headquarters, a school in the center of town,
soldiers came and went to patrols all day, making it resemble a
transit station.

They unloaded the Humvee that was patched on its sides with car
windshields culled from junkyards or simply stolen from vehicles
on the streets. One of the windshields was hit by shrapnel, its
safety glass making it look like a cloudy spider web.

Joseph glanced at it indifferently, even though the modification
had saved his life the day before.

In the old cafeteria, they had set up a mess hall that included, of all
things, an espresso bar. Joseph and his friends got in line for their
post-patrol vanilla lattes.

They didn't talk as patrols came in, some of the soldiers bandaged
and bloody. The barista, brought in by the private logistics
company called Darkstone already knew their drinks. Having been
culled from a highly ranked Seattle coffeeshop, the young man was
making ten times the pay he would get back home.

They sat, enjoying their drinks at one of the tables made for 6th
graders.

"Did you know that a shot of espresso is only good for ten seconds?" Bonner said to a bored-looking Joseph and Darkman.

"You don't say?" Darkman said in his Kentucky drawl.

"It's true. It only holds the magic for a few seconds after it's drawn. Don't believe me? Watch?" Darkman gestured to the espresso machine where a shot was being pulled.

"High-pressure steam shots through the grounds, creating a magic, caramel concoction. You can drink it straight. Beautiful flavor, but as soon as it's poured...watch." Bonner pointed.

Indeed, the espresso shot that was a medium golden brown started turning darker, finally becoming pitch black.

"You see, now the magic is gone." Bonner said with a tone of regret.

A shape obscured Joseph's view of the espresso bar as a man, a civilian named Lester, a contractor for Darkstone, fell across the table, his right arm cut deeply. Blood spurting on everyone nearby.

Medics rushed in, pushing Joseph and his buddies aside.

"Make a hole! Make a hole!" They said as they cut open his shirt, revealing more cuts on his chest and neck.

The arm wound was the bleeder and they went to work on it with a tourniquet.

It was Lester's job to drive the truck that supplied the commissary including the espresso bar. The barista stared in horror as Lester, the man that hired him off the streets of Seattle, lay clinging to life on a child's cafeteria table. It was then that he realized that the great pay really didn't mean so much.

No one was expecting what happened next. A local child, perhaps ten-years old charged into the commissary with a drawn blade. He was so small and fast that he slipped through the soldier's attempts to grab him. He climbed squarely onto Lester's chest and slashed his throat with a knife.

As Lester lay gagging in his own blood, the boy, knife still in his hand, screamed out in Arabic what Joseph recognized as a statement of satisfied revenge against the man that had callously run over civilians on the streets, including his mother. Joseph had heard stories of Darkstone mistreating the local population of most of the cities they operated in. He had never imagined that they were casually running over civilians with their trucks for fun. Now it was this boy with all the rage that could fit inside his being that took revenge on behalf of his and other families, knowing full well he would be killed.

Seconds later, another sergeant, a man named Briggs, brought his Glock to bear and shot the boy between the eyes. The knife fell to the floor with a CLANG.

Joseph stood over the boy that looked like he was sleeping, his eyes closed and his arms crossed over his chest.

The boy's target, Lester, had three medics working on the open throat wound. In spite of their valiant efforts, the man had lost so much blood, there was nothing they could do. He coughed out some of the blood he had swallowed, then his breathing stopped completely.

With the mess hall quiet again, Joseph heard what sounded like a dog whimpering. He glanced up and saw the barista crying and shaking like a scared child. To add insult to injury, he had pissed himself.

Joseph thought of that ten-year old boy. Before the war, that child was probably like any child in America. Playing with his friends, learning how to add and subtract, and eating a dinner cooked by his mother.

If an innocent child could murder after watching his mother get killed for sport, why wouldn'tthe Elephant Man be capable of the same?

THE PIE MAN

A bit later, the Team Lead returned and continued work on Joseph's costume, asking Joseph to do a range of movement exercise, like slow motion jumping jacks.

"I think we're getting closer, mate. How does it feel?"

"It pinches in the armpit, but otherwise, it's good." Joseph lifted his arm and pointed at the offending area under his arm.

"OK, let's fix that. Take it off." The Team Lead said.

After several adjustments like this, the suit was finally ready to field test. That would be tomorrow. The rest of the day belonged to the London Hospital scenes.

At lunch break, Joseph passed several shops that were already open. In one week, they'd be serving the audience, but with this soft opening, they warmed up by serving the actors. There was a shop that sold chicken pie that was irresistible. Joseph glanced in the shop called "Smyth's Chicken Pies" and was impressed by several rows of the savory concoctions. They had lamb and beef pies too, but Joseph stayed with the standard chicken.

"Here ya go, friend." The elderly pie man passed the pie to Joseph wrapped in a newspaper dated 'Sep. 1, 1888'.

"How do you eat this?" They didn't give Joseph any utensils.

"Just dig in with your hands." The pie man gestured with a cupped palm.

Joseph turned the pie to find a good place to take a first bite. This revealed a newspaper headline reading "He calls himself THE RIPPER!"

"Say, you're the guy playing the Elephant Man?" The Pie man said.

"That's right." Joseph said, reading the first lines of the Ripper story on the newspaper.

"Congratulations, my friend. I've been trying for a lead role for years. What's your secret?"

"I just got lucky." Joseph read further, finding that the location of the Ripper murder was just two blocks from the London Hospital.

"No such thing as luck here, Joseph. You must have 'IT'."

Joseph smiled and dug for his Gaslight meal voucher.

"No charge for you. You're money's no good here. Your money isn't good anywhere here anymore."

"Thank you." Joseph said with a twinge of embarrassment.

"They say you'll be the best Elephant Man ever." The pie man said as Joseph left, pretending not to hear the praise. Not wanting to hear the praise. It made him uncomfortable to be congratulated on something he hadn't done yet. He folded the newspaper so that he couldn't see the Ripper story and took his first bite of the pie. It was indeed delicious.

At the London Hospital, Eddie met him at the door with a hearty handshake.

"Congrats mate."

"Don't congratulate me yet. I might end up as a chimney sweep before the week is over." Joseph said, only half-joking.

"You always see the glass half-empty, Joseph." Eddie noted.

"Let's get to work, shall we?"

"Glass half-empty, my friend. Glass half-empty."

A young man, assistant to the Stage Manager, was waiting for him. It was someone he had never seen before.

"You've been very busy, did you get a chance to read the script over?" The Assistant Stage Manager (ASM) asked.

"Of course, I did." Joseph said, feeling a twinge of insult.

"Queen Victoria is on the way. It's a pivotal scene as you know." Joseph said nothing.

"You know..." The Assistant Stage Manager said in a contrite tone. "I've rarely managed one Primary Character in a scene, let alone two. I have to admit, I'm a little nervous."

Joseph could see the ASM's sincerity and was a bit touched by it. "It's ok. No one thought much of me when I got here. I just got lucky." Joseph said.

"You're modest, but you have to know that's not true."

"Look..." Joseph leaned into the ASM. "...I don't want to burst your bubble, but Queen Victoria is kind of a bitch."

"Yes, I know. Everyone knows. All the Prime Actors are terrible. Except for you."

"I'll tell you what's terrible! This fucking scene!" Queen Victoria burst into the room.

"Welcome Queen Victoria." The ASM said through his embarrassment. Joseph hurriedly slid in his dental appliance.

"Fuck you. Let's get to the scene." Victoria waved the ASM away and glared piercingly into Joseph's eyes.

"Very well. Start when you're ready, Victoria." The ASM said. Queen Victoria's face seemed to deflate into a peaceful grin. In an instant, she was in character and Joseph knew he had better not fuck this up.

"We are pleased that you have found a home here at the London Hospital." The scene began.

"Thank you…your majesty." Joseph said in his Elephant Man voice, barely understandable.

"You serve as a true example of English courage, Mr. Merrick. You are an inspiration to us all." Queen Victoria rose and a three Royal Escorts entered the room to bring the queen to her carriage. Victoria turned back to Merrick and smiled as Joseph rose to bow to her. The suit whirred and clicked as it kept Joseph's movements in check.

"I invite you to dinner at the palace one week hence. You may bring Doctor Treves with you."

"Your majesty." Joseph bowed again as the scene ended.

"Back to one please!" The ASM said with a nervous voice.

"Back to one for him. He's the one that needs the practice. Good-bye." Victoria curtly waved and abandoned the stage.

"Yeah, she's a bitch alright." The ASM confirmed.

"It's OK. Can we pull up her hologram and we'll practice some more?" Joseph asked, sensing that this scene was still thin to him.

"Absolutely." The ASM found a remote control and clicked a few buttons that displayed the last scene. The whole room appeared, including the stage manager. He isolated Victoria and the rest of the image faded to black.

"OK. Start!" The ASM said as Victoria came to life again in the hologram.

"We are pleased that you found a home here at the London Hospital." The hologram said.

"Thank you, your majesty." Joseph said in a clearer voice this time, using his tongue to work its way around his dental appliance.

"You serve as a true example of English courage, Mr. Merrick. You are an inspiration to us all." Victoria's hologram rose and she faded in and out as the computer struggled to project a moving target.

Joseph bowed to the projection, his back straining against the limitations of his suit.

"I invite you to dinner at the palace one week hence. You may bring Doctor Treves with you."

"Your majesty." Joseph bowed again as the hologram faded away.

"Again?" The Stage Hand asked.

"Yes. Again." Joseph said rubbing his lower back where the muscle strained against the suit.

"How many times should we do it?" The Stage Hand asked.

"Until it feels right." Joseph said firmly.

Indeed it took fifteen more times before the scene "felt right" to Joseph. He nodded to the Stage Hand who seemed relieved.

"I think that's it." Joseph said, clutching his lower back for dear life.

"OK. We're supposed to rehearse the random sleep interactions." The ASM noted. "We have your bed set up. Please follow me."

"What do you mean?" Joseph was confused. Why was this part of rehearsal?

"Audience members can come into your room, so we have a hologram for that."

"I mean, why do they come? They come into the room and look at me?" Joseph said.

"Really, this is for your benefit. This hologram is an eye opener, taken from two sleep interactions on year one." The ASM gestured to Joseph to follow him down the hall.

"How am I supposed to sleep if people are in my room, bothering me?" Joseph said, mildly annoyed.

"Sedatives. I suggest you take them every night. Now get into the bed and I'll be on the intercom." The ASM started into the hall. Joseph followed him, wondering if the sleep interactions could be that bad. An hour later, he found out indeed how bad they could get after the ASM tucked Joseph into his hospital bed.

Wearing the simplified Elephant Man suit that attached with magnets, Joseph pretended to sleep for about thirty minutes. He began to wonder if the ASM had forgotten about him.

"Are you there?" Joseph called out into the darkness.

"Patience, Joseph. They're coming. They always come." The ASM said through the intercom.

The first sleep interaction came in the form of a family, a gaggle of ten. The matriarch of the group, a pruny old lady with a sour expression approached Joseph's bed first.

"Is that the Elephant Man, Gail?" An old man's voice asked through the darkness.

"Well he's God damned ugly enough." The grandmother approached the bed and poked at Joseph with her foot. At first it was a nudge, then it was a full-fledged kick. Joseph flinched and watched her leg go through him. The hologram was so real in the darkness that he expected to double over in agony. Whoever was playing the Elephant Man this year did just that. A hologram of the screaming actor obscured Joseph's field of sight.

"Fuck!" The actor screamed.

The hologram of a guard appeared.

"What's going on here?" The guard said, breaking character. "Up against the wall, all of you!" The guard extended a baton. Two other security personnel entered the room, ready for anything. The guard leaned down to the hospital bed.

"Are you OK?"

"No…Something's wrong." The Elephant Man actor said, his voice quivering. The guard pulled out his radio.

"This is B2662, we need an immediate Evac of the Elephant Man to the infirmary. He's coughing up blood."

"Affirmative. On our way." A tinny voice responded.

"I didn't think he was real!" The old woman screamed.

"Arrest them." The guard ordered the security personnel who removed zip ties from their back pockets. The family tried to push through them, but were greeted with a face full of mace.

The hologram abruptly cut off.

"That actor, the one before Valor took over, suffered a broken blood vessel in his gut. He had to be airlifted to Miami." The ASM said.

"Did he live?" Joseph clutched his stomach as if he was the one kicked.

"He lived, but he never acted again as far as we know. That's why we had two Elephant Men on year one. Let's continue." The ASM clicked a remote and the hologram continued.

The next scene was a different actor, possibly the replacement for the one that was airlifted. Joseph assumed it was Valor.

Joseph guarded himself, assuming that more violence was coming.

A hologram of a middle-aged woman appeared from the darkness.

She sat in a chair, watching him silently. The effect was more than a little eerie.

"I thought about you." The woman said in a sultry voice that reminded Joseph of Kathleen Turner.

"Many times, I feel like you, but my ugliness is within. If they knew what was under the surface, I would be where you are…locked away." She got up and approached him. Her body was like a dancer's, thin and muscular.

"I know what you need. You need someone who understands where you've been and how painful it is. How lonely." She bent down by his bed. Joseph could hear her breath as if she was there, inches from his face. Her hand reached for the inevitable.

"I know how you feel." She reached for the actor's cock. The Master remained silent as she stroked his cock with her hand, the holograph blanket moving as her hand moved like a piston. The real blanket on the bed remained still as a stone. As the woman whispered something imperceptible, her hand started stroking faster. The Master started breathing hard until he groaned, building up to an inevitable orgasm.

"That's it, baby." The woman said as the actor let out a moan, the actor Joseph assumed to be Valor's body convulsing three times before collapsing. "You see. We ARE connected."

Someone knocked on the door, gently.

"Security., can I speak to you in the hallway, please?" A guard said from the other side of the door.

"Bye." The woman leaned in to kiss The Elephant Man, knowing that the party was about to end.

"You agreed to the terms of Gaslight when you signed the participation agreement. No sexual contact with the actors. Sex workers at your disposal twenty-four hours a day. The actors aren't here for that." The guard said with exasperation.

"But…he's the Elephant Man. No one will give him what he needs."

"No…he's an actor playing the Elephant Man and the problem is that everyone wants him. Please follow me." The guard opened the holographic door wide enough for the woman to follow him.

"They confined her to her hotel room for the remainder of the performance. The ASM said over the intercom. "Shall we continue?"

"By the end of the session Joseph had experienced three lesser assaults and four acts of inappropriate touching, including one woman determined to climb in bed and mount the Elephant Man in his sleep. She was interrupted by security but was strong enough to overcome Valor.

Joseph detached his costume and sat on the bed for a moment. "I had no idea. I'm really in for it. I think I need a drink." Joseph said, feeling a sense of dread descend upon him.

"Go have a drink. Get some rest. Tomorrow we'll finish up here at the hospital. Then it gets interesting." The ASM said before clicking off the intercom.

"Goodnight." Joseph said. For a moment, he sat, enjoying the silence of his set. He realized that his workday had extended well into the night and most of the actors were already partying at the Twelve Bells.

Joseph thought about going there, but found the idea of sitting in the VIP suite to be utterly distasteful. He felt a strong pull to the Glass Paris, but remembered the warning from the Concierge about the place and thought better of it.

The compromise was a drink at the nearly empty hotel bar, so that's where he went.

THE THREE VAMPIRES

As a boy of thirteen, Joseph was enamored by haunted houses.
Not for the scares but for something he would later recognize as
immersive realities.

"How old are you, young man?" The ticket taker asked.

"Fifteen." Joseph said, lying. You had to be fifteen to get in
without a parent.

Joseph's parents wanted nothing to do with something so foolish as
a haunted house.

"You look a little puny to be fifteen." The ticket taker said.

"I was sick last year." Joseph explained.

"All right." The ticket taker took his money and tore off a ticket.

"You be careful in there." He warned as he handed off the torn red
voucher to Joseph.

The haunted house was built inside a warehouse, allowing for a
huge open field inside. The illumination came from a nearby
mock-up of the moon. Across the field, through a forest clearing,
he saw two torches that marked the entrance to the maze. It was
quite a distance, but the path there seemed devoid of any monsters.
Like an auditory illusion, Joseph heard a "tik tik tik" sound
steadily growing louder, just off to his left side.

"tik tik tik"

"TIK TIK TIK"

He glanced over and what he saw first were the reflections of three sets of eyes on him. The faces that framed these eyes belonged to long-fanged Nosfaratu-like creatures that moved in tandem, following Joseph step by step. Their heads seemed to float in the air, devoid of any human expression other than a cat-like predatory gaze.

Fear shot through Joseph like a bolt of electricity. He no longer remembered that he was in a haunted house. This was real. He was about to die.

With his eyes fixed on the vampire creatures, he didn't sense that anyone was behind him. Suddenly a black bag covered his face and he could feel strong arms grabbing him, restraining him. Blinded, Joseph felt the hands around his head and neck. They turned his head, revealing the nice thick arteries within. Through his screams, he felt two cold fingers tapping his neck the way that a doctor would do to express a vein. Then two sharp pricks and the feeling of ice coldness at the site where the vampire bit him. He could feel the dribbling of warm blood as the vampire drew back his fangs.

Joseph's restrainers grabbed him, holding him like a rolled up rug. He was placed into something and a door closed. Then the pounding of nails inches from Joseph's face. Wherever he was, they were nailing him inside of it.

Working his hands free, he discovered a flashlight in the darkness. He shone it and realized that he was in a coffin, complete with bloody scratch marks from previous tenants.

"Help! Help!" He screamed. Screams that echoed into nothingness.

Finally, he tried to push the lid of the coffin open. With all his strength, he managed to get the lid open just enough to fit his hand through. He grasped the lid and finally gained leverage. Just as he began to open it more, Joseph felt something warm, wet and gristly on his fingers. It was a tongue, licking in between his digits. Joseph screamed! With one brutal push, he broke open the casket door. There was no trace of the licker.

At the far end of the hallway, Joseph saw an EXIT sign. He made a mad dash for it, bypassing the normal route of the maze. Through the exit door, he saw the door with a vague glow of sunlight and freedom just behind it. Between here and there, however was a ball pit, filled with those plastic balls found in children's playlands. Lurking waist-deep inside the ball pit was mutated, oily, disgusting clown that laughed like the love call of an insect.

Joseph realized that it might be easier to turn around and navigate the normal maze rather than face down this monstrous ball-pit critter. He also realized that something worse could be waiting for him in the path.

He stepped down into the balls and they clanked like plastic wind chimes.

He slowly moved past the clown who occasionally chittered but didn't move, leading Joseph to believe that maybe it was a mannequin in a suit. Just as he reached the lip of the far end of the pit, he felt two hands grasp around his ankles and felt a huge tug, bringing him down under the ball pit, drowning him in the plastic spheres.

"Hehehehehehehehehe!" He heard the clown chitter as he fought against it.

"No! Get off me! Get off meee!" Joseph screamed as he felt two hands scoop him up by the armpits and lift him to the surface. The oily disgusting clown kissed Joseph on the lips. The smell was like rotten milk and cotton candy.

"Hehehehehehehe!" The clown chittered again as Joseph leapt toward the exit door. Joseph lunged against the exit, landing flat on the dirt outside of the maze.

Actors on their break sat outside in their vampire costumes smoking long cigarettes. As Joseph stood, they applauded.

Joseph rushed to the bathroom and frantically inspected his neck. There were no puncture marks, just the remnants of warm stage blood across his neck and upper chest. He didn't know how they made it seem so real. He was grateful to get out of the haunted house, but part of him wanted back inside. He wanted to inhabit that place as a monster himself. He wondered what kind of person licked a stranger's fingers in the dark. Joseph wondered if that kind of brazen performance lurked somewhere inside of him. With the distance of time, Joseph was certain that the experience was the inciting event. The first step on his path to immersive theater. Many years would pass before this tree bore fruit, but it was firmly in the ground and gestating until the inevitable moment of harvest came.

THE HOTEL BAR

The barkeep appeared thrilled to have anyone to serve as there
were just three peasant women at a corner booth.

"Hello, Joseph." One of them waved at him as he sat down at the
other end of the bar, putting as much distance between them as
possible. Joseph turned his back to them in a rebuke that left the
women with sour expressions.

"Absinthe?" The bartender asked, knowing the answer.

"Yes, please." Joseph smiled.

The bartender nodded, acquiescing to the drawn out process of
creating the beverage. A few minutes later, the drink appeared in
front of him in its glowing aquamarine glory. He sipped it and
immediately missed the Glass Paris. Was it the real wormwood
that made their version so much better? The hotel's Absinthe was
processed cheese to the Glass Paris' flavorful Gouda. He drank it
anyway. The lack of wormwood left him with a headache. This
was exacerbated by the steady CLACK CLACK CLACK of the
telegraph operators in the lobby, already sending messages back
and forth to audience members preparing their trip.

The operators dressed casually, with jeans and sweatshirts and
sipped coffee in paper cups. There would be no such comforts
when the guests arrived where they would have to be in character,
even in the hotel.

"Staying with us another night, sir?" The desk clerk already had Joseph's key in hand.

"Yes. Just one more night. The thought of sleeping in the itchy hay bed in the hovel was less than appealing."

Joseph got in the shower and sighed as the hot water ran down his body. His ghetto-absinthe headache dulled until it was hardly noticeable. His aching muscles still throbbed. He propped himself in bed and flipped through his remote control to find a jazz station. The cramps in his back made it nearly impossible to find a comfortable position.

Joseph considered taking a sleeping pill, but tried to tough it out instead. It was then that he saw it on the TV screen.

"Deep Tissue Massage 24/7" The advertisement was polished with a young girl, maybe ninety pounds working away on a fat middle-aged man with rat-nest back hair.

The service was probably only for the hotel guests, but he decided to call the lobby anyway.

"Front Desk. Good Evening Joseph." The man on the phone said in a purring voice.

"I was wondering. I doubt you have this. I'd like one of those deep tissue massages. Are they available yet?" There was silence on the other end. Joseph thought they were probably rolling their eyes.

"Of course, Joseph. We have someone available 24/7. Shall I send her to your room?"

"Is she strong enough? I mean, my back really is sore."

"Oh yes. I'm sure she can take care of you." The clerk said with a little too much confidence.

"Could you send up a bottle of Merlot please? Something from California?"

"Certainly. Any food?"

"A cheese tray, please." Joseph hoped the cheese would go with the wine.

"Very good. Expect someone in about fifteen minutes." The clerk hung up and the jazz music returned.

The wine and cheese came first. It was a Madera County wine, perfectly serviceable, but nothing fancy. He opened it and poured a little in his glass, letting it breathe as he opened the cheese tray. Some Gouda, some brie, some white cheddar.

"Not bad." He thought as he took his first sip.

A few minutes later there was a knock at the door.

"Did you order a massage?"

The voice was instantly familiar. The massage therapist walked in carrying a robe and towels and Joseph's suspicions were confirmed. It was the Flower Girl. HIS Flower Girl.

"Hello, sir." The Massage Therapist said, smiling.

"Well hello." Joseph said, barely able to contain himself. "Where have you been hiding?"

The Massage Therapist stared blankly at Joseph.

"Oh, I've been at the spa since last week, getting ready for all the guests."

"Do you…recognize me?" Joseph caught her eye. She was friendly, but curt.

"Were you an actor last year? I'm afraid I don't recall, sir. Would you mind putting on this robe?" She handed him an oversized terry-cloth robe and gestured to the bathroom. Another knock at the door as two young men wheeled the massage table into the room.

Joseph ducked into the bedroom to change as his mind raced. Was this a trick of some kind? Was the Flower Girl simply trying to pretend that their night never happened?

Joseph took a deep breath and opened the bathroom door. The Flower Girl was alone and placing blankets on a massage table, her back to him.

"You know. If you don't want to talk about the other night, I understand." Joseph said as he watched her stiffen uncomfortably. "I just thought, we kind of hit it off, you know?" He realized that he might've made a mistake in talking to her when she really wanted to forget it. Joseph felt ashamed, but was glad that he tried to communicate with her. If he didn't, how would he know how she really felt?

The massage therapist turned with a puzzled look on her face, but it was not the Flower Girl. It was another woman. It was someone else that didn't even look like her.

"I'm sorry sir, I'm pretty sure we have never met before. I only flew in two days ago." The woman said.

Joseph suddenly felt dizzy and propped himself against the wall.

"Are you feeling OK?" The Massage Therapist asked, approaching him.

"Yes, my back just hurts." Joseph said, realizing that they might be under surveillance.

Without much to go on, Joseph decided to keep his mouth shut and his eyes open. Maybe he could find the Flower Girl again. If someone was trying to "gaslight" him (the form of mental abuse, not the island) they were wasting their time. He knew who he saw.

Joseph went through with the massage, pretending that nothing was wrong.

When the massage therapist was done, he slid her a tip that she refused awkwardly.

"We can't accept gratuities." She said in an embarrassed voice as she left. Joseph was glad she didn't accept it. She wasn't a real massage therapist and his back hurt more than ever.

Later when he was sitting on the commode, he reached inside the cabinet for a roll of toilet paper. That was where he saw it. The wall at the bottom row where the toilet paper was stacked four high had a gap where the molding was loose. This was not a vent, but a door, a hidden door that he opened to find a crawlspace leaving into the darkness.

He was sure that was where the Flower Girl had made her escape. With this surety in hand, Joseph wondered why The Flower Girl had deceived him. She may have been forced to spy on him. There were too many missing pieces to this puzzle. There would be time to judge her when the picture was more complete. He held out hope that she would come to him again in a place where they weren't being watched. He would tell her how he felt about her and maybe The Flower Girl wouldn't run again.

THE STREET SWEEPER

At the next morning's rehearsal, two male butlers escorted The Ripper to the hospital exterior. The Master was so drunk he was barely able to stand.

The Playwright glanced at Tif. Their eyes met and they nodded at each other. The butler opened his coat, revealing a medical kit with three pen-like devices. He pulled a green pen from the kit and turned a knob before slamming it into the Ripper's leg with his pants still on.

The Butler pulled out the syringe and ejected the medical capsule into the trash.

Within seconds, The Ripper's eyes brightened and he was able to stand on his own.

"Good morning!" The Playwright said with more than a hint of irritation.

"Yes, good morning." The Master said in a groggy, but stable voice.

"Today we are rehearsing the new scenes between The Elephant Man and The Ripper. I thought we'd start out sans costumes, considering the state some of us have appeared for work." The Master looked away, obviously embarrassed.

"I have some below-the-line volunteers that will serve as your audience. Sorry, no holograms until next year.

Keep your focus on the interactions with the audience. We rely on word of mouth to let the storyline spread virally. Make a good impression to help this along, yes? Please get to your starting locations. Keep in mind that the actual start time will be just after sundown." The Playwright said in a harried voice.

One of the Butlers led Joseph to his starting position through the London Hospital.

"Sit on the bed. That's your starting position." The Playwright said over the intercom, leaving Joseph alone awaiting commands over the intercom.

The ASM entered the set with a stack of papers and a harried grin.

"Are you ready?" The ASM asked.

"Yes. Ready." Joseph replied.

"Very well." The ASM left the room and led in the volunteers who waited on the stairwell to Joseph's quarters. There was an awkward silence and Joseph could tell they wanted to speak with him. .

"I just wanted to say…" A young man whose badge read "Street Sweeper" said with a shaking voice. "…That it's a real privilege to work with you, Joseph, even if it's just practice." Some of the other actors nodded.

"Get ready!" The stage manager said over the speaker system.

"Thanks for saying so." Joseph said to the street sweeper. Though he wanted to talk with these young people, the rehearsal was imminent.

"Let's talk later, OK?" Joseph said humbly. The Street Sweeper nodded and smiled. "I'd like that."

"Actors begin!" The Playwright called out over the intercom.

Joseph Merrick studies the photograph of his mother in her youth.
He passes it along to members of the audience.

JOSEPH
Look at my mother.

The audience members share the photograph.

JOSEPH
She walks the streets just below. I want to go see her,
but I am frightened of what she'd say. Should I go see her?

The audience should respond in the affirmative.

JOSEPH
Help me.

Joseph reaches out to a random audience member who will offer to
help him from his bed. Usually someone will.

JOSEPH

I must go see her. Let's go.

The Elephant Man leads the group out of the hospital and into the
street below.
Limping along, he leads them to an abandoned storefront where he
watched Emma (Merrick's mother) ply her trade on the street.

JOSEPH

My mother. She used to hold
me and tell me that my condition
would be solved by the grace of God.
When she said this, I believed it.

A JOHN approaches Emma.

EMMA (to a passerby)
Looking for a sweet taste, dearie?

JOSEPH (to the audience)
A sweet taste? If I were strong,
I could take care of her. She would
Never have to walk the streets again.

The Elephant Man turns to the audience, addresses them
individually. Holds their hands as he shifts from person to person.

JOSEPH

When I was a child, I didn't look like this.

Holds up his malformed, flipper-like right hand.

JOSEPH

I was a beautiful child, my mother
Told me. She would touch my cheek
 and tell me that women would fall
over themselves when I became a man. Then,
a few weeks later, the gray spots appeared
on my skin. At age five, I wasn't beautiful anymore.

A man with distinguished clothes approaches Emma on the street.

EMMA

Hi dearie.

The Distinguished Man whispers something in her ear.

EMMA

Lead the way honey.

JOSEPH

If I approach her just to be rejected all over again.

I would lose all hope.

Joseph follows Emma and the mysterious man down the dark alley. The Elephant Man struggles to keep up with them, holding on to audience members if possible.

Emma and the stranger vanish into a rooming house in the alleyway.

The Elephant Man watches a lantern being lit. The light travels upward to the third floor of the building, vanishes briefly, then reappears in one of the upstairs bedrooms.

JOSEPH
My mother. If I wait here until the man is finished with her, maybe I could speak to her. Will you help me? Be back at ten-o-clock. If I can speak to her in the dark, maybe she won't be shocked. I've gotten so much worse since she saw me last. Please help me? Please help me? You are good friends. The darkness will be an even greater friend. The darkness will help me

regain my mother's love."

The Elephant Man begs the audience members. (Presumably most will return)
"END SCENE!"

Joseph leaned against the wall, completely spent from the performance. He felt the weight and levity of a performance with a live audience. He could feel the emotions coming from them in waves. Several of them were emotionally drained after watching the run through.

"I can't, I can't, I can't come back for this scene again. I can't." A young woman sobbed, hugging The Street Sweeper standing beside her.

"Take a break everyone. Come back in ten." The ASM called out.

"In ten!" The extras replied in response.

Joseph felt disoriented. Usually, he was confident enough to know if a performance was on par. This time, he couldn't tell.

"Did I...do OK?" Joseph asked The Street Sweeper, feeling the pull of his exhaustion.

"Sir...it was very moving. I can't imagine what will happen when you wear the suit." The Street Sweeper said with firm sincerity. Joseph watched the sobbing girl being comforted by him and wondered what she saw in Joseph's performance that he didn't see himself? He couldn't shake the thought that he had missed the mark.

"Correction, let's make it an hour-long break. We'll make it a meal break at the Twelve Bells. Be back in an hour." The Stage Manager could sense that the test audience was shaken. He and the Playwright conferred for a moment. The Playwright took some notes and nodded.

Joseph waited until he was alone in the boarding house before he stood to leave. Outside, the sky was reset to mid-afternoon with a distant storm cloud on the horizon.

Feeling a mental fatigue that seemed unique to Gaslight rehearsals, He decided not to go to the Twelve Bells with the others. Joseph found an empty butcher shop and ducked in. There, among the plastic goose carcasses, he napped on the floor and dreamed of Fallujah.

FALLUJAH AND THE NAVY SEAL

Joseph had seen several SEALS in Iraq, but didn't have a chance to talk to them until he met Larry. Larry was a SEAL waiting for transport to Rammstein hospital when Joseph met him in the canteen. His feet were in casts and he had an IV drip in his left arm.

Joseph was curious about his condition and asked if he could speak with him.

He discovered that Larry had carried one of his fellow SEALS twenty miles to safety, breaking most of the bones in his feet in the process. His buddy who was shot, managed to pull through although he would ultimately be paralyzed.

"People think your body dictates to you, but that's not true. You dictate to your body. You are capable of so much more than you know." Larry said with a knowing smile. "Watch this, Joe." He said.

As Joseph watched intently, Larry's eyes fluttered into the back of his head. His gaze fell on Joseph just before a POPPING sound sent Joseph to his feet.

The SEAL's left arm dropped visibly out of its socket.

Everything in the canteen went silent as Larry's arm hung lower.

"You see. You are the master of your body, not the other way around."

Larry threw his dislocated shoulder against the wall and it made a startling SNAP as it locked back in place.

The SEAL went back to eating his breakfast while the others in the mess hall stared at him in disbelief.

"Not the other way around." He repeated.

THE CANDLE LANTERN

At nine-thirty, the ASM woke Joseph with a firm shake.

"It's time. Your audience is coming back."

For a second, Joseph was disoriented with the plastic butchered rabbits staring down at him.

"Help me up." Joseph reached out to the ASM who struggled to get Joseph to his feet.

"You haven't been drinking, have you?"

"No…" Joseph said in a flat tone. "…Just tired."

"OK. Let's go then."

When Joseph returned, the audience members were trickling back to the building exterior.

Joseph knew what was coming next. He was very interested to see the audience reaction.

As the clock struck ten-thirty, only a portion of the audience had returned. Joseph realized the first parts of the scene might have been too much for some of them.

"We're going with the audience we have." The ASM said over a bullhorn. "Everyone places and get ready."

The Playwright stared at Joseph who averted his gaze until his discomfort finally boiled over.

"What?" Joseph snapped at The Playwright.

"Action, Joseph. Action!" The Playwright gestured at Joseph.

"Thank Christ." Joseph muttered as he seamlessly shifted into character, taking the audience by surprise as he addressed them.

"Thank you all for returning. I never know when I might need a kind hand to help me navigate the stairs." Joseph said as The Elephant Man.
Joseph slipped open the door to the boarding house and gestured for the audience to follow.
"Be quiet please." Joseph warned them.
They entered the building lit by oil lanterns. The lower level was empty.

With Joseph's mother upstairs, he struggled to navigate each step.
Members of the audience helped him as he moaned with pain.
TEM's hip injury would've made stairs a terrible struggle.
With their help, he crested the last step and finally reached the landing.
There, at the end of the hallway was his mother's room, the oil lanterns illuminating the gap around the door.
As Joseph approached the door, someone's heavy masculine feet cast shadows from the other side.
They heard a deep PUFF as the person on the other side blew out the lantern. As he did this, the oil lanterns extinguished.
Audience members gasped, unable to see their hands in front of their faces.

What followed was like an explosion.

A blast of air with what felt like fragments of splintered wood spat across their faces.

With force that would have shamed a professional football lineman, a large bulky figure blasted his way through Joseph and the audience as if shot from a gun. Audience members screamed, taken completely by surprise by such a brutal attack. A few of them cried and asked for the rehearsal to stop. Joseph knew that it wouldn't stop now. Not for the sake of a few tears.

Someone in the audience lit a candle lantern. Its dim glow revealed wet, black footprints imprinted on the hallway floor. With such poor light, it wasn't until closer inspection that they saw that the footprints weren't black but red.

"Mother?!" Joseph cried, quickly regaining his character. He lunged into the room and slid on something wet, landing hard on the wooden floor.
The audience gasped as they trained their candle on the bed. Emma, the Elephant Man's mother was cut to pieces. Ripped from the navel and flayed outward from there, the spine and ribcage were visible as The Ripper had removed the organs down to the empty cavity.

Three audience members vomited immediately. Some started crying, others turned away.

Another was more vocal.

"Out! I want out! Out! Get me out!" A woman in the audience whimpered in the blood soaked corner , curled into a ball. "I didn't sign up for this! You can't do this to me!" She screamed. Joseph saw that she was knee deep in a panic attack. Her speech turning into meaningless gibberish.

"Don't break character" The Playwright's voice bellowed from the ceiling as if it were the voice of God."

"Fuck you. Look at her! She's scared!" A man's voice, (Joseph thought it was The Street Sweeper) screamed in the darkness. Three black-clad men emerged from hidden doorways in the room, inciting more screams.

One of the men covered the Emma's corpse in a thick sheet. Bright LED lights rudely lit the room leaving no question that this was a stage with all of the seams and flaws that any theater set would contain. Flaws visible only in the light.

The men blocked the door, preventing any chance of escape. One of the big men in the audience, a Tradesman, snatched up the terrified girl and made his way toward the door.

"No one leaves until the Playwright gets here." One of the black clad men commanded.

"Bullshit, let me through!" The Tradesman said as he pushed through the crowd to make his escape only to be tazed unconscious, he dropped the terrified woman to the hard floor.

"Oh my God!" Someone in the audience screamed. "We're trapped!"

"Anyone else?" One of the guards yelled, holding up a can of pepper spray made for grizzly bears. A deterrent outlawed for use on humans due to its capacity to permanently blind.

After a few minutes The Concierge appeared in the doorway. The security detail let him through.

"What happened here?"

"10-44." One of the security men said with indifference.

"This first run through was with lights on, right?" The Concierge asked the crowd.

"No!" A collective answer came from the audience.

"Well, what do you expect, you idiots?" The Concierge spat at the guard and turned his attention to the actors.

"Let me be the first to apologize. This is not how we are supposed to handle such a frightening scene. There is supposed to be a lights-on rehearsal first." The Concierge was visibly angered at this breach in policy. He realized that his promise to provide the actors with a safe and supportive environment was a promise not kept on this day.

The Playwright emerged from the security detail and glanced around the room. He gave the unconscious Tradesman a perfunctory examination.

"Get a medic here, please. Security, wait outside, I want to talk to my actors." The Playwright said to the Concierge.

"You heard the man." The Concierge gestured to the security team who holstered their Tasers and retreated to the hallway.

"I'm disappointed in some of you here. I was trying to gauge the intensity of this scene before unveiling it on real customers." The Playwright said in a stern tone.

"If you were trying to gauge it, sir, I would say that you succeeded by the terrified reactions. These are actors. Imagine the audience who don't know what's coming." Joseph said with certainty. The Playwright didn't appreciate Joseph's perspective.

"Go back to the hotel and collect yourselves. Tomorrow, we'll try it again. " With that, the Playwright pointed at Joseph.

"You're out of line, you were wrong and still I have to admit that your performance was amazing."

"Thank you, sir." Joseph replied indifferently as The Playwright left.

Unexpectedly, The Concierge approached Joseph and put his hand on his shoulder.

"My job, first and foremost, is to advocate for you. Not for the Playwright. Not for Gaslight. For you and every other actor. This place, the script, the costumes, none of it matters without you to activate it. Go back to the hotel." The Concierge continued. Have a massage, a good meal. Anything you need."

Joseph knew that "anything you need" was code for a session in the sex dungeon.

With everyone gone, Joseph was alone in the room. He pulled back the sheet and looked down at the body of Emma. It was an amazing feat of mold making. It looked and even smelled like a real corpse.

"Beautiful, isn't she?"

Joseph felt an electric shock go through him. There wasn't anyone behind him just seconds before. He turned to find Emma, the actress, dressed in jeans and a t-shirt, looking down at the model of her decimated corpse.

"Wow, they do quite a job, don't they?" Emma noted, stroking the model in a macabre gesture.

"Yes, they do." Joseph replied

"You want to go for a drink?" Emma asked, nudging Joseph.

"I'm exhausted. I think I'm heading home."

"A rain check then?" Emma nodded and smiled, hiding the sting of rejection.

"Not while you're playing my mother. That's a bridge too far for me." Joseph said reluctantly.

"I see. Well, good night Joseph." Emma left, much to Joseph's relief.

Moments later, the lights went out, forcing Joseph to find his way downstairs in the dark.

He slipped on something on the stair landing. Shining his dim candle on it, he found it was a realistic looking set of lungs.

He picked himself up and slowly made his way back to the stage.

SOMEONE ELSE'S LIFE

Joseph slept hard that night, entering a dream that seemed to last for days as dreams sometimes bend time. He was having a picnic with The Flower Girl. They were on the surface of the island overlooking the steep cliff. Mist from the breaking waves below landed on them in gentle intervals.

"I can't remember a time when I wasn't here." The Flower Girl said, reaching for Joseph's hand.

"Me either. It was like…someone else's life." Joseph said, feeling free in a way he hadn't in many years.

"I love you, Joseph." She whispered to him so softly that he thought it might've been an auditory hallucination.

"Get up!" A rude male voice tore Joseph from the dream. A security guard hovered over him and pulled his blankets away. "Get up, you're late."

At the old apartment building set, Joseph was surprised by the green room they had set up there on the ground floor. There was a working bathroom with a shower as well as a breakfast buffet waiting for them.

In one corner, an automated espresso machine was monopolized by The Ripper who was trying to figure out the secrets of the latte setting.

"Let me help you." Joseph pulled a lever back, allowing him to fish out a jammed espresso pod. He restarted the process and in seconds, he had a latte that was indiscernible from one found in a coffee shop.

"How did you do that?" The Ripper asked with slight indignation.

"Five years slinging coffee." It was Joseph's first post-military job straight out of the hospital. It didn't pay much, but it allowed him the flexibility to pursue acting in a serious way.

"Ahh. Tough gig." The Ripper said before taking a sip of the beverage. He nodded with surprise.

"Very good coffee, but the important question to you is not about that. What do you think of the new scenes, Joseph?"

"Honestly, I am very excited my character is longer being a sympathy whore. I have an arc that puts me on the offensive. For once, The Elephant Man won't be fucked with."

"Well. I don't know how things will turn out, but at least it won't be dull." The Ripper noted.

Joseph glanced around the green room. It was an unfinished room with bare studs. The bathroom was basic. A toilet, sink and cheap plastic shower. At the opposite corner of the room was a folding table, the kind used for camping. Joseph plopped his plate down and carefully took a seat. He noticed that the Ripper didn't follow him.

"Hello Joseph." The Playwright had been sitting across from him. Joseph had been so deep in thought, he didn't even notice.

"Are you ready to do the scene again?"

"I'm ready."

"We had a couple of revolts last night. Actors that had to be replaced."

"What will happen to them?"

"They'll be reassigned. Demoted in pay."

"I see." Joseph said with a shrug.

"Help these actors. They look to you for leadership."

"I understand."

The Playwright stood and slapped Joseph on the shoulder as he left.

"The Elephant Man, twenty minutes." A voice bellowed from down the hall.

"Twenty minutes!! Thank you!" Joseph called back.

Joseph saw the Playwright pass by in the hall working out the scenes with the Ripper who was listening intently and nodding. Joseph stood and started to pace. He was like a horse at the gate begging for the race to begin.

The scene began and progressed much better than the previous night. At the reveal of the mutilated corpse, the audience was disturbed, but stayed with the scene this time. The two new actors hid behind the others, but managed to stay on point.

When they reached the precise moment where everything had previously fallen apart, the audience did exactly what they were supposed to do. They followed Joseph into the hallway where Emma's lungs laid bloody and bare on the floor. Now he could hit his lines properly.

"Who is God to let this happen? Can you answer me?! Is he laughing? Am I his cruel joke? If I was made in his image, then he is hideous, but at least I am not cruel like him! Bringing me within reach of seeking her forgiveness for being born! Instead, she was ripped from me as I stood feet away! Ripped into pieces by this monster in the flesh. What would you do if God insulted you in this way?!" Joseph pointed his paddle-like right hand at the audience accusingly.

"Would you fight back?!" He shuffled over the diced slurry of his mother's lungs and grabbed one of the audience members, a man with a name tag that read "BANKER", by the collar, pulling him down to the floor with him.

"What?! What would you do?!" Joseph screamed at the Banker who looked at Joseph with a terrified expression.

All the man's color drained from his face, noticeable to Joseph even in the dark room.

"What about you?!" Joseph let The Banker go and grabbed someone else, a "SCULLERY MAID" on her tag, pulling her down to the floor, saturating her shirt in blood."

"I'd kill the bastard!" She screamed in desperation." "I'd kill the killer!!"

Joseph let the girl go and turned his attention to the audience.

"Kill the killer! Kill the killer! Kill the killer!" Joseph screamed as he shuffled through the blood to address the audience that recoiled at his approach.

"After I'm done with him, he'll wish he had thrown himself into the arms of Scotland Yard, begging to take him to the gallows."

Joseph approached the audience with brutal rage.

"Bear witness to my quest. Join hands with me and hear that I will have this killer." Most of the audience laid their hands on Joseph's. "I will have my just revenge from the man that stole me away from my mother's love."

"AND...END SCENE!!" The Playwright screamed. Joseph felt his strength give out and he slumped over, trying to catch his breath. The air in the room seemed metallic as if TEM required nuclear fuel to activate inside Joseph's body.

For what seemed like an hour, there was nothing but silence and the sound of Joseph's panting breaths. In his state, with his head down, Joseph heard sobbing from the audience. He felt a firm hand on his shoulder. He knew from the palm's burly weight that it was the Playwright.

"That was CAPITOL, Joseph, just amazing. Look at them." The

Playwright's hands forcibly turned Joseph's head to see the audience members that were turned into shell shocked children at the absorption of the scene.

"You did that, Joseph. To trained actors. If you do that to paying customers…they'll just melt like a candle in a bonfire!"

"Do you want me to pull back?" Joseph asked, for the first time questioning his intensity after seeing its effect on a test audience. He instinctively knew that his level of intensity was what was required. Still, he didn't want to frighten his audience away from the participation needed to make the immersive experience successful.

"What you're doing can't be directed. You just keep doing what your instincts tell you to do. Keep surprising me with my own words." The Playwright folded up his notes and started downstairs.

"That's all for today. I'll message you all tomorrow. Good work everyone." The Playwright said as he left.

Joseph didn't move. Actors touched his shoulder as they left. Last to leave, The Banker kneeled down to him.

"Can I get you home?"

"I just need to sit here. I feel like I blew a gasket or something."

"Are you sure?"

"Yeah. Please go home. I'll be OK." Joseph said, waving the

Banker away.

With that, he left Joseph alone with the imitation candles sending flickering light across the Victorian-era wallpaper.

"Joseph." The voice was so faint that it might've been an auditory illusion, the result of exhaustion. Faint though it was he could swear it was the voice of the Flower Girl. He thought that maybe it was a continuation of his dream.

"Is that you?" He called out weakly. He heard a floorboard creak and waited for the Flower Girl to come up the stairs.

He waited a while longer, but no one came. Finally the candles went dark.

"Joseph, are you still on the set?" It was the Concierge over a hidden intercom.

"I'm still here. I think I need help getting back to my room." Joseph finally realized that he could not get to his feet.

After a momentary silence, the Concierge returned. "I'm coming to get you."

"No." Joseph replied in a whisper.

"I'm coming. No arguments." The Concierge said as the intercom went dead. Joseph knew better than to try and fight with him. He waited in the darkness and soon, he heard the "put-put" of a utility cart downstairs.

Two medics met Joseph downstairs with bottles of cold water and a wet towel. They lifted him on the back of the cart and drove past the hotel to the spa where the Concierge was waiting for him.

"We're taking you to the chamber." The Concierge said with finality.

"What's wrong with me?" Joseph said in a voice he didn't recognize as his own. The voice of an old man.

Joseph didn't want to go back to the isolation chamber after what happened last time. Still, he felt like a rag doll, unable to coordinate him movements.

THE SECOND SESSION IN
THE ISOLATION CHAMBER

The medic punched a few buttons and a hatch opened automatically, revealing a pool of water that misted him with crystallized salt.

"Can you step in or do you need help?"

"I think so." Joseph lifted his leg, but couldn't get it over the lip of the tank. One of the medics had to get in the isolation tank and guide Joseph's legs into the water. Once in the salt water, Joseph felt weightless and movement came easier.

"Do you hear me Joseph?" The Concierge asked over an intercom inside the chamber.

"Yes. Please don't turn the light off."

"We took your vitals. I think you'll be fine once you relax." The medics entered a code into the keypad and the hatch closed slowly, leaving Joseph alone with only a dim-blue light for illumination.

As silent as it was, he could hear his breaths. He could feel the blood flowing through his ears. He felt ashamed that he didn't know his own limits, didn't learn from the past (During a Henry V performance, he passed out in the middle of the battle of Algencort).

The punishment for not listening to his body was a stint in the isolation chamber, a place of illusion in a land of illusions. He tried to quiet the hammer-like banging of his thoughts and listen to the salty water lapping around him. The blue light was noticeably dimmer now.

"Hello, Joseph." A thin voice called out from the darkness of the isolation tank, the corner where the blue light didn't reach. Joseph was sure that, in this moment, he was hallucinating from exhaustion, the way he did on set

"I waited for you, Joseph...but you never came."
Joseph felt a chill run through his body. This wasn't an illusion. It was a man's voice that he recognized from movies he had seen as a child. It was The Master, the real one from last year, Franco Valor.

"I think you want to talk to me. I think you do."
The blue light flared briefly, revealing The Master in full Elephant Man makeup and costume that seemed to be handmade and somewhat crude. With The Master wearing it in this place, it was stunningly effective.
In his weakened state, without makeup, Joseph felt naked in front of the character that he was going to play.

"Why did I walk away from a dream role like The Elephant Man?"

That's what you wanted to ask me. "Why did I flush it all down the drain?"

Joseph felt his breath settle. The sound of water lapping.

"Am I right, Joseph?" The Master said in a clear, deep voice. Joseph realized that the tongue-restricting mouthpiece was the only part of the makeup that he had omitted. He spoke very clearly, making the effect that much more terrifying.

Joseph righted himself, standing on the floor of the shallow pool. "Yes. I have been thinking about that. I was also wondering…why you don't go home. You could go home now if you wanted to." Joseph tried to project confidence, but his voice broke slightly as if he were about to cry.

"This is my home. My role in it isn't finished." The Master said.

"I don't understand." Joseph asked, wondering if the actor was speaking metaphorically.

"No need to. Just consider yourself a placeholder. When I want my Elephant Man back, I will come and take it. When I want anything here, I will come and take it." The Master tilted his head down and descended beneath the salty water. Suddenly the water level dropped hard, about a foot in a fraction of a second, then righted itself, leaving a wake splashing back and forth across the walls and setting off an alarm.

The outer hatch opened and three flashlights shone inside the isolation chamber, illuminating the place where the actor vanished.

There was nothing there. Nothing but the salt water and Joseph.

"What happened in here?" One of the guards called down to Joseph.

"Get me out of here!" Joseph cried, checking the water to see if The Master was still gone.

Later, Joseph sat outside of the isolation chamber across from the grim-faced Concierge.

"He just vanished?" The Concierge asked.

"I told you everything, go see for yourself." Joseph caught the sideward glances the guards were giving each other. They were afraid.

The youngest of the guards was sent down into the pool with a waterproof flashlight. He was shivering as he approached the spot.

"That's it." Joseph said from the chamber door. "Look down."

There was nothing out of place. The floor was continuous, a slab of concrete.

"We believe you, Joseph. We don't know what happened here, but I'm sure The Master was in here with you."

"He would take the role from me when he wanted it. That's what he said." Joseph felt anger mixed with violation. The Master had his chance with The Elephant Man. Joseph wasn't about to give up the role without a fight.

"Don't worry, Joseph. It's just talk." The Concierge said with false confidence that Joseph could smell. "We will protect you."

"Just take me back to my hotel room, please." Joseph said with disgust. If The Master could vanish through three feet of concrete, it stood to imagine that he could do what he wanted anywhere in Gaslight. There was a reason they let him live on the surface and continue to harass the production. They were afraid of him. He was a loose cannon with the fuse lit. He was bound to blow up somewhere.

Back in his hotel room, Joseph lay in his bed. A silent film called "Nosfaratu" was on.

Joseph pushed away the thoughts of his frightening encounter with The Master and put his mental energy toward the next day. The script for the next day had arrived and he had already scanned it.

A knock at the door.

"Come in." Joseph yelled out, knowing who it was.

The Concierge entered with a medic.

"Joseph, you're going to get an injection to sleep."

"I don't want an injection."

"I don't want an exhausted actor. You need to rest, but you're still like a kernel of corn ready to pop. Get a full eight hours, OK?"

"OK." Joseph relented, holding out his left arm. The medic ignored it and went to the right.

"We know your anatomy better than you do." The medic noted as Nosfaratu's face filled the television behind him.

The medic injected him with a big needle, causing the vein to collapse and for blood to spurt out on the fine linins.

"Oopsie." The medic put pressure on the vein and in a moment, it stopped bleeding. Underneath the skin, blood leaked, leaving a purple blotch.

"Sorry buddy. In a couple of minutes, you won't care."

Finding a new vein, the medic injected something warm into his bloodstream. Joseph felt his mind shut down in increments, like that computer in that Stanley Kubrick film. At first he noticed his vision turn hallow, then his hearing. His thoughts became disjointed and his worries seemed to evaporate.

The Concierge put his hand on Joseph's shoulder.

"Sleep well." He said as he left.

Joseph did indeed sleep well, probably better than he had in his adult life. There was nothing but relaxing blackness. His mind didn't race, he didn't think of the incident in the isolation chamber. Even his most terrifying thoughts, the thoughts of what happened in Fallujah were temporarily contained. There was nothing but blissful darkness.

The next morning at the clinic, the doctor confirmed that Joseph was suffering from exhaustion and dehydration. He prescribed three days of bed rest with part of that time being infused with IV fluids. It was a major setback for the rehearsal of the new scenes.

"Hello, Joseph. How are you feeling?" The Concierge asked in a muted voice.

"How are the rehearsals going?" Joseph said, changing the subject.

"It's not the same without you, but we have someone filling in. The new scenes are heartbreaking and frightening at the same time. I think the Playwright really outdid himself." The Concierge leaned in to be out of earshot of the medic and nurse loitering in the corner.

"How long do we have?" Joseph asked in a weakened voice.

"How long do we have for what?" The Concierge replied, wondering if Joseph was referring their time left on Earth.

"For the audience? I've been so disorientated, I've lost track."

"Just a few days." The Concierge said with a relieved grin. "Then there's no turning back."

"I'll be ready." Joseph said without hesitation. "What about you? Will you be 'ready'?"

"No one is ever really ready once the gates are open. Rest and I'll be in touch."

The Concierge started to the door.

"Before you go. I ask for one concession...I think it's only fair."

"What's that?" The Concierge asked suspiciously.

"Let me go back to the Glass Paris. It's the only place here that relaxes me." Joseph asked in a pleading tone.

"Very well, but keep a weather eye on everything and everyone in that place. There are factions inside Gaslight that don't want to see you succeed. Factions that sympathize with the Surface Dwellers." The Concierge sighed at the concession. "It's the one place where I can't protect you."

"I can protect myself." Joseph said with a little too much confidence.

"Only if you know what's coming." With that, The Concierge left.

Later, the doctors released Joseph to return to the hotel. He sat alone in his hotel suite flipping channels on the TV mindlessly. "Only if you know what's coming." The words of The Concierge echoed in his head.

When Joseph finally woke, he glanced at the clock and realized that he had slept another ten hours straight.

There was a meal left for him on a tray with a plastic cover. He lifted it and found steak and eggs, still warm and fresh under the plastic dome.

He felt instantly famished and tore through the meat as if he had been starved. It felt good to have food in his gut again. He could literally feel the nutrition flowing thorough his veins and into his muscles. He stood and didn't feel light headed. His exhaustion was still there to some degree, but it was more of a distant irritant now. Queuing up to replace the fatigue was his ravenous desire to be back on set again.

"Two more days, Joseph." The doctor said over the phone.

"Doc, I feel so much better."

"Two more days." The doctor hung up the phone tersely.

He thought about taking a walk in the extensive hallway, but found a guard outside his door.

"Where are you going?" The guard snapped at Joseph."

"Nowhere." Joseph conceded.

"Please go back to your room, sir."

"I'm bored. I want to get back to the stage."

"Go back or I will assist you back."

"Assist?" Joseph could only imagine how many bruises would result from the guard's "assistance". He wordlessly returned to his room and flipped through the movies on demand. He watched a documentary about a place called "Bombay Beach", then ordered a burger from room service.

"You have a California Burger on the menu and it doesn't have avocado?"

"I'm sorry sir, it doesn't." The attendant said with mild irritation.

"Then it's not a California burger, is it?" Joseph said.

"I suppose not, sir. You know how quickly avocados go bad. We're planning on growing a few trees next year."

"Fine, just give me a cheeseburger with a baked potato, a vodka martini and please make sure it's done medium rare."

"Will that be all, sir?" The attendant asked, coldly.

"Yes."

"Thirty minutes, sir."

Thirty minutes later, room service appeared. It was a young woman, a petite redhead that in no small way resembled the Flower Girl. Joseph almost touched her hand.

"Will that be all, sir?" She asked.

Joseph studied her face and realized that her nose was much larger than the Flower Girl's.

"Yes, that's all. Thank you."

The following day, Joseph felt his strength return. The enforced rest had served him well. At two-hour intervals, a nurse delivered a salty drink to him and charted his urine output.

"How would you rate your urine, one-to-ten, ten being dark and one being light?"

"Two." Joseph told her.

"Pain, ten being highest."

"One."

"Good." The nurse said as she jotted down a few notes. "The doctor will determine if you return to reduced duty tomorrow."

"What's reduced duty?" Joseph asked, feeling a wave of panic wash over him. "No makeup, no wardrobe, a four-hour rehearsal limit." The nurse said without looking up from her notes.

"OK." Joseph said, sounding relieved. There was so much to do.

"The Playwright wanted you to read this." The nurse handed Joseph a packet fastened with a wax seal.

"Changes to the script?"

"I'm a nurse, honey, I don't know what's in the packet." The nurse turned and left, mumbling something unintelligible to the security guard.

Joseph opened the packet by the string and pieces of dried wax fell on his lap.

He removed a script with a title page reading "ELEPHANT MAN: REVISED SCENES".

Skimming through the play, Joseph saw the storyline between TEM and the RIPPER expanded further from the already added scenes. It was obvious the Playwright liked what he saw and Joseph's sudden illness gave the man time to expand the story arc.

The gut-wrenching addition of the murder of TEM's mother had been further developed into something truly hellish, pitting TEM against the Ripper in a clever revenge story that no audience member would see coming.

Joseph read the script straight through, crouched into the reading chair as if he had grown from it.

As he closed the script, he sighed with relief and satisfaction that he was in the hands of someone with full command of this massive story. A writer worthy of his best efforts. This realization gave him chills. He was already riding the crest of the wave after being cast in Gaslight, now he felt that Everest was in front of him and he was about to climb to the top of the world.

On Joseph's last day off, he had been released from his room to take a leisurely walk. His stroll through Whitechapel was noticed by the other actors who started to follow him until they were broken up by some of the guards.

Joseph passed the Twelve Bells, a place that he couldn't make himself enjoy in favor of the hidden nook that was the Glass Paris. He felt a sense of accomplishment that he had convinced The Concierge to expand his leash a little.

The Glass Paris glowed against the backdrop of the dark alley. He saw a few people milling around inside, but it wasn't too crowded. He stood outside of the clouded glass door watching the warm, glowing light coming from the incandescent bulbs inside. It was like a painting that he could sit in front of and watch for hours. The spell was finally broken as two actors stumbled out, unaware that Joseph was there.

Before the door could close completely, Joseph rushed forward and caught it, pausing just a moment before going in.

The Glass Paris was half-full. Joseph thought he would recognize some of the customers this time around, but he did not. Strange since he had met so many unfamiliar actors in the last few days. He thought he would've seen some of them during rehearsals.

"Welcome back, Joseph." The waiter called to him. "Sit at any free table."

Joseph found a two-seater at the center of the room, away from the bookcase that whispered at him last time.

In a few minutes, the waiter came around with his pad and pencil ready.

"What can I get you?"

"Purple this time." Joseph said with certainty.

The waiter nodded and smirked.

"That one's forty dollars. Is that OK?"

"That's steep, but I want to try it." Joseph dug in his wallet and produced three twenties. "Keep the change."

The waiter nodded.

"Thank you, sir."

While Joseph waited for his drink, he kept glancing at the bottle of Black Absinthe on the top shelf.

"Don't even think about it, mate." A red-bearded man nudged Joseph's shoulder from across the aisle.

"They'll fookin' shoot ya if ya try to sip the black stuff and you don't have the title 'DA MASTAH'." The red-bearded man had a deep Scottish accent that, to Joseph, sounded more like Arabic.

"I'm the Conductor, mate." The red-haired Conductor stuck out his meaty palm.

"I'm..." Before Joseph could finish, The Conductor shook his hand and waved off Joseph's introduction.

"Everyone knows who you fookin' are." The Conductor smiled, sipping from his absinthe glass.

"You're a Conductor? Conductor of what?" The waiter brought Joseph's drink. It was bright purple, like a morning glory in the sun.

"Of the train, ya nut?! Didn't you know we have a full-on steam train here?"

"I thought it was a prop." Joseph had seen it in passing, but it was never running, so he assumed it was just there for decoration.

"It's no more a prop than you are, Joseph!" The Conductor pulled out a photo book from his pocket, presenting it the same way that some men keep sexy pictures of their woman to make his buddies jealous.

Joseph flipped through it. It was all photos of the train called "The City of Stalingrad". Joseph only knew this because the Cyrillic had convenient subtitles beneath it.

"Yes indeed, my baby is a Soviet princess. I heard she was to be sold as scrap when Gaslight bought her, somewhere in the Ukraine." The Conductor said, watching Joseph flip through the train porn. As he reached the final page, The Conductor snatched the book back from Joseph, revealing his jealousy of any man possessing his woman for too long.

"After this, I'll take you to see her."

"That's OK." Joseph said, already making a list of excuses to leave without the tour.

"Finish your drink and we'll see if it's still OK, mate." The Conductor laughed and finished the last of his drink. He snapped his fingers and the waiter glanced up at him.

"A Purple over here!" He yelled across the bar.

The waiter did a quick consultation with the bartender before marching to The Conductor's table.

"Let's see your Grant first." The waiter said in a weary voice. The Conductor must have stiffed them before, Joseph assumed.

"Why do you do me like that, mate?" The Conductor dug through his pocket, producing two ten-dollar bills and a couple of Fivers from the Bank of Scotland.

"That's all you have?" The waiter started to offer The Conductor a green absinthe instead when Joseph interrupted him, handing the waiter a hundred dollar bill.

"Give him the purple absinthe and keep the change. "Joseph said sternly.

"Right away." The waiter took the money and scurried over to the bartender who glanced at Joseph and nodded.

"Thank you, mate. Now ya can't say no to the tour of my baby."

As Joseph readied to leave, the bartender approached him with a glass vial in his hand. Joseph's head was still swimming from the much stronger purple absinthe. He couldn't imagine having two of them.

"This is for the road. Try it only when you get home." The Bartender slid the vial into Joseph's hand.

"What is it?" Joseph said, slurring.

"Gold absinthe. For visions." The Bartender smiled and backed into the crowd, vanishing behind a solid wall of late arriving customers.

"Lessgo!" The Conductor barked at Joseph who had forgotten all about the train.

The Conductor led Joseph through the empty gas lit streets to the train station where The City of Stalingrad waited for them. They entered through the first-class car. Joseph could hardly believe that this was a car designed by communists. The seats were massive, plush leather thrones. The walls were covered in purple velvet. The Conductor led Joseph to the front door of the coach leading to the engine compartment. He was instantly hit by hot steam.

"Come." The Conductor called to Joseph who was checking himself for burns.

In the control room, The Conductor opened the firebox and shoveled some coal inside to keep the fire going.

"I just live in the train, mate. No reason to get a room when I have to feed the bitch every three hours." The Conductor said as he closed the firebox door.

Joseph glanced up to a tunnel about a hundred meters ahead. He presumed it to be a false front since it edged up to Gaslight's perimeter wall.

"No, mate. That tunnel is real. That's where we're goin'." As he said this, the Conductor pulled a lever and the train lurched forward, throwing Joseph against the rear wall.

"That tunnel is real, Joseph. Wait 'til you see where it goes." The Conductor said in his absinthe-soaked voice.

"Are you sure you should run this thing? You're kinda drunk."

"Too late, mate!" The Conductor bellowed.

The train's wheels spun and finally caught, moving the City of Stalingrad forward incrementally. The wheels slipped again, prompting Joseph to hang on.

A few curious actors, mostly merchants, came out to watch the train as it gained speed. They came out in their pajamas and robes as Joseph climbed out of the pilot compartment and waved at them. Some of them recognized him, even from the distance and started to cheer. As Joseph turned back to the control room of the train, he didn't see The Conductor. He assumed that the man had bent down to shovel more coal into the burner. That was proven wrong as he heard that mad Scottish brogue coming from the head of the engine.

"Joseph! Joseph! Come man!" Joseph could only see The Conductor's hand waving him closer.

Joseph scooted forward on the catwalk to find The Conductor riding on the cattle grate of The City of Stalingrad, closely resembling a surfer on a wave. The headlight hit the man's head with such a high temperature that it singed his hair every time he got too close.

"Come up here, man! Don't you trust me?" The Conductor yelled back.

Against his better judgment, Joseph crept to the edge of the catwalk and stepped down on the front of the moving train. Feeling the slippery wet surface of the cattle grate, he hung onto the railing for dear life.

"Shouldn't you be...?" Joseph's question was cut off.

"...be what? Running the train?" Joseph asked. This situation paralleled the hundred-mile car ride with his drunk uncle twenty years before. He just hoped that it didn't end the same way, crashing into a ditch with a humerus held together by titanium as a souvenir.

This time, the trusted drunk adult was driving 200 tons of Soviet iron rather than a four-cylinder Dodge Dart.

The Conductor let out a WHOOP-WHOOP as they entered the tunnel.

Joseph was surprised by a giant sheet of black fabric draped a few meters into the tunnel. It hit him in the face, nearly throwing him off the train.

"You all right mate?" Joseph heard The Conductor say. He couldn't respond. He was simply trying to hang on.

The City of Stalingrad's headlight shone into the darkness, illuminating the track immediately ahead of them and little else.

"Watch." The Conductor dared Joseph. Something approached them dead ahead, but it was so dark that he couldn't make it out.

When he finally saw it, he couldn't believe it.

Ahead of the still moving train was a solid rock wall.

Joseph screamed as they kept heading toward catastrophe.

He could perhaps survive if he was in the passenger compartment of the train, but he was like a fly on the grill of a car about to be a stain on the headlamp.

Instead of hitting the rock face, they came to a gentle stop, even thought the sensation of motion continued.

The Conductor flicked a button on what could only be described as a utility belt, flooding the entire tunnel with blinding LED light. Joseph covered his eyes until they adjusted. He blinked furiously, struggling to regain his sight. He squinted and leaned over the starboard side. What he saw prompted him to close his eyes and try to readjust them. What he was seeing seemed impossible. The train's wheels were still moving, but on a gigantic conveyor belt on massive pistons. The whole train, the engine and the two passenger cars were cradled on a simulator.

"Holy shit!" Joseph screamed with excitement and terror at once.

"So eloquent. Isn't that why you got this job. You're good with words?"

"That's as eloquent as you're gonna get from me right now." Joseph climbed back onto the catwalk. The Conductor followed him, seemingly irritated that his only audience member had abandoned him.

Back in the control room, The Conductor downed a shot of foul-smelling gin and flipped a switch to reveal a digital control pad. "Watch this." The Conductor turned a knob and the right side of the tunnel moved in a way a rock wall couldn't move. Like a theme park ride on steroids, an entire Victorian train station lowered and fixed in place. He throttled the steam train back until it came to a stop.

The train was positioned to the edge of the train station and the temptation to explore it was too great.

Not waiting for permission, Joseph jumped onto the platform just as The Conductor turned on the animatronic models.

There was a ticket taker in the booth writing notes in a ledger. A whole line of passengers rose from ports in the floor. There was an old man, a woman and her little boy, two nuns, and a young couple.

As Joseph strolled through the diorama, he could only smile at the audacity of it.

"I'm floored." Joseph said, catching his breath.

"I knew you would be." The Conductor said, taking another swig.

Joseph stepped cautiously through the set. He stood by the nuns and expected them to demand his repentance.

"Sister, did you remember to ask Father Gregory if there was a bathtub there?"

"Of course." The other animatronic said.

"Just checking. That Sister Joanne smelled after two nights on the train. Her facility didn't have a bathtub."

Joseph cautiously moved to the edge of the set. The background sat about ten yards from the man in the ticket booth. Placing his hand on it, Joseph found a cold steel wall that curved like a subway tunnel.

"Come on back, Joseph. Daddy's gonna wonder where his wheels went to!"

Joseph reluctantly returned to the train. Just as he looked back, the entire train station, animatronics and all descended into the ground. In a moment, all that was left was a rock face.

"There's seven different train stations in there, can you believe it?" The Conductor showed Joseph the control with names of different stations imprinted on the dial face. What caught Joseph's eye was the eighth station that was blank.

"Where does that one go?" He asked, pointing at the empty eighth station. The Conductor's demeanor immediately turned sour.

"Who sent you?" The Conductor barked as he yanked the controls away from Joseph.

"No one sent me. I just was curious about the empty space there. Why didn't they put the last station on there? They have a space for it, yes?"

The conductor's anger seemed to deflate. Now he seemed more angry with himself.

"You tell anyone what you see, I'll hog tie you and throw you in the ocean, understand?!" Joseph could tell The Conductor meant business. He also knew that he couldn't resist showing Joseph the

"Big Secret".

"I understand." Joseph said, trying to reassure him.

The Conductor took another slug of gin and put his fat finger on the a button with a double oval. He pressed it.

A blank platform rose from beneath. There was a metal sign that simply read "PLATFORM 8" and nothing else. As if triggered by the platform's presence, the rock wall ahead of them made a huge popping sound. A huge section of it moved forward, clicked, then slid to one side, revealing a hidden tunnel.

Joseph exited the cab of the train and stared into its blackness.

"Where does it go?"

"The ones that know aren't telling me. It may be an escape hatch. Maybe it goes straight to the center of the Earth. Who knows? We're not supposed to go in there, so I don't."

Joseph dug into his belt, finding his LED flashlight. He threw it into the tunnel, revealing that, at least as far as he could see, it was built at a downward angle, possibly going beneath the sea.

"Man." Joseph's curiosity was piqued, but The Conductor had enough.

"Showtime's over." He pressed a few buttons and platform 8 vanished into the ground. The rock wall slid back across the tunnel.

Joseph heard a giant CLANG and the train was free from the simulation cradle, reversing back to the main stage.

When the train returned to the station, The Concierge was waiting for them, looking vexed.

"I disabled the cameras so both of you wouldn't get your asses fired. That's exactly what would happen if management found out about your steam-powered joyride. I say this because I can't afford to lose either of you!" The Concierge screamed. It was the first time Joseph had seen the man lose his cool and he felt ashamed. The Conductor listened with a blank expression, too drunk to care.

"We will pretend this didn't happen. In the meantime, I'll need the keys." The Concierge held out his hand and the Conductor made a sour face.

"I told you that daddy would miss his wheels." The Conductor said to Joseph as he dug for his keys to the locomotive.

Joseph was amused that a beast like The City of Stalingrad used what appeared to be a set of regular car keys.

"I'll give them back when you actually need them." The Concierge pocketed them and silently glanced at Joseph's feet. He seemed to be formulating his words carefully. "Joseph. What you saw."

"I didn't see anything." Joseph interrupted.

"Good. Let's keep it that way. Good night and stay out of trouble. Both of you." The Concierge turned and made his way back toward the Tower of London on foot.

"Well, that was not a boring evening." Joseph said as he stepped off the train. The Conductor didn't say anything. He just watched Joseph leave as he finished off the last of his gin.

THE GOLD ABSINTHE

When Joseph returned to the hotel, he found the forgotten vial of gold absinthe in his pocket. He sat on his bed and opened the top, cautiously smelling it.

Rather that anise being the dominant smell, it was lavender that was the largest note. It didn't seem much stronger by smell than the green stuff so he didn't feel apprehensive when he drank it down.

As he lay in bed, his head swirling from the events of the evening and the alcohol racing through his system, he began to realize that what he just consumed was not like Green Absinthe. Not at all. For a moment, he cocked his head back and the entirety of Gaslight appeared in his mind like a three-dimensional projection floating mid air. He could see all the people and all their roles, like a mental projection of The Nerve Center. He saw them moving like ants navigating a nest.

In that moment, he felt it all make sense, like watching a giant living organism. Without prompting it, the view descended to the lowest levels of Gaslight, far deeper than Joseph had imagined.

Somehow he knew that this was where the sex workers plied their trade. There, he saw a concentration of people like little purple dots on the map. In a room marked 8-210, he saw her.

The Flower Girl's face appeared as if were made of animated neon.
She looked up at Joseph. Their eyes met and she smiled in a way
that seemed completely real.

"Help me, Joseph. I won't make it without you." Her face
appeared clearer and Joseph could see that she had been crying.
Joseph reached into the projection and it fizzled away, the last
visible element, being her eyes. Joseph could sense that she was in
danger. He could also sense that he was the only one that could
help her.

As he opened his eyes and saw the morning sun, he knew what he
had to do. Getting to the bottom floor where the sex workers were,
where SHE was wouldn't be easy. He saw security posted at the
entrance to the one elevator that led down there.

At the hotel lobby, a courier was waiting for him with new script
pages and a wax-sealed card. He opened the letter. It was
unsigned, but in The Playwright's handwriting.

"We can only give you one reduced day. Sorry, but opening day is
almost upon us and these scenes have to be ready." The note read.
Joseph didn't mind. He wanted to get in the fast lane again.

Joseph ordered breakfast at the restaurant, French press coffee and
a croissant, and studied the new pages.

With the hangover lingering, he wondered if what he saw was an alcohol-fuel hallucination or not. In the light of day, it felt that way. Still, it was hard to dismiss it. Did room 8-210 exist? Determining that would be a good place to start.

"Be careful, this is hot." The young waitress warned Joseph as she slid the French Press toward him. The croissant was large and flaky and smelled like warm butter.

She placed a timer atop the French Press set to three minutes.
"You seem like a smart man. You know what to do?" The waitress said. Joseph stared at the waitress and thought about her question.

"Sir?" The waitress said, appearing puzzled.
"I know what to do." Joseph said, forcing a smile. The waitress nodded and returned to the kitchen to pick up an order for the four Street Prostitutes that sat behind his booth.

From where he sat, he could see the elevator and the guard that stood sentinel. He saw a hotel busboy push a small cart with two food domes to the lift. The guard took the man's badge and inspected it along with the food. They pulled the skirt back on the cart. After this intense prodding, he turned a key on the elevator.

For what seemed like an eternity, the humorless guard stood motionless, waiting for the elevator to make the eight-floor journey up to the lobby.

A sudden, rude alarm broke Joseph's concentration.

"AH!" He cried loud enough to be heard by the guard who gave Joseph a cursory glance.

"I thought you knew how to handle yourself." The waitress chuckled as she removed the expired timer for the French Press. "Shall I plunge it for you?" She started to place her hands on the mechanism when Joseph stopped her.

"No. I'll do it." Joseph said, covering the plunger with his hands.

"Very well."

He gently pushed it down. As he did, Joseph could feel the scratchy course grounds of coffee against the metal filter.

He poured a cup and studied its blackness with the slick of natural oils on top. He took a sip and marveled at how good it was. He completed the experience when he took a bite of the savory croissant. In the moment that he closed his eyes to enjoy the rush of flavors in his mouth, he felt someone sit in the seat across from him.

"Hello, Joseph." Even with his eyes closed, he recognized that it was the ASM. He waited for a few more seconds before responding.

"I wanted to eat alone." Joseph said as he opened his eyes.

"I'm not hungry. Just wanted to make sure you get to rehearsal on time. That's only fifteen minutes from now."

"I'll get there, don't worry."

"Please see that you do." The ASM said tersely as the waitress approached.

"You want the coffee to go, hon?" The waitress asked with a

twisted grin.

"Yes, please." Joseph turned the handle of the French Press toward the waitress and smiled.

"Be right back." She said, satisfied at Joseph's imminent departure.

An electric golf cart was waiting for Joseph at the main entry of the hotel. The driver was someone Joseph had never seen before, a young African American girl that looked fresh out of high school.

"I'm to take you to set." The girl said as she studied Joseph's breakfast.

"Did you bring something for me?" She said, only half-kidding. Joseph tore off the end piece of a croissant and handed it to her. She took it gladly.

"Wow, that's really good." She said with her mouth full as she floored the golf cart.

"I'm Jasmine." She said, chewing.

"I thought there were no names here." Joseph said, sipping on his French press in a to-go cup with the hotel logo on it.

"I like my name too much to not use it." Jasmine noted with a grin.

She drove through the streets of Gaslight like a demon. After clipping an ox cart, Joseph finally asked her to slow down.

"Excuse me. I get in trouble if I'm late. You eat too slow." Jasmine said as she rounded a sharp corner, nearly tipping the cart over.

She screeched to a halt in front of the hovel where Joseph had previously collapsed. It looked a lot less threatening during the day.

"They're waiting for you. Good day." Jasmine said in a rushed tone. Joseph got the message and hopped out, still firmly holding his coffee.

When he entered the stage, he was surprised to find the Ripper and the Playwright huddled around the Emma's mutilated remains that looked less frightening in the light of day. He could see the giveaway seams indicating the body had been made from a mold.

"Where is the audience?" Joseph asked.

"There won't be one. The scene is just too intense." The Playwright said with resignation.

"I don't know. I kind of feed off of the audience." Joseph noted.

"Let's just do it and go have a pint, you prima ballerina." The Ripper said contemptuously. "Or do you want to know your motivation?"

"You brutally killed my mother. Do I need further motivation? Your motivation measured in alcohol-by-volume." Joseph spat.

"How dare you!" The Ripper lunged boozily at Joseph who easily grabbed his arm and twisted it into a pain compliance hold, something he used against unruly detainees in Fallujah. Joseph brought The Ripper to his knees.

"Let go! You're breaking my fucking arm!"

"Let him go, Joseph!" The Playwright ordered.

"Only if he's done being a tough guy. Is he done?" Joseph spoke to The Ripper like an unruly child.

"I'm done!" The Ripper cried out, wincing.

"He's done." The Playwright screamed at Joseph who let him go. The Ripper held his sore arm.

"I'm not doing one more scene with this ANIMAL!" With that, the Ripper left the set.

Joseph realized that he might have cost himself the job of a lifetime. He glanced up at The Playwright, half expecting an immediate dismissal.

"I think you went too far Joseph, but that asshole has deserved it for weeks." The Playwright almost cracked a smile.

"So I'm not getting fired?" Joseph

"Hell no. He'll be better behaved from now on I think." The Playwright said studying his tablet. "I'll find someone else for you to rehearse with."

"Can I have an audience?" Joseph asked hopefully.

The Playwright thought about it, stared at his tablet and nodded.

"Give me an hour. Stay here." The Playwright descended the stairs.

Joseph immediately felt ashamed. He could've let The Ripper hit him. It certainly wouldn't have hurt. It was a mistake to let the soldier inside him out of the box, even to put The Ripper in his place. Cracking that door open was dangerous.

"What's wrong, Joseph?" The soothing voice of the Concierge greeted him. It was the voice he needed to hear.

"What are you doing here?"

"I'm here to fill in for negative-eight IQ that tried to punch a decorated soldier." The Concierge said, studying his lines.

"Oh, you heard." Joseph said mournfully.

"Don't be surprised if you have a few fruit baskets at your hotel door tomorrow from cast members he's shit on." The Concierge smiled.

Below them, two rows of hotel workers, maids, busboys and carpet cleaners formed in front of the set.

"What are they here for?" Joseph asked, peering out of the second-floor window.

"Why, they're your audience. That's what you asked for." The Playwright said as he crested the stairs. "Come down and we'll start the scene."

As Joseph descended to the ground level, his audience watched him with quiet apprehension.

They spoke to each other in Tagalog, Spanish and in a language that Joseph didn't recognize.

"Do they...speak English?" Joseph asked, already knowing they didn't.

"No. Shall we continue with the rehearsal or should we join The Ripper at the Twelve Bells. I hear he's already three sheets to the wind." The Playwright pulled up a chair and sat next to the audience.

In the light, out of costume and makeup, playing against a non-actor to an audience that didn't speak his language, Joseph was determined to do what he needed to do. He had something in his bag of tricks. It had been a while since he used it.

He closed his eyes and remembered Larry, the Navy SEAL.

"You want to do what?" Larry sat across from Joseph, his feet still in casts. It was after evening chow and they had guzzled a few.

"Act. I have the GI Bill lined up for Julliard." Joseph said proudly.

"After this place. You may not be welcome in polite circles, my friend. You know what they say..."

"GOOD SOLDIER, BAD CIVILIAN." They said in unison.

"I want to control my body the way you do."

"It's all how you think, brother. All how you think." Larry said with quiet sureness. He studied Joseph for a moment.

"I don't think this thing can really be taught, but I can show you how I do it."

Joseph opened his eyes and he was back at Gaslight. His makeshift audience studied him with a confused expression.

"All right." Joseph said, removing his shirt. The Playwright leaned forward, not understanding.

Next came Joseph's pants and shoes. He tore his shirt, making it into a malleable piece of fabric that he wrapped around his waist as he removed his underwear.

With only the loincloth covering him, she started his transformation into Joseph Merrick, a transformation that involved no makeup or prosthetics.

He seemed to will his body to contort, spine first, then his arms, legs and finally his face that wrenched into a ghastly visage that made some of the hotel workers cover their eyes and clutch each other.

The Playwright tugged the arm of one of the nearby maids. "Your targeted interaction Joseph". He ordered.

The maid looked frightened as The Playwright led her to her starting position. He could feel her shaking through her polo shirt. Joseph turned his eyes on hers. He didn't budge from his character. He was Joseph Merrick again.

"Begin!" The Playwright called for the scene to start.

Joseph was like a racehorse at the gate. Now that gate was flung open wide.

"Look at my mother!" Joseph said in a voice that was pitch perfect without the aid of the prosthesis.

"She walks the streets. I want to go see her, but I am frightened."

Joseph moved toward the audience with his twisted body and dangling and lifeless right arm.

Half of them audience scattered as he came to them, invading their personal space, getting so close that they could smell the French Press coffee on his breath.

He pulled at the old photograph of his mother, a tintype, and displayed it with his shaking left hand.

"Should I go see her? Look at her." The audience didn't need to speak English to make the connection. The picture of his mother in her younger days, the days before her descent into prostitution, Joseph's pleading and warped expression just inches away from them hit the nerves that Joseph targeted. He heard the first tears from the audience. It was like red meat to a lion. Joseph felt something completely take him over. It was as if he was watching from above.

"Help me." He grabbed the hand of a short Filipino maid (the one designated as his target interaction) who screamed and pulled away.

"Won't you help me?" He took the hand of a man (possibly a busboy) this time, pleading, his eyes giant pools of desperation. That man also pulled away. He finally turned to a squat middle-aged Mexican woman who seemed paralyzed as she watched him. Joseph struggled to breathe, forcing himself to hyperventilate. He put the photograph into the woman's hand as if it took the last bit of his strength to do so. She flinched as the tiny weight of the photo hit against her palm.

With a raspy breath he begged her "Help me."

"Te ayudare! Te ayudare!" She screamed. With that proclamation, Joseph embraced the woman like a savior, falling to his knees, sobbing.

"STOP!" The Playwright screamed.

The audience, men and women alike were silent with shock or weeping openly.

They all stood there, regaining their composure. Finally, an exhausted Joseph maintained his Merrick posture as he approached The Playwright to accept his judgement.

"Oh my God." Was all The Playwright said as he clutched Joseph's arm. "That audience, I don't know whether to be envious of them or feel sorry for them." With that, The Playwright left with Emma who seemed in shock from the intensity of the performance.

"Vaminos! Trabajo!" The Playwright made a sweeping gesture to the hotel workers who scattered to return to the hotel. A couple of them glanced back at Joseph, still shaken.

With only the Concierge watching, Joseph untwisted him face and body. As he returned to his normal form, his skin turned red as blood. The Concierge thought he might be having a heart attack as his body made jerking movements. He wasn't having a seizure, to The Concierge's relief he was only crying.

The Concierge hugged him, realizing the depths from which he had to dig. This rehearsal killed off the last of The Concierge's doubts about Joseph delivering the role.

As his crying finally subsided, Joseph was embarrassed and nudged the Concierge away.

"Don't tell anyone." He asked The Concierge.

"Of course but Joseph, emotions are a gift, not a weakness. Being vulnerable is your power and no one, I mean nobody on this planet could do this job better than you. I'm sure of it as sure as I am breathing." As The Concierge said this, Joseph thought he was being condescending.

"Stop blowing smoke up my ass." Joseph snapped.

"No. I give false praise to no one. I'm just so excited Joseph. So excited at what we're about to do."

"What about The Ripper?" Joseph said, still worried about his confrontation with the acting Master.

"He's a day trader and only The Master because we needed to save face after what happened. The man who played your role last year, he was a real Master. He could bring the audience to their knees. Still, I swear to you, Joseph. You are better." The Concierge said leaning to Joseph so that others wouldn't hear such gushing compliment.

Joseph glanced at The Concierge silently. He didn't know how to respond.

"Are they coming back?" Joseph whispered.

"Coming back for what?"

"To finish the rehearsal."

"That ball is no longer in play. You knocked it over the wall. Enjoy the rest of your day." The concierge smiled and slapped Joseph on the back.

Joseph returned upstairs to the set where the corpse mock-up of his mother waited for him.

He stared down at the messy foam rubber representation with the eyes hanging out of their sockets. As ugly as this scene was, he found the loneliness and horror of this room somehow uplifting.

THE RAIN MACHINES

Joseph wandered the streets of Gaslight as clouds gathered in the sky.

A huge PING, like a high-pitched bell, sounded off from every corner of Gaslight.

"Attention. Attention. We will be testing the rain machines for the next hour. Please plan accordingly." A woman's voice said.

A few minutes later, a soft sprinkle began. Before long a cold breeze joined in and made the rain exponentially more unpleasant, prompting Joseph to find shelter inside the hotel.

He went directly to the bar that was fuller than he had ever seen before. He glanced at the elevator to the sex dungeon where one guard stood sentinel.

"What'll it be?" The bartender, a middle-aged woman with a Rubinisque figure and a deep Scottish accent said as she dried her hands with a large rag.

"What IPA's do you have? Something interesting?" Joseph asked, studying the taps. It looked like a pretty boring selection, but he couldn't see it clearly.

"I have this really interesting twenty ounce bomber from Palestine. Just be aware that it's strong as hell." The bartender slid a special menu on the bar for Joseph to peruse.

"That looks really interesting." Joseph said, grinning at the audacity of the beer. A triple IPA no less.

"I'll have one."

"Very good, sir." The bartender left, presumably to fetch the beer from the hinterlands of the cellar. After what seemed like an eternity, the woman reappeared holding a large green bottle.

"Courtesy of the ladies at the end of the bar." She said.

Joseph leaned forward to find a blonde and an Asian girl waving at him. Reluctantly, he approached them.

"Thank you for the beer." Joseph said limply.

"I hear you have a suite." The blonde said with a twinkle in her bedroom eyes.

"I just wanted to say 'thanks' for the drink." Joseph said with a polite grin.

"Then, Invite us up to your room and tell us privately" The Asian girl purred.

"I don't think so."

"Aw." The blonde moaned with consternation. "My friend and I wanted to show you our...butterfly collection."

Joseph studied the women, trying to place them. He hadn't seen them before.

"I'm tired. I think I'll be heading home."

"Where you going?" The blonde snapped.

"Told you he's a fag." The Asian girl said loud enough for the whole bar to hear.

Joseph realized that he might need to start drinking in his living quarters.

"Good night." He said to the bartender who nodded at him. As he left, he could hear a few people laugh.

Joseph woke to a light rapping on his door. He glanced over at the scenery diorama outside his window. The projected moon was full. It was the middle of the night.

"Joseph…" The voice, a male voice whispered.

Opening the door, a shockingly thin young man cowered against the jamb, trying not to be seen.

"It's the middle of the night. Who are you?"

"A friend…a friend from downstairs."

He was too tired to see that he had the special Eros pendant with a gold chain, the same kind that Joseph found in his shirt pocket. He understood the 'downstairs' reference. Downstairs meant The Flower Girl.

"Well. What do you want?" Joseph asked his "friend" from downstairs."

"You have someone down there that you would like to see. I can help you get through the guards." Friend said, eyeing the inside of Joseph's room, trying to drop the hint."

"Why would you want to do that?"

"Don't concern yourself with that. My benefactor wants to help you see her. She want to see you. She needs you."

As Friend said this, Joseph struggled to maintain his composure, not caring about who the "benefactor" was or their motivation for helping.

"How soon?" Joseph leaned in to Friend, causing the young man to take a step back.

"Soon. It's very dangerous for me to be here. I have to go." Friend said, glancing down the corridor.

"Room 8-210. Does it exist?" Joseph asked desperately. Friend froze, looking confused. "Does it?!" Joseph questioned loudly.

"Well, that *is* her room."

At that moment, hefty footprints vibrated the floor and two burly guards appeared from around a corner.

"Gotta fly. I'll be in touch." Friend said as he sprinted for the emergency exit.

The guards quickly closed in on him, their massive frames shaking the foundation.

"Get inside!!" The fat one pointed his sausage-like finger at Joseph.

"Good luck!" Joseph yelled at the guards. He waited for them to circle around, empty handed. He didn't have to wait long.

"What did he want?" The fat guard panted in a Russian accent.

"He got the wrong room." Joseph lied unconvincingly. His worst acting job to date.

"You sure about that?" The guard with a bulbous nose asked suspiciously.

"I'm sure." Joseph replied with trepidation.

"If you're lying, we'll be back." The bulbous guard's purred darkly.

"Good night, gentlemen." Joseph said, closing the door.

He glanced down at the table and saw the unopened bottle of Palestinian beer. Joseph popped the top and poured a little into a glass.

He sat, savoring the beer, taking small sips until it was all gone. All the while he thought about his recent vision and the appearance of Friend.

Someone in the Gaslight inner wanted Joseph to find her. In the end, it didn't matter. All that mattered was that The Flower Girl was reaching out and wanted to see him and needed his help. If he didn't hear from Friend soon, he would go down there himself. Let the goons try to stop him.

In the meantime, he continued to sip slowly realizing that this beer from an occupied land was one of the best he had ever had.

OLIVE BRANCH

The next day brought a long rehearsal that was supposed to be a fight scene between TEM and The Ripper. When Joseph arrived, the ASM handed Joseph a note.

"FROM THE OFFICE OF THE PLAYWRIGHT
The Ripper is refusing to leave his hotel suite. Another actor will be rehearsing with you today. PW"
This didn't surprise anyone.

"Hello. I'll be The Ripper today." A young man shook Joseph's hand. Under his arm was a bone saw that gave Joseph pause. The Stand In noticed Joseph's discomfort.
"This is as sharp as a butter knife. You get a weapon too." At that, the Fight Choreographer, a pale-thin man with dreadlocks planted a hatchet in Joseph's hand.
"Hello, I'm Gary, but as there's no names here, just call me TFC." The Fight Coordinator said.
"Hello." Joseph said as he stroked the blade of the hatchet that was not only dull, but plastic.
"Look, I just can't do this properly if you're not in costume, Joseph. I don't care what the Concierge said, get in costume. You need to feel the weight of it to properly act this scene."
"Did you hear that, makeup department?" The Fight

Choreographer spoke into a microphone attached to his lapel.

"I did. Send Joseph over!" The voice of the Team Lead replied.

A golf cart screeched to a halt next to Joseph.

"Go. See you shortly." The Fight Coordinator said in his rapid-fire voice.

The wardrobe crew hurriedly scrambled to gather the Elephant Man costume that had been at the cleaners.

As they added layer upon layer, Joseph felt every pound.

The Team Lead adjusted the costume a few different ways before he put the headpiece on.

"There you go. Go get 'em Tiger." The Team Lead said as he slapped Joseph on his back hard. There was so much costume in the way that Joseph could hardly feel the impact.

Joseph returned to the rehearsal where TFC ordered he and the stand in to do the fight scene at half-speed. Even in slow motion, Joseph found himself panting from the extra weight.

"Practicemyfriend! That'sthenameofthegame!" TFC rattled off the words like automatic gunfire.

It was becoming apparent that the stand in would be doing most of the physical scenes for The Ripper who had yet to leave his hotel room.

In any ordinary production, The Ripper would already be fired. His status as a celebrity with the title of "Master" complicated things greatly.

Right after rehearsal, Joseph called The Concierge and asked if he could apologize to The Ripper personally. The Concierge reluctantly agreed under that condition that he would accompany Joseph.

They met by the Telegraph office and it felt like a funeral.

"Have you thought about what you'll say to him?" The Concierge gestured to the nearby gift shop.

"You can get him more to drink." Earning a stern glance from Joseph. "Just kidding." The Concierge conceded.

"I think I'll just tell him the truth. I didn't wake up in the morning wanting to put my hands on him, my military training just, you know, kicked in."

"Bring him some Courvoisier. Trust me. He'll forgive anything for that."

Joseph cradled the box of liquor in his hand like a baby as they rode the elevator up to the penthouse.

The Ripper's room was a suite. One that could be had by primary actors such as he, Victoria and more recently, Joseph.

The Concierge knocked at The Ripper's door and waited.

Finally the intercom mounted to the wall croaked out.

"What?!"

"It's The Concierge. Can I come in?"

"Fuck off." The Ripper barked.

"Look, I have the key and came come in, but I'd rather you let us in." The Concierge didn't really have a key. He hoped that The Ripper was too drunk to know that.

Joseph could feel the thumping on the ground as The Ripper stomped to the door and tersely opened it. When he saw Joseph, he moved to slam the door. The Concierge caught it just in time and barged his way in.

"Before you flip out, Joseph has something to say." The Ripper started to retreat to the bathroom to lock himself in. The Concierge grabbed him by the shirt and held on.

"You're going to listen!" The Concierge glanced at Joseph. It was his cue.

"Look, I'm very sorry about how I reacted. I have some issues that I'm dealing with from my military deployment in Iraq. I try to keep my cool, but when someone gets physical, that's when I lose control. I'm sorry." Joseph handed The Ripper the bottle of cognac. He took it grudgingly.

"The play is hurting without you. Please come back." Joseph finally got eye contact from The Ripper. Joseph could tell that he wasn't and would never really be forgiven. It took a great deal of restraint for Joseph to make a supplication to this prima donna who had no business holding the title of Master.

"All right." The Ripper said to The Concierge, avoiding further eye contact with Joseph. "Just keep your mad dog on a leash."

"Very well." The Concierge said, glancing at Joseph. "Let's go.

We'll all be back to work tomorrow. Things will all be copesthetic." The Concierge smiled through his discomfort. It was obvious he was done with The Master too. They left.

In the elevator, The Concierge broke the silence.
"Thank you for your restraint. I know that you don't like him."
The Concierge said apologetically.
"No, I don't like him. That really doesn't matter, does it? We have a job to do." Joseph said as the elevator chimed.
"My floor." Joseph said, leaving The Concierge alone.
"Good night, Joseph." The Concierge said as the elevator doors closed.

That night, Joseph ordered room service and a bottle of merlot. The waiter arrived with a cart.
"Good evening, sir." The waiter said in a soft voice. "May I open your bottle of wine?"
Joseph nodded, not looking at him.
The waiter uncorked the wine and held it out for Joseph to sniff. Joseph smelled the cork and nodded. He was irritated at this formality as he just wanted to get to drinking.

The waiter began to pour. The man smelled bad, like boiled onions. Usually the waiters smelled like they were all dipped in lavender.
"Sir, have you thought about my proposal?"

Joseph glanced up, realizing that he had heard this voice before. It was Friend, unrecognizable in his waiter's coat. He pulled the tablecloth aside, revealing a hidden compartment, just big enough for a man to crawl into.

"You can see her tonight. Who knows when I can come again." Friend said. Joseph studied the skinny kid's arms. They had track marks all over and a budding infection at the triangle of veins at the top of his right forearm.

"Let me finish this glass before I crawl in that thing." Joseph said, gulping down his merlot.

"Whatever floats your boat." Friend said, rubbing his infection.

Joseph stared at the compartment and thought about all the things that could go wrong. How much trouble he could get into if he was caught. Still, the desire to see the Flower Girl again was overwhelming. He finished the glass of merlot for courage, then crawled in the secret compartment like a magician's girl and put his life in the hands of Friend.

The elevator to the dungeon was the first gauntlet they had to pass on the way to room 8-210. He had seen the stone-faced Russian guards do a rude inspection of a food cart from his vantage point at the restaurant. A similar perusal would nail him for certain.

Joseph felt the cart slow and he tried to stay still and breathe quietly.

"Hello, Gregor." He heard Friend say. By the sound of it, he knew Gregor. The spoke like familiars.

"You deliver food?" Gregor muttered in a heavy Russian accent as he lifted the metal dome covers from each dish.

To Joseph's horror, he saw a thick hand grab the curtain just inches from his face.

"Wait. Didn't you see I got you something?" Friend said.

"What you have?" Gregor asked in a suspicious tone.

"Volga cake. I had the kitchen make some for you and your friends." Friend said as he removed the cake from its box. Joseph watched tensely as Gregor's hand let go of the curtain.

"What you want?" Gregor's suspicious tone intensified.

"I don't want anything." Friend said in feigned surprise.

"Nothing free here. I take it, but you get nothing back, understand?"

The elevator bell DINGED and the door opened. Friend pushed the cart in and as the doors closed and they started to descend, Joseph could breathe again.

"Volga cake?"

"I had to think of something." Friend responded, teeth chattering nervously.

I thought they had us." Joseph whispered.

"Me too." The skinny kid replied as he wiped the nervous sweat from his forehead.

The door opened and a guard checked Friend's identity card. The guard at this checkpoint must have assumed that Gregor had checked under the cart. He let them go on with a cursory glance.

Officially, the sex dungeon wouldn't open until the customers arrived, but there was plenty of activity already.

"Not so hard." A man's voice cried out breathlessly from a distant room. They passed another room with intermittent sounds of bodies slapping together.

For what seemed like hours, the cart rolled onto a lumpy carpeted surface that Joseph surmised as shag or possibly carpet remnants throws at odd angles that barely offered comfort from the thick cold concrete.

After hitting the largest lump yet and nearly getting stuck, the cart finally reached its destination.

The skinny kid stopped the cart and pulled aside the curtain.

"Room 8-210, right there. Joseph craned his neck through the curtain and saw the room. Looking back, he saw that they were in a dead-end hallway. It was a dirty and smelly place. The overwhelming odor was mildew, so strong that Joseph wondered how anyone could think of sex in this environment.

The sex workers lived in this sunless moldy place. The Flower Girl lived here.

Joseph rolled out of the cart and crawled across the moldy carpet to room 8-210. He found the door unlocked and he dashed in. The skinny kid wasted no time putting distance between him and the room. Joseph heard the cart rattle clumsily across the carpet remnants. In a few seconds he couldn't hear it at all.

With the immediate danger over, Joseph's senses returned to normal. The smell in this room was burned in Joseph's memory from Iraq. The smell of a field hospital filled with enemy soldiers dying of necrosis.

"Hello?" Joseph said into the darkness.

"Hello, Joseph." A sweet but weak voice whispered back. "I'm glad you came."

Joseph's eyes strained in the pitch dark. For a moment, he thought that he saw phantom shapes moving across the room.

"Can you turn on the lights?" Joseph pleaded, afraid that the phantoms might be the only occupants in here with him.

A match struck in the darkness and he saw her outline as she lit a single candle. He could finally see the room in the growing flame. Though this room was new, it seemed purposefully designed to look like a flophouse complete with old carpet and mattresses from the early eighties.

The Flower Girl sat on the bed. It appeared that she was wearing a diaper. Her face and arms were bruised and her bottom lip was swollen.

"You wanted to see what I really am. Now you see it." The Flower Girl said in a weak voice.

"What happened to you?"

"They hurt me. I think I'm dying, Joseph. I can't feel below the waist." The Flower Girl seemed resigned to her fate. She had no medicine in her room. It was as if she was dumped in this room to get rid of her.

Joseph shuddered to think what they did to her.

"Will you let me look at it?" Joseph asked, hiding his dread.

Wordlessly, she lay down on the mattress allowing him to undo her diaper. As he did, the smell hit him. Dying flesh on her genitals that had been torn open from vagina to anus.

It was black with rot. When Joseph was assigned to Africa to protect UN inspectors, a village of women had been similarly injured by a rival tribe as an act of terror and revenge for perceived slights. It was called a fistula and could only be corrected by surgery.

"Oh God." Joseph felt a wave of sickness wash over him. Sickness and confusion.

"I snuck up to the surface with an assumed identity. They eventually found me…sent me back. They punished me."

The misery of the scene was more than he could bear. He started to cry.

"Don't. I'm just so glad to see you again. I don't want you to be sad." The Flower Girl drifted in and out of a dream state.

"I'm going to get you out of here." Joseph said, with the knowledge that it may be too late.

"You know all I thought about was you not wanting me anymore." The Flower Girl croaked as she faded.

"Of course I still want you." Joseph said, choking back tears.

"You just hang on. I'm going to get you flown out of here. Get you help."

"They won't allow it." She said.

A light rapping at the door interrupted the moment.

"It's the boy. He wants to take you back." She said.

"What's your name? Your real name, so I can tell them who you are."

The Flower Girl shook her head.

"Joseph, people like me don't have names." As she continued speaking, a foreign accent slipped out of mouth. It sounded Russian.

"My only name is 'Asset-334'. The only name I've ever known." She said with an increasingly building Russian flavor. The next sentence she spoke was not in English.

Joseph took her hand in his and asked her to look into his eyes, snapping her back to reality.

With her hand in his, he saw something familiar on her wrist. Something he saw in Iraq and thought he'd never see again. It was a tattoo of Prometheus. The mark of the notorious Marmaladov gang. Scum that had human trafficking down to a science. The Flower Girl was their property. That meant that everyone in this dungeon was their property.

"Just hang on, OK?" Joseph touched her face.

"You'd better go or the guards will be podozritel'nyy." She said, slipping into her mother tongue again.

Friend knocked on the door again.

"Come on Joseph!" He said as loud as he could without attracting attention.

Joseph squeezed The Flower Girl's hand and opened the door, finding an impatient kid pointing at the cart angrily.

"Get in, NOW!" He admonished Joseph who dutifully climbed in. He glanced back at The Flower Girl who blew out the candles, preferring to stay in the dark.

Again, Friend pushed the cart through the halls of carpet remnants and past the disinterested guards

The elevator bell dinged and opened to Joseph's floor where the friendly smells of the hotel flooded in to greet them.

Distant smells of baking bread wafted through the ventilation system along with the fragrant oils burning at regular intervals in little hotpots.

Friend opened the door to Joseph's room and rolled the cart inside. As soon as he heard the door shut behind him, Joseph let out a huge sigh.

"I can't believe you all live that way." Joseph whispered.

"I have to get back to the floor before head count." Friend said, ignoring Joseph's commentary.

"Goodbye and thank you." Joseph said, holding out his hand.

Friend awkwardly shook it as if he had never shaken hands before.

"You can help her?" He asked.

"Yes. Or die trying." Joseph said with a gravity that assured to the kid that he meant it.

"What's your name? The name they gave you?" Joseph asked.

"Asset-889." The skinny kid responded with a humiliated expression. "I have to go." He turned his cart around and left.

Alone, Joseph stood at the center of the room for a moment, still processing what had just happened. He had no idea he was screaming until he fell to his knees. Tears ran from his eyes and snot from his nose.

"Is everything OK in there?" Someone said as they knocked on the room's door.

"Go away!" Was all Joseph could say.

"Are you sure?"

"Yes!" Joseph gasped.

Joseph crawled into his bed and stayed there, the smell of the sex dungeon still in his sinuses.

The next morning, Joseph met The Concierge in his office and admitted what he had seen and done.

"You know, you could be fired for going down there unescorted." The Concierge said in a sympathetic tone.

"I don't care." Joseph snapped.

"...I have nothing to do with what happened to her." The

Concierge said with a pleading gesture.

"I don't care. She has to be evacuated or I'm done." The Concierge knew that Joseph meant it.

"You present us with a real dilemma Joseph."

"Get her medical EVAC or find yourself another Elephant Man. I don't give a shit." Joseph took off his PRIME ACTOR security badge and tossed it on the Concierge's desk.

The Concierge studied it with a gloomy expression.

"This is a human life. She doesn't even have a name, just a number?" Joseph said more as a condemnation than a question.

"You don't understand, Joseph." The Concierge said. His pallor getting whiter by the moment. "I'm the advocate for actors here, but there are dark forces at work here, Joseph. I think you just don't understand the danger. If I help this girl, will you promise me that you won't breathe a word to anyone. It's not just your neck on the line if you catch my drift."

"I know all about the 'dark forces'. I've dealt with them before."

"Promise you won't talk about this." The Concierge asked again.

"I promise." Joseph said without hesitation.

"Well, Joseph, I hope you're a man that keeps his promises." The Concierge said with resignation.

"So you'll help her?"

"Yes. Now will you go back to rehearsal?"

"Yes. Keep me updated and give me proof that she's OK." Joseph stood to leave.

"Very well. Please go. They're waiting for you at makeup."

"Thank you." Joseph nodded, relieved that The Flower Girl would get help. He thought of the hundreds of sex workers down in that basement. The Flower Girl was only one "Asset". There were so many others, each one of them with a tragic slave's story. He felt profound disappointment that the revolutionary theater that was Gaslight was just a front for human trafficking. If the Marmaladov gang was really in charge, the must not have recognized him. Joseph knew that if they did, they would've killed him the second he set foot on the island. Payback for what happened in Fallujah.

As Joseph left for rehearsal, The Concierge sunk in his chair, mapping out a plan to justify a medevac for a sex worker that would otherwise be left to decline and die. The Concierge tried to suppress the thought that he was complicit in the Flower Girl's suffering, but couldn't. He was guilty, as was everyone who tolerated this cruel activity without reporting it. Joseph was the only one that did the right thing. That realization was especially damning.

That night, Joseph was delivered a telegram with a QR code printed on it.

He stuck it under the well-hidden reader on the hotel TV set and the title "SLIDE SHOW LOADING" swiped across the screen.

On screen were a series of photos of The Flower Girl being taken from her room in a wheelchair, escorted past the hotel to the giant elevator to the surface to a waiting plane. In the last photo of her , she looked back at the camera. To Joseph, it seemed like she was looking at him. There was one photo after that of the plane taking off against the sunset.

Joseph breathed a sigh of relief that she was on her way to safety. He reserved celebration, knowing that they might have yanked her off the plane before takeoff. Still, he thought of the Concierge's promise and knew he would keep his word.

Joseph considered a long-term plan. A plan to blow the whistle on what was happening here. Eventually, he would have a chance to get the story out. The struggle for him was waiting for that opportunity to present itself.

THE COIN

The following day, The Playwright held an all cast meeting in the streets of Whitechapel. He stood on the roof of Twelve Bells, megaphone in hand, and glanced over the crowd of actors that resembled the audience at a rock concert rather than a cast.

"THREE MORE DAYS!!! Can you feel it coming?!" The Playwright screamed over the bullhorn.
"Hell YEAH!" Someone screamed from the crowd.
Raucous cheering followed.
"Nine weeks. That's how long this experience will last for our guests. There's never been anything to compare to this experience in length, scale or talent. This year...we will make theater history with attendance, storyline quality and spectacle. These last three days of rehearsal...use them well to prepare for opening day. Thank you!" The Playwright clicked off the megaphone and stepped down into the Twelve Bells through a hidden door.

A groundswell of cheers punctuated the end of the address as dozens of stage assistants flooded the streets holding flags with character names printed on them ten per flag.
Joseph didn't need a flag. The Playwright himself came to supervise the rehearsal. He led Joseph and the Ripper into the Twelve Bells and sat them down at a table.

"Boys, I just can't figure out who is going to live through this conflict. The Ripper's death makes sense because he abruptly stopped killing after the Fletcher woman, his last victim according to history books. Still, The Elephant Man's story would be that much more tragic if he was killed trying to get vengeance for his mother.

"I think the Elephant Man should die. He's frail. It wouldn't make sense any other way." The Ripper noted.

"What do you think, Joseph?" The Playwright asked, knowing that The Ripper wasn't going to ask for Joseph's opinion.

"I think The Elephant Man should kill the murderer of his mother and die with the secret." Joseph said as the Playwright nodded.

"You're full of shit, Joseph!" The Ripper snapped at him. The rebuke was something Joseph expected.

"Tell you what…" The Playwright took out a gold coin about three inches in diameter and held it in his palm.

"Heads, the Ripper dies. Tails, the Elephant Man."

Without waiting for a reaction from his two actors, The Playwright flipped the coin in the air. When it landed on the table, it bounced in a way that a coin shouldn't bounce, causing Joseph to wonder if it was real.

It twirled, but rather than falling on heads or tails, it came to a rest on its edge.

All of them sat, staring at the coin with blank expressions. Joseph didn't know the odds of a coin landing on its side, but he was sure it was pretty low.

"Well. I've never seen that before. Let me flip again." The Playwright gingerly picked the upright coin from the table and prepared to toss it. This time, The Playwright tossed it high, almost to the ceiling. It landed hard on the wooden table and bounced up again about two feet in the air before landing like a sure-footed gymnast, twirling a bit and coming to a stop again on its edge.

It felt like the air was sucked out of the room. The Playwright tried to speak, but only mumbled something unintelligible. Even the Ripper was stunned to silence. The coin landing on its side once was possible, though extremely rare. Landing twice in a row was a mathematical near-impossibility.

Rather than trying again and risking the fabric of space and time, The Playwright left the coin where it was.

"I think this speaks volumes." The Playwright finally found his voice.

"The ending cannot be written. It can only be resolved in the active play"

"What do you mean? Are you saying we should actually try to kill each other?" The Ripper said tersely.

"No. I'm just saying, the right course will come to you in the immersion."

Joseph took this to mean that the Playwright was leaving the
conclusion of this arc in the hands of the actors.
"This is outrageous!" The Ripper growled.
"Your rehearsals are done now. See you on opening day,
gentlemen." With that, The Playwright stood and two bodyguards
appeared from the darkness of the Twelve Bells. They had been
there the whole time.

"Unbelievable!" The Ripper spat as he jumped up from his chair.
He pointed his bony finger at Joseph.
"If you caused this..!" He gestured to the still upright coin.
"…somehow!"
The Ripper stormed out of the Twelve Bells, not waiting for a
denial from Joseph.

Joseph waited for a moment, watching the coin. Joseph finally
stood, leaving it on the table.

That afternoon, The Glass Paris was empty. The place was empty
except for a lone couple sitting in the patio. Joseph sat at his
favorite spot at the far back. The waiter almost missed him there.
"Welcome back. I'm sorry to say that we're out of purple
absinthe." The waiter said apologetically.
"I don't think I could handle another one of those." Joseph

admitted. "Just a green one, please."

The waiter nodded to the barkeep that poured the four ounces of emerald liquid before sitting it under the ornate water dispenser for its slow transformation.

In a few minutes, the drink came to Joseph's table almost glowing. He didn't drink it right away, staring at the aquamarine beverage as if it were a crystal ball. Finally, he took a drink and the sweet taste of anise flooded his mouth.

He drank it slow. Nursing it for an hour or so, waiting for someone to come into the absinthe bar. The couple sitting outside finally went home, leaving him as the sole customer.

Finally, Joseph called for the check. The waiter approached Joseph and took his empty glass.

"Another?"

"No. Just the check."

"Someone has beat you to it." The waiter said with a knowing grin.

"Who? Who beat me to what? Joseph replied, boozy and confused.

"I think you know, sir. I think you know."

The waiter started cleaning up in preparation for closing. The bartender sang an old French song as he cleaned glasses.

Joseph glanced around the room, wondering if he'd see the exiled

Master staring at him. There was nothing. At least not any obvious sign that he was being watched.

"There are dark forces at work here, Joseph." The words of the Concierge played in his head.
"Dark forces." Joseph said aloud as he left the Glass Paris.
A deadbolt lock turned behind him. He glanced back and saw that all the lights were off in the bar.

After vacating the hotel in favor of the straw bed of the freak show, Joseph paid a visit to the wardrobe department at first light.
Inside, a small army of workers were unboxing uniforms and hanging them on a dry-cleaner's conveyor belt.
"Fishmonger number three." The wardrobe master said into his headset.
The conveyor roared to life, turning until the Fishmonger's place on the machine came to bear. An assistant lifted the plastic-wrapped suit onto the slot with a grunt, looking visibly relieved to be free of the burden.

"Oh." The Wardrobe Master stepped back from his computer.
"What can we do for you, Joseph?"
"Is my costume ready?"
The Wardrobe Master seemed stunned and unsure.
"Joseph, your costume is in five parts and weighs almost eighty pounds and needs to be cleaned nightly. We usually wait for the

Team Lead to call for it."

"I can wait." Joseph found a stool and sat down as The Wardrobe Master muttered a command to one of his underlings. Two assistants left the building, presumably to collect Joseph's costume in all its elements.

During the wait, Joseph watched more costumes getting stacked onto to conveyor. "Physician", "Street Sweeper" "Teacher" then finally "Flower Girl".

"Can I see that dress for a moment?" Joseph cried out in a voice of embarrassing desperation.

"Are you gonna wear it?" TWM asked.

"Please, just for a second."

The Wardrobe Master reluctantly handed over the recently mended dress.

He put it to his face and inhaled, smelling the faint odor of patchouli.

"What's this about?" The Wardrobe Master snapped.

"Someone I knew wore this dress. I can still smell her."

"Give it back to me. We'll have it rewashed."

Joseph reluctantly handed the dress back and returned to wait at the uncomfortable stool.

The hypnotic flow of the conveyer belt continued, putting Joseph in a sleepy state.

"It's here!" The Wardrobe Master barked at Joseph who was nearly passed out.

The two assistants carried the costume in thick wooden hangers.

"Would you like help assembling the costume?"

"Yes. I want to get used to the weight."

"Very well. Get undressed and my assistants will help you."

The assistants started with the pants and worked their way up. The shoes had been changed. They were standard tennis shoes with leather sewn into the tops. The padding was extra thick, probably to address the foot fatigue.

There was a rough-hewn undershirt covered further with a canvas-like overcoat.

"I assume you can wait on the hood?" The Wardrobe Manager asked, holding the dirty Elephant Man hood like a dead cat.

"I don't need it now."

"OK. We'll tuck it away until showtime. Now if you don't mind, we have hundreds more costumes to inventory.

"OK." Joseph replied, nodding with gratitude.

Joseph stepped outside and felt the full force of the extra pounds on him. He imagined the experience to be similar to the field pack that he carried into battle. Add to that twenty-five pounds of makeup that he was deferring, it was like carrying a whole other person.

Joseph spent the next hour walking the perimeter of Gaslight, getting used to the bulk and weight. He didn't notice that he was wheezing when a cart pulled up beside him.

"You know that most people would find self-flagellation easier." The Concierge said as he set the parking brake on his cart. "Hop in. I don't want to see you exhaust yourself again." Joseph stood there, sweating, panting, and seemingly oblivious.

"That wasn't a request, Joseph." The Concierge said tersely.

Heading back to the freak show, the Concierge seemed more relaxed than Joseph had ever seen him. Now that the new season was about to begin, The Concierge could finally let the Stage Manager take the bulk of the work. All of the work, really. He didn't tell Joseph that he would be leaving the island soon.

"Sure you won't take a room in the hotel tonight?" The Concierge asked.

"I go by the same rules as everyone else." Joseph said, rejecting the thought of the VIP lounges and hotel suites. He only wanted the same treatment as those making the minimum contracted wage.

"Very well." The Concierge said, patiently waiting for Joseph to disembark the cart. Joseph grunted as his muscles protested. He was sore.

"See you in the morning…Elephant Man."

Joseph glanced back, but didn't respond.

BAMBOO

That night, Joseph slept deeply. The kind of sleep where dreams grow. He dreamed of his mother. She died when he was eight and he rarely dreamed of her anymore. In the dream, he was a child again, sitting at the dinner table. They were eating Chinese take-out and he was fumbling with his chopsticks as she laughed. They had barely made it home with the old VW bug in desperate need of an engine rebuild.

Soon, without warning, she threw away all the cutlery in favor of the bamboo chopsticks without explanation. Joseph would sneak in plastic sporks from school but eventually he got so good with his chopsticks that he could even eat cereal with them. Joseph wouldn't eat with anything else but the chopsticks until he left home for college. They kept the memory of his mother alive. When he left for college, he felt that he had grieved enough and he ate with a fork for the first time in over a decade. He cried uncontrollably as he ate the pancakes at Denny's.

He stabbed the flapjacks and brought the pieces to his mouth in broken chunks covered in tears.

THE LAST FREE DAY

Joseph woke up before the "sun" rose on that last free morning before the audience arrived.

"Good morning." A slight middle-aged lady with a food cart presented Joseph with a menu.

"I have coffee and pastries and a hot breakfast sandwich. If you want something more elaborate, they're serving breakfast at the Twelve Bells.

"Sandwich and coffee would be great."

The woman nodded and dug into the hot side of her cart. Steam rose, against the coolness of the morning. She put a sandwich on a paper plate and then poured Joseph a cup of coffee.

"Cream and sugar?"

"Yes."

She added the condiments quickly and handed him the twelve-ounce cup.

"Good luck tomorrow." She said as she packed up the cart.

"I appreciate that." Joseph said, smiling.

The woman moved ahead to serve the bearded lady at the nearby stage. She just took coffee and toasted Joseph from afar. Joseph returned the toast half-heartedly, briefly thinking of The Mutant Queen and wondering what happened to her.

The suit felt no lighter today. Even though he hated the Twelve Bells, he gravitated there, watching the actors and crew grab breakfast.

The Playwright exited with his entourage that consisted of the heads of most of the departments. Joseph hid in the doorway of a bakery until they passed.

Joseph thought about this last day and just wanted it to be over. The parties and the political maneuvering would all mean nothing once the audience arrived.

The audience would determine how the play did or didn't work as much as the cast did. That was the great unknown element in an immersive production of this scale. An audience that refused to participate would result in failure of the idea as a whole. It was the one element the management couldn't really control.

Joseph entered the Twelve Bells and was relieved that he was largely unnoticed.

He passed over the VIP lounge, opting to drink with the unwashed masses at the long wooden bar.

"Irish coffee please." He called out to the barkeep. The bartender wordlessly assembled his drink from ingredients in the well. Suddenly he looked up and recognized Joseph. He promptly moved to throw out the inferior drink.

"Let me taste it first." Joseph reached for the coffee cup and took a sip. The whiskey was truly awful. "Go ahead." He coughed and handed the glass back. "That was terrible." Joseph said, gagging.

The barkeep reached up to a bottle on the top shelf.
"Nothing I could do about the coffee, sir." He said apologetically.
"Just give me straight whiskey then."
"Yessir." The barkeep remade the drink and handed it to Joseph.

He could tell the difference right away. The whiskey didn't have that odor of rancid gasoline the way the rail hooch did. He took a sip and it burned as it went down. It was the good stuff, probably single cask quality. He realized that he should've just had the shot of good whiskey from the start rather than making any pretense of Twelve Bells having good coffee. In minutes, he felt a warm glow in his guts and head and the bar seemed a little more tolerable.

"Why aren't you in your VIP section with the Queen and the Ripper?" The Bearded Lady asked Joseph as she nudged up to him. He glanced up at the two actors in the swanky second floor bar. Their only company was a bartender standing at the ready.

"They can have it." Joseph noted, wondering what the two lead actors discussed up there in their private duchy. "I'd rather just be with everyone else. Doesn't it look boring up there?" Joseph said, still glancing up at his fellow leads.
"Yeah, it does." The Bearded Lady took Joseph's drink from his

hands and downed a slug.

"Damn. That's tits!" She exclaimed.

"I know it is." Joseph said as he regained possession of his drink. There was hardly anything left of it.

"Well, see you neighbor." The Bearded Lady vanished into the crowd. Joseph turned back to the bar and got the bartender's attention.

"Another one, please."

With a new drink in hand, Joseph found the darkest corner of the bar and hid there.

No one else came to bother him until a call was made over the intercom. The Playwright was to address the actors, all of them, in fifteen minutes.

As they exited the Twelve Bells, each actor was given a packet sealed with a dollop of wax and stamped with a message "Do not open until ordered."

The crowd started to gather as the daytime sky became night with a full moon.

Joseph stared at it, knowing it was an imitation. It was hard to believe that it was just a projection.

Joseph couldn't see the Playwright from his vantage point at the front of the Twelve Bells, but it didn't matter. The moon literally became his stage as his image was projected into it. Thunderous applause spread across the whole of Gaslight until the Playwright gestured for silence.

"Tomorrow is day one of sixty-four. Sixty-four days to change the fabric of live theater. There are so many things that set Gaslight apart from any other immersive experience. Much of the heavy lifting of that unique experience falls on your shoulders. The Stage Manager will take over the reigns from team Concierge and will be responsible to keep you on task. The Concierge did a fantastic job this year! We wish him well on his journey back home to Sicily where he has a production of his own to direct." Another round of applause was followed by the pounding of a thousand feet. Joseph was shocked at the news. He thought he'd have The Concierge for another nine weeks. He felt frightened.

"As of six PM tonight the hotel area of Gaslight is forbidden to actors unless expressly directed by one of the department heads. Your sets will be your homes now. The hotel and the comforts within are the guest's neutral space and I ask you to respect that unless otherwise ordered. Now, take the day to mentally prepare, though the veterans from the previous years will tell you…nothing really can prepare you for this. Starting at midnight tonight, you may open your packets and reveal your one-on-one experiences with customers. At six am, the customers will start landing above us and you must be on your game. Actors, I don't expect perfection right away, but I expect you to give it one hundred ten percent. Good luck to you all. I will see you at the party." The

Playwright stepped down and the moon returned to its realistic former glory.

Joseph felt eyes on him. Some were those that believed the Elephant Man to be a cursed role. Others simply wanted Joseph to fail because they had not been chosen. The ones that seemed to support him the most were the new ones, the ones who were still hungry for the Gaslight experience. The ones who still believed in the magic of immersive theater.

THE LAST HOURS

The Gaslight kickoff party was legendary. Every year, the actors got so drunk that the first day of the production was always considered a throwaway.

After tonight, the liquor would be rationed for the lower tier actors though it could still be gotten on the black market. It was rumored that The Glass Paris made its real money in bootlegging.

Joseph thought of going to the Twelve Bells, but decided to stay home and read his one-on-one interactions instead.

Joseph cracked open the wax seal on the envelope and removed a binder with his name on it.

Each page detailed a one-on-one character interaction.

"You are expected to watch for opportunities for one-on-one interactions. These are the truly valuable experience that the audience looks forward to.

Joseph read three of the one-on-one scenes.

SCENERIO ONE

Dressed in the cloak, approach someone who is alone and bring them through the steam alley, taking the back approach to the freak show. When you reach the FS, take them to your living quarters and offer them tea. If they say yes, use the tea in the container marked "special blend". While having tea, bring out a portrait of your mother and tell your guess the history of how she vanished when you were a child, leaving you at a work house. Offer to look at wallet photos of the audience member's family and say complimentary things if applicable.

When tea is finished ask them for help to get into bed. They will most likely want to leave after this, but if they don't, you can pretend to sleep and they will most likely go on their own.

SCENERIO TWO

Roam the streets near the Twelve Bells at night. Tell a random patron that you are lost and need help getting back to the freak show. Take them near the London Hospital where a Page will approach them with a letter from Dr. Frederick Treves (This will be a separate one-on-one). In the letter, Treves will ask your one-on-ones to follow you and report back your living conditions to him in exchange for five pounds.

They will follow you back to your living quarters and it will be up to you to demonstrate how uncomfortable and inadequate your

conditions are. Ask them about where they stay and react with
awe when they describe it. Ask if they will invite you to see their
living quarters. They will most likely say "no", but if they say
"yes", feign hip pain and ask to visit another time.
This should end the encounter.

SCENERIO THREE

You will be in a horse-driven taxi. You will ride in the taxi in a
corner seat. Eventually when the taxi picks someone else up, you
will explain that you have no destination, but are hiding from the
freak show. The taxi will stop at Twelve Bells where you will ask
the patrons to go inside and purchase a bottle of ale for you. If
they come back, pay for the beer and give them a hefty tip. If they
stay in the taxi, talk about your life and ask them to purchase a
copy of your autobiography (hand them a ragged copy).
At this point, the taxi driver will ask you to leave because the freak
show is nearby and that is "Where freaks belong".
Beg to stay and when the Taxi driver calls you a beast. That will be
your cue to leave. If they try to follow you, duck into one of the
escape doors and lose them.

Joseph glanced at the mechanical clock. It read ten pm. Joseph
wound it and then set his costume on the chair next to the straw
bed. Makeup would come get him at 4am and at 6am when the
patrons landed, he would be the Elephant Man.

OPENING DAY

Even deep underground, the actors could hear the rumble of jets landing to drop off the audience then shortly thereafter howling off to make the return trip to Miami.

The first group appeared on the giant platform elevator, each of them straining for a glance of the landscape of Gaslight.

Spontaneous applause erupted as the first timers got their first good look at the enormity of it all.

When the elevator finally reached the ground floor, a mob of people rushed out to explore the world around them as the guides reminded them to check in at the hotel before exploring the site.

"Please return to the hotel. Do not put us in the position of fetching you and bringing you back." The guide said through the bullhorn.

Most of the errant patrons came back on their own. Two college-age kids were escorted back by security.

Joseph didn't see any of this. He was strapped into the makeup chair as the artists worked furiously to get the facial appliances on.

"We're not gonna make the deadline." One artist exclaimed with worry.

"See if someone can guard freak show door. No patrons get through." The Team Lead said, his face frozen with tension.

"I'll send out the word." An assistant responded and called out for help over the radio headset. "Yes, it's team three. We're so far behind. We'll need someone to do traffic control here at the freak show.

"Yes, I know you're slammed. We're all slammed here." Someone from the London Tower responded.

Joseph was fully dressed and made up at seven am. Three burly guards stood at the lip of the tent. They had turned away one early-bird patron.

"We'll do better tomorrow, I promise." The Team Lead said in a conciliatory tone. "Take a look at yourself."

Joseph stood with some effort, fighting the weight of the suit, the makeup and the motion-limiting appliance attached to his limbs. He stared into the mirror in disbelief as he saw himself fully assembled, costume and complete makeup, for the first time.

"I am Joseph Merrick." Was all he could say.

"Yes you are." The Team Lead said with pride. "We got word they want you with HOOD ON for this first encounter, OK?" The Team Lead brought the giant burlap hood over Joseph's deformed skull. The Team Lead flipped on the heads-up display in the hood. Seeing this, the security guards opened the outer curtain of the freak show tent.

"Your public awaits." The Team Lead said, smiling.

Joseph stepped out into the artificial sunlight, walking with the machine-assisted limp that forced accuracy.

A gaggle of audience members saw him first as they rounded the corner from the freak show.

There was a moment of silent recognition as the audience finally realized who it was in front of them.

They approached like a herd of cattle and surrounded Joseph, touching him, proving that the Elephant Man was really in front of them. Joseph felt hot and uncomfortable in this first encounter and pushed through the crowd. They offered no resistance. Joseph realized that they were all reaching for the cell phone cameras that were confiscated and on the heel of that rendered useless without Wi-Fi. They found nothing in their pockets. They all had to learn to start living in the moment. Relying only on memory to capture the memories.

Though this was the first day, it was a soft open as wave after wave of patrons descended the elevators with nearly identical reactions of excitement and awe.

Crowds would surround Joseph and have the same reflexive reach into their pockets for the device that wasn't there. One lady tried to snatch Joseph's hood off, but he managed to swat her hand away. She held her hand, looking butt hurt.

Later, Joseph passed an argument between a Hospitality Manager and a patron, a middle-aged man, over the confiscation of his cell phone.

"Any media device is disallowed!"

"That is my phone. I have the right to text my family!"

"You can send a telegram for twenty dollars US. That is the only communication allowed with the outside world."

"You're kidding?" The patron screamed.

"This was all in the contract that you signed, sir. You did read the contract before you signed it, didn't you?"

"You can't take my property." The patron bellowed, not understanding the futility of his argument.

"Sir, even if you had your device, there's not a single cell phone tower within five hundred miles! Now, good day." The Hospitality Manager barked, leaving the patron reeling.

"No Wi-Fi?" The customer said as he sulked away towards the hotel.

This conversation was repeated dozens of times across the Gaslight stage as people suffered through stages of withdrawals. One young couple couldn't make it through the night and decided to fly all the way back home to South Africa. They said they had unexpected anxiety about abandoning their social media accounts.

Though Joseph couldn't get close to the hotel, some of the servers from the bar confirmed that the lobby was a madhouse of patrons lining up to send telegrams.

"What a racket." Joseph surmised, thinking about how fifty

telegrams would make Gaslight a thousand dollars. At last report, there were four-hundred people in line.

The secret doors throughout Gaslight led to a place that Joseph knew about but rarely frequented. During the run, there was only one safe area for cast and crew to catch their breath and get updates. This backstage area terminated at the London Tower where the command center resided. At the top floor of this tower replica was The Playwright's lavish apartment.

At the common area backstage there were simple comforts throughout. Cots set up in rows, a small food stand with an espresso machine and lots of couches.
The shuttered main cafeteria was set to open tomorrow. Judging by the clatter behind those closed doors, the kitchen staff worked feverishly to open by the breakfast deadline tomorrow morning.

Joseph was surprised to see The Concierge sitting at one of the couches smoking a cigar and sipping brandy from a goblet glass.
"Hello, Joseph." He said in a slurred voice.
"I didn't expect to see you here." Joseph sat next to The Concierge, waving off his offer of a cigar.
"I'll miss everyone. You most of all, Joseph." As The Concierge said this, Joseph felt himself choke up.
"You've been good to all of us. Thank you." He struggled to get the words out.

"Well, you are all out-of-the-nest for better or worse." The Concierge poured Joseph a shot of brandy and passed it to him.

"To Gaslight." He said as they tinked their glasses.

Joseph drank as The Concierge stared at him.

"I knew you were the right actor when I saw you. Now here we are, ready to embark on your journey. Joseph Merrick himself drinking a brandy with me."

Joseph finished his drink and stood, facing the nerve center.

"I should go out and find someone to interact with." Joseph said, starting to make his exit.

"Relax Joseph. The real work starts tomorrow. The guests are struggling with the lack of cell phones, fast food, and thousands of cable TV channels." The Concierge laughed.

"No doubt some have found the bottom floor." Joseph noted.

The concierge froze, mid-sip and didn't look up at Joseph.

"Less said on that, the better." The Concierge whispered.

"Indeed. You know it's wrong."

The Concierge nodded darkly and drank some more brandy.

"Well, good bye then." Joseph's mind turned to the Flower Girl.

He didn't like the vulnerability he felt when he thought of her.

Still it came and it made his mood sad and dark at the thought of her absence.

"Good-bye, Joseph and good luck." The Concierge said, his mood darkened.

Joseph returned to the main stage through one of the secret doors.

When Joseph returned to the freak show, the makeup team was waiting for him.

They removed eighty pounds of wardrobe and appliances and gave him a night mask to wear while he slept. The night mask was soft, light and comfortable.

The downside to this was that it would not survive close scrutiny.

"While the night mask is on, you must stay in your quarters, did someone tell you that already?" The Team Lead asked in an exhausted voice.

"The Concierge did." Joseph said, already missing the man.

"Good job." The Team Lead noted with pleasure.

"Will I have visitors tonight?"

"You might. Now I won't tell you what to do because you're an adult, but we stocked condoms for you, just in case, in the tin next to your bed."

The Team Lead leaned in to whisper something.

"Everyone wants to fuck the Elephant Man." He stepped back as if to emphasize the statement. "If you don't want to…and they won't leave, push your panic button. But, hey, you can make a lot of extra money that way. A lot of actors do."

"I'm making good money already." Joseph said with a grin. "I'll see you in the morning."

"OK. I'll put up the privacy sign if you want." The Team Lead offered this consolation, knowing that it would be ignored anyway.

"Please." Joseph said, reading The Team Leads face with disappointment.

After they left, Joseph sat on his straw bed for a moment, reveling in the first isolation he'd experienced all day. He stood and paced in the room as the gaslight flickered.

He looked up at the place where the ceiling had been broken through and was grateful that he hadn't had a repeat visit like that. Joseph's eyes traced down a seam of the tent and he saw something he hadn't seen before.

He reached under the tent fabric and found a banner stuck to the backside.

"TRINKA-THE HERMAPHRODITE!!" The banner read. There was a drawing of Trinka that almost resembled Marlene Dietrich dressed in a man's smoking jacket and pants.

Joseph wondered how Trinka proved that she was a hermaphrodite. Did she have to submit to an up-close and personal exam by the audience? Most likely, Joseph thought, it was just an androgynous skinny boy or girl with a gender-neutral wardrobe. There was no Trinka this year. Joseph wondered what had happened to her or him.

Joseph slept for a few hours until he had his first nocturnal visitor. It was difficult to tell in the darkness of the room, but it was a slender woman. She stood there watching him for what seemed like an hour before she approached him. Joseph got a better look at her. She was svelte with deep creases in her face that told stories like grooves in a record. She took off her dress and was naked underneath. Her body looked much younger than her face. Her breasts were small and perky and her skin milky.

She spooned against Joseph's back, causing him to tense up. She smelled good and her skin was soft. Still, Joseph wanted sleep and considered weather to break character and ask her to get out. Still, what she was doing wasn't entirely unpleasant. If this was her fantasy, then he could meet her halfway.

He glanced up at the door and saw another women, much younger and a man waiting and watching.

"He's mine!" The woman in bed barked at the couple who reluctantly retreated to find someone else to bed.

Joseph scanned the side of his bed and found the panic button with his finger. If things got out of hand, he could call for help, couldn't he?

"I'll keep you safe, Joseph Merrick. Those bitches and fags won't come near you as long as you're with me baby."

As she said this, the woman grabbed Joseph's penis and stroked it rhythmically, casually as if she had no further plans for it than to have it in her hand like a figit spinner.

When Joseph woke, the woman was gone and the makeup team

was setting up their cart next to his bed. Her smell was all over him. He hadn't even got her name.

"Ready?" The Team Lead tapped him on the shoulder. "Real acting day today, we'd better get cracking." He gestured to an assistant who brought breakfast to Joseph's bedside.

"Eat quick." The Assistant told him.

The Carnie came and made his rounds in the Freak show. The bearded woman was already out, smoking and drinking coffee while the Lizard Man paced restlessly on the stage just beyond hers.

"Good morning, Freaks!" The Carny said in a droll and sarcastic tone. "Another night spent in a dry bed thanks to me. Another hearty breakfast thanks to me. Just remember that, freaks. It's very cold on the hard streets at night."

Joseph watched from behind the womb of his hood and graded the Carny's performance as only passable.

Beyond the Lizard Man was another stage, still empty. The Carny impatiently tapped his cane on the stage.

"Matilda?!" He tapped the stage again. "You lazy bitch, you get one stage. Your public is waiting!

Matilda's stage name was "Crab Woman", named for the shocking angles of her backward-bending arms and legs. She crawled out to stage with great difficulty. She was obviously in pain, her joints swollen purple.

"That's it!" The Carny said with false encouragement as The Crab Woman grunted with each step.

Joseph could take no more and descended the stairs to help the woman before the Carny waved him off.

"Get back on your stage, Merrick!" As the Carny said this, Joseph felt the machine strapped to his body twist and pinch as he tried to make for the Crab Woman's stage. The pinching finally became a sharp, burning feeling that would not be overcome. The pain forced Joseph to his knees. A pathetic scream escaped from his mouth as the wave of pain became concentrated in his hip. The hip that the Elephant Man broke as a child that healed badly and gave him permanent lameness.

As the Carny laughed and Joseph writhed on the ground, a small crowd gathered at the front of the tent, watching the humiliation of the Elephant Man.

"Get up, you sack of entrails." The Carny spat. The small crowd was silent and visibly moved as Joseph struggled to stand as the mechanism simulated all manner of pain in his joints, his skin and his hip.

"See Merrick, you think you can make it in that big world out there, but you're helpless without me."

With that, the Carny exited stage as The Bearded Lady helped the Crab Woman to her chair. The Lizard Man reluctantly gave

Joseph a hand to get to his feet, holding his nose the whole way. "God, you smell." The Lizard Man complained as a small audience surrounded them. Once on his feet, the LM made a hurried return to his stage.

"Sorry for the disturbance ladies and gentlemen." Joseph could hear the Carny say to someone outside the tent.

The small audience gathered around Merrick's stage as he waved them closer.

"Don't be afraid…" Joseph said, addressing the audience off script. "…I am not the one that would do you harm. Step out of the freak show…then you will find your enemies. Those who haven't suffered with their pretty faces and silk suits. They don't know what pain is. They'll stab you and leave you bleeding in the streets. Beware of them. They are the real monstrosities." Joseph said, warning them of the pickpockets and hustlers that roamed the streets of Whitechapel.

Not knowing how to continue, Joseph limped off stage, hoping the audience would simply go away. Instead, they followed him into his hovel.

For a while, he let them watch him struggle to sit on his bed where he sat, staring at a tintype photo of his mother. Realizing that they wouldn't to leave, he pressed forward guided by the outline of SCENARIO ONE from the list of interactions.

"Pass this among yourselves. It's a photo of my mother. I'm afraid it's the only picture I have of her." He handed the tintype to the closest audience member who held onto it for a few minutes, obsessively staring at the image of Emma on the small piece of metal. Joseph wondered what she was doing.

"I've been very rude. I haven't offered you tea. Can I offer you all tea?" Joseph said this with a sweeping motion across the room, making eye contact with every patron.

"Yes." A woman with a mousy voice spoke up. No one else said a word.

"Raise your hand if you want tea." Joseph said raising his left hand.

One by one, everyone raised their hands.

"Twenty cups of tea, my goodness. I shall have to brew it in my stew pot."

Joseph poured a bit of fuel into the alcohol stove and lit it with a match.

The flame was a pretty blue with low intensity. He filled the pot and sat it on the stove to boil.

Joseph fished through his jars, finding a container full of tea.

"I was saving this for a special occasion. Straight from India. I suppose having friends over is indeed a special occasion."

Joseph spooned the tea a scoop at a time directly into the heating water.

Soon, the room filled with floral aroma.

"Now that you've seem my mother, does anyone have pictures of their family?"

The older members of the audience had wallet-sized photos that they fished out for Joseph.

One old lady handed Joseph several pictures of her dogs.

"They look like good companions." Joseph said with one eye on the still-not-boiling pot.

"They are. Oh, am I not supposed to talk? I'm sorry." The old lady covered her face with embarrassment.

"If someone told you that you couldn't talk to me, they just work for the Carnival. They don't want you to know that I make tea, have a photo of my mother and that I like dogs. They want me to be a monster in all of your eyes because that's how they make money." Josephs said to the audience, making the lines up as he went.

Joseph gently handed the photos back to the old woman and tended to his tea that was nearly ready.

Each patron was billed for a kit of necessary items they would need in Gaslight. These kits were waiting in their hotel rooms when they checked in. One of the items in the "Victorian survival kit" was a tea kit with an unbreakable cup patrons were instructed to bring with them at all times. Sure enough, some patrons didn't have cups in their backpacks, forcing Joseph to ask each of these forgetful patrons to wash a filthy cup from his makeshift pantry. "I swear that it's clean dirt." Joseph said as a patron held up a particularly nasty cup to the light.

In what felt like a surreal soup line, Joseph served every person in the audience tea. He deputized the old woman to pass out cubes of sugar to those who wanted it, then sat on his bed with his own cup of tea, feeling like he had just run a marathon with the energy expended just to move about his room.

A middle-aged man raised his hand. He had a sarcastic, snooty expression that Joseph instantly disliked.

"What happened to the Elephant Man last year? I heard the man hurt some people and here we are like nothing ever happened."

It was as if someone farted at the dinner table. Groans from the audience members who had just started to drink their tea.

"I wasn't here last year. I was touring the north of France." Joseph replied without missing a beat, causing snickers from the audience.

"The fellow who played the part of the Elephant Man went batshit crazy last year. He hurt people. You don't have anything to say about that? How do we know YOU aren't unstable? It's said that this role is cursed, you know."

Joseph calmly sipped his tea and stared at the man with his good eye.

"I'm sorry sir. You are confused." Joseph gestured to the other members of the audience. "Do you not think that the gentleman is confused?"

"Yes!" The other members of the audience responded in unison.

"The only cursed roll is the stale one I threw to the pigs this morning."

"I'm not confused. I saw what happened. I was here." With that, the man poured his tea on the ground and stormed out of Joseph's hovel.

"A most disagreeable fellow, wouldn't you say?" Joseph said in a droll tone.

The audience nodded in unison.

"Now, let's enjoy our tea before I must retire. I get so tired lately."

After tea, the audience filed out in an orderly manner, two of them giving Joseph gifts consisting of bags of coffee, tea and candies.

The old lady slipped Joseph a flask.

"Gramercy, mum." Joseph said, taking a sniff of the contents and finding good whiskey inside.

With the audience gone, and the darkness upon Gaslight, Joseph sat alone, satisfied that the second day had gone well overall, even with the ghosts of last year making an appearance.

Soon, the makeup team descended upon Joseph's living quarters and transitioned him to his nighttime makeup. This was the only time where he could see his body as it really was. He studied him naked body in the mirror as they worked on him and realized that he saw a stranger staring back at him. As this realization hit him, he started to lose his balance.

"You OK, Joe?" A makeup assistant held Joseph's shoulder, preventing him from falling.
"Yes. Sorry. I got dizzy." Joseph apologized.

As they finished his headpiece, his thoughts turned to the life he had left behind.
Who was he back in the world? He was no one and no one would miss him. Most likely someone else was living in his apartment and all of his things, as limited as they were, were thrown out into the street.

His years in New York had gained him little in the way of friends or worldly goods. He would just be another actor that vanished in the same way friends vanished on him. Some might wonder what had happened to him. Most would be too overwhelmed by the distractions of The City to really notice.

Gaslight was his home now and he imagined that he would stay forever if they'd let him. He shuddered at the thought of going home. Home. Where would that be after Gaslight? He didn't know.

Joseph felt the evening headgear slide over him. They pulled here and shifted there and finally the eyeholes were in the right place. "OK. We'll see you in the morning." The assistant said as the team departed the hovel.

"All right." Joseph said, knowing that he should expect a visitor before morning.

In twenty minutes, *she* indeed returned. In the dark, she could've been in her twenties. It was only when she kissed Joseph's hand that he felt her wrinkled face. As she redirected Joseph's hand to her breasts, he realized the secret behind their youthful tautness…silicone implants.

Despite the modest interruptions to his sleep, Joseph's nocturnal visitor never demanded full-on sex. She wanted to be touched by him and to return the favor. What he appreciated most was how she guarded him while he slept, scaring off other nocturnal visitors with her vicious possessive tirades. If he wore earplugs, he could count on a solid six hours of sleep. The plugs would muffle her nighttime verbal assaults on curious visitors.

"He's MINE!" Was her favorite. "Fuck Off!" Was a close second. People didn't stick around to see if she would use those claw-like nails to defend what was hers. All the while, Joseph could sleep feeling protected like a clownfish in their personal sea anemone. He could wake refreshed and she would always be gone. She seemed to know exactly what he needed to protect his most valuable commodity of an immersive actor…rest.

Once during the night, she woke up to use the latrine and came
back crying.

Not asking for an explanation, Joseph pulled the blanket so she
could join him and she settled in with him for the night. He didn't
think much of it.

In the morning, Joseph found an envelope with a heart drawn on it.
Inside, there was a letter. Joseph tucked it away unread just as the
makeup team arrived to get him into his daytime makeup,
wardrobe and appliance package. He wasn't sure that he wanted to
read it.

THE DRUGGIST

Joseph limped through the streets of Whitechapel. His daily pages were surprisingly random today, just a collection of random improv scenes. His first scene was a single paragraph.

"Your skin requires liniment to prevent it from breaking down. The pharmacist refuses to serve you until you show your face. You refuse and are asked to leave. Entreat others to buy the liniment for you. Your makeup crew has created skin breakdown on your deformed right hand. Show this to the audience and beg them to buy it for you. Bystanders might engage with the pharmacist."

A taxi picked Joseph up. The driver had an open intercom and started to speak with Joseph as he piloted the horse-drawn carriage from above.

"It's a pleasure to have you on board, sir." The Taxi Driver said with a strong Texas drawl.

"Look, uh…" Joseph stammered.

"Alex, sir." The Taxi Driver replied.

"Alex. I have to concentrate for my next scene. Would you mind turning the intercom off?"

"Oh. Oh. Of course." The hidden speaker crackled and went silent

When the taxi finally stopped in front of the pharmacy, the speaker clicked on again.

"We're here." The Taxi Driver said again with the annoying drawl that was so out of place in Victorian England. It grated on Joseph.

"Can you help me out of the taxi please?" Joseph snapped, his patience wearing thin.

"Oh…sure!" The Taxi Driver said as he descended from his seat. When Joseph saw him, he noted how his voice matched his appearance. The Taxi Driver was short, barely five-and-a-half feet tall with a rodent-like face.

"It's been a pleasure." The Taxi Driver said as he helped Joseph down the three steps.

"Good-bye." Joseph said in character as he dug out coins from the crude pocket sewn into his cloak and put three in the T Driver's hand.

"Thank you." The T Driver said with a voice that was a little too happy and definitely too cowboy. Joseph was glad to watch him leave. He thought about reporting him to the Stage Manager, but realized that, for the smaller roles, sometimes you just get what you can get out here in the middle of the Caribbean.

From the moment that the taxi left, leaving him fully exposed to the audience, people started to crowd him in a way that felt disconcerting. He tried his best to tune them out as he began his scene, but it was difficult. They pointed at Joseph, gawked and moved closer like a human lava flow.

Inside the pharmacy, there were a couple of actors and a patron wandering about. Joseph limped to the desk and handed The Pharmacist a hand-written note.

"This liniment has morphine in it." The Pharmacist said coldly. "I need to see your face to verify you are not under age. Take your hood off."

"Sir...I cannot." Joseph said in his barely intelligible voice.

"Then you can't have the medicine. Good day." The pharmacist returned to his workbench where he smashed elements together with a mortar and pestle.

Joseph stood at the counter, holding his money.

"Sir." He said, trying to coax the pharmacist back. "I need that medicine."

The Pharmacist continued to ignore the Elephant Man, working away on a different prescription.

Joseph pulled back the glove on his enlarged and deformed right arm. The odor of necrosis was overwhelming. The skin was like a rotted fruit with pock marks filled with mold. With the smell released, Joseph felt dizzy and nauseated.

Amazingly, The Pharmacist didn't react to the noxious smell.

"This is what the medicine is for." Joseph said pitifully, fighting his automatic revulsion to the smell. He dry heaved and coughed and luckily managed to keep from vomiting as he continued the scene, heading outside to enlist the help of some passers-by. As it turned out, Joseph never got to the door.

"Give him the stuff, motherfucker!" A patron threw some coins at The Pharmacist who seemed frozen in shock as patrons climbed over the desk to snatch the medicine right out of his hand as another audience member, a young woman with a tie dye shirt slugged The Pharmacist so hard that he fell to the ground with tearful cries for help in a Boston accent

"Here, take it! Take it! This is against Gaslight rules!" The Pharmacist screamed the obvious to little effect. The tie dye woman pushed the jar into Joseph's left hand. Joseph took it, afraid of what the audience would do if he broke character the way The Pharmacist did.

"You need help?!" An old lady with a deep French accent took the jar and opened it. "I was a nurse."

The woman started to rub the medicine, petroleum jelly in reality, into Joseph's infected flipper-like hand, rubbing so furiously that some of the makeup and the necrosis perfume began to dissolve. At that moment, security officers dressed as Victorian-era Bobbies raided the pharmacy, banging on the walls and counters.

"OUT OUT OUT! Everybody out!" One of the Bobbies commanded as the patrons were pushed out into the streets. Two officers slammed the door shut behind them as the rest of the security force barricaded the front of the pharmacy, shielding those inside from the rabid mob that continued to grow.

"Third fucking day." The Pharmacist groaned.

"What just happened?" Joseph asked one of the security officers.

"You tell us, buddy." The bobby replied, struggling to catch his breath.

In a few minutes, The Playwright and Stage Manager entered the pharmacy from the hidden entrance in the floor, accompanied by a doctor. By that time, the audience had discovered other amusements and the barricade was reduced to just one security officer.

"This sort of thing happen before?" The Pharmacist asked The Playwright as the doctor examined his bloody temple.

"Not this quickly. I'll review the script and take out scenes that might provoke this kind of reaction." The Playwright said.

"You think you can act tomorrow?" The Stage Manager asked the Pharmacist.

"Yeah." The Pharmacist replied, his voice inflected by a hint of doom.

Joseph felt a sense of guilt. Anyone hurting the Elephant Man in a scene could fall victim to the mayhem witnessed today. The mob seemed to think that protecting The Elephant Man was their sacred duty. These fanatics seemed to have only a modest hold on reality. The Playwright approached Joseph.

"I'm gonna be busy writing your pages. Until I have new pages for you. You go with the minimal schedule, ok?"

The "minimal schedule" included only the scenes required to move the story along. No one-on-ones, no improvisations. That meant that Joseph's acting day would consist of about two hours of scenes at the freak show and the rest wandering silently through the streets of London, essentially acting as set dressing.

"How long before the new pages come?" Joseph asked, hoping it would be just a day or two."

"Probably a week. Sorry." The Playwright mumbled as a telegraph was handed to him detailing yet another problem elsewhere in Gaslight.

Joseph couldn't hide his disappointment at the delay. There was so much to do in the nine weeks of production, losing a week meant losing story. Losing story meant losing his impact of the play as a whole. The thought of doing almost nothing for a week made him angry and depressed.

"Come on with us. It won't be safe for you in the street right now." One of the Bobbies said, guiding Joseph to the hidden door that they had used to enter the pharmacy from the back stage.

The Bobbies left Joseph at the closed cafeteria.

The only food service he could get was at the small bar where he ordered a beer that he had to drink through a straw to get through his contorted mouth. A Makeup Assistant saw him at the barstool leaned in next to his beer.

"I heard you have a few minimum days."

"Yeah." Joseph replied in a slightly slurred voice. "Apparently I created a near riot during my scene."

"I don't think we've ever seen anything like that since the first year opening day." The Makeup Assistant noted.

"It's nice to be protected." Joseph said sarcastically.

"Well, until your pages come in, stay out of trouble."

"Maybe so." Joseph said as he slurped down the last of his beer.

"I can give you one more…" The barkeep said. "…then I have to cut you off."

"Didn't you hear? I'm on minimum. My acting day is over."

"I don't make the rules. You want the beer or not?"

"OK. Hit me." Joseph pushed the empty glass toward the barkeep. He seemed surprised when he realized the Makeup Assistant was still there.

"Don't you want that stuff off now?" The assistant made an all-encompassing circle with his finger.

"After the beer."

"I'll see you at the freak show then." The Makeup Assistant stood and left.

"Good night." Joseph waved him off as the next beer came.

By the time he finished his second beer, he was sitting in the bar alone with a barkeep that seemed more annoyed by his presence than anything else.

"I'm closing." The barkeep tersely said as he took Joseph's glass away.

Joseph didn't feel the alcohol until he stood up. At that point, he felt thankful for the two-drink maximum as he tried to find his way back through the darkness of Whitechapel bearing the weight of his suit.

Recognizing that he was struggling, a patron who was passing by took Joseph by the arm and led him back to the freak show. Once there, his bedmate was waiting for him with a sour expression.

"Come to bed!" She cried out in a panicked voice. He was late and didn't even send her a telegram ranked high on her list of complaints.

Facing her after everything that happened made Joseph feel incredibly tired. Thankfully, the makeup team arrived just a few seconds after this encounter and kicked the woman out of the room to change out Joseph.

"Well fuck you!" The woman bellowed, sounding more than a little inebriated herself. "I'll go find another old man."

"I didn't know I was her 'old man'." Joseph said to the Team

Lead.

"You could have someone younger and prettier Joseph, why'd you pick her?"

"She protected me and let me get some sleep." Joseph noted, already regretting losing his bed partner.

"So will a pit bull." The Team Lead noted as he readied his jars of solvents. "Ready to get that shit off?"

As Joseph climbed in bed wearing his "Elephant Man pajamas" as the Team Lead called it, he secretly wished that his bedmate would return. She never did and his sleep really did suffer.

The following day, Joseph had a scene scheduled at ten am at the freak show. There was no dialogue. He just had to stand there while the Carnie told the terrible story of Joseph's Merrick's decline from normal child to the monstrosity that he was now.

Even though the scene was very pedestrian, the crowds started to gather in the tent just for the chance to see him. Eventually, the Bobbies had to come out for crowd control as the entrance and exit to the freak show tent became impassible.

Joseph felt a twinge of embarrassment as he watched the dismal crowds at the Bearded Lady and the Lizard Man who at best had half-a-dozen in their audiences.

Joseph caught contemptuous glances from the other freaks as he continued to garner capacity audiences, culminating with the Bearded Lady throwing a tomato from her stage and grazing Joseph on his back before she ran off the stage in a huff.

After the morning scene, there was a short exterior sequence that consisted of walking across the town square near the Twelve Bells in mid-afternoon and another freak show performance at nine pm. With nothing to do until then, he found a hidden door that brought him backstage.

"Joseph, I heard that you cause pandemonium by just showing up." The Ripper said with a snide grin.

"People are curious about Merrick." Joseph muttered.

"Oh, Come on! They're crowding around you waiting for the implosion...the disaster." The Ripper studied Joseph sarcastically.

"Will you be giving them an implosion, Joseph?" The Ripper scratched his head sarcastically.

"I will do my best not to...Master." Joseph said coldly.

The Ripper's posture stiffened.

"Don't go there." The Ripper said, refusing to answer to his title.

"The Master is the leader here of all the actors. Where is your leadership? Is it hidden in your subversion?" Joseph continued. "Is it hidden in that Black Absinthe?"

"I don't drink that shit. As for the other point, you don't deserve my leadership. You or anyone else in this theme park." The Ripper snapped.

"There it is then." Joseph said in an icy voice as The Ripper stormed away.

Joseph couldn't fake his contempt for this man. The Concierge was the closest thing that the actors had to a leader here and he was probably already gone. It made sense that The Ripper didn't drink black absinthe, the rumored mind-expansion effects of the drink would be lost on a narcissist like him.

The accumulating mystery of this "implosion" of the previous year's Master was like an itch that Joseph couldn't scratch. He had to find a way to get the straight story.

ONE DRINK ONLY

Approaching the Nerve Center, Joseph saw his name in red. His once full slate was reduced to three scenes, the morning scene blinking grey to indicate a completed sequence.

He had two hours until his march across the town square. He had enough time for a drink at Glass Paris and possibly a chance to make contact with Franco Valor or possibly the mysterious figure that broke through the roof of his hovel, the one called The Tread Setter.

"A drink? It's the lunch hour, Joseph." The Stage Manager snapped at Joseph.

"I feel jittery and stressed. I'd like an Absinthe."

"You can't work drunk, Joseph."

"Just one." Joseph promised.

The Stage Manager sighed.

"Don't make me regret this. You may take a cab there, then take a cab back to your scene. One drink only. We'll be watching." The Stage Manager said, sounding exasperated. "Be ready for those new scenes. Possibly as soon as tomorrow. You won't have any more time for nonsense after that. Remember to wear your hood." The Stage Manager said hurriedly.

"I'm looking forward to the lack of nonsense." Joseph replied to The Stage Manager's back as the man had already moved on to the next problem. Joseph used the intercom to call a cab, secure in his gut instinct that those new pages were still a week away.

"Tomorrow, my ass." He whispered to himself.

A GREEN ONE

Inside The Glass Paris, Joseph's entry caused a moment of silence by the customers and staff alike. The bartender lifted the drawbridge built into his bar and greeted him at the door.

"Joseph. We didn't expect to see you here."

"Am I still welcome?" Joseph said, realizing that all of the eyes on him were actors in costume. There were no theater patrons yet as The Glass Paris strove to give the actors a few days in peace before allowing the unwashed fanny packers in.

"You're always welcome here, don't be ridiculous." Come and sit. I'll make you a drink.

"Can I have the table in the back?"

Joseph pointed to the homely single-seat table butted against the slanted wall.

"Sure you want that one? I have a better one for you."

"That table is fine."

"I'll make your absinthe then. A green one, yes?"

Joseph nodded as he navigated through the customers to reach the awkward table.

Once seated, he found that the book, *Alice in Wonderland,* was still on the shelf.

Pulling the hardcover out, Joseph scribbled a note and slipped it into the gap discreetly. A proposal of a meeting between him and Franco Valor. He heard the paper fall behind the plaster wall, faintly tumbling down the lathe until it came to rest at some unseen landing.

The emerald drink came on a hand knitted doily.

"Joseph, we got word. Only one of these while on duty."

"If you can call a minimum schedule real duty." Joseph said, picking up the drink. "I thought this place was…autonomous." Joseph jibed, knowing The Glass Paris doesn't have to follow the rules in the strictest sense for reasons still unclear to him.

"You're right we are, but we try to keep the peace. Enjoy." The Bartender touched Joseph's arm and left him.

In his corner of the bar, Joseph slid *Alice in Wonderland* back on the shelf. He sipped his drink, hoping for the book to fall on the table containing a new message. The book stayed on the shelf this time. Joseph drank slow and ignored the stares from his fellow actors. Did they know what he was really doing here? Did they know that he was seeking answers to forbidden questions? They seem to accuse him with their glances and by the time the taxi came to take him to the scene, he was glad to leave The Glass Paris.

THE SURFACE DWELLER ATTACK

"Elephant Man, start scene." Joseph heard in the taxi's intercom.
He exited the taxi to cross the courtyard with the motion-limiting
device bearing down on his posture.

Suddenly a ragged washerwoman screamed from the north side of
the square. She was pointing at him.

He stood there, scanning his memory, sure that he had no
interaction in this scene. It was supposed to be a simple
appearance, walking across the square.

"Monster!! This monster has no place in public!! With decent
people!!!"

The woman reached into her baskets of dirty clothes and threw
them at Joseph who let them hit him and fall to the pavement.
The audience circled around the scene, unintentionally cutting off
Joseph's path of escape.

Joseph felt a sense of panic building inside him. Why was there an
unplanned scene? One that could whip the audience into a mob the
way the drug store did?

"That monster doesn't belong here!!" The washerwoman turned to
the crowd, looking for allies. "He's better off dead!" At this, the
washerwoman hurled a knife at Joseph nailing him in the
prosthetic part of his shoulder.

For a moment, Joseph was sure that he had been stabbed. A warm fluid leaked down his torso. He was unable to verify if it was indeed blood.

He realized the gravity of this emergency as the washerwoman found another knife in her basket and started to fix her aim. An audience member, a middle-aged woman, rushed from the crowd and pushed the washerwoman so hard that she landed on the pavement with a hollow CRACK as her head made contact with the cement. The woman was out cold.

From backstage doors, six Bobbies rushed to the town square and pushed back the crowds. More appeared to secure the scene and take the woman who saved Joseph away for questioning.

A pool of blood grew around the head of the washerwoman. "Medical!" One of the Bobbies cried. Minutes later an electric ambulance took the woman to the hospital. This was the first time that Gaslight itself had broke character this season.

Joseph was hustled into the room with the Nerve Center. The Playwright and Stage Manager were conferencing and went silent when they saw Joseph.

Two members of the makeup team helped him off with his mask as the Stage Manager began the debriefing.

"It's as we feared. That woman is a Surface Dweller. One of Valor's followers. She played the Dog Woman in last year's freak show."

"Did she tell you why she did it?" Joseph asked.

"No. She won't be confessing anything today or ever. We got word from the hospital that she's suffered a massive stroke and died." The Stage Manager said with finality.

A medic approached a silent and shocked Joseph, checking for a stab wound. Luckily the attacker only severed a hydraulic tube that was part of his posture-altering appliance.

"Why would they do this?" Joseph wondered aloud.

"They don't want us to succeed. They don't want you to succeed." The Playwright said with a flavor of doom in his voice. "Next target on their list will be the audience members themselves."

"What should we do then?" The Stage Manager asked, his voice shaking at the prospect that *the problems* were starting all over again.

"We'll need to find someone they trust to negotiate with them." The Playwright said with trepidation.

"Forget about The Master." The Stage Manager said. "He's just a day trader."

"That really came back to fuck us, didn't it?" The Playwright said in an admission wrought with guilt. "Valor needs to be dealt with another way." The Playwright grew silent, his mind racing for a solution. He paced wildly and finally stopped, his mind fixed on a plan. "Call the Concierge back." The Playwright commanded.

"He's in Sicily." The Stage Manager reminded.

"If anyone can get them to talk, he can. Get the plane ready. Take five of your best in the security detail. Joseph. You'll go too. You're out of commission until we solve this problem anyway. With you there, maybe he'll come quietly."

Joseph didn't protest. There was nothing he could do now that the Surface Dwellers were actively seeking his demise. In truth, he felt a level of comfort with the Concierge that none of the other team came close to. He was like a dorm mother that dispensed advice at the perfect moments. The Stage Manager was a doer, not a listener and didn't seem to care about the mental landscape of his actors.

"Someone go and get Joseph's things and get his costume off." The Stage Manager commanded. With that, the Playwright and Stage Manager were hustled away. A team of private commandos entered the room and seemed to be watching Joseph's progress.

What followed was what you could charitably call a rush job to get The Elephant Man costume off. The ASM interrupted them just as they removed the main headpiece.

"Out. Makeup, we're outta time. Joseph will have to get the rest off by himself." He said, waving the harried makeup team away.

"So, The Concierge trusts you?" The Assistant Stage Manager asked Joseph.

"Yes, I think so."

"Good, because we're depending on you. You'll talk to him. If that doesn't work." The ASM shrugged ominously.

"You would really do that?" Joseph asked, not really surprised that they would take such a gentle man by brute force.

"To keep things running smooth. You wouldn't believe what they'd do." With that, a pilot appeared from the elevator looking harried.

"We're warmed up and just waiting on you." The pilot said, breathing hard.

The private soldiers nudged Joseph toward the elevator that led to the surface. They didn't seem to care that pieces of his makeup still hung from his face.

In five minutes they were airborne and on their way across the Pacific Ocean to Sicily.

Over the ocean, there wasn't much to see as there wasn't even moonlight to illuminate the water.

A harried stewardess with sleep still in her eyes brought drinks for the security team and passed out MRE's, which they ate listlessly.

"Sorry we didn't have anything else ready." The Stewardess said in a tired but apologetic tone."

"It's OK baby, we're used to this shit. Just keep the drinks comin'."

"Alright." She said through a yawn.

Joseph guessed that this flight team was kept on standby 24/7. He wondered how many other last minute flights like this had occurred over the weeks.

"You want something? All we have is MRE's with the ham and cheese omelet. Not that bad heated up. I can get you a drink or some coffee or bottled water?"

"Maybe later. I'm gonna get a nap in." Joseph said as he tore off the last of his face makeup.

"You're an actor?" The Stewardess asked, momentarily forgetting that she was not supposed to ask questions.

"Yes, could you get me a blanket?" Joseph said, veering the conversation back to a safer topic.

"Certainly sir. Sorry, sir." The Stewardess opened an overhead bin and produced a thick blue blanket that she unfolded and covered Joseph with.

"I can do the rest, thank you." Joseph worried that the Stewardess might start tucking him into bed like his former freak show bedmate.

The security team drank and talked incessantly about a previous mission that went badly, though Joseph couldn't make out what that mission was. Their voices mutated to hallow noise that, combined with the sound of the jet's engines, lulled Joseph into a deep sleep.

DESCENT

"We are making our final approach into Palermo, Sicily. The stewardess will be passing out passports and emergency currency as well as a return ticket to the Dominican Republic if you should become separated from the group. If this should occur, you will be picked up at Santa Domingo and brought back to Gaslight. Good Luck."

The Stewardess passed Joseph an envelope with "Open Immediately" scrawled on it.

The letter read

"Joseph, your assignment is to infiltrate an immersive theater production called "RED,WHITE AND BLUE" as a paying customer. During the play you must find the Concierge on the third-floor control room. Access it through a hidden door as shown on this map and wait for him there. Convince him that he must return to Gaslight voluntarily or the security team will come for him. He has until the end of the play to decide before we take him by force. We'll be observing your progress."

This note was not signed.

Joseph studied the location of the hidden room on the map as well as on photographs printed on the back of the page.

"I have to take that now." The stewardess held out her hand. Joseph relinquished the paper to her. The Stewardess handed Joseph another envelope.

"That one you can keep, apparently."
She left to fetch more drinks for the security team.
Joseph opened the envelope and found a ticked to *"RED, WHITE AND BLUE: An immersive experience."* Also in the envelope were directions to the play in English and Italian. Joseph was impressed that The Concierge had undertaken such a project and even more impressed that he kept it a secret from his actors.

"This is the captain. Please fasten your seatbelts in preparation for landing."

At the Palermo International Airport it was three pm and the play started at five. Joseph was the only one, other than the pilots to exit the plane. The security team stayed on board waiting for the order to pluck out the Concierge kicking and screaming from his own production.

RED, WHITE AND BLUE

"I'm going here." Joseph handed the directions to the cab driver who read the bottom of the page, avoiding the English version of the directions.

"Oh, very popular. Scary I hear. Like nothing anyone has seen. Not here anyway. Not on this island." The driver responded in passable English.

The driver dropped Joseph off in front of the theater with a billboard-sized sign for "RED, WHITE AND BLUE" with The Concierge's real name on the playwright credits. A name Joseph purposely tried to ignore. Joseph was impressed and proud of him.

There was a restaurant near the theatre so with a couple of hours to kill, Joseph inspected the menu and sat down in a dark corner of the place. On his way to the table, he saw the maître d's desk stocked to the brim with gum, mints and a sets of post cards. He snatched a post card with a silly drawing of a fat old mafioso and stuffed it in his pocket.

Once at his table, Joseph wrote a harried note on it.

"Alfonso Dominguez, Reporter Herald, New York City.
Mr. Dominguez, I am an actor in the play Gaslight. I met you in
Fallujah during the operation to stop human trafficking by the

Marmaladov gang. I was in your security detail. The situation here on Gaslight Island is much worse. Thousands, not dozens. Please come to Gaslight Island to investigate! If you receive this letter and decide to come, send me a telegram containing the words 'Black Absinthe'.
Until then,
Joseph Bickle"

He heard someone approach and hid the postcard. The waiter greeted him in English and passed him a menu in Italian.

"Can you please help me? I can't read this."

"You like lasagna?" The waiter asked patiently.

"Sure." Joseph said, impressed that the waiter also spoke English. He credited the tourist trade but realized the public schools here were probably teaching at the American college level and every student knew more than one language.

"I'll bring some with a wine pairing, with your permission." The middle-aged waiter scribbled something on his order pad.

"That's fine. Bring a bottle please."

"Certainly, sir." The waiter retreated to the kitchen, shouted something to the chef in Italian and returned with a bottle of red wine labeled with a number.

He opened it and let Joseph smell the cork.

"Is OK, sir?" The waiter asked. Joseph nodded, unsure of how sniffing a cork could tell him anything. The waiter poured just a bit.

"Just pour the whole glass. I'm not particular."

"Very well." The waiter said in a cold tone as he filled Joseph's glass halfway.

"Thank you." Joseph said as he took a sip. The wine was a bit bitter and he felt saliva building in his mouth the same way it did from sour candy. It wasn't an unpleasing flavor.

"Can I ask you a favor?" Joseph asked with a hopeful expression.

"What can I do?" The waiter replied.

"Can you post this for air mail and send it with your next outgoing?" Joseph handed the waiter the postcard with a C-note. Almost all of his personal money.

The waiter studied the bill for a moment and realized how much it was. He took it gingerly.

"I will do my best, sir." He said, slipping the money and the postcard in his pocket. Joseph realized that the waiter might just pocket the money and not stamp and send the letter. He let that worry go.

The wine was strong and after three glasses, he was feeling buzzed. The lasagna was like nothing he'd had before. He suspected that it was the cheese that brought it over the top. When the check came, Joseph tipped 100%, feeling no guilt about spending on Gaslight's credit card. The waiter smiled realizing the windfall of an entire day's pay from one customer.

A crowd grew around the entrance to "Red, White and Blue". The performance was still an hour away, but there was a lounge that was about to open according to the chatter from the crowd. They took Joseph's ticket which was apparently a "VIP experience" and he found a seat at the bar. There were cocktail tables where larger groups congregated. His name on the ticket was "Samuels". Glancing at the poster adjacent to the ticket booth, he saw that this was one of several performances in English.

"A cocktail for Mr. Samuels." The bartender placed a cloth napkin on the bar, followed seconds later by a martini with a thin crust of ice on top. This VIP experience wasn't too shabby, Joseph thought as he tasted the drink. It was a perfect martini.

"Five minutes until showtime." An announcer called out over the intercom. Joseph stayed at the bar. Somehow the crush of a crowd was no longer something he could tolerate.
Someone in a black cloak approached the podium on the small stage. He revealed himself as he drew near the microphone. It was The Concierge.

"What if we lived in a perpetual atomic age. If 1950's America lived on in perpetuity? What would happen to the identity of America and the world when the Red Scare was perpetual and patriotism was mandatory? What if the whole world became America of the 1950's? Enter the world of Red, White and Blue..."

The doors swung open and there were a dozen young men and women waiting for them with novel-like brochures. They handed the heavy volumes out to every member of the audience.

"How to become an American!" The pamphlet was titled. The background design was an All-American family gathered around the flag. A young boy saluted the flag. A man in a perfectly pressed suit, presumably his father patted him on the shoulder. Both father and son had perfectly parted hair, slathered in pomade.

Once the entire audience had cleared the first room, the doors closed and locked behind them. The "greeters" seemed to vanish, leaving the only path through a yard filled with plastic pink flamingos. Up ahead, a three-story house glowed invitingly. A man in a long white chef's jacket cooked ribs at a charcoal grill.

The path led through the front door of the house where a blonde woman waited with cocktails and hors d'oeuvres on a tray. She was about thirty and had a wardrobe lifted from one of those funny black and white TV shows from the fifties.

Joseph took a cocktail (a Tom Collins) and made a mental note of where he was in the play. In the diagram of the house, the secret room was on the top floor with the doorknob tucked behind a panel.

If he made a beeline to the room, it would immediately arouse suspicion. He had to make it up there in an organic way.

In the kitchen, a black woman readied trays of food, presumably for them.

"Help you sir? Cold drink? Something to eat?" She dutifully asked Joseph.

"What's going on here tonight?" Joseph asked.

"You askin' me sir? I don't ask those kind of questions. I'm sure you know why you're here. Tryin' to trip me up. I don't know nuthin'." She said suspiciously.

The servant turned back to her trays and arranged them in on the table. It was as if Joseph was no longer there.

"Come on. What are you doing bothering the help?" The Hostess said she doesn't know anything." A middle-aged man chastised him from a hidden alcove.

"Sorry. I didn't know…" Joseph stammered.

"Meeting is in the basement." He whispered to Joseph. He could smell the Old Spice and the starch on his shirt.

"The basement?" Down was not the direction Joseph needed to go.

"Come on. I didn't ask you here for nothing! It was a big risk." The man said in an angry whisper. He pulled Joseph aggressively into the basement.

"You know what I put on the line? Now go sit down!"

There was a group of about twenty audience members seated on folding chairs with a blackboard facing them.

Some of them looked fearful, some overjoyed with the experience. Joseph sat down next to a man with a fedora who was obviously an actor planted within the group.

The middle-aged man with the starched shirt introduced himself as "Comrade Martin". He scanned the group and smiled.

"Thank you for coming. The American Communist Party welcomes you. Though meeting like this isn't technically illegal, we had to be careful and some of you had to have a cover story to make that happen. We appreciate that you did come. All of you took a risk of some kind. Now the capitalist system…" Joseph listened to the man drone on as he studied the basement. In the darkness, he saw someone emerging from a hidden door. The light was so dim that he could only see shapes. It was a woman.

"We have a film to show you that will really open your eyes to the evils of the capitalist society." She said to the audience as she stepped into the light, revealing herself as the hostess.

"Honey. Please dim the lights." The Hostess asked.

"Yes, dear." Comrade Martin replied.

The projector started.

In the moment of distraction, Joseph crept on his knees to where he estimated the hidden door was. There was no handle on the door that was hidden near a tool cabinet. He found the seam and pulled and it opened. With access, to the back stage, h

Joseph stealthily navigated the dark to find a secret spiral stairway. A stairway that led to the third floor.

Joseph navigated the stairways as silently as he could, the metal stairway telegraphed every step no matter how light. At the second floor landing, Joseph heard a door open. An actor from the first floor was heading down the dim stairwell. Much to Joseph's relief, the actor didn't so much as glance up as he passed Joseph. He waited until the actor closed the basement door before he continued up the stairway to the third floor. Joseph nudged the access door and it was unlocked, leading into what appeared to be a closet. Exiting the closet door, the hallway was decorated with route 66 memorabilia and photos of generic 1950's family vacations. There was a photo of one of those wigwam hotels. It was here that, according to the file, a latch would be there to open the door to the control room. With a soft yank, the latch gave way, revealing a joystick like trigger. He pulled it and there was a loud CLICK as the secret chamber opened.

It was a perfectly hidden door, fitted so well between molding and seams that Joseph never would've found it unless he was drawn a map and shown a photo.

Inside the room was a bank of monitors and a long desk with a timeline similar to the Nerve Center on it, but exponentially smaller.

In a corner of this room, a recliner was turned against the wall. It was only when Joseph was almost on the chair when he saw The Concierge curled up on it like a cat, breathing deeply, mumbling to himself as he slept.

Joseph sat on the arm of the chair, wondering if The Concierge could sense that he was there.

"Hello." Joseph said as he sat down next to the sleeping man. The Concierge's eyes opened to slits and he stared at Joseph in disbelief.

"What the hell are you doing here?" The Concierge mumbled.

"How do you sleep through your own show?" Joseph asked.

"I'm exhausted. These actors know what they're doing by now." The Concierge slid on his glasses, removed them and wiped them off, then put them back on.

"But that's not why you're here. What happened Joseph?"

"The Surface Dwellers. They attacked me and hurt some of the guests. They want you to come back and convince them to leave the island."

The Concierge shook his head. "They'd rather die than leave, don't you see?"

The Concierge stood and opened a panel hidden in the wall. Inside the hidden space was a back bag stuffed to capacity. A "bug-out bag" as the CIA called it with everything he'd need to make a quick escape.

"What are you doing?" Joseph said, expecting to endure a long debate about why The Concierge should "Come along quietly". It seemed he didn't need to.

"You came here to ask nicely. There are men on that plane that won't ask nicely." The Concierge knew what would happen if he didn't leave with Joseph. He was leaving for Gaslight one way or another. Joseph nodded in confirmation.

"I have my bag for just this occasion. Let's go."

As they opened the door leading to the hallway, an actor dressed as a 1950's FBI Agent checked himself in the hallway mirror.

"Carlos." The Concierge called to the actor who seemed embarrassed.

"Yes, sir. I was just heading down."

"Tell Blanca to take over for me. I have a personal emergency."

"Will do, Captain." The actor seemed relieved that he wasn't chastised for hiding on the third floor.

Joseph followed The Concierge down the spiral staircase and into a Sub-basement floor that exited to the street through a tunnel.

"It's good to see you again, even under these strange circumstances." Joseph said to the Concierge.

"I was thinking of you. Wondering how you were handling the big role." The Concierge replied.

"It feels like I haven't got started, especially now, since the attack." Joseph admitted.

"Well Joseph, let's fix that."

"OK." Joseph replied. He felt safe with The Concierge by his side again. Somehow, he knew things would be better.

The Concierge put his hand on Joseph's shoulder and squeezed. A black car pulled up. A Sicilian taxi driver leaned out his window.

"Joseph? Is your name Joseph?"

"Yes." Joseph noticed that the taxi driver had a photo of him in his hand.

"They asked me to come get you."

The short taxi driver got out and opened both rear doors.

"Well, come on." The Concierge said as he handed his bug out bag to the taxi driver.

"I should tell you." Joseph said as they took their seats in the taxi.

"…Your play was really amazing. I wished I could've seen it the way the audience did."

The Concierge smiled at Joseph's kind words.

"The audience never knows how lucky they are. They experience something we never will. They experience it like a baby experiences the world. We can only be jealous." The Concierge said.

A few minutes later, they were airborne.

During the flight, Joseph wanted to ask The Concierge about the Flower Girl, but didn't. He wondered if she was OK. If she had surgery. He didn't even know if she was still alive. Later, perhaps over a glass of Absinthe, he would press those questions then. Joseph wondered if he was ready to accept the answers.

THE RETURN

The Playwright met the plane at the tarmac with a party of about twenty people that Joseph didn't recognize. Some of those people had bandaged faces. Arms or legs in casts.

"Evictions already?" The Concierge whispered.

"Surface dwellers?" Joseph asked.

"They went too far in attacking you. The security team had to do something." The Concierge said as the airplane's hatch opened. The fresh smell of tropical air filled the sterile cabin as the flight crew was switched with a fresh one before Joseph and The Concierge were allowed to exit.

As they passed the evacuees, Joseph could see the palpable fear in their eyes. Similarly, the Playwright had a fearful expression for a different reason. His masterpiece was being threatened and if he couldn't turn things around, this could be Gaslight's last year. Joseph was certain the moneymen in Gaslight would have no problem placing blame squarely on The Playwright's head.

"I'm so glad to see you." The Playwright grasped The Concierge by the shoulder. The Playwright's eyes were swollen and red. "Joseph, come here." The Playwright waved him closer. Joseph wondered if he knew about the poison seed that he planted on a postcard addressed to New York City. He wondered if the waiter was working for The Playwright.

"You did very well. I want you and The Concierge to get some rest and tomorrow I'll send you in to talk."

"To whom, sir?"

"The remaining Surface Dwellers. Valor. Who do you think? Now get some rest. You did a great job."

Joseph felt a chill as he realized that he would finally speak to who many consider to be the real Master. He was ashamed to feel a little scared.

Joseph and The Concierge shared a suite recently vacated by an evacuated audience member. They didn't say what the evacuation was for, but surmised it was another Surface Dweller attack. Joseph opened a bottle of champagne left by the absent guests and poured one for the Concierge.

"Isn't champagne usually for celebration?" The Concierge asked, coming out of the bathroom in a Terry cloth robe with the emblem of the hotel.

"It's not for celebration, but to steel ourselves." Joseph said as he passed him the full glass.

"Drink to that." The Concierge said as he gulped it back.

"That girl…" The Concierge said, anticipating Joseph's question.

"The Flower Girl?" Joseph sat up, eager to hear any news.

"She had to get a bowel resection. She almost died. Her anus and vagina had to be removed and replaced with skin grafts. She has a

colostomy bag now and she will never have sex or bear children again." He got it all out in rapid-fire speech that seemed more uncomfortable at each passing word. He glanced up at Joseph, bracing for his reaction. Joseph stared blankly at The Concierge.
"She has to do number two in a bag, Joseph."
"I know what a colostomy bag is." Joseph snapped, screamed actually, causing The Concierge to flinch.
Joseph didn't realize that he was standing with his fists clenched. A stance that obviously frightened The Concierge.
"Joseph. I am on your side." He pleaded, hands raised in acquiescence.
"I'm sorry." Joseph took a few deep breaths to stand down. He felt ashamed. "I'm grateful that you helped her. I think about the others down there. I can't believe what's going on just a few floors below us."
The Concierge recognized that the mood in the room had shifted out of danger and he could talk to Joseph again without losing a few teeth.
"Don't be a hero, Joseph. You were lucky you could help one person out. Like I told you before the forces at work here. They don't play." The Concierge said in a warning voice. Joseph turned away from him, his face to the wall, lost in something.
"I don't play either." Joseph said in a tone that rang ominously in The Concierge's ear.

TRAFFIK

FALLUJAH: THE SECOND IRAQ WAR

2004

With help from a soldier named Joseph, Alfonso Dominguez climbed in the rear of the Humvee. Joseph only knew that they were escorting a journalist to the recently discovered "CATTLE MARKET" of human trafficking. A discovery he made while searching for an insurgent bomb factory.

Days before, he and three other soldiers found themselves in a room filled with children. The only adult in the room wore a western suit and spoke perfect English. He explained that the building was a school for children orphaned by "George W's war". Joseph saw in the children's eyes that it was no school. Suitcases full of rubles on the man's desk was further testament to that.

Joseph glanced at the periphery of the room and saw gunmen training their weapons not on him and his men, but on the children. "You see, everything *is* in order." The man in the suit said in a hushed tone.

"Yes. Sorry to trouble you. Good luck with your school." Joseph gestured to the other soldiers to leave. Joseph knew that he would come back and next time, he would be prepared.

"I heard you boys stumbled on this last week?" Dominguez asked his security detail.

"Yes, sir." Sargent Randy, the leader of the detail replied. "Our man Joe found it. Kids from all over the globe. They have the mark of the Marmladov gang."

Randy slid a file in Dominguez's hands. Inside he found pages of photos of children with the tattoo of a wolf encircled with Cyrillic words that roughly translated into "property".

"How many are trafficked here?" Dominguez asked Randy.

"Dozens. This is just a stop on the way to their final destination." Randy pointed to statistics in the chart.

As they approached the secret warehouse belonging to the Marmladov gang, the soldiers in the security detail loaded their weapons. In the moments before they ruined the day of several Russian gangsters, Joseph stared at one of the photos in the gangster's file marked "sold" in Cyrillic. It was a girl with that tattoo on the back of her arm. She couldn't have been more than eight-years old. He couldn't have imagined that he would meet the child in this photo many years later.

THE SURFACE DWELLERS

In the morning, the security captain called the suite and instructed Joseph and The Concierge to come to the lobby.

The Concierge was quickly encircled and briefed. By the time Joseph got close enough to hear anything, the conversation was over.

"Joseph…get ready." The Concierge said, strapping on a bulletproof vest.

"For what?"

"We're going to the surface. Get ready."

Audience members watched the security team led by The Concierge as if it were part of the show. The audience watched as the fully armed team ascended on the platform elevator like Christ into the heavens. Joseph breathed a sigh of relief when they were out of the audience's sight.

"Joseph. They plugged in another actor to do basic Elephant Man scenes while you were gone. That man was killed last night." The Concierge said with a gloomy tone.

"HE did it, didn't he? Franco Valor." Joseph asked, knowing the answer.

"All these actors were recruits of mine." The Concierge broke in. "I'm going to try and talk them down. If I fail…"

"You won't fail. You're very persuasive." Joseph said, trying to reassure him.

The elevator rose into to concrete shelter that led to the airstrip. The jet was gone, back to the mainland for a crew switch out. At the moment, they were cut off from the outside world.

"There's a trail." The Concierge pointed to what appeared to be a deer trail. Being the only one familiar with the surface dweller encampment, The Concierge led the security team through the brush until they were at the lip of a cliff with a sixty-foot drop to the sea under them.

"What's this?" The Security Commander asked impatiently.

"This is where we wait." The Concierge said.

They didn't have to wait long. A black-cloaked tiny figure was affixing stairs into rock wall. He or she (it was impossible to tell through the cloak) reached the final tread and placed a wooden pole into a slot in the rock. This pole supported the safety rope that would be their only salvation from certain death if they slipped.

The cloaked figure stood patiently, silently waiting for them to descend.

"That's the person who broke into my room?" Joseph said to The Concierge.

"Yeah." The Concierge nodded.

"You're lucky you woke up in your bed and not in hell. That's

The Tread Setter. Valor's personal guard. Formerly Trinka, the Hermaphrodite from the freak show."

Joseph remembered the sign that he found in his hovel.

"What do we call her-him?" Joseph asked.

"Zie, zir, zirself." Use gender neutral pronouns if you don't want to be shark bait." The Concierge said in all seriousness.

Each step was just a plank, but The Concierge assured him that they were a marvel of DIY engineering. They didn't know exactly how they were constructed, but these stair treads could shoot an anchor into rock, wood, almost any solid surface and hold the weight of an adult. The Tread Setter could create a path with these that would provide access to almost any part of the Gaslight stage, including Joseph's room. Not only was zie good at this, zie was fast.

On the way to the stairs, Joseph passed The Tread Setter who seemed like one of those horse jockeys, possibly weighing 75 pounds wet. It was difficult to see a face through the cloak. The Tread Setter didn't move at all, resembling a sentinel positioned to guard the sea.

The treads led to a cave opening that would otherwise be inaccessible. It provided a safe landing for the party, but that was all. A closed steel door led to the deeper part of the cave where the Surface Dwellers waited.

With everyone on the landing, The Tread Setter descended and shuffled through the party to reach the steel door. Zie used an old key to unlock the door and open it with a firm push.

Zie gestured for them to enter.

They entered a passage lit by a string of dim garden lights, probably pilfered from the Gaslight set.

This led to a stone chamber housing a long table occupied by a row of Surface Dwellers, all with faces veiled in black cloth. In their silence, the effect was frightening.
The Concierge gestured for the others to stand back as he moved forward to engage the ghoulish Surface Dwellers.

"I came to negotiate for a peaceful evacuation of the island." The Concierge said to the silent hooded figures.

"Very good. We will help you evacuate." A booming voice pierced through the darkness. From one of the lightless hidden alcoves, The Master appeared, his face obscured in the hood that he used when he played the Elephant Man.

"We will financially compensate you for what you've been through. We'll relocate you. Provide you with therapy to reenter the real world." The Concierge said.

"This is the real world. This and the stage below us. We've earned the right to be here. Every actor has earned the right to be here." The Master said with surety that Joseph found to be chilling.

"That's a fantasy Franco…"

"Don't call me by that NAME!!" The former Master snapped. "That name died when you brought me here. Everyone's name dies and is reborn when they become part of this place, even if they don't know it yet!!"

"Living in this cave is one thing. Interfering in the Gaslight production. Harming our guests. Threatening our actors. That's becomes a different thing entirely." The Concierge's voice grew dark and filled with gloom. The next step would not involve negotiation. The next step would not involve conversation at all.

"You brought Joseph." Valor approached Joseph and placed his hands on his shoulders.

"Joseph, your Elephant Man is good. It's so good that I had to take action when they tried to replace you with that cheap knockoff. An oafish man with a southern accent and not the slightest idea of who Joseph Merrick was. That's what makes us different, Joseph. We inhabit this part." The Master finally let Joseph go. He backed away, pacing in and out of the darkness.

"As good as you are Joseph, I play him better. I play him better and I refuse to let him go. I'll give you a good part. Something else." The former Master said to Joseph who stared at the silently at the man. He began to understand the magnetism that others had described. The man seemed to have his own gravitational pull.

The Concierge placed a large envelope on the table and scanned the hidden faces.
"Please read our offer. You'll find that it's quite generous."
"Bless you and your generous offer." The Master said sarcastically. "I suggest you leave while you can."

Joseph was perplexed that although the security team was fully armed, it was them that seemed to be at the disadvantage here. He could sense that the guards were more than anxious to get back to the safety of the stage.

"Let's go and give them time to consider our offer." The Concierge waved toward the guards who hurriedly turned to leave the cave.

As they were retreating, Joseph heard the former Master's deep voice call out to him.
"Joseph."
Joseph turned and watched The Leader pull his hood off, revealing the face of the Elephant Man. In the darkness it looked as real as

seeing Joseph Merrick in the flesh. Illuminated by the lapping flame from the torches, the effect was intense and surreal.

"You're always welcome here." Valor told Joseph with chilling sincerity. "Maybe when they abandon this place to us, we can have YOU play The Ripper." The former Master said as he slipped in and out of the darkness.

"Who would we be playing for?" Joseph asked what he thought was an obvious question.

"For ourselves…" The Master answered. "…What other audience do we need than each other?" He said with a twisted grin.

"Joseph!!" The Concierge barked at Joseph. "Come on!!"

As he turned to leave, Joseph heard Valor give him a final warning. "Just leave Merrick to me."

The lights seemed to dim and on cue, the room faded to darkness.

When Joseph reached the surface, the Tread Setter leapt into action disassembling the stairway to the Surface Dweller's cave. Pulling each tread out of its stone firmament as zie descended to the cave.

"What do you think?" Joseph asked.

"There's no negotiating with them. All this did was warn them what was coming. Fucking waste of my time I say. I can't believe I'm missing my production for this nonsense." The Concierge spat venomously. Joseph had never seen him so angry.

Later that night, after the debriefing with the Stage Manager and the Playwright, The Concierge met with Joseph in the hotel suite.

"They're doing it tonight. Taking the cave by force." The Concierge said bitterly to Joseph after the meeting concluded.
"I don't understand this at all. These people could've been cleared out a long time ago. Why the wait?" Joseph asked.
"Joseph, these people are more dangerous than you realize." The Concierge said, exasperated by Joseph's lack of understanding about the way things really worked at Gaslight.
"Why? Why are they dangerous? In my previous life, I dealt with *real* danger. If this was Iraq, he'd be extracted on day one, chopped up into tiny pieces and made into fish food."
"We're not in Iraq, Joseph. The battlefields here are the cubic inches between your ears." With that, The Concierge put down his drink and left him alone in the suite. Joseph thought about what The Concierge said and surmised that he probably was right. The battle for the mind is what really mattered in Gaslight.

THE RAID

Conducted at midnight, the raid netted all but two of the Surface Dwellers who sat bound blindfolded and gagged at the edge of the tarmac waiting for the plane to return from the Dominican Republic. The Master, of course, wasn't caught and neither was the Tread Setter. The two that held the most sway in the "battle for the cubic inches".

"Things will go back to normal?" Joseph asked as the jet came into view.

"No." The Concierge replied flatly. "The most dangerous ones are still here. Things will not be normal. Not until they're caught and evacuated."

The security force lifted the detainees by the gait belts around their waists and loaded them one-by-one into the plane.

"Aren't you going with them?" Joseph asked the Concierge.

"I'm staying for the run..." The Concierge kicked angrily at the dirt. "...not that I have a choice in the matter."

"I'm sorry." Joseph said, thinking about The Concierge's play. He wouldn't even know how it was received until they let him return to Sicily a full two months from now.

"I'm sorry too. At least you have the green light to start acting again. I've read the new script and it's good stuff, Joseph. I know you'll run with it." The Concierge nodded, confidently.

"I for one am glad you're staying. I felt lost without you here."
Joseph smiled and The Concierge threw his arm around him.

"Thanks." The Concierge started to leave, then turned back. "You
really liked my play?" The Concierge asked in a doubtful tone.

"Loved it. I can't wait to go again when I don't have a mission to
kidnap you." The Concierge smiled and left Joseph alone in the
empty room.

Joseph was allowed to stay in the hotel until his scenes could be
restarted in the timeline of the play. Without his makeup, the only
ones that recognized him were the actors, crew and a few of the
servers.

He had a dinner of bangers and mash and went to the front desk to
get some towels. Before he could get there, he felt a hand on his
arm.

"Hello again, sir." Joseph grinned, glad to see the butler again.

"Tif! How are you?" Joseph was slightly overwhelmed at seeing a
friendly face.

"Better than you, sir, from what I heard." Tif replied with concern.
"Are you well?"

"I'm fine. I'm out of commission while they deal with the current
difficulties, but in a day or two, I'll be back."

"Yes, difficulties. Very unpleasant." Tif smiled and pointed at
Joseph's packet. "My intercom number is inside. Call me any
time, sir. I'm at your disposal." Tif said with a short bow.

"Thank you, Tif." Joseph said. He started feeling hopeful again. Hopeful that this experience wouldn't come to a dark end as so many other events in his life.

When Joseph returned to his suite, he found a carved wooden elephant sitting at the center of the bed. He picked up the elephant and found a card taped to the base. He tore it off and opened it, finding a strange symbol inside...two offset ovals. He had no idea what the symbol meant, but he felt oddly sure that he would soon find out.

The next morning, Joseph got a detailed note slipped under his door marked for his eyes only.

Joseph- ROLE of THE ELEPHANT MAN

You are hereby given notice that your role is scheduled to resume tomorrow morning. Given the circumstances, you are given the option carry a weapon with you if you feel it necessary, but with all of the time lost due to the recent crisis, it is imperative to makeup for lost time. I will meet with you after a 4am makeup call and we'll get The Elephant Man back on track.
Best,
The Playwright

Joseph would have a few more hours of freedom. He didn't even consider carrying a weapon that could injure someone in the audience. Whatever happened was just going to happen.

At 4am, the makeup team woke Joseph with a breakfast cart. The Team Lead was bright and alert. Joseph guessed he must have been up since 2am. He wondered if the man ever slept.

"Welcome back Joseph. We all missed you."

"I missed you too. It was an interesting break in the routine."

"I heard you saw the Concierge's play?" The Team Lead said with a wry smile.

"I don't know if 'saw' is the right word, but what I did walk through was amazing. I'm just sorry that he couldn't stay until the end of it." Joseph took a slug of the espresso and smiled.

"Beautiful. How do you make such good coffee on this island?"

"You wonder how I get up when everyone's going to sleep? That's how." He nudged the espresso cup for emphasis.

"Finish up and get in the shower. We have a golf cart to take you to the stage."

"You have a bullet proof vest in my costume?" Joseph said, joking.

"In fact, we do. Only five pounds of Kevlar. Go ahead and finish breakfast and wash up. We'll wait in the lobby."

The make-up team left and Joseph studied his huge breakfast, opting to finish his amazing croissant with the coffee and polish it off with the Irish bacon.

The shower was abbreviated, but refreshing and when he got down to the lobby, Joseph was ready to rock and roll.

They got to the makeup area and were received with applause by the crew. This surprised and embarrassed Joseph, but he considered the jubilation to spring from the crew's relief that the Surface Dweller threat was abated. He remembered what The Concierge said and considered that any celebration was premature with The Master and The Tread Setter running around.

Once in the chair, Joseph discovered the identity of the man who was killed. He was not a stranger to Joseph, but a struggling actor from Joseph's New York days off Broadway that he knew fairly well.

"You knew him?" The Makeup Assistant pointed at the photo of the man that Joseph knew as Rafonovic.

"Yeah, I knew him." Joseph noted sadly. "He was always dealt the bad hands in life. So unfair."

Rafonovic wasn't a great actor and had some bad luck with keeping a roof over his head with the low-paid ensemble work. Joseph thought about the time that he asked to stay on the couch. He made a bullshit excuse because he didn't have the nerve to tell Rafonovic that his poor hygiene was the reason for the refusal. He always smelled and Joseph didn't want that scent imprint on his sofa.

Rafonovic probably was overjoyed at the opportunity to take on a lead role, even just for a few days. He wondered if he had any family and if they had been notified.

"Could you let The Concierge know that I have to speak with him?" Joseph said to the Team Lead.

"Oh, certainly." The TL said as he finished the last of the latex application. "…But I think the Playwright wants to speak with you first."

In moments, The Playwright entered with his entourage. He had a copy of Frederick Treves' book "The Elephant Man and Other Reminisces" in his hand.

"Joseph, are you ready to dive in?" The Playwright unfolded a few script pages from his pocket.

"I'm always ready." Joseph said boldly.

"Good, because I want to do the train scene today."

"Today?" Joseph doubted he could be ready for a new scene, but said nothing.

"Yes. Take a look at the scene and call me if you have questions." The Playwright was handed a telegram and retreated to a corner with his assistants to have a conference. In the interim, Joseph had a chance to read the scene in its entirety.

After the Carny took Merrick to Belgium, the Elephant Man

exhibit was shut down by the police and the carnival man took most of Merrick's money before sending him back to London by ferry and then train.

The train trip was documented in Treves' book as one of the lowest moments for Merrick. Without food and water and already weakened, Merrick arrived in London in a near-death state, unable to communicate his needs. One of his only possessions was Treves' card that he received in the doctor's first abbreviated examination of Merrick. This rescue by Treves marked the transition of the Elephant Man from sideshow freak to Treves' patient at the London Hospital.

This scene was one of the few in the play that frightened Joseph with its intensity.
"What a reintroduction." He said to the Playwright.
"I know you're excited about acting on the train. It's really a sweet toy." The Playwright knew he had the hooks in. Since he and The Conductor had their drunken adventure on the train, Joseph was dying to get back on The City of Stalingrad.

The audience members lucky enough to see this scene in person would be chosen by random lottery and notified by telegram. The rest of them would have to view the events projected on the ceiling. This would be the first time Gaslight would use video to bring the hotly anticipated events to the most people possible.

Some turned their nose up at the blatant use of modern technology, but The Playwright agreed that this was one breach of accuracy that would be tolerated.

"I'm very excited." Joseph admitted.

"I knew you would be. Get yourself in the zone, you'll be leaving soon." The Playwright slapped Joseph in the shoulder before his entourage pulled him away.

"Good luck Joseph!" The Playwright waved at Joseph as he vanished into the access tunnel.

The makeup department paid special attention to make Joseph look starved and injured. Joseph was given a special spray that imitated the smell of the Elephant Man's putrid smelling flesh after several days without a bath.

"Only one spray at a time." The Makeup Assistant warned. "Any more and you'll suffocate yourself and anyone close to you."

"Joseph. The transport is ready." The Team Lead gestured to one of the doors with the "no admittance" sign scrawled into the wood. These were the doors that led to the secret pneumatic pod that led to the train chamber. This was something not mentioned by The Conductor.

Joseph felt a rush of excitement that was akin to the anticipation of opening Christmas gifts as a boy.

Past the "No Admittance" door there was a hydraulic lift that descended deep into the lower floors, possibly past the level of the sex dungeon.

Next to the lift was a small platform that was stationed by a pale young man in a parka (The temperature there was downright freezing).

A pod emerged from the darkness. It closely resembled a roller coaster car.

Joseph was surprised that it was only built to accommodate one passenger and only had a small windshield for protection.

Indeed, the pod may have been a recycled roller coaster after all.

The pimply operator helped Joseph with his seatbelt as another car rolled in behind him.

"If you want to keep your hands, make sure they're inside." The kid warned Joseph as he pushed the button releasing the car and thrusting it forward.

The car descended into a dark tunnel that, from what Joseph could tell, was just large enough to accommodate the pod. In the darkness, Joseph swore he could, at two sections of the ride, feel the tunnel ceiling brush up against his hair.

It was a straight shot lasting about two minutes, finally terminating at the train station carousel where dozens of actors playing Belgian passengers waited for the train to arrive.

As Joseph's pod came to a stop, the actors started to applaud Joseph, provoking him to check his posterior to see if The Playwright was behind him. No one was there. They were clapping for him.

Joseph exited the pod with the assistance of another pimply operator. Stepping to the platform, actors approached him and shook his hand.

"It's an honor to work with you, Joseph." A middle-aged lady in Victorian schoolteacher garb said.

"This is a real privilege." A young man (a peasant) was next to approach.

"I'm flattered, but honestly I haven't had a chance to earn your respect yet."

The Schoolteacher shook her head.

"You've done more that you think, Joseph. I was here last year." The woman said as she showed Joseph a massive scar across both her arms that told the story of Valor's violent attacks. "You give us hope. Hope that Gaslight will last a few more years…after what happened."

Thinking of Rafonovic, Joseph turned to address his fellow actors. "I'm going to have a memorial to the actor that was killed while filling for me as The Elephant Man. I'm going to request that it be Saturday after most of our shifts are done. If you could make it."

"I'll be there." The young man said, putting his right hand up without hesitation. Soon more hands went up until finally all of the actors promised to be there.

"Thank you. This man. I knew him. I would hate to have an empty room at his memorial."

"Train arriving." The voice of the Stage Manager boomed from the intercom. "Standby."

The lights that were painfully dim brightened instantly. The rear projection kicked in, revealing a daytime scene of the train station at Dover. Joseph glanced behind him, watching the scene of the old city and its costumed animatronic characters.

"Wow." He whispered to himself as the overhead light imitating the sun turned on and grew in power.

Finally, the vibration of the train grew beneath their feet until it finally emerged from the tunnel, belching steam. The train ran the length of the dark chamber and came to a stop at the far end just before the tunnel terminated.

The huge cradle raised below the tracks as soft arms descended and clasped onto the train and tracks with a huge SNAP.

Joseph glanced up and saw The Conductor. Their eyes met and he smiled so brightly that Joseph couldn't help but laugh.

"Oy, laddie!" He exclaimed, taking a hit from his flask.

"Standby." The Stage Manager warned.

The train was moving as a simulation now, gently vibrating the cars. The platform filled with steam and the actors froze, waiting for direction.

"Begin on the Dover stage." The Stage Manager called over the loudspeaker.

The actors started to mill about the platform as Joseph remained motionless. No one would come closer than ten feet to him.

With the train at a complete stop, Station Masters started to take their positions for the embark/debark process. For that brief moment, the actors only had an audience of themselves as the train windows were in a closed position. It was a surreal moment and Joseph had to pause to watch the scene. The actors, animatronics, the rear projection and the steam train on its simulator combined to create a near-perfect illusion.

Finally, the curtains raised on the passenger compartment of the train, revealing the entire scene to the audience inside.

Even through the train's thick walls, a series of audible gasps accompanied by applause could be heard by the actors.

Actors disembarked and left the platform via a hidden corridor leading to the transport pods.

"Aboard!!" The Station Agent called out and the line to enter the train formed with Joseph carefully taking his place at the rear. The other passengers stared at Merrick in his strange robe and hood. When he finally reached the embarkation, the agent stopped him.

Joseph huddled over pathetically as the Agent asked him questions about his destination.

"Do you have your ticket, sir?"

Joseph dug into his pocket and produced a crumpled ticket. The Agent punched two holes in it.

"You are in third class. Back of the train." The Agent yelled as if Merrick was hard of hearing.

"God help us." The Agent muttered as the Elephant Man boarded.

As Joseph entered, he was crowded by curious audience members that blocked his path to the third-class section of the train. Remembering the odious spray given to him by the makeup crew, Joseph dug into his pocket and turned the spray towards himself, spritzing one time as instructed.

The ghastly odor that came from the one application of this substance was enough to send audience members screaming. The smell was a combination of rotten meat, urine and shit, all left to fester. Joseph gasped for air, thanking God that he didn't accidentally spray himself twice.

He had no trouble making it to the rear of the train now. As he did, he could hear actors break character to lament the horrible stench as well as unprepared audience members dry heaving.

Joseph found a spot at the very rear of the last coach that was meant to carry luggage. Suddenly, a light much brighter and colder than the others appeared behind him, casting hard shadows on the wall of the cabin. Joseph realized that the cameraman was just behind him. Joseph found a nook just large enough to collapse into. A single audience member followed him, but no one dared approach him yet.

"All Aboard!!" The Station Agent screamed from the platform. Moments later, the train's door slammed shut and they felt the first lurch as the window curtains slowly closed on the passenger compartments.

"Give him some space. People. He obviously wants to be alone." The Conductor firmly commanded to the audience.

"Can something be done about that smell?" One of the third-class passengers asked with a hint of desperation in his voice.

"Why yes." The Conductor said in a sarcastic-but-cheery voice. "Buy a second class ticket."
The third-class passengers groaned at this answer.
"Now back up everyone. Back up."

The train gained "speed" on the simulator and they started moving at what seemed to be quite a clip.

Joseph remembered from the time estimation on the script that this scene was expected to last ten minutes. He figured it was time to start attracting attention and possibly interacting with some of the audience.

Joseph tried to lift himself to an upright sitting position and calculatingly collapsed the way he'd practiced, almost falling into himself.

"Treves described the Elephant Man's posture perfectly. Use that as your tool." The Team Lead said as he coached Joseph for this scene. "Remember that when Treves was finally called to the station to deal with Merrick, he thought the Elephant Man's arms and legs were broken. That's how flat he was. Start that process on the train. Fold your limbs so you resemble something foreign. Not human."

It was good advice. Joseph imagined himself to be a crab and his legs were like jack knives.

Joseph wished that he could be up in the control room knocking some back with The Conductor, hearing his crooked laughter and his Scottish brogue.

Instead he remained motionless except for his left hand that was clutched to the horrible-smelling spray. Every time the audience got too close, he gave himself another dose, forcing them back to the front of the car.

"Is he dead?" One woman exclaimed. It sounded like she was crying.

"I can't stomach that stench." A man said, covering his mouth with his shirt.

Joseph hated the smell, but loved the effect it had on the audience. He made no noise, but was endlessly amused at how they crept forward toward him only to retreat with another dose of the noxious stuff.

Finally, Joseph heard a small dog barking over the hidden speakers. That was his auditory cue that the transition was coming for the train to be released from the simulator and run on its own power on the return to the Gaslight stage.

Though Joseph couldn't see it from his prone position, he could hear a hum. This was followed by a brief sensation of weightlessness accompanied by a thumping sound then the feeling of motion resumed.

The blinds on the train windows opened but there was nothing to see yet except the wall of the tunnel. Suddenly, the train roared out of the darkness and into the nighttime stage of London. The audience was positively giddy as they approached London Bridge

Station.

"Look at them all!" The young man, an audience member nearest to Joseph said, pointing at the masses of people waiting for the train to arrive. "There's hundreds of them."
"Everyone wants to see this scene. How lucky we are, hey?" A female patron added.

Joseph was afraid to raise his head to look as the train came to a stop with a HISS, presumably at the London station.
"London Bridge Station!!" The Conductor screamed. The doors flung open, causing a crush of people into the train.
The audience inside the train pushed to get a better look at Joseph, prompting him to spray another dose of the foul smelling substance. As horrible as it was, the smell did little to stop the audience from crushing into him.

"Make way. Make way!" A row of Bobbies pushed people aside and ejected a few from inside the train. Joseph heard The Conductor's voice.
"I don't know if he's dead or alive, but he certainly smells like a corpse." The Conductor exclaimed with disgust. "I'm not going near him."

"Don't think we like this either, but you ARE going to help us." One of the Bobbies barked at The Conductor.

Joseph held out his left hand weakly through his cloak with Dr. Treves' card clutched between his fingers.

"Can you get up on your own?" A bobby said, nudging Joseph with his foot.

The officer lifted a corner of Joseph's hood and gasped.

"Jesus, Mary and Joseph." He exclaimed before vomiting all over The Conductor and an audience member.

"I just cleaned these boots!" The Conductor spat.

One of the policemen took the card and read it aloud.

"Someone go fetch this Dr. Treves. Maybe he'll know what to do with this creature."

In ten minutes Joseph heard Treves being hustled through the massive crowd.

"Let the doctor through! Let the doctor through!" One of the cops barked.

Joseph heard the clacking footsteps, indicating the higher quality of shoes that a doctor could afford.

"He hasn't spoken at all, Doctor." The Conductor said.

"If he did, you wouldn't be able to understand him anyway." Dr. Treves said with a calm voice. Joseph enjoyed hearing Eddie's voice again. He had missed the early days of rehearsals before everything got so crazy. From what he could tell, Eddie had come a long way with inhabiting his character.

"Let's get him to the hospital." Eddie commanded. "Find a cart. Something strong enough to hold him."

Eddie leaned down close to Joseph's head.

"Hang on Joseph, I'm taking you somewhere safe."

"Thank you." Joseph muttered weakly in a nearly unintelligible voice.

One of the porters found a luggage cart sturdy enough to get Joseph to the street where they could get a horse-driven cart to take him the rest of the way. The Bobbies gagged and held their breath as they lifted Joseph atop the cart. As they rolled him off the train and onto the platform, a burst of applause came from the audience that packed the station to see the scene.

"Make way! Make way!" The Bobbies commanded. Joseph felt hands touch him as he was rolled through the station. "We love you Joseph!" Someone in the audience yelled, causing the applause to intensify. The outpouring of emotion was always surprising to Joseph. To many of these people, Joseph wasn't an actor, but the real Elephant Man. In their minds, they were transported back over a hundred years and experiencing the actual events…meeting the real person.

Joseph thought of the warning in the welcome packet that everyone received before entering Gaslight. One of the disclaimers in the "Terms of Experience" contract was the warning that "Audience members have reported a higher instance of mental illness issues upon returning home from Gaslight, exacerbating pre-existing conditions as well as inciting new disorders (specifically schizophrenia). You consent to attend Gaslight with full knowledge of these risks." The contract read.

Joseph was transported to the London Hospital. They brought him into an evaluation room where Treves removed the Elephant Man's hood and cloak to the gasps and applause of the audience. Once the nurses saw and smelled the Elephant Man in his full horrible visage, three of them ran screaming, leaving the two old minders to help Treves with the examination.

This was Joseph's cue to have a full-on asthma attack.

Joseph began gasping for air as Treves barked orders for various medicines and machines. In the end, they attached a steam respirator to Joseph's face.
"This is going to help." Treves said through Joseph's earpiece. Bring the breathing back to normal."
Joseph slowed his breaths in increments, but maintained the panicked look in his eyes.

"He's stabilizing." Treves said with relief. "I think he'll be all right now, at least as far as his breathing is concerned. Can we find him a bed?"

The elderly nurses glanced at each other with an expression of doom.

"You can't expect the other patients to tolerate bedding next to this man. Can you put him in the isolation room?" The Old Nurse said.

Treves nodded in agreement. "Very good. Let's get him there. As quietly as possible, please."

"Yes, doctor."

One of the Old Nurses brought TEM to the isolation room. They moved slowly with the horde of audience in tow. Two Bobbies let TEM and the Old Nurse in the isolation room and closed the door behind them, allowing no one else through.

The Old Nurse sighed with relief.

"That was great! I have to get back." The woman hugged Joseph and then opened the door leading to a hidden spiral staircase.

Finally, with The Elephant Man tucked away in the isolation room and the gate locked from the outside, Joseph could finally stand and walk off the cramp that had built in his hips and shoulders.

Eddie appeared from the same spiral staircase that the Old Nurse had exited from. The man couldn't contain his glee.

"That…was fucking AMAZING!! AMAZING!!"

As dour as Joseph's moods were recently, even he had to smile. He had never had such a reaction with almost no words of dialogue. In coordination with the flawless function of the train and the Gaslight set itself (not to mention the enthusiasm of the audience) he had just experienced a once-in-a-lifetime piece of immersive theater.

"I have to admit…that was sweet." Joseph finally relented. "You did a great job Eddie. You've really advanced in this part."
"Thanks Joseph. Let's have a drink, what do you say?" Eddie took out a flask and found two small glasses on the nightstand. He poured two shots and they slugged it down together.

"Ahhh." Eddie said. It was Scotch. Peaty Scotch that Joseph was ill prepared for. For a moment, he felt his throat close off and his lungs burn. This unpleasant moment was followed by a warm trickling feeling throughout his gut.
"Hah, sorry. Not everyone's ready for the milk of the highlands. We have the rest of the day off. What will you do with it Joe?"
"Um. Maybe I'll roam as an audience member. I saw that Hamlet was playing at the local theater tonight."
"OK. I've got an appointment on the bottom floor. Beautiful blonde with a Russian accent."
A wave of sickness came over Joseph. He didn't know that Eddie was a customer of the sex dungeon. The thought of that place immediately put him in a foul mood, though he did his best to hide

it from Eddie.

"Tell me what you see down there." He asked Eddie.

"You haven't been?" Eddie seemed surprised.

"Not exactly."

"They have anything you want. Anything." Eddie whispered even though they were alone.

"Who is 'they'?" Joseph asked, turning Eddie's smile into a sneer.

"Never mind. Forget I mentioned it. You have a good time watching…Shakespeare." Eddie slapped Joseph on the back, and then made his exit through the spiral staircase. He paused, glancing back at Joseph.

"You coming?"

"Na. I'll hang out here for a minute. It's quiet here in my new home."

"Good night, then." His mind already on his appointment in the dungeon.

After sitting in silence for a while, as his head pulsated.

Later, Joseph would navigate the narrow tunnel to the green room, get his makeup and costume removed and then check out some street clothes and just explore.

Theater Dispatch NEW YORK CITY
THE PREVIOUS YEAR

This Friday marks the opening of *Falstaff*, an immersive experience on the scale no one has ever seen before will open in an abandoned five-story office building in Red Hook. The production from the formerly Minneapolis based theater company Head Water took a huge leap with a McMurphy grant to create the largest immersive theater experience we have yet seen in America. "Fallstaff", based on Shakespeare's "Henry V" is not like anything the Bard could have imagined. You, the audience member are King Hal and the actors treat you as such. There are a whopping sixteen storylines going on at once, one for every five-audience members, making it physically impossible to see the show in its entirety. In addition to the immersive aspect of the production, it further challenges the audience by setting *Henry V* in a department store in the middle of a hostile buyout from a rival.

The show is three hours long, not including the pre-show in the lounge.

This play is headlined by a Brooklyn newcomer, Joseph Bickle who plays Falstaff an embattled district manager trying to keep his store alive despite the apathy from the employees who know about the impending hostile buyout from the French department store

"Dauphin's".

This reporter was one of twelve journalists invited to the preview show and I found the experience to be simply overwhelming. In this five-story building, there was simply no safe harbor even from the elaborate sets that suck you in and threated to devour your entire three hours. After going down this rabbit hole, I forget this wasn't a puzzle room. I could walk out any time I wanted. Still it seemed like I was rifling through the dark secrets of Henry's father, Henry Sr., the former CEO of the department store who deposed the founder, Richard King from the company on a trumped up sexual harassment charge from young women that were paid to falsely accuse. The falsely condemned Richard, who started the company from his garage, couldn't cope with being ousted from his creation and they found him hanging in the garage where it had all started. Richard continues to torment, even with Henry Sr. gone, haunting his son during this hostile takeover from The Dauphin Company.

I was fortunate or unfortunate enough to be confronted by this specter and led through a hidden passage for a one-on-one experience with this ghost that left me shaken and feeling remorseful in the way that I found unnerving.

It was a disturbing feeling as if someone had gone inside my mind and replanted a memory of a repressed crime. What followed was a tremendous performance by Bickle who led the audience who dared to follow him into the dark underbelly of corporate America.

I found it disorienting and exhilarating at the same time.

I can't say that this production is for everyone, but I can be sure of this. Attend *Falstaff* and you will never forget the experience.

Jason Conroy – Theater Dispatch

Internal Memo

Head Water Theater Company

"Falstaff"

Production Staff's Eyes Only

Joseph Bickle aka "Falstaff" has been suspended for multiple complaints of over-aggressive one-on-ones with audience members. During questioning over the complaints, Joseph revealed his struggle with drug addiction that had interfered with his judgment and created an acting environment where he lost control and pushed or hit audience members. He checked himself into a rehabilitation facility and will need to be replaced. Please do not encourage cast members to discuss this incident at least until out of court settlements can be negotiated with the victims.

Thank you for your cooperation.

R-Ridley---Playwright "Falstaff"

After his firing, Joseph knew that his theater career was finished. Maybe he could negotiate a new future as a scrubber of toilets or a custodian at the local high school.

He had dreamed for so long of acting in a play that really broke through. What he didn't plan on was becoming an opioid addict after a simple prescription for his Iraq War injury

For eight weeks, he lived his dream until he lost control. The audience members didn't show his character the respect he deserved. They talked over him, yelled out for their friends, Complained that the immersive experience was "the dumbest thing they'd ever seen". It was too much for Joseph in his addled state and he acted out.

Now job offers that were in the pipeline after *Falstaff* dried up. Phone calls weren't returned. Friends avoided him on the street. He was a pariah.
He spent one afternoon studying the classified ads looking for any job he might be qualified for. He had his apartment for another three months and desperately wanted to stay in New York City.

At the height of despair, staring at the want ads for jobs wouldn't even cover half of his rent, Joseph closed the paper and sipped a cold cup of coffee at the greasy spoon diner in Bed-Stuy. He didn't notice the man pulling up a chair at his table.

He glanced up and saw a man in a black trench coat sitting across from him. He looked like a butler with his stiff posture and piercing eyes and receding hairline.

"Hello, Joseph." The man said in a deep purring voice.

"Look…are you a collections agent? The only acting job I can get is at a haunted house. I have nothing to give you." Joseph said in a shaky voice. The man with the piercing eyes watched Joseph silently.

"You know my name. What's yours?" Joseph asked. The man didn't look like any bill collector he had ever seen.

"Where I come from, names are not important. My official title is 'Actor Outreach Executive', but you can call me *The Concierge.*"

Email Message
From Joseph Bickle

Dear Concierge of Gaslight,

After considering your interest, I would like to discuss it with you in greater detail before you leave New York. I am available all day tomorrow. Please call or e-mail me when you get a chance.

Thank You

Joseph Bickle

TEXT MESSAGE

REPLY From

Concierge @Gaslight.gs

Joseph, I am at the airport. If you are serious about joining
Gaslight, drop everything and come. I will hold the plane for you.
Reply in the affirmative and I will send a car right away.

TEXT From Joseph Bickle

I'm in. No need to go home. There's nothing there I want to take
anyway.

Minutes after sending this final text, a Mercedes pulled up by the
curb. Joseph checked his back pocket where he always carried his
passport. Like a good soldier, he was prepared for anything.

"Joseph Bickle?" The middle-aged driver asked.

Joseph nodded and the driver exited to open the rear door.

"Do you have any bags sir?"

"No. Nothing." Joseph said as he got in.

"Very good sir." The driver shut the door firmly.

They pulled into La Guardia's private jet terminal and were waved
onto the tarmac to a medium-sized jet with an all-white paint
scheme.

"You must have some important friends." The driver said. "They
don't usually let us drive on the tarmac.

The Concierge emerged from the plane and waved Joseph in as
soon as the car came to a stop.

"You'd better go. Good luck sir." The driver called back to Joseph.

The car drove away and Joseph felt a momentary sense of panic. He had one last chance to flee. Flee back to what? There was nothing here for him now. He boarded the plane with the vague gnawing feeling that he would never see New York City again. As he entered the jet, The Concierge greeted Joseph at the door and quickly showed him to a seat as a flight attendant closed and sealed the main hatch.

"They were holding this plane for YOU?" A middle aged, balding man snapped at Joseph.
"Yes, we were waiting for him. Do you have a problem with that?" The Concierge's piercing eyes served him when he was charming, but served him better when he was pissed.
The middle-aged man seemed to wither under his gaze.
"No. No problem." He squeaked.
"OK then. We were waiting for him, because I knew that he would come to his senses and join us. I held the plane because I knew this actor had something that we could use that would strengthen our community. I have an instinct about these things." The Concierge bowed to Joseph who was a bit stunned. This man that he just met today had more confidence in him than anyone else in his life. What was his basis for that, especially after the failures and the addiction problems? Why did he have more confidence in

Joseph than Joseph had in himself?

IT'S COLD

With Joseph cleaned up and dressed in civilian clothes, he roamed the streets of Whitechapel, thinking about how to spend his evening. As his mind cleared, he remembered his promise to memorialize Rafonovic.

St. Phillips towered over Whitechapel and was one of the buildings that was only open when enough actors could be dedicated to it. Sunday morning service was the only scheduled opening other than two funerals during week three and five.

The Father was a real priest and kept an office and a confessional open on the rear entry of the cathedral.
Before heading back, Joseph made a stop at his office and found it closed.

"Hello, may I be of assistance?" A soft deep voice called out from a dark hallway. It was the priest.
"Hello Father, do you know who I am?"
"Should I?" The Father said. He was younger than Joseph by perhaps five years. Joseph was glad he didn't address him as "my son".
"I play the Elephant Man." Joseph said. The Father's eyes lit up with recognition.

"Oh! Joseph. Welcome. Welcome. Please step into my office."
The office was decorated immaculately as if it were lifted from a
historical photo. There was just enough room for Joseph to
squeeze in as the bench seat was crammed beneath a slanted
ceiling that accommodated the second floor stairs just above. He
could hear the creaking on the treads as someone walked upstairs.

"A control room right above us. They wouldn't let a big space like
this go to waste." The Father lit a pipe and took a few puffs.
"So, what can I do for you?" The Father broke character, revealing
a hint of a Jersey accent.
"Rafonovic. The man who was killed. I knew him."
"Ah, tragic. I'm very sorry. I heard they cut his face off. They'll
have to have a closed casket." The Father said coldly.
Joseph's face dropped. He didn't know that they defiled the man's
body.
"I didn't know that." Joseph whispered sullenly.
"Ah, I just remembered. I wasn't supposed to tell anyone that."
"Rafonovic, he doesn't have any family. I'd like to do a memorial
for him."

The Father shook his head immediately. "They've shipped his
body out to the States. We're a working theater production now.
We can't do that."
If they hadn't flown me out to run an errand, none of this would've
happened. Gaslight owes the man a memorial because there is no

one back home to even claim the body."

"Take it up with the Stage Manager. I can't make that kind of decision."

"If they say 'yes', would you do the service?"

"No. I wouldn't. I wasn't contracted for funerals." The Father stared at Joseph with impermeable coldness.

"What's your price?" Joseph asked.

"More that you could afford. You may go home with a check, but you came here poor. I know you don't have any money." The Father stated bluntly.

"How do you know that?" Joseph leaned in and literally felt colder as he got closer to The Father. "Thank you for your time." Joseph said, letting himself out. He didn't want to spend another moment around this man.

The Father puffed on his pipe and didn't respond to Joseph's exit.

Joseph strolled around the church and through the streets of Whitechapel, finally entering the London Hospital set through a secret door. In the isolation ward, he was all-alone in perfect silence, alone with his bitterness. Joseph felt fresh rage in several directions. Payback was on the menu both for The Master and (to a lesser extent) The Father for denying closure for Rafonovic. Soon, he could hear thumps from the performances downstairs, but nothing else. He was alone with his thoughts for just a few moments before the makeup team came and the audience would be able to watch the Elephant Man sleep. He savored this moment of solitude.

Soon enough, the familiar footsteps of the makeup team grew louder up the spiral staircase.

"Joseph!" The Team Lead greeted him as he stepped through the secret door.

Joseph returned the greeting.

The Team Lead gestured to his assistants and they came at Joseph with the night costume.

"Sorry for the assembly line. We're behind tonight.

"I get it." The process pulled and pushed Joseph, making him feel like a t-shirt in a washing machine. In all of thirty minutes, they were done and packing up.

"Have a good night Joseph. Remember, we'll be watching all night." The Team Lead pointed up at the infrared camera hidden in the corner.

"Good night." Joseph said to each of the makeup artists as they left.

As the last of them went down the spiral staircase, Joseph heard the gate on the downstairs open with a metallic creak. He got into bed, hoping he would have a little more time to himself. Instead, they came almost immediately.

This was a complete difference now with the security

improvements. The audience had to stay behind a blue line now, a distance of about five feet from Joseph. They were good at policing each other if one of them got too close.

"Remember what they said!" One of them warned a woman who got too close.

"You'd be fined." Another said.

Joseph slipped in earplugs at midnight when the turkeys finally started to thin. He hadn't slept so soundly since the first night at the freak show.

The next day morning, Joseph heard the gate close and lock downstairs.

A few seconds later, he heard the metallic steps on the circular staircase.

The Team Lead entered with a hearty "Good Morning!" and a breakfast tote filled with pastries and thermoses of coffee.

"We have a different craft service for the hospital. I hope you like it as much as before. "

Joseph glanced down at the pastries; a croissant with shaved almonds, a bagel with a tin of cream cheese, and a cinnamon roll that seemed to still ooze from its innards.

"It looks amazing. How's the coffee?"

"French press, the Team Lead said with a grin. It's good. I'm sure I can get espresso tomorrow."

"It's fine. French press is great!" Joseph took off his headpiece and started to make a bagel on his end table.

"Take ten minutes to eat. We have to unpack everything anyway."
The Team Lead said as he unlatched the suitcase containing the
Elephant Man's cloak.

The bagel was fresh. With cream cheese and French Press coffee,
it was exquisite.

"What scenes do you have today?" The female assistant asked
Joseph.

"Today I stand naked in the exam room all day while the doctors
do my examination." Joseph groaned.

"Well, I'm just glad that the poor man had a perfectly normal cock
or I'd have to glue a Frankenwiener on you." She said.

"Glad you won't suffer through that." He said, hoping to change
the subject.

"Hey, I'm a professional. I do what I gotta do." The assistant said
with a grin.

"All I have to say is they better have that stage heated." Joseph
thought back to his experience acting in *Equus* during a Cleveland
winter.

"We'll put you in a hospital gown." The wardrobe girl rifled
through a bag and found the gauzy white robe.

"Can you stand in position for very long? It looks terribly
uncomfortable from what I can tell." She asked.

"When we rehearsed this, I had a break every thirty minutes. That
seemed to be enough to shake off the aches and pains." Joseph

could feel his knees and hips twinge as he said this.

"Good luck, Joseph." The Team Lead said as he gestured to his assistants. They quickly gathered their things, echoing their leader's well wishes for Joseph as they filed down the stairwell. The Team Lead closed the door behind him and Joseph could hear them bumping their equipment as they traversed the stairs.

A few moments of silence passed. There was a bit of commotion from the lower floor and Joseph could feel footsteps ascending rather than descending. The room's door opened. It was The Stage Manager.
"Morning." The man gave Joseph a perfunctory grin and studied him up and down. "Looks like you're ready for the day."
"I hope so."
"Sure. Absolutely. Now Treves will come in and fetch you in about ten minutes to take you to the exam room. You saw the script?"
"Yes. Please explain the time limit. I think I understand, but…" Joseph asked.

"The audience will only see five minutes at a time. Security will man the front and rear of the room. After the five minutes, the crowd will be ushered out and a new one will be let in. We can do breaks when needed. We'll just leave the room closed and have them wait in the cue.

"Same script...all day?" Joseph asked.

"Correct. Just don't get an erection if your see someone you're attracted to. That's really breaking the forth wall harder than necessary." The Stage Manager laughed.

"I'm a professional. My body is my professional tool. You won't have that kind of problem." Joseph said, slightly offended at the crude humor at his expense.

"Good. Well, get ready. Good luck today."

With that, the Stage Manager took the secret stairway down and a message squawked through the intercom.

"Elephant Man is live!" An assistant said over the speaker.

Within seconds, the audience filed in finding Joseph standing in the middle of the room looking through them. A white light illuminated from the floor, designating the safe spaces that the audience could stand. They did their best to stay behind this line. A hospital guard reminded anyone who came too close to Joseph.

A single person climbed the stairs. Joseph could feel the footsteps through the floor. The door opened and it was Dr. Treves wearing a white lab coat and a file of papers tucked under his arm.

"Good morning, Joseph. Are you ready?"

"Yes, Doctor Treves." Joseph said through the constrictive mouthpiece.

"Very well."

Joseph was led by Treves to an exam room. The audience followed them down and were joined by a larger group waiting on the ground floor. The hospital guard instructed the audience to form a line and wait for word from him as Treves brought the Elephant Man into the empty examination theater.

The makeup crew rushed to Joseph, placing him on a platform marked by a black "X". They took the nightshirt off, leaving him completely naked.

"It's cold. I asked if we'd have proper heat." Joseph said bitterly. He could see the goosebumps forming on what little skin was visible through the makeup.

"We'll take care of it now." One of the assistants promised. Feedback squawked over the hidden intercom as it switched on.

"You all ready?" It was the voice of the Playwright.

"Yes, but it's a little cold for Joseph. Can we turn it up a bit?" Eddie said toward the hidden microphone.

"Got it. Good luck. Make sure to take your breaks." With a click, the intercom was turned off.

"Thanks." Joseph said to Eddie.

"Shit man, your nut sack is vanishing into your stomach. Let's get some heat for you." Eddie noted, making Joseph laugh. He realized that he so seldom laughed that he felt embarrassed at the show of vulnerability.

"It's good to see you loosen up a bit." Eddie said to him.

"Yeah, maybe I should run around naked and cold all the time." Joseph noted, only half-kidding.

"Ready in 30 seconds." The voice of the Stage Manager called out.

"Game time." Eddie said, his hands shaking.

"Deep breaths." Joseph said, nudging Eddie.

"Ten seconds." The Stage Manager called. This was the last warning. At zero seconds, the doors flung open.

Two hospital guards took count as the audience filed in until the crescent-shaped, two-level observation platform was full. The scene was live.

"I'm glad to see that you came, fellow physicians and esteemed specialists. As you have been informed in my letter, this poor individual, called 'The Elephant Man' has a combination of maladies that I have never seen before." As Eddie said this, antique slide projectors listed his maladies from his enlarged head, cauliflower-like skin growths, curved spine and deformed limbs.

"With all of these horrible afflictions, could you, dear colleague approach and examine this man. Maybe with our combined knowledge, we could determine the cause of this combination of illnesses. Come. One at a time."

As they were instructed by the guards, each audience member got an up close and personal look at the Elephant Man. A guard thrust a pencil and clipboard in their hands and encouraged to write a diagnosis.

For a few moments , each audience member participated as expected, looking him over, sometimes only glancing at Joseph before jotting down some notes and turning them over to the eager Dr. Treves who piled the findings in a stack on his table. Then the first problem began.

The smell of the Elephant Man's rotting skin was piped in by a series of tubes. After almost no smell being disbursed, a sudden surge of the offensive odor hit just as a middle-aged woman stepped up to observe Joseph. Even thought he was preconditioned to tolerate this odor, Joseph momentarily gagged. The woman was instantly overwhelmed and projectile vomited all over Joseph's legs.

"Don't worry. His necrosis is a bit much until you're used to it." Treves chimed in, cleaning off the Elephant Man with a rag. A guard rushed the woman outside. The smell of the necrosis combined with vomit was so vile, several patrons refused to approach Joseph.

The second event involved a woman that had obviously had too much to drink. Joseph wondered why this woman who was barely able to stand was allowed to get in line.

She glanced at his naked body and fixated on his penis.

"Why is his cock normal? That makes no sense!" She slurred.

"The man's genitals are normal, Doctor." Eddie tried desperately to stay in character and move the woman along.

"Did you run out of makeup for his dick?" The woman reached out and grabbed Joseph's member in her hand in such a way that one of his testicles were entangled in her fingers and bulged out painfully as she tightened her grip further.

Joseph was in trouble.

"Madam Doctor…" Joseph said in a kind tone that did nothing to betray his feeling of horror at becoming a eunuch. "…I think I can speak for Dr. Treves and remind you that what you have in your hand is not your medical specialty."

The drunk woman stared at Joseph blankly and then broke out in a giggle that expanded into belly laughter that made her forget the tender cargo she was holding. She loosened her grip just enough for Joseph to slip it out of her hand. Sore, but not permanently injured.

Joseph snapped the fingers on his left hand, signaling that he wanted the room cleared.

"Exam is over! Thank you doctors."

The guards herded the audience out the door. Once the last of them were out, Joseph called up to the intercom.

"Listen! You have to screen out the fucking drunks!" Joseph yelled at one of the guards. "I almost lost the fucking plural on my balls!"

When the guard looked at the Stage Manager rather than listening, to him Joseph grabbed him by the shoulder and cornered him, leaving him nowhere else to look.

"If you think this is easy, you get your ass down here and let people yank your junk! I depend on you to do one thing!" Joseph yelled as he got up in the face of the increasingly frightened guard.

"We hear you, Joseph. If you want to blame anyone, blame me." The Stage Manager said in a placating tone, trying to decelerate Joseph's anger.

"We will make screening for inebriation a top priority from now on. Just one more thing we have to do."

"Well, I'm sorry for the inconvenience." Joseph spat as he broke off from his confrontation with the guard.

"Take a minute and we'll let the next group in." The voice of The Playwright came over the loudspeaker. "Joseph, do you think with the extra vigilance we can get back to the scene?" The Playwright said with a concerned tone. Joseph felt embarrassed, remembering the times when he couldn't keep his cool. It was an incident similar to this one that almost cost him his career. He took a deep breath, closed his eyes and reset himself. When he opened his eyes, he was calm again.

"Are we ready to go?" The Stage Manager asked impatiently.

"Yes. I'm OK. Sorry to the guard there. I was out of line." Joseph said in a contrite voice. Joseph looked back at the guard who nervously nodded at him.

"Very well. Get situated in thirty seconds." The Stage Manager ordered.

"Watch it with that rotting smell!" Joseph added."

"It's always like that at the start." The Stage Manager noted.

"Fifteen seconds. Everyone." The Assistant Stage Manager called out.

The doors flung open and it was the same wide eyed, half-drunk customers ogling over him. The smell, horrible as it was still didn't dissuade audience from touching him. As the third group began, Joseph begged the stage manager to impose real consequences for those who groped him if for no other reason than it was ruining his chest prosthetic.

"What do you suggest, Joseph?" The Stage Manager barked angrily.

"Confine them to their rooms for a day. Don't you do that when they break the rules?"

"Really, Joseph?"

"Have them warned and follow up on it. I can't do another eight weeks like this. Aren't you supposed to protect us?"

"Very well. Guards will you please warn the audience of the rule regarding the Elephant Man and the consequences of room detention if they don't follow it?" The Stage Manager ordered.

"Yes sir." The Lead Guard responded and slipped out to the hallway to address the turkeys in line.

"Are you happy now?" The Stage Manager snipped.

"You see the problem with drunks in the audience yet? You shouldn't serve drinks until later in the day."

"Thirty seconds, Joseph. Don't complain. You got what you wanted. Get ready. Fifteen seconds." The Stage Manager was pissed.

Before Joseph could formulate a comeback, the doors flung open to a new batch of "physicians".

The first two-thirds of the group went as expected. Inspection, the writing of a diagnosis, and then turning it in to Treves for perusal.

Later in the day, a short, curmudgeonly man, was writing notes, inspecting the Elephant Man a bit closer than the others. He dropped his pencil and when he bent down to get it, he lunged forward putting Joseph's dick in his mouth.

For a moment, everyone was silent, making the event even more disturbing as the sucking sounds filled the room, causing most of the audience to turn away.

"Sir." Joseph said as calmly as he could. Realizing that the dental prosthesis was in the way, he yanked it out to facilitate speech. He was dumbfounded that no one else said anything or did anything to defend him, like it was all part of the act.

"Get off my dick old man!" With Joseph's limited mobility, he still managed to push the man off of him, his teeth scraping against his penis upon exit.

"Fuck!" Joseph said, glancing down as his embarrassingly erect dick with red scrape marks that made it resemble a candy cane.

"Clear the room!!" Eddie finally screamed, standing in front of Joseph, protecting him from any further harassment.

"Clear the room and arrest that man." Eddie pointed at the old man bitterly.

"Guards!" The stage manager barked over the intercom.

Two guards helped the old man to his feet and escorted him through a hidden door. The rest of the audience just stood in place, looking too shocked to move.

"Show's over." Joseph said angrily. "The guards will show you out." With the audience still motionless, Joseph lunged at them with a primal scream that caused several of them to run for a door, any door. One of them went through the hidden door, the one that the old man was led down after his arrest.

The rest of them filed out in a slow, guilty shuffle.

"A medic is coming, Joseph." The Stage Manager said in a hushed tone.

"Jesus Christ." Eddie said in disbelief.

"Am I bleeding? I can't see it."

Eddie bent down to check and shook his head.

"It's red, but he didn't break skin." Eddie said as he grimaced, feeling sympathy pain in his own groin.

Moments later, medics arrived and disinfected Joseph's scrapes. The makeup team came shortly afterward and started removing the prosthetics.

"I heard what happened. I'm sorry Joseph." The Team Lead said in a consoling tone.

"I just want to go home."

With the makeup off and his wound disinfected, someone in the makeup crew threw a robe over him. Rather than exiting out of the secret passage, Joseph went right out the stage door to the hallway where the next group still stood in line.

"Why are you still here?" Joseph barked at them as guards tried to bring him back into the room and out of sight. He shook them off and the audience gasped.

They started applauding him, making him even angrier.

"Why are you clapping? The scene is ruined!"

Joseph stormed away, the turkeys still applauding.

A Guard manning the door to the isolation ward saw Joseph coming at him out of costume and frantically searched for his keys, opening the door just in time as Joseph pushed inside his dwelling.

"Joseph?! Joseph?! Joseph?!!" The Stage Manager screamed over the intercom. Just before Joseph ripped the intercom from the wall, he heard the Playwright say "Leave him alone for a while."

Joseph pushed a chair against the door, then a chest of drawers against the hidden access. He flung himself into bed and felt the ache between his legs. He felt ashamed that he had reacted the way he did. He should've been calm and let the guards handle things. He hated losing control like this, even under these circumstances. He heard the isolation ward door close and lock. They were finally protecting him from the slobbering masses. The stress had exhausted him. He slept hard and didn't dream.

BEHIND GLASS

The next morning, the Stage Manager arrived with the makeup
team.

"We realize that we could do more. To be honest, we didn't
expect this kind of behavior from the audience. This kind of thing
has occurred before, but it was very rare. So, you'll be behind
glass when you do your scene today. They won't be able to touch
you."

Joseph was relieved though he still felt uncomfortable.

"Are you satisfied with the results?"

"I'd prefer to wear a loincloth."

"Very well, but consider that the normalcy of the Elephant Man's
genitals are part of his diagnosis by Treves himself. His dick and
his left arm...the only normal real estate on the man. When you
look at it that way, you cannot consider it gratuitous."

"Very well." Joseph understood his reasoning, but it still left him
unsure.

"You'll have a good day today, Joseph. Don't worry about a
thing."

The Stage Manager left down the secret stairway, allowing the
makeup team to start their session.

"Did you get some sleep?" The Team Lead asked with genuine
concern.

"I did actually." Joseph said distantly.

Joseph was lost in thought. One of the assistants helped remove
his nightshirt. He stood, naked in front of the team, the marks on
his penis scabbing over.
"Breaking character." He said with the same inflection as
admitting he had cancer. "I just feel like I let everyone down."
"It was an emergency, Joseph. You were being assaulted. You're
supposed to break character." The Team Lead reminded Joseph.
"I know. I still feel…weak. Undisciplined." As Joseph said this,
he felt himself tearing up. He wasn't used to such bare admissions
except at his Narcotics Anonymous meetings.
"Weak and undisciplined are the last words I would use to describe
you Joseph. The last words."
They worked on Joseph for another hour before he was ready for
another day of medical inspections.

Before Eddie arrived to take him downstairs, Joseph asked the
Team Lead for a slug of whiskey from the hip flask he knew he
kept hidden in his cart. The Team Lead slid it to him discreetly
and Joseph slugged down two good swallows.
"OK, now I'm ready." He said, grinning.

"You'll do fine." The Team Lead nudged his shoulder and
grinned. He gestured to his people and they started to leave.
"Thanks." Joseph called to them as they descended the stairwell.

Joseph could hear the downstairs padlock open and the creak of the heavy metal door. He assumed it was Treves coming to fetch him. He stood at the center of the room with his hospital gown on, ready to start twelve hours of immersive theater.

To Joseph's surprise, it was the Concierge that entered the room instead.

"Hello, Joseph."

"What are you doing here? My scene is about to start."

"I just wanted to talk about yesterday."

"Well, I'd rather just move on, you know.."

The Concierge flipped open a phone with a projector.

"Just watch."

The image was of a security camera showing two guards escorting the old man who assaulted Joseph into his room.

"He had two guards posted at the door. When they went to check on him, they found this."

A body cam on of the security showed one of the men delivering a tray of food to the prisoner.

They were met with complete darkness. Every light in the room smashed in.

The guards scanned with flashlights and found a hole in the forced perspective window that looked over a three-dimensional model of Whitechapel. Looking down into the hole, they revealed treads mounted to the outer wall of the hotel that consisted of a dark metal mass at the outer barrier of Gaslight. There was a six-foot gap between the hotel wall and the retaining wall that was the barrier before the bedrock.

The stair treads trailed down to a room just below on the third floor. That illusion window was also busted out.

"They found the body of the man. He'd been pushed. Assassinated by The Tread Setter." The Concierge said glumly.

"Holy shit." Joseph sat down on his bed, looking deflated

"Please take my advice. Don't let these bastards ruin the experience of our audience or yours as an actor. Showtime is in fifteen."

"Fifteen!" Joseph dutifully called out.

"That's what I want to hear. Good luck, Joseph." The Concierge closed the hidden door behind him, leaving Joseph alone with his thoughts. He was grateful for the visit.

He closed his eyes and breathed, projecting his thoughts to the day ahead of him.

"One minute." The Stage Manager called out over the intercom.

Joseph thought of the video that The Concierge showed him. His mind kept returning to the stair treads fixed into the outer shell of the Gaslight structure, like the leavings of a mountain climber on the face of El Capitan. The chasm the Tread Setter braved on zir escape was truly frightening. A black void that seemed to go on indefinitely, the only break in the darkness, tiny pinpricks of light leaking out of the forced perspective windows of the hotel

A security guard came and led him down to the stage. Just before he reached the bottom of the stairs, he was in character, entering the audience zone as The Elephant Man.

A row of Bobbies could nearly keep the crowd in check as they clamored over each other just to get a look. Joseph continued to the examination room, ignoring their applause.

Once in position behind the glass barrier with the scene about to start, Joseph saw a hole in the ceiling and could make out an unoccupied stair tread. Was that hole there yesterday? If it was, The Tread Setter might have seen the incident with the old man and made the decision to act. Did zie kill the man for what he did to Joseph? Perhaps there was another reason.

"You're on!" The Stage Manager called out over the intercom. The door burst open as patrons filled the room up to the marker that lit up on the floor. Joseph noticed quickly that the audience was not paying attention to the marker the way they did before. Soon they crammed the room, coming into physical contact with him on the edges of the glass barrier. He didn't react to them. He stared straight ahead, maintaining his composure.

Joseph waited for the guards to push their way through and thin out the herd. They paused the scene until enough patrons stayed in their designated zone.

"Get behind the illuminated line!" They barked.

Joseph remained motionless. He took a deep breath as Treves entered the exam room and greeted him.

"Mr. Merrick, good morning. We will start the day with an examination by my esteemed colleagues. I hope you are up for that."

"I am, Dr. Treves." Joseph answered.

"Very well."

After three groups went through the exam room without incident, they took their first short break. They all glanced at each other, reluctant to jinx the smoother-than-expected performance.

"They're looking at you Joseph as a barometer for the health of Gaslight." Eddie observed. "...You coming back after yesterday and being co calm and on the mark. They sense that and respect you. In turn, they respect Gaslight."

"Maybe." Joseph considered. "Or maybe it's just the glass barrier."

"I like to think it's you." Eddie said.

As the day progressed, Joseph's confidence returned and he asked for the glass barrier to be removed.

"You sure about that?" The Stage Manager asked Joseph.

"Yeah. If something does go wrong, I'm ready ."

"We'll be watching them."

"So we can remove the glass?" Joseph asked impatiently.

"Yes." The Stage Manager said, gesturing to the guards to cart the barrier away.

"Take it through the audience." Joseph told the guards. "I want them to see that they have my trust again."

The guards glanced back at the SM who reluctantly nodded.

When the guards paraded the glass barrier through the waiting audience, some of them applauded. Others seemed melancholy, perhaps because they were embarrassed of their collective behavior the day before.

When the guards returned from disposing of the barrier, they stood at the door to the exam room and waved over the next group to go in.

Now that they were halfway through with group number four, Joseph felt a bit of elation. So many things had not gone as planned. Now they were finally making progress and the story was moving forward as it should. He thought about the arc of his character and the responsibility that he bore to follow the story as the Playwright had intended. It was during these thoughts that the mishap occurred.

A woman took her turn observing the EM. She started to write her findings, all the while getting uncomfortably close to Joseph prompting him to snap the fingers of his left hand. Before the guards could reach the woman, she fainted, fell forward and tore off Joseph's leg prosthetic, sending it across the floor in two pieces.

"Alright folks, we'll need to clear the room." The guards commanded as another guard emerged from a hidden door carrying a metal shield to a dazed Joseph. The shield not only protected Joseph from physical attack, but it was so large as to completely conceal him from head to toe.

"Please exit the room folks." A door guard motioned the sheepish audience back to the hallway.

Moments later, the makeup team burst through the hidden door. The Team Lead took one look at the prosthetic and clutched his hair in frustration.

"FU-UUUK!!" He said, pulling his hair so hard that you could see the pale scalp clearly beneath. "Well that's toast." He barked, knowing that it couldn't be fixed, at least not on the island. Medics were waved in by the guards and they placed the unconscious woman on a gurney.

"What happened?"

"She came up close and seemed to try to tell me something. Then she fainted." Joseph reported.

"She didn't attack you purposely?"

"No. I really think she just fainted."

The medics took her vitals then glanced up at Joseph.

"She didn't faint, she's not breathing." The medic said as he felt for a pulse.

With that, the medics started CPR while one of the door guards called the Stage Manager.

"Medics performing CPR. She had no pulse. That's right. I can't tell. Sir, this just happened. Hold on." The guard said with panicked breaths.

The Medics unwrapped a boxy item from their cart. It was an AED unit. Joseph had seen them before in his Brooklyn pharmacy and in one of the off Broadway theatres where he briefly performed.

One of the medics cut the woman's shirt open while the other unraveled the pads leading from the AED. He peeled stickers from the pads and stuck them on the woman's skin.

"Get back." The medic commanded.

The machine beeped and started talking in a mechanized voice.

"Pads attached, yes or no?"

The Medic pushed the "YES" button.

The machine hummed.

"Clear a space around the patient." The AED warned.

"There is no pulse. Preparing to shock." It's mechanical voice said.

"Stay back everyone." The Medic echoed the machine's warning.

"Shocking now." The mechanical voice said with a calmness contrasting the Medics who spoke in frantic tones.

The woman's body convulsed, arms stiffening.

"Analyzing. Do not touch patient."

The room fell into silence.

"No pulse. Preparing for shock."

Eddie nudged Joseph.

"If they don't come around after two shocks, they usually never come out of it." The medic mumbled.

"Shocking now." The AED decreed.

The woman's body convulsed again, her tongue sticking out. Suddenly, she started coughing. Her eyes opened. Her blue face regaining normal pallor after her body's momentary death.

"Ms. Pikel. You had a heart attack. We're taking you to the ER." One of the medics told her in a nervous voice.

Ms. Pikel gestured to the Medic to come closer.

"You don't need to speak." The Medic said as the woman pulled him closer to her, whispering something in his ear.

The Medic turned to face Joseph. He looked confused.

"She wants to talk to you." The Medic said.

"What on Earth about?" Joseph's voice quivered at the thought. This woman was clinically dead just a moment ago. Why would she want to talk with him now? He leaned over to her, removing his mouthpiece so she could understand him.

"I saw you. In the land of the dead." She whispered.

"I'm glad you're feeling better. They'll take you to the hospital now." Joseph said nervously, unsure how to react to what Ms. Pikel said.

"You told me not to be afraid. Thank you." Ms. Pikel's eyes closed. The Medics pushed Joseph away and measured her vitals.

"She's just sleeping. Time to move her to the hospital."

The Medics transferred Ms. Pikel and had no choice but to bring her through the main hallway, through the crowd.

"Clear a path!" The Medics shouted as they attempted to get to the front of the London Hospital where the double doors would allow an exit with the gurney. Joseph watched this through the dirty pane window.

"What are they doing? Do they think this is part of the play?" Joseph could hear the ambulance approaching, sirens blaring. A security team emerged from the ambulance pushing the crowd back until the medics could do their job and get through the crush of people.

They loaded the woman inside and the security team walked the ambulance through the streets toward the hotel where the small ER was housed.

"London Hospital Team…" The Playwright's voice called from the intercom. "…What would you like to do? Do you want to continue with two more performances or should we call it a day?"

Joseph and Eddie glanced at each other. Eddie looked wrung out. The guards and nurses seemed to have the "thousand-yard-stare" that went way beyond exhaustion.

"I think we should stop. In fact I think we should move on to another scene. This one seems to be...ill omened." Joseph said with resignation as someone finally covered him with a blanket.

"Unfortunately, I agree with you." The Playwright sighed over the speaker.

Eddie looked especially relieved as he heard this.

"OK. Let's move on. The next scene will be your mother's story, Joseph, then some one-on ones. Eddie, you'll have the outbreak of consumption scene and we'll get you both back together in week three. Now go home everyone. Relax a little tonight and wait for further instructions in the morning." The Playwright's voice clicked off the intercom.

"Sir, before you go." Joseph said with trepidation.

"Yes?"

"Can you point your security camera at the upper ceiling on the north-west side of the room?"

One of the security cameras whirred as it pivoted and zoomed. It stopped at the hole made by The Tread Setter, paused and zoomed in further.

"Dammit." The Playwright mumbled. "Well, we're out of this room anyway."

"Do you think this is why we have a dead customer?" Joseph asked coldly.

"I have to go gentlemen. Good night." With that, the camera turned to its original position. The intercom was off.

The makeup team disassembled Joseph's costume in about an hour and brought him civilian clothes.

Once changed, he took the exit through the lobby of the London Hospital. The actress playing the elderly Night Nurse gestured for Joseph to walk softer. The Elephant Man's rustling gait was difficult for him to shake off. He could see the actors (playing patients) sleeping in the next room and did his best to tread lightly.

Outside, a flower girl (not his flower girl) greeted him with a few pretty miniature roses and baby's breath wrapped in butcher's paper. He paid her a few shillings and thanked her with a smile. She wondered why he was so nice to her.

He still thought about his Flower Girl as he blended into the nighttime audience. He wondered what she was doing now that she had her freedom. He wondered if he'd ever see her again. He wondered if she had chosen a new name for herself.

With a few hours of freedom ahead of him, Joseph tried to find something to distract him that didn't involve absinthe. Up ahead, he saw a crowd gathered. It was a theater. The performance was

Hamlet.

He got in line and dug in his pockets hoping that he had enough money for a ticket. In seconds, he felt a tug on his arm. One of the pasty-faced actors, a short-middle aged man smiled up at him.

"It would be an honor if you would come in and see me play Claudius." The actor said as he touched Joseph's shoulder.
"How could I turn down such a warm invitation?" Joseph smiled. This was just the distraction he needed and he followed Claudius through the backstage entrance.
Inside, Claudius led him into the dressing room where he presented himself to the other actors who were busy with makeup and wardrobe.

"Let me introduce our guest tonight. Joseph, the actor playing this year's Elephant Man." Claudius bowed proudly as the others turned with delight and embarrassment.
"Oh my God!" Ophelia exclaimed, turning to see Joseph and smearing her makeup in the process. Hamlet rushed to Joseph and bowed.

"We are honored with your visit. Are you staying for the play?"
"I was about to buy a ticket." Joseph sheepishly started to dig into his pocket.
"Put your money away. We have a special booth for VIP guests.

Follow me please." Claudius led him through the dressing room to a creaky stairway leading to a posh sitting room."

"It's reserved for Victoria when she wants a dose of Shakespeare. With the new actress playing that part. The room stays unused. She can't be bothered."

"Thanks so much." Joseph noticed a valet bringing a bottle of mead chilled in an ice-filled bowl.

"I just wanted to say. We've all been watching your work with great interest. The Elephant Man is the most difficult role on this massive stage. You make it look like child's play." Claudius said, almost in supplication.

"I can promise you, all I can think about is that I'm messing it all up. That I'm not worthy for this part. Sometimes the weight of it is overwhelming." Joseph admitted.

"If I may say. I think that's why things went so wrong last year. He was arrogant, thought he was too good for the role. He held the rest of us in contempt. You are humble and gracious and incredibly talented." Claudius continued.

"That's very kind of you, but I only was brought here for a minor part. I just got lucky." Joseph said, slightly embarrassed.

"There is no luck with The Concierge. He knows you better than you know yourself." Claudius stepped back and bowed again. "Enjoy the show, Joseph."

The gaslight lamps were just bright enough for Joseph to read the label on the bottle of mead. It was purposely meant to look like a product of Victorian times, though there was a small patch of labels that contained the required information for the modern world. It was small and could be easily missed. "18% ABV:Product of Grenada" next to a QR code. Joseph didn't know that Grenada produced Meade. He poured himself a glass, filling it half way before taking a sip. It had a beautiful and subtle sweetness, not as overpowering as other meads he had tried. The alcohol bite was there, burning his throat slightly as he drank.

The seats filled steadily as Joseph began to feel the buzz from the honey wine. He saw patrons dressed in Victorian clothes but also saw quite a few in t-shirts and shorts, sporting fanny packs. They glanced up at him, wondering why this plainly dressed man was sitting in the royal booth. He backed away into the shadows, hoping that no one would recognize him.

The gaslights dimmed and the curtain opened to applause. Joseph sipped on the mead, gradually approaching the lip of the Royal Box, leaning over it in full view of the audience.

Joseph leaned back in his chair and became lost in Hamlet's familiar opening scene. The night patrol encountering the ghost of their murdered king.
"Something is rotten in the state of Denmark." Marcellus proclaimed.

"Something indeed *is* rotten." Joseph considered.

Later, as the scene with the traveling troupe of players approached Elsinore, Joseph laughed as he finished the second glass of mead. "This is a play within a play within a play." He whispered to himself. Someone shushed him contemptuously from the lower level.

When Hamlet finally concluded, a valet came to fetch him and bring him down to the backstage. Joseph staggered down the stairs and took a deep breath, entering the dressing room applauding the actors.

"Well done. That was beautiful." Joseph said with more than a slight slur.

The company stood in a line, still in costume and bowed at Joseph. Claudius' mood took on a serious pallor as he started to speak.

"We know you were friends with Rafanovic. He was in our company doing small parts when he got the call to play The Elephant Man." Claudius said in a dour tone.

"You wanted to have a service for him. You were denied we heard." Claudius continued.

"That's true. I felt…bad about what happened to him. Partially responsible. Maybe a little more." Joseph admitted.

"We wanted to do something for him, but he was reluctant to make friends here. He was not the easiest person to work with." Hamlet noted, looking embarrassed.

"That was nothing new for him. He didn't like people very much. He got most of his small parts because he showed up on time and didn't complain about the shitty money." Joseph remembered.

"We want to host his memorial. We hope you'll officiate it." Hamlet said in a solemn voice.
"I would really appreciate that."
"We'll do it after midnight so we don't get in trouble. Is that OK?" Claudius asked.
"Of course. Any way you want to arrange it." Joseph glanced up and saw Rafanovic's locker. Some of his oversized clothes were still in it.

"Friday would be best. We don't perform on Fridays." Claudius noted.
"You know, I have to admit. I have no sense of days anymore. What day is it anyway?"
"Monday, Joseph. Today is Monday." Hamlet said, smiling.
"You're not the only one suffering from Gaslight time."
"Well. I should go. Thanks again." As Joseph bid goodbye, the Shakespeare Company bowed. Joseph didn't quite know what to do.

As Joseph exited to the street, he started to cry. So rare was a genuine act of kindness. He was sure that Rafonovic's abrasive demeanor rubbed these actors the wrong way. Even so, they wanted to honor him. It seemed the right thing to do for any actor that died in the line of duty.

After walking the streets for a while, reflecting on the sweetness of the Shakespeare Company, he realized that he was recognized by some of the performers on the street. They paused their scenes just to watch him as the audience members stood in silent confusion, incensed that their one-on-one time with the actors was being interrupted.

"Why are you looking at that man?" One fanny packer asked a Lamplighter who had paused his performance to watch the tearful Joseph pass by.

"Sorry, I was just about to tell you the benefits of whale oil." The Lamplighter said, restarting the interaction.

Joseph spotted a hidden stage door and disappeared behind it, releasing his tears in the darkness, just out of sight.

LEAP AHEAD

The following morning, the make-up team greeted Joseph with breakfast as usual.

"Ready for today?" The Team Lead asked.

"What's so special about today?" Joseph felt confused.

"We leap ahead to the new scenes today." The Team Lead glanced at his assistants, looking confused.

"The first of the Ripper encounter scenes. That's today. Didn't you know?" The Team Lead said, surprised that Joseph wasn't prepared. It wasn't like him.

"Shit. How did I not get the memo?" Joseph felt a cold panic rush through him. How had he become so distracted that he didn't look at the scene list for the day? He felt ashamed and panicked.

"Please can someone get me those pages?" Joseph asked desperately.

"Sure. Just a minute." The Team Lead opened his folder and produced five pages of dialogue-heavy script.

"Fuck." Joseph said with dread.

"I'll need that back when you're done, OK." The Team Lead said, feeling Joseph's panic building.

The scene took the Elephant Man's mother's brutal end and created a revenge trajectory that completely changed Merrick's arc in Gaslight. Joseph realized that the new scenes were meant to be the lynchpin of the whole production. The pressure on Joseph and the current Master was massive, especially since the Team Lead's script (a version that Joseph was not supposed to see) detailed massive cuts to scenes taking place concurrently with Joseph's. This rerouted resources to the new scenes and guaranteed a massive audience. At what cost? Thirty scenes cancelled and two hundred actors put on the sideline. Their hard work thrown into the abyss. It made Joseph feel sick.

"Here's your scenes back." He said, handing the pages back to the Team Lead like contaminated waste.
"You got it? That was a lot to absorb."
"Yeah. I got it. Maybe a little too well." Joseph said with more than a hint of sarcasm.
"Hold on." The TL removed a stray piece of spirit gum from Joseph's cheek. He nodded and started for the exit. "Go get 'em." The TL said as he and his people descended the spiral staircase. In a moment, a stage assistant appeared to lead Joseph through the maze-like backstage to the bathing room where he would begin his scene.

THE FIRST RIPPER SCENE

Joseph's makeup was waterproof today so that he could take a bath. This was only for these occasions as it didn't allow the skin to breathe.

They poured a lukewarm bath for him as he got in carefully.

"Feel any leaks?" The Makeup assistant asked.

Indeed, Joseph did feel a leak near his right calf where the cold water seeped in with its frigid tendrils.

"Right leg. I feel a leak."

"Can you live with it?" The Makeup assistant asked in a contrite tone.

"Yeah."

"The nurses will dry you off then transition you to street clothes. Good luck."

In minutes, the scene began with Joseph in the tub, the loose skin on his back scrubbed by the nurses.

The audience was always accompanied by security now, the same ones as in the hotel that made no pretense to blend into the Victorian surroundings the way the Bobbies did.

They filled the room in a semicircle, staying within the confines of the designation audience zone.

The nurse scrubbed Joseph's back, washing off the deeply imbedded dirt within the cauliflower-like folds of his skin.

Though he had only been in the water for a few minutes, it had turned deep brown and smelled like a sewer, all part of the sensory effect. Another nurse brought in the London Times and began to read it aloud.

"He calls himself 'Jack the Ripper'. Terrifying isn't it?" The nurse washing Joseph shuddered. The nurse with the paper went on. "It turns out that he likes to target certain kind of ladies that we won't mention in front of our patients."

The nurses went on talking to each other in hushed speech while Joseph addressed the audience directly, breaking the fourth wall. "Prostitutes. They mean prostitutes. My mother walks the streets here in Whitechapel, though I've never seen her. Right where the Ripper finds his victims. What can I do to help her? Question is, will she even allow me to help her?" The Elephant Man said, glancing at the sour-faced nurses.

The nurse with the scrub brush finished and grabbed a towel starting to dry the EM's head.

Joseph turned to address the silent and enraptured audience.

"I've asked a friend from the freak show to help find my mother. He's meeting me in the back alley." The Elephant Man continued "Mr. Merrick, please stand up so we can dry you off." The nurse with the scrub brush commanded.

When Joseph stood naked as a matter of course, some of the

audience gasped at his nudity. Joseph was surprised that they would react that way after the previous examination room scene. It was likely they were part of that group turned away on day four and five when the scene was cut short.

The nurses dried Joseph off and helped him exit the tub. They went to fetch his robe and hood and Joseph approached the audience, causing some of them the recoil at his horrid visage.

"I have to find my mother." He made intense eye contact with each member of the audience. "It's far too dangerous for her to ply her trade when this Ripper character is out there."

"But she abandoned you!" Some woman from the audience shouted. A security guard glanced at Joseph who shook his head. He didn't want the woman removed. They continued.

Joseph walked straight into the audience causing several of them to whimper in surprise, still shocked at his nudity. He grabbed the woman from the audience and pulled her into the actor-only zone.

"Where did you hear that lie?" Joseph questioned the woman in a gritty tone.

"I...I...I." The woman stammered.

"You...you...you shouldn't judge. It was I who drove her away. It was my fault she had to sell her body on the streets." Joseph burst out in tears.

"I'm sorry." The woman said, patting Joseph on the shoulder.

"I must be wrong. Please forgive me." She confessed. Though

she might have read that The Elephant Man's mother had coldly abandoned him in a workhouse, her argument withered as Joseph sobbed at her feet.

Now it was her that was crying, begging for forgiveness. Some in the audience were confused and frightened, some were moved by Joseph's display of love for his fallen mother. Joseph gently pushed the woman back into the audience.

"Don't worry. You'll be safe there. The Ripper won't see you. You'll all be safe if you stay inside the lines. Once you leave them, I can't protect you." Joseph said in a cryptic tone.

The nurses approached Joseph with his clothes and started to dress him. When his underwear, cloak and hood were on properly, Joseph was handed his cane.

"If you want to see, you'd better come with me." Joseph said to the woman.

Joseph made a hasty dash to the stairway and the woman followed him with the rest of the audience behind her.

He descended down the stairway to a dark corridor. He moved so fast that the crowd had a hard time keeping up. The sheer weight of them bowed the floor and stairway as they followed The Elephant Man.

In the back corridor, there was a man waiting for Joseph. He was dressed like a Frenchman with his frilly cuffs and shirt collar.

"Prove to me that it is you." The man said, his accent more than apparent.

Joseph took his hood off. The man recoiled slightly.

"It is you." He said in barely-masked disgust.

"Now it's your turn to prove it to me." Joseph insisted.

"Touché." The Frenchman pinched both sides of his cheeks and pulled past the point that any normal skin would stop. He stretched them out until they were translucent.

Joseph turned to the audience and spoke to them. The Frenchman froze as he addressed them to offer exposition.

"The Frenchman was also called The Rubber Man. I had heard about the former freak from the continent. I heard that was good at finding people for the right price." Joseph turned back to The Frenchman who instantly reanimated.

"Right then. What did you find?" Joseph asked as he planted some coins in the Frenchman's hand.

"Your mother is a whore called Emma". She has no pimp so she is difficult to track down. I found her in Whitechapel near the Twelve Bells practicing her trade."

"That's where the Ripper killed his two victims." Joseph noted, remembering the article in the London Times. "Thank you. I will try to find her."

"A word of advice. Keep your hood on when you do." The Frenchman pulled on a black cloak and slipped away down the alley, back to the freak show.

Joseph turned to the audience again.

"In my condition, it will be difficult to find her, but I'll do whatever it takes to keep her safe. In the meantime, you go and find Emma and tell her that her son desperately wants to see her. Good-bye for now. Good-bye and thank you."

With that, Joseph stepped backwards into a hidden door. A door that he knew with his eyes closed. It had a built in flash that temporarily blinded the audience so they couldn't see Joseph push the spring balanced mechanism that shot him into the backstage like a bullet from a gun.

Backstage, Joseph felt a sharp jolt of pain. The spring door had flung him onto the concrete floor. Joseph felt his right shoulder where he landed, hoping that it wasn't broken.

In the dark corner, he could see someone holding the air mattress that was supposed to break his fall.

"Hello, Joseph." A high-pitched voiced called from the shadows. Joseph glanced up the dim wall and saw stair treads attached to the surface.

"I handled that old man for you. You're welcome." The Tread Setter said as zie stepped from the shadows.

"Don't you dare hurt the guests using me as a justification."

"I didn't hurt him. I killed him. I know you know my history."

"You were Trinka."

"Was. Past tense. That man. He did the same thing to me." As the Tread Setter said this, zie seemed far away, lost in a humiliating memory. "As a part of my freak act, I had to prove that I was indeed a hermaphrodite. That's when he lunged forward. You think they did anything to protect me? You think they'd ban him from Gaslight for life? No. He kept coming back and I could do nothing about it." The Tread Setter said, zir voice shaking. When he attacked you, I couldn't let him get away with it again. So...you're welcome."

Joseph didn't thank The Tread Setter.

"Gaslight is nothing but a front for human trafficking. Your Flower Girl, she was created for one purpose." The Tread Setter stated the obvious. "We want this world for the actors. A world we can make together." The Tread Setter stepped closer to Joseph. "Join The Master and we can make this into our own paradise." Zie said, touching Joseph's cheek with a tiny smooth hand, looking deeply into his eyes before pushing his face away.

The Tread Setter bolted up zir makeshift stairway, each tread falling after zir steps.

The Stage Manager ran into the dark room followed by several guards.

"Was that?!"

Joseph picked up one of the fallen stair treads and answered the Stage Manager's question.

"This is fucking ridiculous." The Stage Manager muttered to himself. Joseph tried to get up, but couldn't between the pain in his shoulder and the weight of the suit.

"Are you hurt, Joseph?"

"My shoulder. Help me up?"

The Stage Manager pulled Joseph by his chest prosthetic. Once on his feet, Joseph felt stronger, though there was still a nagging pain in his shoulder.

"Go to the clinic. You'll need an X-ray. Can you walk ok?"

"I'm fine." Joseph waved off the clinic idea.

"You go. If it's fractured, you can make it much worse. Go get an X-ray." The Stage Manager ordered. "Elephant Man coming in for urgent care copy."

"Clinic copies that message." A tinny voice called out from the other end of the walkie-talkie.

"Go." The Stage Manager shooed Joseph away. "We'll be watching so you don't get lost along the way."

"Fine." Joseph said in a frustrated tone. "Waste of time." Joseph muttered. Waste of time or not, Joseph's left shoulder continued to hurt with greater intensity all the way to urgent care until by the time he got there, he could barely speak through the pain. The medical team was there with the makeup team waiting for him. They quickly ushered Joseph back to an exam room where they removed the many components of his costume and makeup.

An X-ray tech rolled in a portable machine and she sandwiched

Joseph's shoulder between two sheets of glass.

"I heard it was the Tread Setter." The Team Lead whispered to Joseph.

"You heard correctly." Joseph said, wincing through his discomfort."

A machine buzzed behind him.

"Take all this costume stuff with you." A nurse ordered.

When the room finally cleared, the X-Ray tech told Joseph to hold still as she fired off a series of X-rays.

In a few moments, they removed the glass plates and a radiologist was tsk-tsking the results.

"There's the crack right there."

"Ah. You're right, sir." The physician, Dr. Patel, noted.

He approached Joseph and sat down on a nearby stool.

"You have two choices. Treat it the traditional route and you will not be able to wear this apparatus that alters your movement."

"What's the other choice?"

"The other choice is you let me perform a pretty simple surgery where I essentially glue the small crack together, returning your load carrying capacity back to almost normal."

"Is there a downside to option two?"

"I won't lie to you, Joseph, the risk is bruised or severed nerves, partial paralysis of the arm and unfortunately, lots of pain."

"Sounds great." Joseph thought about the possibility of paralysis of his left arm, living with pain long after Gaslight was over.

"OK. Let's do the surgery." Joseph said, willing to do anything to get back to the stage.

"Very good." The doctor said, waving to an assistant who presumably gathered surgical tools.

"The drill. Make sure you have extra batteries." The doctor called from across the room. "Got it." The assistant yelled back.

"We'll get you prepped for surgery." The doctor said as several nurses emerged, two of them with carts.

One of the nurses came at Joseph with a collection of needles and tubes.

"Lay down on the operating table Joseph." The nurse said. Joseph was shocked how narrow and cold the table was.

"How long will I be under?" Joseph asked.

"Oh this is just local anesthesia. You'll be awake through the whole procedure." The doctor said as the nurse handed him a drill with a mean-looking bit. He pulled the trigger twice and smiled for emphasis.

DEEP ACHE

After the surgery, a groggy and aching Joseph was escorted to his room in the London Hospital. The stairwell had been vacated so the audience wouldn't see anything that might compromise their experience. His shoulder had a deep ache that felt like perpetual cold. He guessed that was the glue still drying inside him.

The next day, Joseph was not allowed to leave his room. He was brought books, videos and a cart filled with food and drinks.

In the late afternoon, The Concierge came up the secret stairway. "We missed you today." He said, forcing a smile.

"I appreciate that. Will you let me go back tomorrow?"

"Yes. But there is someone that needs to see you tonight. It's urgent. Will you make time?" The Concierge said as he took another drink.

"Of course. Can you tell me what it's about?"

"I'm afraid not." The Concierge noted. "See you in the morning." With that, the Concierge left, leaving the door unlocked for Joseph to explore the night if he so wished.

In spite of the pain, Joseph wanted to be out among people. He gathered his civilian clothes and decided to explore a distant corner of Gaslight near Buckingham Palace, an area he could not otherwise visit with all of his scenes taking place on the opposite end of the stage.

In a few minutes, he was on the main boulevard looking for a taxi. He hailed a cab and asked the Taxi Driver for recommendations. "Ship and Turtle Tavern! Been around since 1377, sir."

"That sounds great!" Joseph liked the name right away.

"It's a long trek, sir. Just to warn you." The Taxi Driver said with a worried expression.

"Driver, I have nothing but time tonight." With that, Joseph was on his way.

The ride through Whitechapel was jammed with stop and go traffic as audience members roamed the grisly streets.

Leaving the district, Joseph breathed a sigh of relief as the crowds thinned and they picked up speed.

They traversed neighborhoods that were unfamiliar to Joseph. There were other guest hotels that were integrated into the surroundings and run *in stage*. Unlike the main hotel, in these places, there was no break from the play. In fact, Joseph remembered seeing large scenes taking place in the script. Scenes with actors imbedded as guests in the hotels.

These establishments ranged from six-room flophouses to majestic edifices. Joseph admired the audience members that would choose to stay in these places, but if he were in their shoes, it'd be a trip too far down the rabbit hole.

Feeling a touch of motion sickness, Joseph closed his eyes and listened to the CLOP CLOP of the horse's hooves against the cobblestone streets. It was a sound that would've been relaxing if he weren't thrown about so much in his seat.

Once he was hurled against the side of the cabin and a nerve in his repaired shoulder cried in protest.

"Fuck!" Joseph screamed.

"Everything OK, Guv?" The Taxi Driver called to him.

"Yeah. Yeah." Joseph replied, wondering if this excursion was really a good idea.

Suddenly, the taxi slowed.

"Sir. Sir! Buckingham Palace if you want to look." The Taxi Driver called down to him. Joseph opened his eyes and saw it off to the left.

With a long row of gaslights across its steel fence, Buckingham Palace glowed against the backdrop of the dark street. Across the endless scape of rooms, there was one light on in the palace where Joseph could make out a female silhouette. It appeared that she was drinking a glass of wine.

"My God." Joseph said, marveling at the sight. Marveling at the attention to detail. He immediately wanted to get inside.

"Stop please!" Joseph called out to the Taxi Driver.

"Sir?"

"I'm an actor. Perhaps you don't recognize me out of costume." Joseph stepped out of the cab and showed the Taxi Driver his identification.

"I see." The Taxi Driver said, studying the card.

"Wait right here."

"There's no way in there, sir." The Taxi Driver warned.

Joseph didn't bother to knock at the front door, opting to find a hidden access door at the adjoining guard shack that was unoccupied.

Once in, LED lights illuminated a tunnel that went under the front yard and into the palace.

As he progressed further, motion detectors turned lights on just ahead of him until he reached the end. He stood at the tunnel exit and stared into the darkness, letting his eyes adjust. Finally, he could just make it out. He was standing in a giant empty box. Buckingham Palace was a roomless blank space with a long stairway leading to a platform that was lit from behind with a bank of dimmed movie lights.

Joseph started the long trek up the stairs, taking a break twice to catch his breath.

When he finally reached the platform at the top, he saw her sitting at her table, the glass of wine by her side.

It wasn't Victoria, but a Stand-In who continued to read her book, sip her wine the way a queen might.

"You're not supposed to be up here." The Stand In said tersely.

"I had to see what was inside 'Buckingham Palace'. I had to see my queen." Joseph sat at the stair landing trying to recover from the climb and wondering how this old woman had managed to make it up here without having a cardiac event.

"You're the 'Elephant Man' aren't you?" She said, keeping her eye on her book. "Well, that doesn't impress me. There are a lot of us living on fixed income that will just be happy to walk out of here with a few thousand dollars to your million."

"I'm sorry to have interrupted you. I'll go now." Joseph said, realizing that he had let his curiosity get the better of him. He turned to make the descent down the dark stairs, no longer afraid of having a heart attack but wary of a fatal slip and long tumble down the dime-store version of the Odessa Steps.

"You come back again, you bring some tea and cakes." The Stand In said. He didn't think he would come back, but wrote himself a mental note as he descended, keeping a firm hold on the handrail on the way down.

"I'm not making a million dollars. Not even close." Joseph grumbled, embarrassed at his wealth as compared with the majority of his fellow actors. Of course in order to cash in, he'd still have to make it home where an overdrawn bank account patiently waited for him.

"Hello, sir. Did you see what you wanted to see?" The Taxi Driver asked, seeming to sense Joseph's disappointment.

"Let's get moving, driver." Joseph said as he climbed in the passenger compartment.

"Very good, sir." The Taxi Driver clucked at the horse that started forward. He didn't ask more questions about the palace.

By the time he reached the restaurant, he was already tired.

"I see why you warned me." Joseph said to the Taxi Driver.

"I have to end my day. I'll send someone to take you back if you give me a time." The Taxi Driver flipped his logbook open.

"Give me about an hour. I'd go back home now, but I don't think my stomach could take back to back buggy rides."

"Understood, sir. Have a good evening." The Taxi Driver said as Joseph passed him a fifty-dollar gratuity. He tipped his hat, smiling. "Much appreciated, sir."

Joseph nodded and smiled as the driver clopped away.

THE SHIP AND TURTLE TAVERN

The Ship and Turtle was old in a way that the pyramids were old. To put it into perspective, William's Shakespeare's grandfather wasn't born yet when the first customers stopped in for a pint. The oldness of it was like a time capsule in the surrounding buildings that were modern by comparison. The outside wall seemed to be built with hay and mud. Inside, the glow of gaslights were supplemented by the whale oil lanterns that had lit the pub for generations.

Once inside, the surprise that greeted Joseph was a giant tank filled with turtles. Cooks plucked the reptiles from the water.

"Turtle soup!" The bartender called out to Joseph. "Best in London."

Joseph nodded and bellied up to the bar. The bartender stopped drying his mugs and approached Joseph.

"What'll you have?"

"Turtle soup and a pint of beer. Stout if you have it."

"If we have it? Don't insult me, sir." The bartender laughed as he poured a jet-black pint. He let it sit for a minute before placing it in front of Joseph.

Joseph took a sip and marveled at the flavor of the beer. It was like drinking darkness itself.

One of the waiters brought the turtle soup and Joseph was immediately struck by the savory aroma. He had never had turtle before, but he didn't imagine that it would smell so delicious.

"I know you." The Bartender said, losing his accent.

"Look, I'd like to stay on the down low if I could. I've had a rough week." Joseph said, hoping the conversation didn't have to go farther.

"Of course." The Bartender watched him, grinning. Joseph found it impossible to eat with this man hovering over him with a shit-eating grin.

"I'll give you twenty dollars if you wouldn't do that." Joseph said as he slid a bill out of his pocket.

"Do what?" The bartender seemed to be caught off guard. Joseph grinned, trying to remain patient.

"I have hundreds of people stare at me like a bright shiny object all day. Can I have a break from that on my time off?" Joseph slid the bill to the Bartender who took the money with a sour face. He turned his back and picked up more glasses to dry.

Joseph tried the soup and it had somehow lost its enticing aroma. He put down his spoon, realizing that his mood had darkened, making it impossible to enjoy his food.

"Sir! What are you doing here?" A familiar voice called from just behind him. A warm hand landed on his shoulder.

He turned and was pleasantly surprised to see Tif.

"Why Tif, how are you? It's been a while."

"I'm the butler at the Courtesan Hotel. They have me on the other side of Gaslight from you." Tif said, smiling.

"Look, Joseph, I'm not here by accident. They need you back

home. I have a golf cart with our name on it." Tif said.

Joseph considered the ride back on the horse drawn taxi and realized that the golf cart would be like riding in a Rolls Royce by comparison.

"What's wrong?" Joseph asked, sure that there was another disaster waiting for him back in Whitechapel.

"I'm afraid I don't know, Joseph. Do you want some time to finish your soup?" Tif asked, admiring the dish.

"No. Let's go." Joseph said, glad to leave the pub.

"If you don't mind." Tif took the bowl and took a large gulp of the soup. He licked his lips with satisfaction after finishing half the bowl in ten seconds.

"Forgive me. I can't afford the stuff and I love the turtle soup." Tif said, almost glowing.

"Bartender, can we get a bowl of the turtle soup to go?" Joseph asked the man who maintained his sour expression.

"You want it to go? Go the river and catch one." The Bartender snapped. Tif nudged Joseph and shook his head.

"Let's just go, sir."

They pushed through the dense crowd and finally made their way to the entrance where the golf cart was waiting for them. Sitting in the plush leather seat, Joseph felt overjoyed to have a little taste of modern luxury. Tif took off through the dark London streets, beeping the horn to get the attention from the audience that packed the streets like bowling pins ready to get knocked about.

Finally resorting to the siren and lights, Tif managed ten miles-per-hour at best all the way back to Whitechapel.

As they passed Buckingham Palace, Joseph leaned out to see The Stand In still at her place high in Buckingham Palace.

"There's nothing in there. Just a shell." Tif said, ignorant of Joseph's journey into the "palace" on the way to the Ship and Turtle Tavern. Joseph let him continue, telling him about the long dark stairway leading to the platform where someone stood in for Victoria having her evening wine. Joseph feigned surprise and amazement as Tif described the facade of Buckingham Palace, revealing a bit of history about the original plan to build the massive interior of the queen's home to facilitate a separate immersive experience. According to Tif, the original construction of Gaslight had gone so far over budget that the interior was scrapped just as they were starting construction.

"One day, they'll finish it." Tif said optimistically.

Tif pulled up to the secret tunnel leading to the London Hospital and entered a code on the golf cart's dash keyboard. A hidden garage door built into a blacksmith shop rose up, revealing the descending tube that would be their route.

Down in the tube, Tif could floor it. He zipped along, stopping only at crossroads, sometimes not even then. When they finally reached the underground entrance to the London Hospital, Joseph was surprised to find The Concierge waiting for him.

"Thank you, Tif for bringing our wayward rooster back to the farm." The Concierge waved at Tif who nodded back. Joseph shook Tif's hand.

"I hope you'd come back to these parts soon." Joseph said.

"Certainly, sir."

With that, Tif sped off, presumably returning to his hotel.

"How's your shoulder?" The Concierge asked with a grin.

"What happened? A disaster I presume." Joseph said, bracing for bad news.

"Why on Earth do you think its bad news?"

"It always it, isn't it?" Joseph responded.

"A plane just landed from Miami. There's someone that very much wants to meet you." The Concierge said coolly.

"I'm tired of parading myself around for the bigwigs." Joseph snapped at The Concierge who didn't react.

"Just go up to your room. You'll be briefed there. Don't worry about rehearsal. I'll tell them you have a special assignment."

"Fine." Joseph threw his hands in the air and stormed to the stairwell. He turned to dress The Concierge down further and realized that he wasn't following.

"Aren't you coming?" Joseph asked, puzzled. The Concierge simply shook his head.

"I think you need to do this yourself." He said to Joseph.

"Fine." Joseph said, stomping loudly up the stairwell with the double door marked "live stage".

On his way up to his room, Joseph was flanked by guards as well as a curtain that hid his ascent from the rabidly curious audience. He was now recognized out of costume, making anonymity increasingly impossible.

When he reached the isolation ward, the gate was closed behind him and locked. The guards folded up the curtain and Joseph could hear the audience starting to file towards him. Fearing that he would be seen, he ran up the stairs and entered his room.

In his attempt to avoid the crowd, Joseph had forgotten that someone was waiting for him in his room. It was still dark and silent, leading him to conclude that whoever wanted to see him had gotten bored and left. It was in that moment of relief at being alone that he heard someone breathing in the darkness.

Fearing that it was the Tread Setter or worse, The Master, he grabbed the heaviest thing he could find, a stone paperweight and prepared to attack.

What he found was a women with her back turned to him. She was very slender, almost gaunt and a full foot taller than the tread setter with long wavy hair. She was dressed in gauzy clothes that hung loose on her thin frame.

"Hello?" Joseph cautiously approached her.

She turned and for a moment, he still didn't recognize her until she smiled. It was the Flower Girl, at least twenty pounds lighter on a frame that could scarcely stand to lose any weight in the first place.

"Hello Joseph." Her smile was a brave front, but she crashed like a waterfall into tears. She fell to her knees weeping and Joseph rushed to catch her.

"Thank you….thank you…" She said and repeated as she pawed at him. She had thought of this day as much as Joseph had.

BOND

When she could finally form a coherent sentence, she told him how close to death she was when she was medevaced to the hospital in Miami. Upon arrival at the ER, she went into cardiac arrest. They had to cut out more than half of her intestine that had succumbed to sepsis.

The doctors assured her that she was very lucky to be alive.

"Why would you come back here, after all you've been through?" Joseph asked her, perplexed that she would even want to leave the safety of the US.

"We have a bond, Joseph. You saved my life. I want to come back to the states with you. In fact, I won't leave until you do."

"You're a foolish woman." He hugged her. "But I'm so glad you're foolish. All I could think about was seeing you again."

The Flower Girl leaned in to hug Joseph and cried fresh tears. He could feel the lump of the colostomy bag as he put his arm around her.

They ordered champagne and dinner that came with a butler to serve them.

When he struggled to remember her Asset number, she revealed that the Concierge helped her legally change her name and get a passport. The latter was a bit complicated as the last time she had been in the US was when she was seven. That was when her mother sold her for a kilo of heroin and she was trafficked to the Middle East, eventually ending up in the hands of the Marmaladov gang.

She showed Joseph her American passport. Instead of completely jettisoning the only name had known (Asset) she repurposed it..

"I held my name up to a mirror and that's when I knew, I would make it as a reminder of where I've been and what I've been through. It was a palindrome for my new name...Tessa."

Joseph had resigned himself to never seeing the Flower Girl again. Now they were together, catching up as if she had been on a vacation to Europe rather than on a medevac that was nearly too late. He was happy and proud of her. Proud of her bold choice for her new name. Proud of her for escaping the Marmaladov Gang, an organization that had liquidating human property down to a science.
"Tessa." He said it aloud and liked it even better.

As she finished a second glass of champagne, Tessa's Russian accent started to creep out.

That night, she wanted to give herself to him.
She explained that after the surgeries, traditional sex was no longer possible, but if Joseph was patient she would show him that she

could please him.

Joseph assured her that she didn't need to prove anything to him.
He was just happy to be with her.

"If you love me like I love you, this is something we have to do."
Tessa said firmly as if the glue between them had to be set tonight
or run the risk of never bonding.

She undressed and Joseph was shocked at how thin she was. With
fifty percent less intestine to absorb nutrients, keeping weight on
was very difficult, she explained.

A catheter tube emerged from just above her pelvic bone, leading
to a leg bag that collected urine.

Tessa's vagina appeared like a Barbie Doll's, bare skin; the
structure surgically removed and sealed shut. He could see the
colostomy bag strapped to her side. She saw him looking at it and
immediately turned to hide it.

"I'm ruined." She said, starting to cry. "Can we turn the light off.
You shouldn't have to see me like this." She said, sobbing
uncontrollably. "How could I hope you could ever love me.
Look at me! I'm destroyed!"

Joseph approached her and put his arms around her thin body.
"I love you even more Tessa… and I don't care about any of that."
Joseph said without hesitation. "I think I've always loved you. I
was just looking for you my whole life. I never want to lose you

again."

"You mean that?" She asked desperately. In disbelief.

"You know I do." He said, kissing her.

"They you will let me please you. You won't turn me away?" Tessa asked in a voice that overflowed with anxiety. The fear of rejection.

"Of course not." Joseph said gently, trying to put her at ease.

She impatiently undressed Joseph and found some lotion to lubricate him. Tessa lay on her back and pulled the tape off her colostomy bag, revealing a stoma site, essentially a hole where her intestine had been rerouted.

"Please, don't stop me." She cried.

"I won't, Joseph promised.

Joseph held her hand and moved to her and they became one.

He stopped twice to ask if he was hurting her. Tessa continued to guide his movements and told him not to stop again until she told him to.

She seemed to be in a trance for a moment, her eyes rolling in back of her head before opening suddenly.

"OK, you can come now." She told him.

Joseph moved slowly this time, forming a "T" pattern with their bodies. Finally he reached an orgasm.

"Stay in for a second." She told him as she grabbed a towel. As

she pulled away from him, she slid the towel on her stoma site.
He asked her if she was ok.

"It started to hurt at the end, but it's ok. Most of it was nice. So good to have you inside my body." She said, obviously in a more than a bit of pain.

Joseph could tell that it hurt more than she was letting on. She went into the bathroom and cleaned up and reattached her colostomy bag. Joseph stripped the bed and then took a shower while Tessa poured them both more champagne.

"That was intense." She said, taking a slug directly from the bottle, bypassing the glass.
"Yes it was." Joseph admitted.
"Come here Joseph" She kissed him.

They drank champagne and ordered more gourmet meals and went to bed

Tessa woke him up at three in the morning, her skinny elbow digging into his chest.
"Are you sleeping?" She asked.
"Not anymore." He said, weakly chuckling.
"Last year, the Master reached out to us. He made all these promises. To people like us. Truth is that he just used us. Gave us false hope. Sex slaves were nothing to him. We weren't even

human. He betrayed us the first chance he got. He's certain to do it again if given a chance."

"Try not to dwell on it." Joseph told Tessa. "He won't hurt you anymore."

Tessa didn't talk again until the imitation sun rose in the window. Then it was just the pleasantries of the morning. They spoke little. Room service brought them a lovely breakfast of crepes with mascarpone and coffee. Joseph ate silently but his head was fully engaged with the images that Tessa painted in his mind. Hundreds of people suffering as slaves down there in the dungeon. The immersive play…the beautiful art the actors and crew created together was rendered foul by the suffering of these people. For each plane filled with audience members, another landed filled with sex-tourists. A parasite built upon something pure.

There was a knock at the door. Joseph turned and called for them to come in.

"Telegraph for you, sir." A young telegraph agent handed Joseph the yellow cards with just a two words on it.

"Black Absinthe".

Joseph studied the words silently and Tessa realized that something was going on. He couldn't tell her about the letter to the reporter. The poison letter was received and the paper was indeed *on* the story. He was sure that his telegram was intercepted by someone in the Tower of London. Weather or not it arose suspicion remained to be seen.

"Are you all right?" Tessa asked with a concerned expression. "Yes, now that you're here." Joseph put the telegraph on the table and hugged her. They stayed that way for the whole morning. Tonight he had to say good-bye to Rafonovic. Who knew what he'd have to say good-bye to tomorrow.

Joseph skipped lunch, opting to sit quietly with Tessa. On the nearby wall there was an ornate metal mirror that stood about six-feet high. He stared at it as Tessa napped in his arms, looking at their reflection for a long time. She seemed so content in his arms. Like she had never suffered a day in her life.

He turned her arm revealing the tattoo given to sex slaves of the Marmaladov gang. He wondered if Tessa was there when his platoon raided the trafficking hub in Fallujah or if she was already moved on to her final destination in Russia.
He closed his eyes and thought of those children watching him and his fellow soldiers as they arrested the ringleaders and their guards, the ones they hadn't killed. He searched in his memory for Tessa's deep sad eyes. Eyes he would've recognized anywhere at any age. He couldn't find them as he scanned his memory, recalling the cages where the children were contained. He came out of the memory exhausted and followed Tessa into a deep nap.

CUBE OF SUGAR

In the late evening Joseph woke as Tessa got up to answer the door. It was The Concierge and another man that Joseph didn't immediately recognize until he saw the cart that he pushed to the kitchenette. It was a liquor bottle with the unmistakable green glow of absinthe. The Concierge had brought the Bartender from Glass Paris.

"I thought we'd have a drink." The Concierge motioned to the Bartender who rummaged under the cart for the accouterments of the cocktail. The crystal glass, slotted spoon, cube of sugar, a bottle of water with a narrow nozzle and of course the absinthe itself.

"I've missed the Glass Paris." Joseph said with a genuine smile. "More than you know."

The Bartender positioned the slotted spoons over the glasses and placed a single cube of sugar over each with tongs.

"How are you, Tessa?" The Concierge kneeled down to where she sat.

"It's good to see Joseph again." She nodded, looking emotional.

"The play goes fast. Faster than you think. Then you can go back to New York. Start over." The Concierge held both of their hands. For a second, Joseph envisioned him as a priest about to bring their hands together in marriage.

"How do you feel about that, Tessa?" The Concierge asked.

"I can't even imagine." Tessa said. Tears of joy filled her eyes. The Concierge hugged her and her tears slowed at his warm embrace.

"Can I get a job? An acting job?" She asked meekly.

"Of course. Anything you want…" The Concierge seemed surprised by this.

"…but let's discuss it later. Joseph needs to get to a memorial service. If he's ready."

"As ready as I'll ever be." Joseph stood, making a mental checklist of the clothes he picked out for himself.

"I'll leave you then. Meet me at the tunnel, Joseph?" The Concierge leaned down and hugged Tessa goodbye.

"See you in a minute." Joseph nodded at The Concierge as he left.

"Do you want to come?" Joseph asked Tessa.

"Not really. I'm still feeling tired. The trip took a lot out of me."

"Get some rest then." Joseph kissed her and went to the closet to find his suit waiting for him. In minutes he was transformed.

"You look amazing, baby." Tessa said, half asleep.

"I'll be back before you know it." Joseph leaned down to kiss her. She was snoring as he left.

MEMORIAL

They took the cart through the labyrinthine tunnel. They didn't speak until Joseph put his hand on The Concierge's shoulder.

"Thank you. Thank you for keeping your word about Tessa."

"Don't thank me. Thank how much they value you Joseph. That's the only reason Tessa is sitting in your room and not in the coroner's vault. You have to know that." The Concierge said in a dark tone.

"Still, you stood up for her and for me. Thank you."

The Concierge smiled and said nothing. Nothing needed to be said.

Soon they were at the sterile underground entrance to the wing that housed The Shakespeare Theater.

They entered into blackness until a motion detector flipped on very dim LED lights that illuminated the path.

They passed the secret entrance to the barber shop that was marked "B-4" with a hand scrawled sign "Smitty's Barber Shop" beneath it.

After five more doors, they reached the entrance to the "Shakespeare Theater T-7"

As they pulled the door open, they found a dozen actors from the troupe waiting for them as well as a few of the actors that Joseph met during the train platform scene.

"Joseph! Mr. Concierge." Claudius said.

"Good to see you again, Claudius." The Concierge shook the man's hand.

They entered the theater proper where more actors were seated and waiting for Joseph. He didn't recognize everyone, but nodded to them in appreciation.

"Thank you for coming. Especially at this late hour." Joseph said as he took the podium.

"Mr. Rafonovic wasn't what I would call a close friend. We hadn't seen each other in years. My last recollection of him was that he got fired from that Scottish play for playing King Duncan while drunk on schnapps."

This incited a few laughs.

"It was quite the fall from the engaged and disciplined young man as I knew as a drama student. I tried to keep track of his performances that started to dwindle as his reputation was weakened by his addiction. One year, I didn't see his name at all. I wondered if the worst had happened. Instead of reading the trades, I started reading obituaries, looking for his him in car crashes or suicides.

When I returned from a break, just a few days ago, I discovered that Rafonovic was not only taken from us, but it was while he played Joseph Merrick. You can imagine the internal turmoil that left me with. He died while representing me as well as Mr. Merrick.

I thought the least I could do for him was to gather some friends and say a few words because anyone who steps on the stage and bears their soul is our brother…our sister.

Mr. Rafanovic had no family but us actors. We will miss him.

Joseph bowed his head as he completed his memorial, leaving the stage to polite applause.

Claudius took the podium next and told a few lighthearted stories about Rafonovic, most of them to do with his grumpiness.

As the eulogy was wearing down, Joseph noticed someone watching him from back stage. A bearded man wore all black with black sunglasses in the dark stage. His face was expressionless. For a moment, he thought it might be the Playwright with a glued-on facial hair, but he finally decided it was not. The eulogy was concluded by passing around schnapps, Rafonovic's favorite drink.

"Skol!" They screamed as they downed the shot.

"Thank you everyone and bless you Rafonovic, wherever you are." A final bit of applause and the small crowd dissipated, presumably to go to bed before the wardrobe and makeup bell, just five hours away.

The bearded man backed away with unnatural movements that

couldn't help but catch Joseph's eye.

When he started to follow the bearded man, The Concierge grabbed Joseph by the shoulder and tried to pull him back.

"We have to get you back to your room." The Concierge pleaded.

"Follow me or don't." Joseph said tersely as The Concierge realized that something was wrong and he had better follow.

They snuck behind the stage curtain to a dark hall. They followed a winding passageway that led to a dead-end of a black-velvet curtain. Footprints, presumably of the bearded man stopped cold just before the velvet barrier.

"What the?" Joseph said as he approached it. As he was about to pull it aside, the fabric fell to the floor. The Bearded Man, was standing tall in the rafters training a stun-gun on Joseph. He fired, sending hooks into Joseph's flesh followed by the rude clicking sound as current ran through his body.

Joseph fell to the ground in seizure-like convulsions. As he continuously shocked Joseph, The Concierge ran to him and pulled out the Taser. As he did, someone slipped a cord around his neck and pulled it just tight enough to keep him immobilized. With both Joseph and The Concierge stunned, The Bearded Man stepped from the shadows.

"What do you want?" The Concierge asked desperately, feeling the noose tighten and pull him to the left. The one holding the cord turned him like a dog on a leash so he could be seen. It was Valor, The Master.

"Wait!" The Concierge pointed to the bearded man. "I thought...Who are you?!"

Valor gestured to the bearded man who pulled the facial prosthetic off revealing that it had been Rafonovic the whole time.

"You?" The Concierge said incredulously.

"Very kind words at the eulogy." The Master said smiling. "He made an excellent recruit, Rafonovic did. He's shared so much about Joseph. Your golden boy wasn't the boy scout I thought he was."

"What...do you want?" The Concierge asked again with a raspy voice, feeling his throat close.

"What do you think I want? I want The Elephant Man back. I want to lead the audience into the revolt that you denied me. I want Gaslight for the actors, by the actors, something that you of all people should've supported

"Call the makeup crew. Tell them they have to suit me up or Joseph will wake up in hell." Valor pointed to the still unconscious Joseph.

"Security. They'll stop you." The Concierge warned, but ended up sounding impotent.

"Call the makeup crew!"

"As you wish." The Concierge replied, his eyes never leaving the former Master.

IT HAS STARTED

The Team Lead gathered his group at the secret meeting at the police station. They brought their full array of Elephant Man makeup and prosthetics and several changes of clothes.

"Why are we here with the crash cart, Cap? An Assistant asked him said with an exhausted tone.

"We got an emergency call from The Concierge. Bring the cart is what he said and that's what we'll do. Something has happened. Are you ready?"

His five assistants nodded. They had already worked sixteen hours, but The Concierge wasn't going to ask for help without a good reason.

"We stay here and wait for him."

"Did something happen to Joseph?" The Third Assistant asked with a hint of worry in her voice.

The Team Lead just shook his head. He knew as much as they did.

The lights dimmed. The kind of dimming that you saw ahead of a blackout.

"That's not a good sign." The Prosthetics Expert groaned.

Finally, the lights cut out completely followed by gasps from the makeup team.

"It's been so long…" The voice of the former Master filled the room. "A year in fact."

The Makeup Team knew that voice right away. They were unable to contain their fear.

"NO!" The Third Assistant cried.

From out of the darkness, a light shone on the face of The Master, his tattered Elephant Man makeup stitched together with glue and hemp.

"You know what I want."

Another light shone on Rafonovic who held a pistol at the makeup team.

"Make me beautiful again." Valor purred.

ISHKATAY

Joseph woke inside the sensory deprivation chamber in near
complete darkness. Only the faint glow from the LED lights in the
water offered any perspective. The Concierge floated next to him
unconscious as his body bobbed like a top in the salt water.
Looking closer, Joseph saw that he'd been bludgeoned by
something and was bleeding from his right eyebrow.
Joseph found the door leading to the outer chamber and as he
feared, it was locked.
Joseph remembered when The Master appeared from seemingly
out of nowhere. There had to be a hatch on the floor of the
isolation chamber. He dove beneath the buoyant water that fought
against him the whole way. To his dismay, he felt along the space
where The Master appeared and felt nothing. The floor appeared
seamless. Finally, he couldn't fight the salt water's buoyancy and
had to surface.

Suddenly, a dark mass shot up from the seamless bottom of the
concrete pool.
A light appeared from the surface of the pool illuminating two
silvery eyes fixated on Joseph.
"He tried to stop me." A voice croaked from the shadows. "...but
I was too quick for him."
Finally, Joseph realized who the croaking voice belonged to.

It was The Tread Setter, sporting livid bruises around zir throat. Joseph knew right away that the Master had tried to kill zir for something zie was about to do. Zie approached him slowly, the dim light revealing the broken blood vessels in zir eyes.

"Joseph…" Zie said with zir sandpaper voice.

"Yes?" Joseph didn't understand. Zie looked half-dead. Was zie coming to kill him?

"I follow you now." The Tread Setter said as zie fell into Joseph's arms, gulping for air through zir inflamed throat.

Joseph held The Tread Setter's tiny body in his arms.

It was hard to believe, holding zir, that this person that weighed maybe a third of Joseph's mass could strike such fear in others. At the moment zie looked as helpless as a child.

After a while, The Tread Setter's breathing calmed and zie could respirate normally again.

"Where I emerged from the water. I want you to stand there." The Tread Setter said weakly to Joseph.

Fighting his mistrust of zir, Joseph edged closer to the spot where zie exploded from beneath the water.

"A little to your left." The Tread Setter whispered. "Then a little back." Zie continued. Joseph dutifully followed the instructions.

"Good." The Tread Setter said, apparently happy with Joseph's navigation to just the right spot. Zie clung onto him tightly with zir arms and legs wrapped around him like a vice.

"Ishkatay!!" The Tread Setter yelled.

They seem to be shot through a gun into a space that was weightless and black.

In the seconds that it took to travel in a way that Joseph still couldn't identify, he could feel the Tread Setter's heart beating like a cat. A rhythmic pitter-patter tapping against his chest.

They landed, also in the water. Also in a dark area.

After a few seconds of disorientated searching, they found each other in the darkness. A dim light clicked on overhead and they could see each other.

They were in a cube, about twenty feet in diameter. From all appearances it seemed to have no other function than to be part of this strange water-transport system. Joseph could see the circular tube that probably served as the launching spot to the isolation chamber. There were three others that Joseph presumed to transport to different destinations judging from the hard turns the tubes took to different parts of Gaslight.

The Tread Setter pointed to the hidden hatch in the wall that resembled something from a Jules Verne book. Zie struggled to zir feet, leaning against Joseph. Joseph turned the latch on the door and pushed.

What they found was completely unexpected. On the other side of the door was a food cabinet inside the green room area. A secret way into the backstage. The whole wall pushed to the side, giving them enough room to transition into a pantry.

It was Joseph that found them first. Dead bodies. The security guards that The Master targeted first. As they stepped toward the carnage, their shoes became coagulated in blood.

"It's started." The Tread Setter croaked out.

TAKEOVER

The stage, in front of The Twelve Bells came to life. Spotlights focused at the center of the courtyard and the entirety of the sky faded to black. A crowd grew, following the lights to a platform where the lights converged.

An elevator rose from beneath, lifting the former Master dressed as The Elephant Man into the middle of Whitechapel.

An audience gathered to watch, mostly out of confusion to this unscheduled Elephant Man performance. Some of them knew right away that something was wrong. This was not Joseph. This was someone else. Even through all the makeup, they could see it.

"Citizens of London!" The Master bellowed in his Elephant Man dialect. "You have read about my plight. Some of you have come to see me at the London Hospital. Some of you have come to see me at the freak show. They will try to take me away again. Can I count on your protection?" Valor scanned the audience, reading them. "They come to take me away again. They come to torture me like they always have. The only thing between them and me is you, dear friends. Please don't let them do this. Haven't I suffered enough, dear friends?"

As he said this, three Guards approached to take Valor into custody.

Watching this scene from a video monitor in the green room, Joseph and The Tread Setter were transfixed.

"What happens next determines everything." The Tread Setter said in zir raspy voice.

On screen, they watched the audience grab the guards and bring them down into prone positions. They looked up to the Master who congratulated them.

"Please don't do it." The Tread Setter whispered.

From beneath his coat, Valor produced a miniature bludgeon that looked like a toy baseball bat and handed it to a woman who helped to hold one of the guards down.

"Don't listen to him." Zie said.

The woman hesitated, unsure of what to do.

"Who has used you?" The Master purred. The woman listened, but didn't look at him. "Parents, your employer, your boyfriend, your children, your church?"

The woman shook her head, resisting his words.

"That man is anyone who has used you. He will use you again and again. This is your only chance to stop him. Your only chance to stop him with my protection. Take him out. He deserves it. He has deserved it for so long."

Valor's words were hypnotic. The woman glanced up at The Master and realized that he was staring at the scars on her wrists.

The multiple scars. He knew everything about her. He knew how those users made her want to die. Made her try to die. Rage, long buried, swelled inside her. The guard became the personification of everyone that derailed her life.

Without further hesitation, the woman slapped the wooden bat across the face of the guard, bashing his nose into his sinus cavity. The Guard didn't scream. He only flailed his hands out and felt at the hole in his face before the woman hit him again, this time smashing his jaw.

The Master held the woman's hand and took the bloodstained weapon from her hands, placing a pause on the carnage.

"These were your oppressors. There can be no mercy for what the oppressors have done to you. With me, they won't hurt you again. As long as you follow me, you can have your revenge and I will protect you. I will protect all of you."

With that, The Master dropped nine more bludgeons at his feet.

"The first that take these in their hand will be my warriors against oppression." The Master crossed his arms and waited for those people to pick up the bludgeons and become his first enforcers. In seconds, all of the bludgeons had been spoken for. Valor was now The Master again in name and in power.

"We've just lost Gaslight." Joseph said.

"That's right." The Tread Setter agreed.

THE SEED

When Joseph and Tread made it to the streets of Whitechapel, they saw how fast everything had gone wrong.

The Master's voice blared over the speaker system.

"Don't concern yourself with the blood. Everything has been approved. Don't concern yourself with the blood, everything has been approved." It was a recording of The Master repeated again and again like a nightmare.

The scene in front of the Twelve Bells told the story. Every one of the guards assigned to Whitechapel lay dead on the streets, beaten to death with bats.

Joseph recognized some of the guards as men and women that protected him when he was threatened by Surface Dwellers just days before.

"Does this surprise you, Joseph?" The Tread Setter asked. "All The Master had to do was to plant the seed. It was the audience that made it grow.

"Don't concern yourself with the blood, everything has been approved." The recording continued to repeat.

"Where did they all go?" Joseph asked.

"I think they're searching for you. We have to stay out of sight, Joseph." The Tread Setter said, pulling at him.

"You go. I have to find Tessa." Joseph said, staring down at one of the dead guards, a woman that he remembered from the London Hospital scene.

"He'll kill you." The Tread Setter sounded scared. It was so uncharacteristic of zir to be frightened of anything.

"Maybe, but maybe not." Joseph continued to the sound of a massive crowd just a block or two ahead of him.

"Good luck." The Tread Setter said, knowing that zie was in even greater danger now that zie had betrayed The Master. If he caught zir, there would be more than just bruises on zir neck.

Alone on the bloodstained street. Joseph went straight to the sound of the mob. He prepped his mind to enter the character of The Elephant Man, but realized the futility. He was in a dirty, wet funeral suit. Worse than being naked.

"Joseph." A woman's voice whispered from across the street. Joseph glanced over to find the Third Assistant holding a bag. Keeping low, she approached Joseph, her eyes searching for incoming threats. Finally, she reached Joseph.

"I'm sorry I can't help you more." The Third Assistant said through her fear.

"Thank you. Get out of here before you get killed." Joseph said as he took the bag.

"Good luck, Joseph." The Third Assistant ducked as she ran to the hidden door leading to the green room.

Joseph opened the bag and realized why she took such a risk. It was The Elephant Man's hood and robe. There was nothing else. No makeup, no prosthetics. Just a hood and cloak and whatever talent Joseph could bring to bear.

DO IT

"Audience of Gaslight, this is The Playwright! This play has been hijacked! Do not cooperate with this man!" The Playwright's voice warned desperately over the speaker system. This message had little effect on the roaring crowd. By the time he had said it twice, the intercom link was severed.

Entering the square just ahead of the Tower of London, the crowd parted as they saw Joseph in his cloak and hood. Across the narrow row carved out in the audience, the two Elephant Men faced each other across the distance, like a nightmarish gunslinger showdown.

"Joseph." The Master said, his voice echoing across Gaslight, entreating him to listen. "We need you on our side."
"What happens if I don't want to be on your side?" Joseph asked cautiously, steadfastly in character. The Master wasn't even trying to maintain the Elephant Man dialect at this point.

"Funny you should ask." The Master snapped his fingers and Rafonovic led Eddie by a rope tied to his neck. He still had his Treves costume on, though it was tattered. His face was a collection of bruises.
The Master ten personal guards surrounded Eddie, bludgeons

ready in their hands.

"Look at him." He spoke to his personal guard. "He is yours to take."

"DO IT. DO IT. DO IT. DO IT. DO IT." The Master's Followers chanted.

They raised their bludgeons, ready to strike. Suddenly someone got between them and her prey. It was Joseph. It was The Elephant Man. The play continued once again. Now it was a play of thousands with only one person doing any acting.

"Don't!!" Joseph cried as he covered Eddie, shielding him from attack.

"Dr. Treves is a good man. I would be dead if it wasn't for him. Please show mercy on this man." The Master saw what Joseph was doing and realized that he was not going to break character, something that he hoped Joseph would do, making this game a contest of persuasion through the craft of acting. It was obvious that he had underestimated him.

"Dr. Treves. Dr. Treves." Joseph said as he leaned in to completely cover Eddie with his misshapen body.

"Mr. Merrick. Don't put yourself in danger on my account. This mob wants me and will have me, even if that means hurting you." Eddie said, also clinging to his character through his fear. He was, in all seriousness, acting for his life.

Joseph turned back to the mob and scanned them with angry eyes that shocked them.

"For most of my life, I didn't know what it meant to have a friend. I only understood it in the most abstract way because of my condition. In the course of him plucking me from a nightmarish existence, Frederick Treves became my friend. My very first friend. He is more valuable to me than he will ever be to you. I may be bent so far out of shape that people call me a freak. I may be weak and sick, but I will use every last drop of my energy to protect my friend from harm…so DO YOUR BEST!!" Joseph stuck his chin out, daring the audience to land a blow on him. None of them did.

"I thought so." Joseph turned his twisted body and leaned down to offer Eddie his misshapen right hand. Eddie took it and Joseph helped him get to his feet.

With both men standing, they embraced like old friends reuniting after a long separation. The audience broke into spontaneous applause that resulted in a new batch of audience members to come to watch the scene unfold.

The elation created by this scene between doctor and patient didn't extend to The Master who was in real danger of the crowd turning on him.

ABANDONMENT

On the surface of the island, The Master's thugs led the Concierge to the tarmac where the jet was being loaded to capacity with the management team of Gaslight as well as the terrified Ripper and Victoria. Both primary actors reduced to sniveling children as the Master's guard locked eyes on them. One of the guards, an old man, approached the Ripper and held the bludgeon to his chin, forcing him to look into his eyes.

"The Master? You?" The old man lunged his bludgeon forward, cracking against The Ripper's jaw, bringing the defunct Master to tears.

Customers who were wealthy enough to pay a premium stood in a huddle, looking hopeful that the Stage Manager would take their money in exchange for a coach seat, even a place in the aisle. The price kept rising to extract every last dollar from the highest bidder. The going rate for evacuation was a million-five. In a few minutes, it was likely to double, finally resulting in the luggage being tossed from the underbelly of the plane to load more bodies in the plane.

The Playwright came out of the plane to meet the Concierge with a dour expression.

"I saved you a seat." The Playwright said gesturing to the plane.

"What about your audience? You're just going to leave them here?" The Concierge said with contempt. "All that we agreed to after last year to protect our audience. It was all just words to you."

"What do you want me to do?" The Playwright scoffed. To the Concierge, the man he thought he once respected appeared to him like a carpetbagger. Ready to abandon his people at the first sign of trouble.

"I'm staying." The Concierge muttered in disgust.
"He'll kill you. You know that." The Playwright reminded him.
"If I do make it out of here, at least I'll be able to look in the mirror." The Concierge said with unmoored bitterness.

They stared at each other for a moment, the silence broken by one of the billionaire's being held back at gunpoint by Rafonovic.
"FIVE MILLION DOLLARS FOR A SEAT!!" He screamed at The Playwright.
"Give him my seat. I know how much you value gold." The Concierge told The Playwright.

The Playwright nodded to the Stage Manager who waved the billionaire over. They didn't need to ask if he was good for it. They knew everything about their customers. Routing and account numbers were the first order of business at Gaslight.

"You asshole!" A woman screamed from the sequestered huddle. She tried to claw at the billionaire but the guards pushed her back. The Concierge finally recognized the woman as the billionaire's girlfriend. When they arrived at Gaslight, they were arm in arm, seemed madly in love. Now he boarded the plane and didn't look back to tell her good-bye.

"Good luck." The Playwright said to The Concierge who didn't respond. Finally the Playwright and his personal guard boarded the plane as the jet powered up.

The plane turned to face the sea. The leftover millionaires hoping for a ride threw rocks and dirt at the plane. Two of them tried to get in the way and were run over.

One rock hit a turbofan with a spark. The rock disintegrated and the plane took off anyway, despite a trail of smoke from the targeted engine.

The Concierge wondered if the plane could gain altitude if that engine failed. He watched as the plane continued flying, continued gaining altitude. Eventually all they could see of it was a trail of smoke that ascended into the stratosphere.

"What do we do now?" One of the millionaires asked The Concierge.

"Any of you have a satellite phone?" The Concierge asked, knowing they didn't. They stared back at him blankly.

"Go you your rooms and barricade yourself inside until this is all over."

"Until what is all over?" One of the millionaires asked.

"You'll know." The Concierge muttered as he heard the elevator rise to the runway level. "When it's over, everyone will know." Three men led by Rafonovic approached to arrest The Concierge. The millionaires were left alone for the moment to contemplate what this man called "The Master" had in store for them.

THE APPLAUSE

Joseph's riveting performance had enraptured the audience when
The Master interrupted. He approached, then got between Joseph
and Eddie, making it impossible to complete the scene.
He suddenly ripped Joseph's hood off, revealing Joseph's naked
face.

"This man!" The Master began as Joseph Merrick. "Has stolen
my identity to make you feel sorry for him." The Master plunged
his left hand into Joseph's pocket. Joseph felt the weight of
several coins drop only to be scooped up again by The Master. He
held the fistful of coins above his head.
"My savings! I was to use this to find my mother. This imposter
thought nothing of stealing that dream from me."
The audience was silent, watching intently. It was impossible to
know whose side they would be on. Joseph had no makeup. The
Master's face was perfectly done, better than Joseph's best day.
The smart thing to do would be to throw down the robe and run.
Joseph instead checked the feeling deep in his gut and followed it.
He would stay and fight. He would stay and act.
Joseph took off the robe, leaving him only in a loincloth.

Positioning his body in the twisted position of The Elephant Man,
he envisioned the lame arm and the drooping jaw of Joseph

Merrick and assigned his body to act, using what he had learned from the SEAL in Fallujah. His mind was in charge of his body, not the other way around.

He strained muscles to the point of snapping. Everyone watched with morbid curiosity as Joseph contorted so much that his joints came loose in two distinctive *pops.*

He had dislocated two bones by sheer will, his right shoulder and the right side of his jaw. The latter changed his face completely, enticing screams and gasps. Even The Master in his wildest imagination didn't expect this. It was a complete transformation without the aid of makeup.

Joseph's eyes glared at The Master who started to take a step back. Joseph lurched forward, looking so horrific, the audience turned and ran in terror. The Master matched Joseph's steps. Finally, Joseph's jaw drooped further, causing his tongue to hang out like a livid worm. It was too much, even for the great Franco Valor. He reached into his pocket and frantically pushed the button on a remote control. The remote control to a bomb.

ON THE TARMAC

For the millionaires standing at the tarmac still bitter about not getting a seat on the last plane off the island, they ended up flying through the air in a way they had never expected, one piece at a time. The Master had just blown up the runway, effectively cutting off the island from the outside world.

The Concierge felt the explosion as the elevator descended to the stage floor. As he looked up the elevator shaft, dirt, debris and human flesh rained down on him and the thugs guarding him. The thugs were covered in blood and screamed as it got in their eyes and blinded them.

"This is who your leader really is." The Concierge muttered to them in disgust.

ON THE STAGE FLOOR

The Master ran, as did the terrified audience, as chunks of the
Gaslight roof rained down from above.

Eddie held on to Joseph who was grasping his dislocated jaw,
unable to speak.

A taxi approached them and Eddie gestured desperately for it to
stop. Miraculously, it did.

"London Hospital, quick!" Eddie screamed as he pushed Joseph
into the coach.

"Yessir." The Cab Driver said and he clucked his tongue at the
horse. Even at top speed, the old mare still wasn't very fast.

Joseph pushed his jaw back in place and made a sudden swinging
motion against the wall of the coach. A hard *snap* made Eddie
wince at the realization that Joseph had just popped his jaw back in
place.

"That hurt." Joseph mumbled, massaging the stretched muscles
and ligaments.

In a comparatively easier move, he leaned his shoulder against the
back of his seat and pushed. A dull, hallow *pop* signaled the
resetting of his shoulder.

"Hey." Eddie said to Joseph who slouched in his seat. "You saved
our asses. Thanks."

"That trick…" Joseph winced as his nerves sent waves of pain
across his face. "…is a one time deal."

"It bought us time, but we need a plan if we're gonna beat this guy." Eddie said desperately.

"OK. You have any ideas? I kind of blew my wad with that last one." Joseph said, struggling to speak.

THE NERVE CENTER

The Plan, as it turns out, came to them. The Tread Setter stopped the horse by making a mysterious clucking sound. The Taxi Driver knew better than to complain as zie and Tessa climbed inside.

"Tower of London." Zie whispered to the Driver.

Tessa hugged Joseph.

"They arrested The Concierge." The Tread Setter said as zie pounded the ceiling, signaling the Taxi Driver to get moving. He obeyed, most likely out of fear.

As they entered the Tower of London, they were surprised to find the entry doors unlocked and the controls abandoned.

The Nerve Center at the heart of the Tower was blinking red at the site of every dead body in Gaslight of which Joseph counted thirty-two.

"I can't believe he didn't take this room first." Joseph muttered.

"His obsession for the last year in that cave was winning over the audience, that's all that mattered." The Tread Setter said.

"His mistake is the first good news today. Look." Joseph pointed to a white dot marked "UNKNOWN" on the board

"He's waiting for me at the hospital."

"Look for The Concierge." The Tread Setter said and they all scanned the board for his blinking name.

Joseph found him easily. He was being held in the observation room in the hospital, the same room where The Tread Setter had watched Joseph's scene from a breach in the ceiling.

"Got him. He's using him as bait." Joseph said.

"You rattled him, Joseph. What did you think was going to happen?" The Tread Setter said sullenly. "Well let's blind the man at least." Zie passed stair treads to each of them. Zie raised her tread over zir head and smashed it into the console. With the others joining, in, the room became a shower of sparks as the Nerve Center's screen flickered and finally went dark.

"Now, we're all blind together." Joseph said with finality.

"Blind and isolated on this island with a madman." Eddie whimpered. "What are we gonna do?"

"We'll keep acting. Stay in character. Stay in character and bring the audience to our side. The audience is the only power that matters now. It's our only chance." Joseph said darkly.

"It's a psychological battle now. And you underestimate him at your own risk. He knows how to manipulate the audience. He knows how to manipulate anyone." The Tread Setter observed. As zie said this, Tread recalled how The Master had pulled zir into his orbit, made zir feel important and loved before he asked zir to kill on his behalf, like a thespian Charles Manson.

"While we're all talking, The Concierge is in danger." Joseph broke in. "Trap or not, I'm going to get him back. Are you with me?" Joseph's said, his eyes filled with the fire of a soldier.

THE LONDON HOSPITAL

In The London Hospital, The Master's patience had come to an end. He gestured to his thugs to force The Concierge to his knees. "Where's Joseph? He should've come by now." He said in a smile that seemed too wide.

"I don't know." As The Concierge said this, The Master grabbed the man's wrist, shoving his own smart watch in his face.

"Look at it." The Concierge cried. Indeed, the watch was blinking a pixelated "NO SIGNAL" against a blue screen.

"He's probably in the control room, wouldn't you say?" The Concierge said with a hint of irony.

"I think we'd better give the audience something. There's nothing worse than a bored audience. Devil's workshop, yes?" The Master said as he turned to one of his Guards and calmly ordered The Concierge's execution.

"Are you sure about this?" The Guard said, looking apprehensive.

"Do you have the guts or don't you?" The Master said, grabbing The Guard by his shirt. "They are useless to us. The ones in the basement too. Cut off the rotten fruit. Do it now."

The Concierge was rudely dragged toward the secret door where he was sure he'd be led to his execution in front of a cheering horde.

In that long walk through the hallways littered with pieces of wardrobe, The Concierge thought of Joseph, Tessa and Eddie. He thought of the audience abandoned by the creative team of Gaslight. He thought about the death of Gaslight itself, assured by the actions of The Master and the inaction of The Playwright. The last thing that The Master said was chilling. "Cut off the rotten fruit." referenced the ventilation system that piped in breathable air to the sex dungeon.

The Concierge was sure that he was going to suffocate them all. "They are useless to us." He had said.

The great experiment that was Gaslight was about to be destroyed from within. It was impossible not to see the failures that rotted the concept from the inside out and revealed the deal with the devil the management made when they trafficked in human flesh.

The thought of their suffering and his failure brought The Concierge to tears.

He knew and didn't say anything. Was he afraid? Yes. That didn't make his self-loathing any less biting. He was complicit in everything that happened there. He was about to die with that regret drowning any of the good work he had done. At that thought, he cried.

"Look." One of the thugs spun The Concierge around, displaying his tear-stained cheeks to the other guard.

"Spit on him!" The thug said. Looking up at the recently recruited guard, The Concierge recognized him as an audience member. A man in his early 20's that owned a huge software company. The

Concierge thought it was ironic that this man who funded a charity to benefit the mentally ill was about to spit in his face.

Spittle flew across The Concierge's cheeks and dribbled down as the thug laughed.

Joseph, who was watching from the darkness of the corridor had enough. With a tread still in his hand, he bashed the spitting guard across the temple just a little too hard. Soon bleeding in his brain ensured that the software company would have to find new leadership. By the time their CEO came home, he would have to be fed through a tube and toileted five times a day.

The Tread Setter took care of the thug, knocking him across the gut first before delivering a stair tread to his jaw. Both men were out of the fight before they hit the ground.

For good measure, Joseph hawked a good one on the spitter's face.

"You OK?" The Tread Setter studied The Concierge for any sign of injury.

"Yeah, yeah." He came out of what appeared to be a trance. "I have to tell you something. Something that I heard him say."

As The Concierge relayed what The Master was about to do, Tessa clutched her face in disbelief at the thought of her fellow Assets, some of them who she had known since childhood being suffocated because The Master considered them to be "useless".

"There's still time to help them. I know a way down there. A way that *he* wouldn't know." The Concierge said with heaving breaths. "But we have to hurry because the back door I'm talking about is an hour away on foot and the air goes stale down there very quickly."

There was nothing left to discuss. They made their way through the tunnels as quickly as their feet would take them. Their destination was at the far side of Gaslight, past Buckingham Palace. With the Nerve Center destroyed, The Master was blind in the underground tunnels. They could move with impunity as long as they watched for the golf carts carrying recently recruited guards. This necessary evasion cost them time. They reached their destination in two hours and change.

They reached a spot in the tunnel that seemed like a pockmarked wall. The Concierge reached into a hidden handle, something that Joseph wouldn't have seen if he was looking right at it. The Concierge pulled off a panel and uncovered the hidden place.

As The Concierge opened it, LED lights that may have gone unused forever illuminated a slide that descended into unknown places at unknown depths.

One of the lights illuminated a sign reading "EMERGENCY ACCESS TO SUB-BASEMENT".

There was nothing but a single seat facing sideways with an overhead belt, like the kind found in racecars.

"What the hell is this?" Joseph asked.

At that moment, The Concierge heard it. One of the carts somewhere in the tunnel. With the labyrinth of tunnels, he couldn't tell if the cart was coming closer or going away.

"No time, get in." The Concierge ordered.

Joseph strapped himself in the chair. He stared straight ahead into a black wall. It seemed like one of those dark rides at a carnival. The ones that drove the cart right into a pair of doors disguised as a wall that banged and shot open as the cart crashed into it. A green light illuminated above his head and Joseph discovered how close to a carnival ride this contraption really was.

Instantly everything went dark, followed by a feeling of weightlessness as he clutched the arms of the chair and held his breath as he endured the ceaseless fall. In seconds that felt like hours, Joseph saw the first hint of light. The chair started to level out and the speed of his fall slowed culminating in the surface turning completely horizontal. His seatbelt unlatched automatically as the ride terminated at a room of foam padding and summarily ejecting him against the soft surface. Joseph looked back, his head spinning as he watched the chair vanish into a hole in the floor, presumably to return to its home at the tunnel loading zone.

"Jesus!" Joseph stumbled trying to regain his balance.

One by one, they endured the same drop into the abyss, finally ending in The Concierge sliding with such velocity, he nearly smashed against the unpadded far wall.

The room had several emergency procedures posters. Hurricane, fire, disease outbreak…no instructions on dealing with a major revolt. There was a mini-stash of emergency food and water rations, first aid kit and a strange device that looked like a kitchen tool.

On the wall of the escape room was a diagram displaying means of escape from Gaslight.

The Elevators
The Main Escape Stairwell
The Alternative Escape Stairwell at the Hotel
The Train

"The train?" Joseph asked aloud.
The diagram displayed the mechanism that made up the various train station simulations. There was, however, a blank station that was indicated as an escape route. Included in the train method of evacuation was the strange symbol that Joseph had seen before, the offset double oval.

"How many people know about the train?"
Joseph asked the Concierge.

"The Stage Manager, The Conductor, the Head of Security if he's still alive, the Playwright…and myself."

"Could The Master know?"

"Doubtful, but you never can be sure." To Concierge conceded.

"Where are we anyway? We seem to have fallen forever." Tessa asked Joseph.

"We're at the lowest level. Your former home, Tessa." The Concierge said in a dark tone that sent a chill through her.

"Would he really hurt them? The 'Assets'?" Tessa said with a breaking voice.

"All he had to do was push a button." The Concierge said, preparing Tessa for what she might find behind the metal doorway leading to the sex dungeon.

"What are we waiting for?!" Tessa screamed as she rushed to the door, turning the metal ring to unlock the nautical-looking passageway. Joseph joined her, putting all of his weight on the turn ring until it finally started to move.

The Concierge steeled himself for what was coming. When the door's lock finally clicked open, Joseph pulled it open. It hissed as the air in the escape room came into contact with a vacuum in the dungeon.

"Close it! Close it!" The Concierge screamed. Tessa was closest to the door and fainted. The air inside the dungeon was stripped of its oxygen. The Master hadn't just stopped the flow of oxygen, he tripped the fire suppression system making the remaining air poisonous.

The escape room's ample supply cache included two firefighting respirators with a supply of oxygen that would last a few minutes at best.

"Can you hotwire the air circulator?" The Concierge asked the Tread Setter as Joseph picked Tessa off the cold floor, her eyes fluttering open.

"Maybe. I'm not sure." Zie replied.

Joseph pushed the second respirator in zir hands.

"Maybe is better than nothing."

The Tread Setter secured the respirator to zir face, pulling the strap as tight as zie could. Joseph continued to turn the maritime wheel that unlocked the door.

As the door cracked open a vacuum sucked the air from the escape room. The air in the dungeon was foul, smelling of vomit and excrement and dispensed halon.

"Good luck!" Joseph said, coughing as the Tread Setter slipped through the narrow opening. As soon as zie was through, Joseph spun the mechanism closing the door, saving what little air they had left.

In the darkness of the dungeon, the headlight on the respirator revealed to The Tread Setter the totality of The Master's disregard for the lives of the Assets. It also put zir face to face with the terrible choice that zie made following the man as long as zie had. Just ahead, a pile of desperate Assets lay on their backs with their mouths and eyes open, frozen in their last suffocating breaths. The Tread Setter felt sick for their suffering and the role that zir might have played in it, however peripheral.

Still, there might be survivors in this room clinging to life. Zie had to get the air circulator running and zir own air supply was very limited.

Scanning the dungeon, the red emergency exit signs were still illuminated. Navigating through the dead and dying, zie saw the *auxiliary air circulator* near one of these exit signs and decided this was the best chance zie had.

Using the tools in zir small utility kit, zie waved a voltmeter over the wire feeding into the circulator. The line was cold. Waving it over an artery of wires, the voltmeter chirped like a sick bird. One of those wires was the one zie needed. It was still live. The Tread Setter's joy at this discovery was short lived as the oxygen supply on the respirator spat out one last shot of air before dying.

The Tread Setter reached back for zir number two respirator and fumbled to switch them. In those seconds, zir vision became hazy and tunnel-like. As zie secured the new respirator and switched it on, zie realized that something was very wrong. The oxygen was only coming out in an uneven sputtering supply. There was nothing else to do but continue the repair attempt and hope that zie didn't black out.

In the escape room, everyone sat in tense silence, hoping to hear a knock on the metal door.

"I'm going in there." Joseph finally proclaimed.

"Zie has both respirators. If they have ten minutes of air supply each, zie has thirty more seconds of air left." The Concierge calculated.

"I should've gone." Joseph mumbled.

"You wouldn't know what to do, Joseph, Tread does." The Concierge reminded him.

"I'm going in." Joseph said, starting to open the metal door.

"NO!" The Concierge tried to stop him, but Joseph threw him off. He hit the concrete wall hard, knocking the wind out of him.

The door opened to reveal a small hand lying against the metal. It was the Tread Setter, and zir respirator had failed completely. There was something else in the thin air, the CHUG-CHUG of the auxiliary respirator piping in a small but critical amount of fresh air from the surface.

"You did it." Joseph said, removing The Tread Setter's mask. "You did it!"

Zie smiled, but didn't speak, the oxygen deprivation invoking a temporary spongy paralysis.

In about an hour, the air became saturated with oxygen.

The Concierge flipped on the battery-powered emergency lights and passed flashlights around.

In the moment before they started searching for survivors, Joseph stood at the precipice to the dungeon taking in the enormity of the carnage.

"These are human lives. Why not at least let them free to the surface?" Joseph said, trying to comprehend the type of person that would commit mass murder for the sake of convenience.

"You don't understand how The Master thinks." The Concierge said in a matter-of-fact tone.

 "It's easier to push a button and make the problem go away."

With that, the overhead lights flickered illuminating the dungeon's depressing scene. Hundreds of Assets lay motionless on beds, chairs and the floor.

The room filled with desperate moaning as the oxygen-starved victims came back from the brink of suffocation.

"Breathe. Breathe." Joseph held a young man in his arms, his color returning with each new breath.

"What's your name?" Joseph asked gently.

"Asset…1…3…3…6." He panted.

"I'm Joseph. We're going to get you out of here when you're strong enough."

"Thank you." 1336 said weakly, his eyes drifting in and out of lucidity.

Of 1200 of the slaves, about 500 hundred of them were suffocated to death. About a hundred of them were alive, but unable to respond and were presumably brain damaged. The remaining approximately 600 Assets came back to lucidity after cheating death.

After three hours, Joseph was able to marshal the strongest of the Assets to lift the injured ones out of the dungeon and into the auxiliary escape stairwell.

After three hours of climbing, they finally reached the top and flung the doors open to the tropical night.

Tessa tearfully collapsed on the grass, recognizing many of her friends were among the dead. Joseph held her as she sobbed. One of her best friends, a female Asset, was brought to the surface, still breathing, but passed away before they could lay her down.

For Tessa, this treatment had been her whole life. This was the life of all of the Assets. They were disposable and had no families other than each other. These disposable people were her family.

In the fresh tropical air, some of the brain addled returned to life. Most of them weren't that lucky and stayed in a comatose state, probably forever.

As the survivors sorrow turned to rage, they looked to Joseph as their savior and pledged their loyalty to him. It wasn't revenge that they were after, but justice. The Master had to answer for the deaths of their friends.

To Joseph, Tread was the real hero, but knew that the praise would only make zie uncomfortable. Despite zir hypoxia, Tread was already solving the next problem of contacting the outside and informing them of the carnage.

"The telegraph office is locked and under guard, but I know another way in there." The Tread Setter knew every hidden door in Gaslight and where there wasn't one, zie could make one up. "He'll be waiting for you." Joseph reminded zir that The Master knew zir tricks.
"Maybe. Maybe not." The Tread Setter smiled in a way that Joseph couldn't help but find charming. He was just glad that zie was on his side.

"Joseph, were you expecting someone?" Eddie called from the lip of the nearby cliff.
"No!" Joseph could tell that Eddie had seen something. He rushed to the edge to investigate. The Tread Setter and The Concierge followed.

Joseph could hardly believe what he saw. It was a small yacht, about twenty-meters long, wrecked against the rocks, the emergency lights still blinking.

Joseph thought of the journalist Dominguez. He hoped that the writer wasn't on that boat.

"There's no point in going down there now. We'll wait until first light for our answers." The Tread Setter said with finality. If anyone knew of the challenges of traversing the side of the cliff it was zir.

That night, those that were strong enough set up a makeshift triage on the surface near the destroyed airfield. They used anything they could salvage from the basement, bringing up thin mattresses and warm blankets to comfort those still too weak to move as well as the Assets still unconscious. The dead were left in the basement for now. No one had energy to spare for the dead tonight after the long climb up the emergency stairs.

Luckily, the night was calm and the temperature was mild. The oxygen was thick, almost chewable. It felt so good to be out of the thin air of the dungeon.

Exhausted, Joseph lay on a foam pad waiting for Tessa to join him. Eventually she collapsed into his arms, crying herself to sleep after seeing so many of her friends destroyed by The Master's cruelty. All Joseph could do was hold her. He couldn't say that everything would be OK.

The Tread Setter and Joseph left camp at first light carrying backpacks filled with heavy duty stair treads that would support Joseph's substantial weight.

Standing at the edge of the cliff wall, Tread felt the place in the rock that would support the all-important first tread. It went in with a crunch as the internal hooks imbedded into the stone. "Feels solid." The Tread Setter said as zie hopped onto the tread repeatedly, making Joseph feel queasy just looking at zir testing her handiwork over the precipitous drop.
"Please don't do that?" Joseph said, looking nauseous.
"Do what?" The Tread Setter said as zie did a little dance on the bare tread that hung over the cliff. Joseph could tell that zie was having a little too much fun.
"Put in the next one already!" Joseph screamed, covering his eyes. Each time zie affixed a new one, the Tread Setter got a little faster. As Joseph followed zir down, handing zir treads from his own pack; he felt the plank bow under his weight. Tread told him that, in theory, they could hold his weight, the weight of the pack with ten pounds to spare. With the sharp rocks on the beach below, Joseph didn't find this very encouraging.

When they reached the beach, they had just two treads to spare. The Tread Setter smiled at zir handiwork and hopped onto the rocky beach.

A tread was used to climb through a breach in the yacht's hull.

Inside the yacht, Joseph found a dead man lying next to the steering wheel. Judging from his uniform, Joseph assumed that it was the skipper.

"I'm going below. Stay here in case…" Joseph said as he opened the dark corridor to the engine room and a howling sound greeted him from the emergency power system that was about to give up the ghost.

As Joseph descended, Tread noticed something off about the skipper's face. Zie knelt down and turned the man over to get a better look at his face. Tread saw something that made no sense. It was a wire that ran through the skipper's jawline.

"Hello?!" Joseph called out in the dim chamber.
As he was about to leave, he saw movement in the darkness. He crept forward to investigate, hoping that he had just seen his own shadow.
Reaching the engine, he stepped into a puddle of salt water. Here at the far end of the engine room, it was very dark. Joseph could barely see his hands feeling for obstacles ahead.
"Hello?" He repeated, wanting desperately to get this over with and return to the upper deck.
In his moment of distraction, he didn't notice the hand that slid out

of the darkness, interlocking fingers with Joseph's. It was so unexpected that Joseph couldn't scream.

The Tread Setter had searched the upper decks and found two more bodies, both crewmembers. Both of them had been shot in the head.

"Tread! I need you!" Zie heard faintly from the lower deck. Something about the tone of Joseph's voice worried zir. It seemed frantic, out of control, very unlike him.
The Tread Setter's heart started racing as zie grew closer to the door leading to the engine room.

"Joseph?" Tread called into the darkness. Immediately, zie could tell that something was wrong. Joseph was straining against something, his breaths rapid and short.

As Tread got closer, zie saw it. Two bloody hands had hold of Joseph's and were squeezing hard.
Tread grabbed the last stair tread from zir backpack and stabbed it into the darkness, estimating where the unseen person's head might be.
CRAKK! A hallow sound echoed through the engine room.
A bearded man covered in cuts fell forward sending Joseph flying back onto the floor.
The man was stunned, but still conscious.

Zie raised the tread to hit him again and Joseph stopped zir with both hands.

"Don't!"

"Why not?!"

"That's the reporter!" Joseph screamed. "It's Dominguez. He said he was coming to investigate the island. I sent him a letter when I was in Sicily.

"Pleasure to meet you again, Joseph." Dominguez muttered cupping a fresh cut delivered by The Tread Setter. "Sorry that I didn't recognize you. It's been so long."

"It's ok. We have to go." Joseph gestured for Dominguez to follow.

Joseph ascended to the control room to see the face of the skipper again.

"He's a surface dweller." The Tread Setter croaked. "One of those kicked off the island. This is why they should've killed them all." Zie turned the man's face, revealing a wire imbedded in his jaw.

"He wired his jaw back together." Zie said in a matter-of-fact tone.

"Are you saying, those Surface Dwellers. The ones that were arrested and evacuated…"

"They wanted to be caught. It was all in the plan." Tread admitted. "So they could perform missions out in the world to help Valor. Missions like stopping a reporter from discovering the truth."

"Shit!" Joseph realized that he had sent Dominguez into a trap.

"If The Master knows Dominguez is here, he's dead for sure." Tread warned Joseph.

"I was trying to help the Assets. I was trying to do the right thing." Joseph said in a pained voice.

"No one cares if you feel bad, Joseph. The Master knows what he's doing. He knows how to seduce people to his side. He seduced me into believing all sorts of things. Then you came along and I saw him for what he really was. You think I don't feel bad about what I did? What matters is that this man has to be stopped. I thought you were the man to do it. Am I right or am I wrong?"

"You're right." Joseph said, sensing Tread's waning faith in him.

"Good. Don't underestimate The Master again." Tread warned Joseph.

A whirring sound was followed by complete darkness as the emergency power supply finally quit. On the wall, a yellow blinking light was the only visible illumination. It was something that Joseph recognized right away.

He approached the blinking object that resembled a bulky cell phone with a globe light on top.

"What's that?" Tread said, confused.

"It may be our last chance to get help from the outside. Follow me." Joseph grabbed the blinking object.

They followed the visible sunlight to the upper deck. Joseph flung open the door to the outer deck.
"What are you doing?" Tread seemed even more confused as Joseph threw the object into the sea.

It dropped into the water and bobbed up like a buoy, blinking furiously, letting out a single desperate cry like a drowning child.

"That's an EPERB." Joseph said, watching the blinking object as it pitched in the water. "Satellite distress signal as soon as it hits the water."
"And that means?" Tread still looked puzzled.
"It means that eventually someone will come and help." Joseph said, feeling a sense of relief.
"Question is, will help come in time." The Tread Setter said in a grim tone. Joseph didn't like this. He wondered if there was something that Tread wasn't telling him. Was there a final reckoning of some kind that was inevitable, coming sooner than later. Would the rescuers come only to find a Jonestown-like scene waiting for them? It solidified the realization that time was not on their side and The Master had many more tricks up his sleeve.

They brought Dominguez up to the main deck where they could finally get a good look at him. When they saw the wound, it was clear why there was so much blood. He had been shot in the head, most likely by the imposter that posed as the skipper. By a stroke of luck, the Surface Dweller was a bad shot and only managed to graze Dominguez's skull.

"You're lucky to be alive." Joseph mopped blood from the bullet wound as well as the gash from Tread.

"I don't feel so lucky." Dominguez grunted as he tried to sit up. Joseph helped Dominguez to sit against the wall of the control room.

"Is anything broken? Can you walk?" Joseph said, knowing that they couldn't carry him up the cliff. The stairs were already straining under Joseph's weight.

"I don't know. My head hurts." Dominguez put his fingers on the wound and could feel his exposed skull.

"Don't do that! Infection!" Tread snapped. Zie poured iodine over a bandage meant to go against the wound.

Tread pressed the wet gauze over Dominguez's head with little sympathy for his screams. Zie wrapped the bandage around his head, tied it off and proclaimed it done.

"Let's see if you can walk." Joseph helped Dominguez to his feet. Though he was bruised, shot and cut, nothing was broken. Joseph was relieved. "We have to get you to the surface, there we can explain everything. A lot has happened since I sent you that letter." Joseph told the reporter.

Joseph had hoped that the boat had radio equipment, SAT phones, anything like that, but it had all been cut out and probably thrown overboard by the Surface Dweller. Luckily for them, The Master probably didn't have a clue what that little box on the wall was or he would've ordered the EPERB destroyed.

The journey up the cliff was slow going with Dominguez close to tears at every step. He could sense that Tread just wanted to shank him rather than deal with his bitching about the climb, especially because zie was stuck behind him, collecting the stair treads as they ascended.

"Why is he important to you?" Zie screamed bitterly.
Joseph warned Dominguez that he had better get his ass to the top or Tread would ditch him over the edge and not give two shits. Believing him, Dominguez took a deep breath and overcame his fear in a big way.

When they finally reached the last tread, Dominguez collapsed on the edge of the cliff only to have Tread hop on him, holding a small knife inside his lip.
"No one's gonna carry your ass here, got that?" Tread said, deadly serious. Joseph was certain zie would cut him as a reminder of their conversation.

"We need him." Joseph calmly reminded Tread as Dominguez

tasted the end of the Tread Setter's blade. "To bear witness to everything that happened."

Joseph pointed at the rows of injured Assets under a makeshift tent.

Dominguez saw the dozens of people, some looked like they were sleeping, other seemed to be broken animatronics with their eyes turning independent of each other, their bodies shaking involuntarily and muttering gibberish.

Joseph could see that Dominguez was overwhelmed.

"These were the lucky ones. The others are still in that basement I told you about. Dead."

Dominguez pushed away Tread's blade and zie let him go. Tread could see that he understood the gravity of the situation.

Joseph hugged Tessa and gave her the first aid kits from the boat. She seemed exhausted from caring for her friends.

"Take a break." Joseph pleaded.

"I will in a little while." Tessa promised, knowing that she wouldn't.

Joseph invited Dominguez into his tent and they talked until the sun went down. He told the reporter about The Master's bloody coup of Gaslight. How he tried to kill all of the Assets. How he expertly honed in on the right members of the audience to mold into his enforcers.

"Just like that experiment at that school." Dominguez said with recognition of the pattern. Joseph didn't know what he was talking about.

"There was an experiment. They gave one group of guards a little bit of power, made the others play prisoners and it got ugly fast. They quickly forgot that it was an experiment." Dominguez realized they didn't know what he was talking about. "Never mind. Tell me more about what happened"

Dominguez furiously took notes, shaking his head at each dark revelation.

Dominguez put down the notepad and took a strange object out of his pocket. Something metallic about the size of a deck of cards.

"What's that?" Joseph asked, curious about the object.

"I brought a digital camera outfit with me. The salt water destroyed them. I always carry this little mechanical Rollei with a roll of black-and-white film just in case something happened. In the hundreds of times I've been on a story, I've never had to use it." Dominguez said, twirling two of the knobs on the camera and took a shot before Joseph knew what he was doing.

"If you only have one roll of film, don't waste it on me."

"Joseph, you are the story here." Dominguez smiled as he stuffed the tiny camera back in his pocket.

"There were so many things to talk about. I forgot to tell you something. Something important." Dominguez's mood seemed to darken. "On March twenty-first, there was a mayday call. An unlisted jet had lost an engine and was going down about 200 miles from here. It was presumed to have crashed, but no trace of it or the passengers were found. Was that when the managers of this place evacuated?"

As Dominguez said this, his pad and pen were back in his hand. Joseph had lost his track of dates weeks ago. Dominguez seemed to sense this.

"About a week ago." Dominguez noted.

"I think that was when they took off. Time's funny here, you know."

"I understand." Dominguez smiled, taking another note as he spoke.

The Concierge joined them in the tent delivering a wax-sealed envelope to Joseph.

"It's from The Master."

The air in the tent got heavy as they waited for Joseph to open it. Joseph studied the large creamy envelope and gingerly pulled the string that tore through the seal.

The inside of the envelope was a pitch-black card. The message written in silver ink.

"The Glass Paris 2:30pm tomorrow. Come alone." Joseph read to himself, then closed the envelope. The Concierge knew The Master was probably laying a trap for Joseph.

"He wants you there alone?" The Concierge asked.

Joseph didn't need to answer.

"If you go in there, there a good chance you won't come back." The Concierge warned.

"I dunno. The Glass Paris has always felt safe to me. I think I'll be OK."

The Concierge bristled at this.

"Just keep your eyes open and you might come back in one piece. If he's calling you for a meeting, maybe you have something he wants."

"I can't imagine I have anything that he would want." Joseph said, feeling puzzled.

"I'm surprised at you Joseph. The most valuable thing in your possession is you. He wants what you brought to the role." The Concierge said.

"His role. I think he was clear about that." Joseph said with a dark voice. "He wanted to play Merrick."

"Just keep your eyes open. I'm more concerned about his thugs than The Master, honestly." The Concierge stood and started to return to his nursing duties.

"So you'll go?" Dominguez asked Joseph.

"Yes. I'll go. Alone. Let's find a place for you to rest." Joseph said with finality.

As Joseph finally convinced Tessa to get some sleep, they rested under the clear night sky, watching satellites pass over them, shining brighter than any star. He wondered if it was the one destined to carry the distress signal from the EPERB to whoever could come to help them.

Soon, he heard Tessa's sleeping breaths and he turned to watch her. He thought of the terrible life that she had endured and how she still managed to be a good person. Joseph slid his arm around her and soon they were both sleeping, breaths synchronized together.

The next morning, Joseph had a hearty breakfast culled from the Surface Dweller's cave. Tread's former cave home was stockpiled with survival stores. Powdered eggs, instant coffee, freeze dried crackers and portable desalination units alone with other odds and ends from MRE kits and camping food packs.

Tessa brought Joseph crackers, MRE peanut butter and a cup of black coffee that Joseph added sugar to.
Joseph was amazed how good such a simple meal tasted and credited it to the circumstances.

When Joseph finally spotted Tread, emerging from the cave with a box of MRE's he couldn't hide his joy.

They hugged and Joseph thanked zir for the help. The Tread Setter was visibly shaken.

"I heard about that meeting." Zie said. "You know that it's probably a trap. I don't want you to go."

"Somehow, I don't think that's true." Joseph didn't know why he felt this way, but he felt it with a certainty that unnerved him.

"Joseph…" A shrill voice called out to him. It wasn't a voice he recognized.

He turned to find two muscle-bound thugs standing at the lip of the elevator. By their stance, Joseph could tell that they could bring him in by force, possibly with a broken bone or two.

"My ride's here." Joseph said to a tearful Tessa. He kissed her and strode out to meet his fate. The Concierge, Eddie, Tessa and The Tread Setter gathered together and watched Joseph descend with his brutish escorts. Dominguez took pictures though the tent. In the last photo, Joseph saw him and stared directly into the camera just before he descended into his fate.

THE MEETING AT THE GLASS PARIS

As Gaslight came into view, Joseph found his greatest fears realized. Rows of shallow graves lined the streets. Blood covered the cobblestones along with occasional pieces of hair-covered scalp. Joseph estimated that most if not all the regular security forces, the one actually employed by Gaslight, had been killed. Some of the audience members were in chains and appeared to be in some kind of drug stupor.

In just a few days, The Master had turned Gaslight into a hell that Pol Pot or Chairman Mao would be envious of.

The Master's "personal guard" encircled The Glass Paris. They all glared at Joseph who realized that there might not be a meeting after all. Perhaps they were there just to beat him to death. Suddenly he saw the door open to the bar and Rafonovic appeared. "He's expecting you." He said to Joseph as he held the door open. Joseph passed him with a piercing glance.

The inside of The Glass Paris was empty except for the Master who sat at a center table and the jittery bartender.

Something was different about The Master. Gone was any remnant of the Elephant Man. He had changed character and was wearing the wardrobe assigned to Jack the Ripper. The character the previous Master had abandoned at the first sign of trouble.

The Master glanced back at the bartender, looking slightly irritated.

"Get Joseph a drink please and another one for me."

"Yes sir. Right away." The barkeep said without hesitation.

The Master studied Joseph's shabby visage and clucked his tongue.

"You came to meet me looking like this? I should send you back."

"I'm sorry, but rescuing the Assets from suffocation has made it difficult on my wardrobe and hygiene routine." Joseph said in a cold voice.

"You should've let them die, Joseph. Now you'll be saddled with a thousand parasites. If they come down here, my team knows what to do with them." The Master promised with a smile.

"I'm sure the Assets have some ideas about what to do with you as well." A visible chill went down The Master's spine as he considered this. "Thanks to you, the number is actually closer to six hundred."

Joseph's drink came. The Master's did too. The legendary black absinthe only allowed to The Master.

Joseph held his green absinthe up fearlessly for a toast.

"Cheers" Joseph said as The Master met his toast with a wince.

The Master said as he took a modest sip, knowing better than to gulp this dark concoction down.

"What's it like? The Black Absinthe?" Joseph asked, more curious than he let on.

"A revelation to my consciousness. I feel sorry for the unwashed masses who will never feel what I feel when I drink it." As The Master said this, he kissed the absinthe glass.

"They say the experience depends on what the drinker brings to it." The Master said. Joseph could that oddly reassuring, though he doubted he would ever test out that theory.

He sat his glass down, then waved at Rafonovic who brought him something wrapped in paper. It looked like a piece of meat from the butcher shop. As he handled it, Joseph realized thankfully that it was just a script from the play and not someone's vital organ.

"The only reason you're not dead right now is because I need you, Joseph. I painfully concede that you are the superior Elephant Man. Try to understand that I have rarely met an actor that could outperform me in any role. Congratulations, Joseph. Your talent has saved your life...so far." The Master said in a whisper. Joseph couldn't believe what he was hearing. He was sure that The Master would fight to the death to take the part back. There was something that Joseph was missing. The Master wasn't one to cave in this way.

He watched The Master's eyes as the black absinthe took effect.

They became glassy. His pupils dilated. For a moment, he thought he might pass out in front of him. The effect passed in a few seconds and he was as focused as ever.

"I read the Playwright's script with the new Ripper scenes. I have to say that it is brilliant work." The Master flipped through the pages of the script. He seemed to almost be in pain at the admission of anyone else's talent.

"I agree. Brilliant." Joseph conceded easily. The new scenes were inspirational and deserved to be performed (maybe next year if Gaslight even existed by then). Performing them under these circumstances, however, was insanity.

"I see you pause. What's your hesitation?" The Master demanded an answer.
"What happens when the performance is over?" Joseph countered. The Master took another sip of black absinthe and let Joseph stew in silence for a while.

"Who says it will end? New scenes will be written. The Ripper and the Elephant Man forever enmeshed by the murder of Merrick's mother. There is no end to that kind of pain. The thirst for revenge would be unquenchable."

Joseph's mind went to the EPERB he threw into the ocean. If his message was received, they could conceivably expect a rescue in a few days.

"You don't have a choice, Joseph. If I can't entertain my children one way, I will find another shiny object."
Two Personal Guards pushed The Concierge into the Glass Paris. He had been beaten and his black cloak was torn.

"Stop!" Joseph screamed. He saw where this was going. He was going to torture The Concierge until he got what he wanted
The goons held The Concierge's hand down on the wooden bar.

"Watch." The Master said, smiling.
"I'll do it!" Joseph cried out.
"I know you'll do it." The Master replied and nodded at the goons. One of his Personal Guards unstrapped a hatchet from his belt holster and held it over his head. Joseph thought that this was still just a scare tactic until he brought it down.

The sound reminded Joseph of a butcher cutting the ribs from the carcass of a hog. The bones crunched with finality followed by hypersonic screams. The kind of screams that could not be suppressed.

"Enjoy your drink. I'll see you at rehearsal." With that, The Master knocked back the remaining black absinthe and left with his Personal Guard flanking on all sides.

As he closed the door, half of The Concierge's hand, fell with a thud on the floor. The barkeep used a clean bar towel and his belt to apply enough pressure to stop the bleeding. They hadn't cut the hand off at the wrist, but in the center of the palm where it would cut through four bones and immeasurably more nerve endings.

"God-damn motherfucker!" The Concierge spat, his face beet red. The barkeep pulled a bottle of bourbon from the well, popped the top and handed it to The Concierge.
"Drink this. You'll feel better."
The Concierge grabbed the bottle and belted a shot back.
"Feel better?" The barkeep asked.
"Fuck no!" The Concierge snapped back.
"Take another slug."
The door swung open and Rafonovic appeared.
"Time to go." Joseph said.
"Wait!" The barkeep held a small torch in his hand, the kind used to light the absinthe sugar cubes on fire. He handed the Concierge an absinthe spoon and grabbed his hand.
"Bite down on that." The barkeep commanded.
The Concierge did what he was told. The torch ignited and the screaming began anew. The sizzling sound of cauterizing flesh and the disturbingly delicious smell of barbecue filled the room. Joseph had to hold The Concierge down until he went limp, passed

out from the pain.

The bartender leaned against the bar and shook his head in disbelief.

"The Glass Paris in supposed to be neutral territory. There will be consequences for this insult."

"I don't think The Master is afraid of your rules." Joseph said as he checked The Concierge's pulse. "I think you'd better tell me about The Glass Paris. About who you really are…otherwise I can't help you." Joseph said this with a finality not lost on The Bartender.

"Think of us as ambassadors, Joseph. Diplomats of the underworld that keeps the owners of Gaslight in check. We are supposed to be protected." The barkeep said in a low desperate voice.

"You will be protected." Joseph promised.

"For that you will have powerful allies when this nightmare is over."

Joseph stuck his hand out to the bartender.

"Promise. I want to hear you promise." Joseph demanded. The bartender took his hand, grasping it hard.

"We promise." The bartender said in a deep, serious tone.

"Break it up! Let's go!!" Two burly thugs stood at the door. Rafonovic waited for them just outside.

Joseph nodded at the bartender as he left The Glass Paris.

On the elevator up, surrounded by The Master's Personal Guard, Joseph got close enough to Rafonovic to whisper to him.

"Are you enjoying this, Ricardo?"

"You got your big chance. Well this is my big chance, Joe. I'm someone now. I'm someone and you can't take that away."

"The only one that can take your due away is you; don't you understand the disaster you've enabled?"

The elevator dinged and shuddered as it stopped at the surface. The thugs pushed Joseph off and the car quickly descended.

Tessa was waiting for him. She touched his face, unsure if he was really there. Their eyes met and with the surety of Joseph's safety, Tessa fell in his arms.

They lay together in their tent, unable to sleep. She didn't ask him any questions.

"Three more of them died." Tessa said. "They just never woke up. *YA prosto ne mog nichego sdelat.*" She said.

"I'm sorry baby, what language were you speaking?" Joseph asked.

"What do you mean?" She asked, clueless that she had just spoken Russian.

"It doesn't matter. Let's try to get some sleep." Joseph said as he leaned over to kiss her.

From The Journal of Alfonso Dominguez.
Gaslight Island
Interview of Trafficked Individuals at Gaslight Sex Slave
Operation
Asset 9011

The slight young man, no older than twenty is one of the lucky
ones. He was resuscitated after nearly being suffocated by Franco
Valor along with hundreds of others trapped as slaved in the lowest
levels of the theater experience known as Gaslight. What most
people think of as sort of theme park for lovers of immersive
theater is really just a front for the notorious Marmaladov gang,
familiar to my readers from my reporting in wartime Iraq.
In Fallujah, I had seen their trafficking operation first hand.
Ironically, the children trafficked there may well have ended up
here in the middle of the Caribbean. A private island with no laws
where the gang could operate unobstructed. Sadly, in the process
of Valor's violent revolt here, these slaves have been further
victimized. Rather than granting them their freedom, Franco Valor
attempted to get rid of them instead by cutting off the air supply.
Asset 9011 was rescued just in time. Hundreds of others weren't
so lucky. My first interview with one of the Assets was with 9011.
Though I would like to call him by his name. He insists that he
never had one.

DOMINGUEZ: "Do you remember a time before you were enslaved by the Marmaladov gang?"

9011: No.

DOMINGUEZ: No memory of your mother or father?

9011: No.

DOMINGUEZ: Did you know that something was wrong about the way you were treated?

9011: No. Everyone had to serve customers.

DOMINGUEZ: What did you know about the outside world.

9011: Only what I could learn from my customers. One of my regulars would tell me about books. Sometimes he would sneak them to me. I had to read them very fast because the boss would confiscate them.

DOMINGUEZ: Do you remember what your favorite book was?

9011: Oliver Twist. I felt like I had a lot in common. I wanted nothing more than to have a name. A real name. I would be Oliver if I could.

DOMINGUEZ: What if I told you that you could?

9011: I don't understand.

DOMINGUEZ: Now that you're free, you can choose any name you'd like.

Asset 9011 seemed blindsided by this revelation. He began to sob at the thought of choosing his own name. He was too overcome to continue the interview.

This Concluded My First Interview with a Sex Slave of Gaslight Island.

In the middle of the night, Joseph sat up and watched Tessa sleep. He had too much on his mind to go back to bed, so he wandered outside taking in the cool ocean air.

Nearby, he saw the Tread Setter in zir tent, a lantern illuminating zir face in an orange glow. Zie looked at Joseph and gestured for him to join zir.

Inside zir tent, he could tell that zie was agitated, and like him, couldn't sleep.

"Only the stupid ones think the normal play is still unfolding. The problem is that The Master gave all the stupid people power." The Tread Setter said.

"You should've seen the graves." Joseph said soberly. "Dozens of them in the streets where we used to act for people's amusement."

"So it's true. You're going back to do the scenes?" The Tread Setter asked. "They know how to pull my strings. They were going to hurt The Concierge. You know what? They ended up hurting them anyway."

"Doesn't surprise me." Tread said numbly.

"Did you think he would take it this far?" Joseph asked the Tread Setter, unsure if he wanted to hear the answer.

"He waited so patiently. So quietly. Until it was time not to be quiet. Up until the very end, he knew that someone like you would come. Someone who could give him the ultimate challenge worthy of his talents. Well, here you are." The Tread Setter poured

Joseph a shot of brown liquor and handed it to him. "He realized that someone like you was needed to take him to the next level. To get to a level higher than Master."

"What's higher than The Master?"

"Only he knows. The Tread Setter said as zie held up zir shot glass

"Salud." Zie said with finality.

"Salud." Joseph took the shot.

The Tread Setter pulled Joseph down by his shirt and kissed him. Momentarily stunned, Joseph pulled away and saw that zie was crying. It was not a kiss of lust or love, but the kind of kiss you give someone on the way to their own execution.

"You'd better go." Tread said, wiping away tears. "Yeah, you'd better go." Zie gave Joseph a gentle push backwards, zir eyes on his until he was clear of the tent. The Tread Setter closed the tent flap leaving Joseph outside in the dark.

The next morning, Joseph was shaken out of bed before sunrise by The Master's thugs.

He hurriedly dressed and kissed Tessa who was huddled in the corner of the tent. The Personal Guards made so much noise in the arrest that they soon had an audience as Joseph was led forcefully to the waiting elevator.

As they descended, Joseph kept eye contact with Tessa until the surface dropped away. He felt a jolt against his calf and didn't realize until he hit the ground that he'd been struck by the guards. Two hits to the body and one to the face and he blacked out.

JOSEPH AND THE OLD MAN

As Joseph's company was getting ready to make the move to Mosul, Joseph went on a one-man patrol close to the lair of the Marmaladov gang. He carried his M-16 fully loaded with a grenade launcher as well as a Glock sidearm. Extra ammunition hung from every pocket.

When he found himself at the abandoned lair, Joseph saw the leavings of the trafficked children strewn across the dirty concrete floor. Shoes, dolls and fragments of toys were stark reminders of the children kept here before the raid.

Dominguez had published the article to great notice in the human rights community. Joseph himself was mentioned (unnamed) in the article.

With this matter dealt with, Joseph should've felt at ease. His instincts told him that there were more roaches in the walls. His concerns fell on deaf ears in the command center.

"Joseph, we ran them out. It's done." His commanding officer, a beetle-like man name Kohl said exasperated. "This is becoming an obsession with you and an obsession for you is not a good thing."

"Mister…Mister!" A tiny voice called out from the maze-like rubble of a ruined house.

Joseph's eyes searched for the source and finally found a tiny child, a boy of about seven, hiding behind a pile of metal scrap. This boy was not Iraqi.

"Mister, you come for the bad men again? They came back."

The boy led Joseph to an adjacent building that was guarded by four men in tank tops. It was easy to see by their tattoos that they were in the Russian mob.

"They guard now, day and night." The boy told Joseph.

"You stay here. Under no circumstance will you follow."

"Yes, sir."

Joseph screwed on a silencer onto his pistol and made sure he had a full clip.

He didn't waste time with these thugs. Two in the chest, one in the head. Only the last one had a chance to react and get a shot off. Joseph felt the bullet graze his arm as he fired a hallow point into the gangster's brain.

Russian voices screamed from inside. The clattering as they grabbed their weapons.

"Go the back way!" The boy pointed to an alleyway that was now unguarded.

Entering the building that was a former beauty salon, Joseph found children, dozens of them bound and gagged, whimpering on the floor.

With the eight gangsters huddled at the front door, training their weapons toward the street. Joseph got within two meters of the men before one of them finally realized that there was someone behind them.

As they swiveled around to confront Joseph, he opened fire.. In a flash, Joseph had emptied his full clip of twenty-eight bullets into them. Even with the gags on, he could hear the children cry with terror.

Joseph reloaded his weapon and gave each of the men a bullet in the head before turning his attention to the children.

From a nearby closet, Joseph heard whimpering cries. Thinking it was a child, he opened the closet door to find an old Russian man, fumbling to aim his revolver at Joseph who kicked it out of his hand, breaking the man's wrist at an odd angle.

Joseph emptied the old man's revolver and stuck it in his back pocket.

He grabbed the broken wrist, and ignored the howls of pain. Joseph found the tattoo identifying him as a member of the Marmaladov gang. The old man cried and mumbled something in Russian.

"I will let you live. You just tell them that if they traffic children in Iraq, the same thing will happen again."

The old man's fear dissipated. His face became an edifice of defiance now that he realized he was going to be spared.

"They will come for you. Wherever you are. You will not be safe in America. You will not be safe anywhere." The old man said weakly.

"Neither will you." Joseph grabbed the old man by his good wrist and put a knife handle in it. The old man didn't understand.

"You'll cut every child loose and set them free. Do it now." Joseph said as he brought out the confiscated pistol.

"Fifty caliber. If you shot me with this you would've blown my head off."

Joseph loaded a round and pointed it at the old man's shattered hand.

"I suggest you follow my order."

One at a time, the children were freed. They spoke many different languages. Even when Joseph gestured for them to run, they hung on to his legs desperately.

The old man glanced at Joseph bitterly.

"You are some Santa Claus, young man."

"You just tell your boss what I said."

"What is your name, young man? So he can pay his respects in return."

"Joe. I'll let you figure out the rest." Joseph picked up one of the crying children and hugged her. He brought them all back to the base. He could feel the vibrations of their shivering on the drive back.

GONE WAS THE JOY

Medics had to give Joseph a shot to wake him enough for makeup.
As he regained consciousness, he realized that the guards that had
abused him were dead on the floor, both shot through the temple.
"I'm sorry, but I have to give you a stimulant. If your heart seems
the jump out of your chest, please let me know.
Joseph nodded as The Medic injected amphetamines into Joseph's
veins. He felt himself instantly return to life as his memory of the
events reemerged along with the pain.

He glanced up and the hotel staff had a breakfast cart with them
filled with treats as well as a coffee pot in a cozy.
In the room too was the makeup team. Gone was the joy that was
so evident before in the course of their job, replaced by hammered
misery as the team was chained to the wall, each of them given two
buckets, one for meals and one to defecate in.
Joseph couldn't believe that the people most trusted to pull off the
characters of Gaslight were treated with such profound disrespect.

"We're glad to see you alive, Joseph. We'd heard…" The Team
Lead said sullenly.
"Never mind about that. I'm alive and you all are too. That's
something to be thankful for."
"Indeed." The Team Lead said as he gestured to the chain that

bolted them all to the concrete wall.

"You're…"

"Slaves. Yes, Joseph, we're slaves." The Team Lead said grimly as the Elephant Man cart was rolled to him by an Assistant, the blonde young woman whose chains were a bit longer than the others.

"We're only alive because he needs us." The Team Lead said.

The assembly of Joseph's costume was essentially the same except for the prosthetic mouth and legs that helped Joseph walk and talk like the Elephant Man.

"He said you didn't need them." The Team Lead said.

Joseph felt a bit insulted that he wasn't consulted about this change, but lack of respect was what he should have anticipated.

Joseph used the considerable time in makeup to study his lines. During this time, he had started to get used to the sounds of chains and the steady sobs from actors and crew alike.

One actor was carried into the makeup room, missing the right side of his face.

The makeup team was ordered to make him presentable.

"I can't make him presentable. He's dead." The Team Lead told the guards who beat him for talking back. They ended up dumping the body into the dungeon with the corpses of the dead Assets.

A woman entered the room; she had a slight build and was probably in her mid-20's. She introduced herself as the new Stage Manager.

"I heard you fell down. Are you fit to act?" She asked Joseph in a barking tone. She looked familiar to him. She might have been the girl that watched him closely at the Freak show.

"I didn't fall. I was..."

"Obviously, that will not happen again. Here..." The Stage Manager interrupted as she dug into her pocket and produced a pill bottle. "This will get you back in line."

Joseph took the bottle and read it through his foggy vision.

"I'm not taking narcotics. I'm a recovering addict. Didn't you read my file?" Joseph felt alarmed and dirty even touching the bottle...a bit excited too. It was that little bit of excitement that worried him the most.

As four people worked on his makeup, Joseph studied the scenes from where their performance left off several days ago. At the emotional climax where The Elephant Man swore revenge on The Ripper, the new story continued with The Elephant Man escaping the London hospital at night to search Whitechapel for his mother's killer.

In the original script, Frederick Treves goes out after his patient and experiences his own storyline as his searches the Twelve Bells for his patient, ultimately finding himself confronting a freak, The Lizard Man, that had worked with Merrick at the side show and forcing him to take him to Merrick's hiding place.

"Is the Twelve Bells still operating?" He asked the Team Lead. "No. The Master shut it down. The only place left to get a drink is the hotel. The Glass Paris is only for The Master and his personal guard." The Team Lead said.

"The Twelve Bells had a troupe of forty actors. Where did they go?" Joseph asked, already knowing the answer.
"Call the guards over." Joseph motioned to an assistant who pretended that she didn't understand. "Call them." Joseph insisted.
When the Guards approached, Joseph showed them the script.
"We need Eddie, The Lizard Man and the entire troupe that made up the Twelve Bells to do this scene. We also need the makeup team to be able to move around at will to do their work, not chained to the wall." Joseph waved the pages in front of the Guards.
"You are in no position to demand anything." A Guard said.
"Oh yes I am. The Master wants these scenes. We must do them as written. Go tell him." With that, Joseph waved away the makeup crew that was scarcely half-finished.

"I'm not going to act if we can't be faithful to the material. Go tell him that."

"He'll order me to shoot you if you said something like that." The Guard said, grinning.

"You saw what happened to the Guards that beat me up?" Joseph said, knowing that the Guards threatening him now realized that he was protected, kind of like Gaslight's version of a MADE MAN. They knew he was untouchable.

"You'll wish he ordered me to shoot you. I think you'll be begging for it after we're through with you." The Guard said, bluffing clumsily.

"Go tell him what I said and stop embarrassing yourself." Joseph turned away from the Guards who glanced at each other, unsure what to do. Finally, they left, presumably to deliver the message.

"I hope you know what you're doing, Joseph?" The Team Lead said, his voice shaking with fear.

"There's a tribe in Africa that confronts prides of hungry lions consuming their kill without carrying a single weapon. They have the nerve to stand up together. The lions see that, don't know what to do and they run away, leaving their carcass. The tribe just goes up and grabs it and takes it home."

"How long does that ruse last?"

"As long as they stand together." Joseph said with satisfaction.

"Are you saying you're not afraid of lions?" The Team Lead asked.

"Not while I'm stealing their dinner. Not while we're standing together. We are standing together, aren't we?" Joseph asked with a smirk as he produced a flask from his pocket and passed it around.

The Team Lead took a drink, smiling. He realized that if anyone could save them, it was Joseph. The feeling of doom evaporated and tears began to drop from his eyes with the realization that he stood a good chance of seeing home again.

An hour later, four of The Master's Guards burst through the double doors. The makeup team paused, realizing that this was the first time they saw the guards carrying pistols (similar to Rafanovic's) in crude belt holsters. It was well known that there were no weapons on the island. Joseph wondered where they had come from.
He wondered if they were about to be beta tested on him.

"The Master says that your demands will be met. Be ready in three hours." The Bald Guard commanded. The guards turned and left.
"Good Job." The Team Lead said with relief as he fell against the wall, his legs turning into rubber.
"Guess we should continue the makeup?" Joseph mentioned casually.
"Guess so." The Team Lead grabbed the next appliance for Joseph's face and took a deep breath.

"Take another swig and you'll feel better." Joseph said, pointing to the flask.

The Team Lead indeed took two more swigs. A warm feeling swept over him and his focus came back.

Down in the stage, the Twelve Bells was being forcefully repopulated with actors that had been repurposed as slaves for the Gaslight's new power class of "collaborators".

The whole thing was a rushed job, but it brought some actors to tears to be on their stage again.

The sets with finished interiors had been turned into apartments for those loyal to the master. It was like their own little fiefdoms, complete with servants culled from people who were fellow audience members just a week prior. The implied promise was that, with their loyalty, those on The Master's side would enjoy their status well past the end of the season. They would go on and on, drunk with power they never had in real life. Even the power to take a life.

As the last member of the creative team still on the island, The Concierge was ordered to direct the new scenes. Joseph considered this one of the few decisions by The Master that made sense, considering The Concierge was a playwright in his own right.

The Concierge met with Joseph in the green room and they hugged briefly. His hand had been properly bandaged in the clinic. The Concierge marveled at how perfect Joseph's makeup and costume were.

"Seeing you gives me chills, Joseph." The Concierge said. "What's going on out there?"

"Crowds are gathering. The Twelve Bells is an activated space again." The Concierge said with relief.

"Let's activate this whole popcorn stand, what do you say?" Joseph said in a tone that The Concierge found funny and chilling at once.

"You want to share your plan? It seems like you have one."

"Just watch me and follow my lead." Joseph said with finality.

"I'm ready to start, are you?"

"Yes, Joseph. Ready as I'll ever be." The Concierge clutched the pages of the new scenes.

"Alright. Let's do this." With that, Joseph was escorted to a golf cart that would transport him to the Twelve Bells.

At the doorway, Joseph began his mental transformation to the elephant man just before the audience could see him. By all definition, it was seamless. After all that had happened, he was owning the role again.

With the cameraman following him and his image projected a

hundred-yard-wide image on the roof; the audience could see him across the entirety of Gaslight. Cheers, the like that you would only hear in stadium rock concerts reverberated across the stage.

A space opened up as people made way for him to reach his cart. As the cheering continued, Joseph waved to them. One of the Guards helped Joseph to his seat and they drove to the front of the Twelve Bells. As Joseph exited the golf cart, a spotlight fell on him. He turned back to the audience and waved at them again, inciting another wave of cheers before turning back to the Twelve Bells and taking his place, a spot marked with a blue "X" just ahead of the front door to the pub.

A second spotlight fell on another cart carrying The Master, standing like Victorian Julius Caesar on a chariot. He didn't wave and the crowd didn't cheer him. What he wanted from them, Joseph realized, was to be feared. Judging by their reactions, his wish had come true. They were intimidated to silence. Fear was, after all, his most valuable currency.

The Master was escorted through the crowd in the garb of a gentleman that could be a doctor or an aristocrat. He entered the Twelve Bells without so much as glancing at Joseph.

Joseph wheeled around fighting the weight of the makeup to get a good look at the audience around him. There was a sense of palpable relief from them now that The Master had entered the Twelve Bells. Members of the audience reached out to touch him. This contact was usually brief and the guards would quickly swat them away, seemingly resentful of the love displayed from the audience. Joseph finally rested at the blue "X" and waited, his body shivering with anticipation. He heard a whistle and his eyes followed the sound. This was The Concierge's signal indicating he was about to start. Joseph gave him a thumbs up. With that, the scene began.

RESTART

"All I had!" Joseph projected through the stage. His voice came back as an echo through the silent audience.

"...was her! My mother!"

Joseph turned and faced a random audience member, a middle-aged man who shivered as their eyes met. Joseph grabbed the man by the collar accusingly.

"You saw it. You saw what he did!" He paused to take a strained breath. Unseen by Joseph were images of the murder projected on the ceiling of Gaslight, hundreds of feet above for the benefit of those who had forgotten the bloodbath of that scene. He could hear the crowd reaction and knew what they were seeing.

"She was within reach! As poor as I am, I could've taken care of her. Brought her off the streets. I missed saving her by one day? How is that possible?" Joseph accented his soliloquy with tears that descended into sobs. A woman in the audience close to Joseph reached out and hugged him. He didn't resist, embracing her in return.

"You have always been my friends." He broke away from the woman to address the crowd.

"I was filled with hope and inspiration once. Now I am bitterness and revenge made into flesh." Joseph felt the words of The

Playwright come to life inside him.

He entered the Twelve Bells, rendering his scene viewable only by
the projection on the roof. Only a tiny percentage of the audience
were allowed inside the pub and only because they had won the
lottery drawing to be there.

"Where are you. The CUR that calls himself the Ripper in the dark.
What name do you give yourself in the light? I will give you a
new name with my blade."
Joseph unsheathed his knife, a four-inch steel blade with a bone
handle. He re-sheathed it and glanced around the room, with fierce
concentration. A shark looking for a fish.

The bar patrons turned to stare at the Elephant Man.
"Hey, that freak can't drink here!" The Butcher (who just had
been freed from slavery) delivered his line with exquisite
callousness. Joseph quickly produced two coins in his left hand
and clinked them together.

"If the freak wants a drink and can pay." The Bartender said to the
Butcher. "Mind you bid'ness." The Bartender admonished the
crowd with a mad-dog glare. Joseph nodded and approached the
bar.

"Pint please." He said softly and handed over his coins. In a moment, the barkeep returned with a foamy beer.

"I think your friend is in the den." The Bartender motioned to a cave-like room adjacent to the main hall.

There, he could see that someone *was* waiting for him.

"I'll help you with that beer, mate." Joseph recognized that voice as the Lizard Man.

The cameraman followed them to the den.

"Hi Joe. Good as hell to see you again. Sorry about the circumstances." The Lizard Man greeted the Elephant Man with a salute only known to workers at the freak show. Three fingers over the eyes. A symbol of their life in the shadows. Joseph returned the salute with his left hand.

"Me too." Joseph said as a coughing fit overtook his speech.

"You're not doing that well…are you?" The Lizard Man asked, sensing a budding case of pneumonia.

"Doctor says I'm dying slow. That's why there can be no delay. I have to find this Ripper while I still have my strength."

"Joseph. Let the coppers handle it."

"Coppers don't care about a freak and his tart mother. What did you find out?" As Joseph spoke, his face bore how he had changed. Gone was the victim, the meek and scared freak. In his place was someone determined, focused and without a care of the opinions of others. The Lizard Man was afraid of Merrick for the first time.

"This Ripper. He comes here. Some say he was a surgeon in his previous life. He has plenty of money."
"I don't want revenge on the wrong man. How do you know?" Joseph said, scanning the room.

"His first victim. Daisy Nottingham. The whore's bairn was hiding in the closet watching the whole grisly nightmare. The kid came to me with the account. Nearly fainted when the man walked into the Twelve Bells." The Lizard Man said. "He's like a ghost, Joe. He seems to only come out to drink and kill. The child drew this picture of him." The Lizard Man handed Joseph a crude but effective child's rendition of The Ripper, complete with the top Hat and the cane. The effect of the drawing wasn't lost on the audience outside as Joseph heard audible gasps from the massive crowd.

"What will you do with your mother's body? Will you bury her?" Joseph thought about it for a moment, then looked down at his one good hand.
"What can I do for her now? He stripped her flesh so clean there's nothing but a mound of cartilage in a dress."
Another wave of sounds from outside, this time, nervous laughter at Joseph's line delivery.

"No sir, revenge is the only service she deserves." Joseph said with finality.

"I have to go, Joseph. Do you need help getting back to the hospital?"

"I'll just finish my beer before I go."

"Alright friend." The Lizard Man clasped Joseph's shoulder as he left.

As the door opened, the cameraman stayed with Joseph. A few desperate audience members snuck past the Guards and made a beeline to Joseph's booth. They were jittery and unsure of how to start the conversation. Joseph was unsure what rules The Master was enforcing these days, but if these audience members didn't address him in character, he would simply ignore them. He might ignore them anyway.

"We saw you at the freak show." A middle-aged woman blurted out awkwardly.

"Good for you. If you're going to stare at me that way, at least get me another draft." Joseph turned his gaze toward to woman and her group of housefrau friends. She seemed to recoil as his eyes met hers.

One of the audience members, a timid man in his early twenties with a shock top of red hair was quickly overwhelmed by the gravity of Joseph's eyes and retreated to the other side of the room.

"Go get me a beer, fucker." He heard the gasps from the audience outside before the woman reacted.

"I'll get that beer for you." The woman promised, digging in her pocket for a coin as Joseph turned his attention to finishing his beer he already had.

After taking a sip, he glared at the woman's remaining friends staring at him dumbstruck.

"Well, sit down before you fall down." Joseph said in a surly voice.

Again from outside a reaction that permeated through the walls. The laughter of thousands.

Joseph put his empty glass down and brought his right arm up to the table letting it fall with a THUMP.

"You want a little show?" Joseph said to the housefraus as he started upwrapping his severely malformed arm. He could see the women grow progressively more terrified as the skin began to appear and the alien-like appendage was visible with its flipper-like appearance and mottled skin.

"Look at it. That's what you wanted…isn't it

"Want to shake my hand?" Joseph thrust the flipper at them. This was the first time that Joseph saw one of them crying with revulsion.

"Here's your beer." The woman slid the beer to Joseph and pulled her friends from the booth in a panic.

As they left, uproarious applause shook The Twelve Bells. This was not what anyone had expected. This was a man filled with rage. This was a man who had had enough of the whole fucking world and refused to be a victim of it anymore. Joseph felt his character do something other than inspire disgust and pity. The Playwright had charted a new character arc. It was the badness inside the Elephant Man that was finally emerging. It was badness that probably existed somewhere inside the real man after being the victim for his whole life. It was the badness that the Merrick deserved to feel and Joseph knew it.

Moment by moment, Joseph felt the acting and on the heels of that, felt Gaslight retake him through some kind of powerful magnetic force drawing him to an unknowable black hole. Did the Master know it would have this kind of effect on him? Certainly he didn't know that of himself. Everything before now seemed to be a false start. The real scenes had, Joseph realized, truly began.

Joseph was alone with the cameraman. He started on the beer and was surprised at how good it was.
"About halfway through the pint, a dark theme started to play over the loudspeakers in the bar. All of the actors in the bar froze where they were. Time had stopped and whatever Joseph was about to see would be witnessed by he alone.

At first Joseph thought it was a boiler starting to overheat until he realized that it was a musical score. The use of music or sound effects were completely forbidden by the Playwright, but The Playwright wasn't here. From Dominguez's account, The Playwright might be at the bottom of the ocean with the rest of the creative team, brined inside a jet plane at the bottom of the sea.

Then it finally happened. With a flash of red light a figure strode through the bar like a demon just escaped from a hell dimension, seeming to float two feel above the floor, The Ripper looked just like the child's drawing with the cloak and the stovepipe hat complete with the bag of surgical tools carried in his left hand. "Joseph Merrick…" The Ripper's voice hissed over the speaker system. The Ripper's mouth made no attempt to lip-sync to the dialogue, making the effect ever more haunting and surreal. At this, Joseph stood and fearlessly approached the Ripper.

"You should thank me. I destroyed the womb that created you." The Ripper hissed in the voice over that played across Gaslight. This had no effect on Joseph who stood in mute rage. "Don't you want to thank me?" The Ripper continued as he turned to face Joseph, his eyes glowing from the firelight.

"Come closer." Joseph drew his blade with a sharp CHINGGG sound.
"That would be too easy. I want to see you run to catch me before I find another womb to add to my collection." The Ripper's voice over declared as he looked down on The Elephant Man.

Joseph lunged at the Ripper. Though he had read the script, he had no idea how this was supposed to work. What would happen when he actually reached The Master with his knife?

As he stabbed at The Ripper, a mist shot downward from the ceiling. He stabbed into nothing. The Ripper had vanished. In addition, the actors in the Twelve Bells started to move again. Going about their drinking and carousing like nothing had happened.

The dark cackle from The Ripper filled the whole of Gaslight as the camera stayed on Joseph's face. The audience burst into spontaneous applause as the cameraman's lights cut out. Everyone, including Joseph, froze, leaving the few audience members allowed to watch the scene in person that much easier to spot and remove to the outside. When the Twelve Bells interior was out of sight of the audience, The Concierge waved his hands, indicating that they could move and talk freely. No one from the audience could see them.

A burst of applause from the actors was directed at Joseph. Some of the actors approached him for a hug or to shake his hand, one or two of them kissed his hand as if he was the Pope.

"You have no idea what you rescued me from. Thank you. Thank you." The Barmaid said between sobs. The Butcher told Joseph that he had been "given" to a young couple of Valor loyalists as a slave. They seemed to take great pleasure in beating him for the slightest infraction. He showed Joseph welt marks on his stomach where he had been flogged.

"Who are these people?" Joseph asked, feeling a burning in the dark places in his mind.

"They're just rich, horrible people. Their father owns a company that makes drills or something." The Butcher explained.

"How many of you were "given" to other actors as slaves?" Joseph asked the room. It was one thing for an ignorant audience member to buy into this crime, but for an actor to betray another actor in this manner. It was unthinkable.

About a third of the hands went up. Joseph was disgusted.

"We'll deal with them when this is all over. Until then, keep your head down and keep your parts going. The more you do to engage the audience, the more indispensable you'll be. Be actors that they can't afford to lose. OK?"

"You are the actor we can't afford to lose, Joseph!" One of the actors screamed from the dark corner of the room. Joseph didn't react to this and made his way toward The Concierge to discuss the next scene. The trek took quite a while as the performers fell over each other just to touch him.

COLD SWEAT

Tessa and The Tread Setter watched the scene from a small monitor hacked into the A/V transponder. The image of Valor as The Ripper had visibly unnerved zir. The Tread Setter turned away from the monitor, shaking.

"What's wrong?" Tessa put her hand on Treads shoulder. She couldn't see that zie was crying.

"I loved him." The Tread Setter said sharing a rare confidence with Tessa.

"It's hard to break free from someone that intoxicates you that way. I did it, but it was hard. I had to leave a part of me with him. Part of me that I'll never get back." Tessa watched The Tread Setter's stony visage crack and wondered if she should hug zir, but decided to wait for Tread to initiate it. Zie never did.

In the middle of the night, Tread woke in a cold sweat. Zie couldn't sit by and wait for the help that the reporter had promised. The only way to contact someone directly would be through the telegraph office, the most secure room in the entirety of Gaslight. The Master ordered it closed and guarded around the clock. Zie made a plan to penetrate the impenetrable.

The emergency stairwell had collapsed into rubble half-way down. A purposeful demolition ordered by The Master. There was another way down that The Tread Setter knew about, but zie had no idea if that one was sealed off as well or, even worse, booby-trapped like one of those tunnels during the Viet-Nam War.

This was an access tunnel, demanded by electricians to reach critical junction spots as the tangle of power cables came to a central hub. This access tunnel was not included in most of the records and was difficult to find if you didn't know where to look for the entrance. Tread had used it last when zie was asked to spy on Joseph when he first arrived. The time when Tread had snuck into the freak show to watch him sleep.

With any luck, the tunnel would still be intact and unspoiled. With any luck, no one would see zir on the descent. Tread gathered a bug-out bag packed with survival gear and headed to the entrance to the tunnel. When zie got there, there was already someone waiting for zir.

"I downloaded the blueprints before I got here." Dominguez smiled, revealing a large map of the Gaslight superstructure.

"What are you doing here?" Tread asked, puzzled.

"I thought I'd poke around. Maybe you know how to get this hatch open?" Dominguez clumsily pulled at the access hatch. The door didn't budge.

The Tread Setter flipped three buttons around the porthole-shaped entrance and the hatch slid open revealing a channel bored into the darkness.

"After you." Tread gestured to the entrance.

DRY

Joseph was led into a closet sized room where a couch waited for him. With his makeup finally removed, he was too exhausted to do anything but collapse after the full day of acting for survival.

He was grateful to see all of them, but he felt squeezed dry. Beyond exhausted. Within seconds of lying on the couch, he was asleep.

"Call time is zero-six-hundred hours for makeup." The brash guard said before leaving Joseph alone.

As Joseph drifted to sleep, he thought of The Master, slumbering in the King's suite in the Tower of London. Sleeping in the horsehair mattress reserved for the ultra-rich guests.

By contrast, he was in a janitor's lounge and would probably wake up with a sore neck. Still, he felt that, of the two of them, he was the luckier. The question that popped in his head as his brain finally relaxed was "Will I ever be this sad and happy at the same time again?" With that, he went to sleep and didn't dream.

PERPETUAL NIGHT

A new day broke in Gaslight, but the moon was still high in the sky. During the night, The Master had decided that the remainder of Gaslight would be experienced as perpetual night.

The Concierge made a general call for actors and crew for a morning pre-show meeting to be held at the cathedral. He put out a call for the hotel workers as well, but only managed to get a small delegation of them to appear.

The Concierge took to the pulpit and scanned the remains of the Gaslight team, a good portion of which were surely spies for The Master. In addition to this, six brutish guards sent by The Master lined the back of the church.

"Good morning, thank you for being here on short notice." The Concierge said in a bright tone that attempted to make the best out of the situation.

"I just wanted to start by acknowledging the makeup team and all of their hard work." The Concierge gestured to the makeup team sitting in the front row. Applause broke out from the pews as the team stood and raised their hands, revealing the red welts on their wrists, injuries created by the manacles that were recently removed.

"Thank you also to the tradespersons who came. The construction workers, the electricians, the hotel workers. We are all in this situation together." The Concierge glanced toward The Master's thugs guarding the exits of the cathedral and his face darkened. "You people that are putting the shackles on us, enslaving us, preventing us from leaving the island. You were customers before this pirate took over our beautiful production. Just because there is no law on this island doesn't mean there will be no consequences!" As The Concierge said this, the guards glanced at each other. The meanest of them, a bald fat man that owned a chain of car dealerships in the outside world, pulled out his knight stick and started toward the podium.

"OK asshole!" The bald guard's eyes glowed with rage as he made his way down the center aisle, finally facing the unflinching Concierge at the pulpit.

"You got a big mouth." The bald thug raised his baton to strike The Concierge, all the time unaware of the construction worker approaching him from behind, holding something in his thick glove.

A hand covered the bald thug's face. Surprised, the thug shook the hand away, unaware that the man, a concrete worker, had just covered his face in lye. He raised his knight stick again and the pain hit. A chemical burn that was immediate triggering pain that increased exponentially by the second. His screams were the rare sound that only happened in instances of extreme pain, the kind you hear if you witnessed someone trapped in a burning car as their skin popped open like an overlooked hot dog.

The other thugs abandoned their comrade and tried to escape. The actors that met them at the door revealed their hidden sticks, homemade shanks and their bare fists. By the time they had the Guards on their knees, the actors had these men surrounded. Having already disarmed them, the thugs became who they really were. They begged for their lives, some started to cry. One Guard defecated on himself.

The screams from the bald thug had ceased. The man's face was burned off and though he was technically still alive it was only a matter of moments before his scarred airway fused together, suffocating him.

The Team Lead approached the Guard that had shit himself and displayed the beet red injuries on his wrists. .

"What should we do with them?" The Concierge asked coldly.

"Do we have those manacles handy?" The Team Lead pushed his injured wrists against the thug's face. "Hamburger. That's what they turn your wrists into. Hamburger."

The Guards were led away by a group of women, all barmaids from the Twelve Bells, to a room where they would stay until the end. Shackled, their skin infected and some suffering with sepsis before they were done.

Joseph entered the room in full costume and makeup just as the Guards were marched away to detainment. He spat on them with disgust as if they were a horde of roaches.

"This is the best that The Master can do? If you want to see character, look for those who said "NO", who refused to cooperate. Those are the ones with real strength. Those people are US!" Joseph paused for a moment and was surprised to hear applause coming from the pews.

"Keep the plan close to your chest. Good luck today people and remember the tears shed by those that you feared only this morning. You'll be seeing a lot more of that kind of Capitulation. Their bravery is built on a house of cards and they are fresh out of aces." Joseph raised his left hand and made a fist. Cheers broke out again. The new day was about to begin. The *plan* was under way.

TRINKA

In sixth grade science class, Trinka finished assembling an electric
drone for zir final project. Zie wrapped copper coil around the
rotating arms of the motor then positioned a tiny microphone near
the landing gear. Trinka sat back and smile, knowing that zie
would get an "A" for this assignment. The teacher had even
discussed the possibility of Trinka patenting some of zir
assignments. The solar well pump that zie created with ten dollars
in supplies was a masterpiece if the teacher had ever seen one. In
science, none of the students had ever come close to Trinka's
inventions.

Zie stepped outside the classroom into the courtyard, holding the
drone above zir head.

Trinka smiled as the propeller blades sprang to life.

"Ishkatay!" Zie screamed, and the drone shot up into the sky.
Ishkatay, the name of zir Jack Russell terrier. Sometimes zir only
friend. Since Ishtakay died, Trinka immortalized zir name inside
zir inventions. In that way, zir friend was still with zir in these
moments of triumph.

Trinka spent zir lunch period following Jason, a boy that zie liked
in English class. In the sixth grade, Jason was the tallest boy, with
deep green eyes that made zir weak when zie looked into them in
passing. Trinka felt a burning whenever zie followed him. Zie

wanted him alone, in zir bedroom where zie would straddle his huge frame and kiss his full lips for hours. The thought gave Trinka an erection and made zir wet at the same time.

When Trinka came out as genderqueer, there were protests from parents about zir choice to use the boys' bathroom. It got so heated that the Vice-Principal of the school was assigned to escort zir to and from class after a parent attacked zir, smashing a grapefruit in Trinka's face. Disturbing hate mail was sent to Trinka's home, eventually causing zir family to call the FBI. Months passed and things seemed to calm down until Trinka started to like Jason.

One day, zie gathered the courage to talk to Jason. It was after school and they were both there to attend the basketball game. When he went into the boys bathroom, Trinka followed him, hoping to talk with him on the way out, maybe get his phone number. Trinka wondered if zie should act more feminine to attract him. With zir army surplus clothes and zir crew cut hair, zie realized that it would be a stretch.

As zie entered the bathroom, zie saw Jason huddled in a corner, shaking with fear.

"Jason, what's wrong?" Trinka asked, just as the bathroom door slammed shut.

Hugging the walls were several parents. Trinka felt zir body lift up in the air as if it were propelled by a spring. The sensation of tugging and the sound of ripping fabric was followed by a feeling of cold below the waist.

"Panties. This freak has panties on." A mother's voice observed angrily.

Then those were gone too, ripped off of zir followed by gasps from the parents.

"Gawd damn, look at that mess!" One of the dads exclaimed, face to face with dual genitalia.

"Get the camera." One of the moms yelled.

All the while, Trinka watched Jason with his back turned. Zie could tell that he was crying.

A FLASH FOLLOWED BY ANOTHER!

"Freak!" The dad holding Trinka suspended in the air brutally hurled zir against one of the stalls. The last thing that Trinka remembered was the feet shuffling out of the bathroom.

"Trinka's hurt." Jason moaned as he was dragged out.

Later that day, the photographs of Trinka's sexual organs were broadcasted to every parent at the school. After being released, from the hospital, zie never went back to junior high, zir parents opting to home school.

They saw something change in their child after that incident. Even after the parents were charged and convicted, zie never returned to zir old self. Each of the parents in the bathroom that day would have a visit from Trinka over the years.

Five years after the incident, Zie finally did kiss Jason's full lips as his slept. When he woke, he found both of his parents strangled in their beds. Photos of their genitals tacked to the head of their bed with the spray painted message on the wall.

"Freaks"

On that night, Trinka ran away to start a new life, first as a circus freak and in due course, The Tread Setter.

THE TREAD SETTER AND THE TELEGRAPH ROOM

The night before, while Joseph was sleeping in the janitor's office, the Tread Setter broke into the hotel, navigating a small crawlspace just under the floor.

Dominguez tried to follow Tread until he reached a point in the crawlspace that wouldn't accommodate his girthy frame.

"I can't go any further." Dominguez whisper-yelled to Tread.

"Stay right there, OK?" Tread ordered Dominguez. There was certainly no way that he was going forward.

"OK."

Tread shuffled ahead, the dim lantern around zir neck throwing shadows in the honeycomb like understructure.

"Hey, Tread!" Dominguez called to zir.

The Tread Setter turned back, thinking that something was wrong. Instead, zie saw a camera pointed at zir and heard a dull "click" of the shutter. Dominguez smiled, knowing he had a great shot. Tread thought of a few ways zie would cause the reporter pain when they got back to the surface.

"Good luck." He whispered. Tread ignored him, kept going.

On zir hands and knees, Tread estimated that the hotel lobby was probably just above. There was an access panel that zie gently lifted and there it was.

The telegraph office was guarded by a single thug armed with one of those crude handmade pistols that probably didn't fire.

The telegraph handsets sat dormant.

Tread shuffled forward and emerged inside the telegraph room. On the operator's desk, desperate notes paper clipped with the twenty dollar fee, hoping that someone would eventually come back to send the messages.

Crawling low on the floor, The Tread Setter grabbed the cord leading to a telegraph handset. Zie slowly reached up, watching the back of the guard's head through the window. What zie couldn't see was that the handset shifted forward as zie moved the cord. It fell, smacking hard against The Tread Setter's chest and landing with a clatter.

A shooting pain went through Tread's chest as the unexpectedly heavy handset left a purple impact mark on zir sternum. Overriding this was the fear of discovery by the Guard outside who turned to investigate the noise.

He couldn't see the motionless Tread Setter. He scanned the telegraph room like a snake then finally turned back to face the drunk patrons at the hotel bar.

Sighing with relief, Tread grabbed a pair of electrician's pliers and cut the red power line and the black ground wire as zie took a tablet-like object from zir backpack.

Tread attached the wiring to the portable battery unit and flipped a switch to initiate the power up sequence on the telegraph system. In a few seconds, zie could hear the wires ignite with a steady electrical hum.

Zie straddled the control panel and cautiously pushed the Morse handset, making one long BEEEEP.

Zie nodded at this with satisfaction.

In theory, all that was required was a simple SOS call sent over the shortwave. Though the message would be heard across the globe, it meant little if no one was listening.

The Tread Setter began transmitting the SOS in earnest; zie cradled the handset and hoped that none of The Master's goons were monitoring outgoing signals.

Zie saw a figure pass the frosted windows of the telegraph booth. A tall muscular figure leaned in. It was a different Guard this time. He cupped his eyes against the window, prompting Tread to stop zir transmission. He stared for a while, seeming to scan every inch of the telegraph booth. Finally, he lost interest and vanished from Tread's limited field of view. Zie held zir breath as long as possible then gasped. When The Tread Setter was sure no one was watching, the distress call began again.

MISSING TIME

The Tread Setter woke to a searing pain at zir shoulders and wrists.
Zie blinked quickly, trying to clear the mucus from zir eyes.
"Hello darling." The Master said in a cooing voice. He was
dressed as the Ripper, ready to start his day in a world with no
daylight.
"That was very naughty what you did down in the telegraph office.
You know what this project means to me."
Zie tried to follow The Master as he circled zir, feeling dizzy and
drugged.
"You shared my bed all year. Planned every part of this takeover.
This is blood on your hands too."
"It was a mistake…it was a mistake to believe you when you
promised you'd have mercy on the workers. It was a mistake to
listen to you!" Tread groaned out through the fog of the
medication.
"You did once. You believed in me completely. Now you try to
bring in the outside world into the heaven I created here on Earth."
The Master tsked at the Tread Setter and pressed a button,
lowering zir to the ground in a numb heap.
"I won't allow you to help Joseph again. You have to realize that
he wants this actor's paradise just as much as I do."
"You can't get inside his mind. That makes you afraid. Afraid
that he's better than you. More intense than you. More

everything…"

"No one is better than me." He leaned down to the Tread Setter and clutched zir chin in his hands, forcing zir to look into his eyes. "Just watch and I'll prove it."

As The Master said this, the dual screens of Gaslight, one for The Master (for the moment just a still image of The Ripper) and one for Joseph projected onto the wall.

Incarcerated in this room, the Tread Setter would see what everyone in Gaslight saw. Zie wondered how The Master planned to prove his superiority.

As a motorized taxi pulled up to the cathedral, the giant roof projection showed The Tread Setter hanging by zir arms.

Joseph turned to The Concierge, his eyes were the only visible sign of his panic and indignation. It was impossible to do anything else in the mask and prostheses.

The Concierge nodded at him discreetly.

"I'm on it, Joseph." He whispered. "Just stay on task. It's going to be a hard day and *they* are watching.." The Concierge gestured to a row of Guards stationed on the street. All of them watched Joseph like a wolf watches a lamb.

"You have a gift for understatement." Joseph replied, squeezing The Concierge on his shoulder. "See you on the other side of this."

"God willing." The Concierge added.

The Taxi Driver opened the rear door.

"Sir. We have to go." The Taxi Driver said in a heavy Australian drawl.

Joseph navigated into the taxi.

"Safe and sound." The Taxi Driver said, satisfied that Joseph was seated without so much as a blemish on his makeup.

"OK then." Joseph waved at the crew at the stairs of the cathedral. He felt that this might be what the lunar astronauts felt when they bid their final good-byes to the ground crew. They did the job that made the flight crew's job possible. Instead of charting an unexplored celestial object, he was set to explore the unexplored country within his mind. Without proper preparation and a lot of balls, this journey could be a one way trip.

For the opening scene at the London Hospital. Joseph was escorted to his bedroom where Eddie and the nursing staff waited for him in a cleared stage. For the moment, the audience had to wait outside.

"Good morning everyone." Joseph said, exuding more confidence than he actually possessed.

"Good morning Joseph!" Eddie and the nurses said in near unison.

"Ten minutes." A voice called out over the intercom.

"Anything we need to discuss before we get started?"

"We're just going to take your lead. I think that's what we're all doing." Eddie said.

"I don't know if that's a good thing or not." Joseph said, smiling.

Eddie nodded at one of the nurses and she brought out a fifth of whiskey and poured shots for everyone in hospital drinking glasses.

When everyone was finally served, Eddie held up his shot glass for a toast.

"To Gaslight. A wonderful idea made a dangerous idea in the hands of the mad."

He slugged his shot down and everyone followed his lead.

"Places. Everyone…places." The intercom chimed in, breaking the mood.

"Good luck." Joseph said with the best smile he could manage beneath the makeup. He gathered his props and stood by the door, waiting for the moment.

"Ready…and…ACTION" The Concierge said over the loudspeaker.

The day (in perpetual night) was underway.

THE NEW DAY TWO

Joseph stepped out of the London Hospital wearing his cape and hood. He carried a meager bag of his belongings. Dr. Treves chased after him desperately through the throng of onlookers. A cameraman followed them with a stabilizing harness to soften the movement as he tracked them through the street.

"You can't go Joseph. Your lungs can't take being out in the damp and cold. You'll die if you leave the hospital."
Joseph swung around to face the doctor with a cold expression.
"I'm dying either way, doctor." Joseph said as he leveled his cane at the doctor like a weapon. The act of aggression left Treves stunned. He silently watched as The Elephant Man vanished in the crush of unwashed masses in the Whitechapel night.

"Come back." Treves said weakly as the mass of the audience swept forward like a wave, following Joseph through the streets that lived in perpetual darkness.
In the Red Light District, Joseph looked for someone to act against to further the scene. Joseph found a target group of four in the audience that looked like they were together and brought them into his orbit. They were about to experience the most coveted interaction at Gaslight, the one-on-one with Joseph Merrick.

"My mother took me to this place when she couldn't afford a room. A secret room above the butcher shop once used to dry soup bones. Come."

Joseph grabbed the hand of the matriarch of the group. She might have been mother to the kids in their twenties, maybe an aunt. The grey haired man in the group might have been her husband and father to the kids but he looked too old. Perhaps he was their grandfather.

Joseph led them to the alley behind the butcher shop and pushed his hand through a knot in the wood. After fishing there, he pulled a hidden cord and the secret door popped open.

"Go." Joseph commanded, allowing the four audience members in with the cameraman behind them. Finally, he addressed the audience left behind in the alley, a gathering of about one hundred. "You'll keep my secret, won't you?" He asked them like a kid asking classmates to keep the clubhouse password from the teacher.

They all nodded mischievously as Joseph closed the door behind him, vanishing from their sight but still projected on the ceiling of the Gaslight stage above them.

Unseen by Joseph, The Ripper exited a posh brownstone flat and seemed to float through the dark street with his own audience following. There was a bag of tricks in his right hand. An assortment of knives that could make for quick dissection of any human of any size.

Joseph couldn't see exactly where The Ripper was headed, but he could feel him deep in his gut. For the moment, his attention was focused on his audience of four.

"My name is Joseph Merrick. Please don't be shocked when I remove my hood." The one-on-ones huddled together as if they had never seen Joseph in makeup before. It was somehow different in this place, in close proximity in a forgotten old room. They acted like they were seeing him for the first time.

He removed his hood and they audibly gasped. The brother and sister recoiled.

"Finally, I can breathe." Joseph said as he flung the hood away, unintentionally hitting the cameraman.

"Now that you know my name…what are yours?"

"I'm Katie." The woman spoke with a shivering voice. These are my two oldest kids, Randy and Lisa. This is my dad, Max."

"Pleased to meet you." Joseph extended his left hand and they each shook it briefly. "If you don't mind. We'll need to climb." Joseph opened a small broom closet and revealed a hidden spiral staircase. The family followed it up to the next floor.

The secret room was built for this scene. Though Joseph had seen it under construction, he didn't have the opportunity to do an actual rehearsal in it with all the recent turmoil. He just hoped that they actually finished the room the way it was described in the script. If they left a bunch of construction junk up there, he would have a hard time pretending that power tools existed in the Victorian era. Luckily for him, when he ascended, he had the finished set at his disposal, complete with his mother's bed that she had hidden in this place.

The room was very small and shabby, but it had a great view over the Red Light district of Whitechapel. A perfect place for Joseph to watch for hooded figures carrying suspicious looking black cases filled with sharp objects.

On the nightstand was a candle that Joseph lit with a green match. The cameraman's light dimmed as to not spoil the mood. On his mother's nightstand was a photo of a young boy, perhaps two years old. There was something a bit off about the child's face, but it could be credited to the cheap tintype photography of the day.

"That was me." Joseph said, sounding prideful of his once near normal appearance. "Every year, I got worse until she couldn't handle me anymore." Joseph paused for a moment and was able to telegraph his pain through his nearly expressionless face. "No one could blame her." He picked up another picture. One image of his mother, holding him as a baby.

"I keep telling myself that I didn't drive her into her…fallen position. In reality I knew I had." Joseph said in a voice soaked with guilt.

He gently returned the photo to the nightstand and turned back to the family who looked like deer in the headlights. He stared directly at the mother and made a surprise move to hold her hand. She took a step back and found herself against the wall, unable to escape.

"God bless you." Joseph whispered. "God bless every woman who bears a child." He let go of her hand and backed away, leaving her shivering in the arms of her father.

"The man that took my mother from me is out there. My promise to her is simple. To get revenge for what he did. When he comes back to this cross street, I will be there waiting for him."

Joseph moved to the window and studied the bustling street below him.

"Katie, come here. I want you to see." Joseph said to her. The woman remained pinned by fear against the wall.

Joseph pointed at the street below.

"My wish is being granted sooner than I thought. Look for yourself."

Curiosity nullified the fear as the family inched forward to peer down on the intersection.

There, standing at the crossroads was a figure that seemed to darken his surroundings as if the evil he carried was draining the light away. It was The Ripper staring up at them.

Katie gasped at the frightening visage of the man.

Joseph turned to the family and bowed as best he could.

"It is time. I bid you farewell. My destiny awaits on those dark streets below."

"Mr. Merrick." Katie stopped him.

"Yes?" Joseph wasn't expecting this.

"Confucius said that 'Before you embark on a journey of revenge, dig two graves." Katie touched Joseph on his chest. Right at his heart. Joseph knew the quote and was moved that an audience member has chosen such appropriate words for his situation.

"My grave is already waiting. That bastard down there doesn't need to be buried. Bless you." Joseph ran downstairs. Katie exhaled deeply and the family stayed in the secret room, watching for what came next.

THE CROSSROADS

Joseph found himself in the empty crossroads, he found himself surrounded by the sound of sharp footsteps from every direction. He thought that he saw the tail end of a cape trailing around an alleyway to the north, but it could've been anything. As he prepared to follow, a fog rolled in seemingly on cue.

He bolted forward, hoping to find the owner of that cape before the fog completely obscured his vision.

The cameraman had lost him. Joseph could see the bulbous glow of his LED light and he seemed to be moving in circle. It was a hopeless endeavor. In seconds, not even his glow was visible.

Faintly, Joseph heard the sound of what seemed like dripping water just ahead. As he drew closer, he realized that the sound wasn't water at all.

He followed it into an open doorway where he discovered a woman lying on her bed. He could only tell it was a woman because of the torn dress that hung from her dissected body. In reality, the sound was blood draining to the floor from an open vein in the woman's neck, blood pulsing out as her heart pumped. It was here that the cameraman finally found Joseph again. The audience who were able to see this on screen, gasped with terror.

The horrible thought that this woman was still alive in this condition made Joseph fight back his urge to vomit right there on the floor. He hoped that this was just a prop, but it looked far too real for that to be true. And the smell. The room was filled with the smell of death.

Upon closer inspection, the Ripper victim had her vagina removed with the precision of a laser, the wound was cauterized, indicating that The Ripper didn't want the woman to die right away, burning the walls of the cavity so that she wouldn't bleed out for a little while anyway. On top of all that, her eyelids were removed.

This was too much for the cameraman who fell to his knees, vomiting. Somehow he managed to keep the carnage in the frame.

The woman reached her hand out to Joseph. He held her hand and came closer, nearly slipping on the blood-soaked floor
"I'm afraid you're going to die soon." Joseph said in his softest voice. The woman's lidless eyes followed him. They had dried out to the point that there was a glaze forming over them.
"The end will come soon. I'll stay here with you."
Joseph continued to hold the woman's hand until her breathing became shallow and she entered death spasms, culminating in a shivering then one final breath.

Joseph's hand started to tingle. Rapidly, the shock's intensity multiplied tenfold and Joseph's snatched his hand away. It was then he saw the servos and tubes inside the realistic and terrifying animatronic. It was the make-up department's crowning achievement.

Joseph realized that the next body that he would find would probably be the real thing. Humans would take the place of the expensive and finicky animatronics if he allowed The Master to go on with his carnage. The Master, Franco Valor, The Ripper, whatever his role or title, he had to be stopped. There wasn't enough time to wait for a rescue to reach them. He had to act to get close to The Master. Close enough to slice his throat. That was the only rescue that Gaslight needed.

A sardonic laugh seemed to descend from the heavens. It was The Ripper mocking him as if from a nightmare dimension.
"Hello Mr. Merrick." The Ripper droned. "Are you enjoying the tour of hell that I made for you? I hope so." Joseph exited the killing room and the fog lifted as soon as he stepped into the alley.

"I can't say you are worthy adversary, but you are certainly entertaining. Come to The Glass Paris. I have something I'd like to share with you." The Ripper laughed and it echoed through the audience-lined streets.

As the Ripper's voice faded, another one called out his name from the dark streets. It was the Lizard Man, limping toward him. Something had happened.

"Joseph. You have to stop this insane plan of yours."

"Why would you say that?" Joseph said defiantly.

"There's forces at work here that you don't understand." He said in a guttural voice.

"He's just a man." Joseph replied defiantly.

"No…that's where you're wrong." The Lizard Man clutched at his chest and retreated as a new plume of fog rolled in.

"This man…this place…you can't change what's been set in motion! Forget revenge. Save yourself." The Lizard Man said as he finally vanished in the fog, leaving a trail of bloody footprints.

Joseph stood in the foggy street, struck by a gut feeling that he was standing at a dark crossroads. A river Rubicon of his soul that could set him on the same path as Franco Valor. Joseph's Rubicon was a place called The Glass Paris. There, The Ripper waited for him to cross.

THE SECOND MEETING AT THE GLASS PARIS

When Joseph arrived at the Glass Paris the cameraman had found him again. He saw that the bar had been closed in anticipation of the new meeting between Joseph and The Master, not The Elephant Man and The Ripper.

He saw The Master there at the center table. He already had a Black Absinthe in his hand and was sitting with someone that he assumed to be Rafonovic. As he stood at the door of the Glass Paris, he expected Rafonovic to open the front door for him, but instead the bartender had to let him in. The bartender had a ghostly pallor and avoided eye contact except for one panicked glance that made Joseph's heart skip a beat. The cameraman stopped shy of the door. This meeting was not for public consumption. Neither was the assassination planned by Joseph.

"Come and sit while he makes a drink for you." The Master waved the bartender over, not looking at him.
Joseph cautiously approached and sat down, his eyes so focused on The Master that he didn't see that Rafonovic was very much dead.

"Hello Joseph." The Master finally turned toward Joseph with his piercing and unblinking eyes.

"I suppose we could recycle your eulogy for Ravonovic." As The Master said this, Joseph turned toward Rafonovic and saw that his throat (all the way to the larynx) had been torn out. He had an almost white pallor and a facial expression that seemed to be frozen at the moment of his doom. Joseph wondered what Rafonovic did to deserve it. He probably did nothing. This body in front of his was no animatronic.

The bartender brought a glass of Absinthe to Joseph. It wasn't the usual green color or even the variant purple, it was black.

"What's this? Where's the Green Absinthe?" Joseph asked, confused, knowing that the black stuff was only consumed by two people. The Playwright and The Master.

"Why?" The Master asked sarcastically. "You think those rules matter anymore?"

"I'll have my usual if you please." Joseph said politely but firmly. The Master snapped his fingers and the bartender immediately went to work making a new drink.

"Why are we meeting? Why aren't we acting right now? Why are we burning up this time here?" Joseph asked.

"Rush, rush, rush. Is that all you know, Joseph?" The Master said with a sigh. "Don't you understand that time doesn't matter anymore in Gaslight."

"You can't keep the outside world out forever. These people have families, some of them rich and powerful. You think they won't come?" Joseph watched for any sense of concern on The Master's face. There was none.

"I have a deal for you, Joseph. I'll let you and your friends go and as much as it pains me, I'll let Tread go too."
"Bullshit."
"Just finish Act III." The Master said his smile fading. "I can't do Act III with anyone else." The Master continued, making a rare show of vulnerability.

If the scenes so far were simple arithmetic, Act III was complex calculus. Joseph sensed that The Master and he shared a common fear of it, as if they were reciting a mysterious incantation that only they could speak, summoning a demon that might be out of their control.

Joseph's drink came and he took a sip. As he did, Ravonovic's limp body slumped over and fell to the floor. Neither Joseph or The Master reacted.

"I have a better deal." Joseph broke the silence, almost frightening The Master. "I'll leave the island after we finish the scenes that we agreed we'd finish. In the mean time you won't hurt anyone else." The Master was perplexed by this reply.

"Don't flatter yourself, Joseph. You're a day trader. You can't wait to go back to New York and pick up a new addiction. The Master threw a manila folder at Joseph.

"What's that?" Joseph asked with apprehension.

"That, boy, is insurance."

Joseph opened the folder. There were three photos of The Tread Setter. Tread was hanging by her hands. Zie had been beaten. One of Tread's eyes was black and swollen shut. Joseph realized that the planned assassination would have to wait until he could get Tread to safety. He wondered what had happened to The Concierge. He had promised to "take care" of Tread.

"My former lover is very good at causing trouble. Zie'll be in a secret place until you fulfill your obligation." The Master leaned forward, tapping on the table rhythmically, glancing around the room. "You know, we will miss you when you go. I think this place won't be the same without visits from The Elephant Man."

With that, Joseph leaned in to The Master, giving him pause for a moment.

"You know what I've learned over the years?" Joseph said, his eyes distant, looking through The Master in a way that the man found unsettling.

"What?" The Master asked, trying to mask his nervousness.

"Everyone eventually has to settle their bill. Even those who thought it was all free." Joseph said, eyes drilling into Valor. The Master leaned over to Joseph and snapped his fingers at him. "You'll complete scene three. You don't have a choice." With that, The Master left, flanked by his security detail.

Someone approached him from behind and Joseph moved like lightening, holding a knife to the perceived attacker's throat. "Please, Joseph. It's me." The bartender held his hands up, pleading. Finally, Joseph realized who it was and lowered his blade, to the relief of the barkeep.

"They told me you have to report to your starting position. I'm sorry, I don't mean to rush you." The bartender said, still shaking.

"It's OK." Joseph said, looking stunned. "It'll all be over soon."

"You know, if you don't mind me saying. The Master was right." The bartender said.

"What do you mean?"

"The Glass Paris WILL miss you. You've always seemed to belong here."

"I think you"re right." Joseph said, certain he'd never see The Glass Paris again.

"And something else you were right about." The barkeep continued. "His bill will come due."

Joseph wondered what the barkeep meant by that. He put it out of his mind and went to his opening mark.

SCENE THREE

As the scene began, a shroud of fog descended over Gaslight. Joseph felt a chill run down his back as The Master began the scene by taunting Joseph over the speaker system.

"Little Jackie sees you coming FREAK...Little Jackie sees everything...Little Jackie is everywhere." The sinister voice of the Ripper sent chills through the whole of Gaslight. The fog made it impossible for Joseph to see where The Master was and what he was doing. He could only see the shadowy figures of the audience against the cobblestone streets and the hazy glow from the cameraman's LED light. Joseph took a deep breath and began by addressing the audience standing in front of him.

"It is fog like this that hides the act of a monster. How brave would the monster be once a light is shone on him and he can no longer hide in the crevasses? What does the monster feed on when there is no other sustenance? The monster...the external and internal beast feeds on fear. Once we no longer fear him, the monster will no longer be fed...and will die. Inward and outward." With that Joseph took a handheld mirror and looked directly at his own reflection. He swallowed hard and continued.

"I wasn't always able to do this." Joseph said, taking a deep inward breath. "But after the inhumanity I've seen, my visage really isn't so terrifying." Joseph turned the mirror toward the audience and approached them, causing some of them to retreat.

"Look for yourselves. Can you look and know that you are not a monster? The Ripper must not own a mirror. I will make sure to place this one in his dying hand."

Joseph sprinted through the fog, a move totally unexpected by the cameraman. In just a second or two, The Elephant Man had vanished. Joseph heard the audience applaud his performance from every direction.

Through the alleyways near the Twelve Bells, Joseph found himself in the heart of Whitechapel at an octagon-shaped place that abutted the ass end of several buildings, creating an impassible dead end. As he paused at the center of the octagon, he could see the light of the cameraman grow brighter as he searched for Joseph in the darkness.

Gaslights from the backside of the buildings ignited and grew more intense, just barely penetrating the fog. The light was just enough to reveal five shadowy figures, each of them the terrifying visage of The Ripper. This effect was further intensified by the back illumination coming from the cameraman's light, making them seem like beings from hell.

He heard the distinctive "CHING" of metal blades being unsheathed. Each of these apparitions turned a blade in his right hand. What was supposed to happen at this point in the script was a physical confrontation between the Ripper and the Elephant Man that leaves the Ripper injured. Obviously, The Master was trying his hand at rewriting.

Rewriting to bring Joseph's life and influence on the audience to an abrupt end. The accuracy of Scene III no longer seemed to matter.

It was all just a death trap, just as Joseph had expected.

The five Rippers surrounded Joseph in the fog. He could hear their labored breathing and their heavy steps.

Knowing what was about to happen, Joseph unsheathed his blade to fight back, unleashing torrential cheers from the audience of Gaslight.

The Rippers lunged at him swiping their surgical steel at him. Joseph wasn't about to wait to be cornered by five blades. He rolled on the cobblestone to avoid a direct stab.

He saw a shadow above him and thrust upward into resistance that could have only been flesh. A raw scream blasted from above him and Joseph heard a blade drop on the cobblestone just as a deeper fog descended, making it impossible to see. Joseph went to the sound and grabbed the surgical knife, giving him two weapons in which to exact vengeance.

Again the audience cheered for The Elephant Man, unaware that this fight was not choreographed. It was real and Joseph was still very much in danger. What these Ripper Knifemen didn't know was that they were the ones at a disadvantage.

Though many years had passed since Iraq when he last engaged in hand-to-hand combat, it came back to him in an instant.

Joseph almost felt sorry for the Knifemen, pressed into this battle. Shoulders split open, guts spilled out on the cobblestone, and the fog was laced with arterial spray and vibrated by the cheers of the audience.

He stood defiantly over the five Knifemen as a new camera came into range, lighting their faces. They were Guards all of them, before that they were members of the paying audience, before that they were by all appearances, normal citizens of the world.

Joseph screamed gutturally at his triumph, fully unaware of a sixth Ripper emerging from the fog, dagger in hand. The whole of Gaslight let out an audible gasp as Joseph, too deep in the aftermath of the fight, couldn't hear the attacker from behind. He turned to see the knife coming at him, knowing that he couldn't defend himself in time.

A sudden THUNK sound from behind the attacker. The would-be

killer's knife slid out of his hand. Joseph watched as the man's frozen expression of pain grew exponentially as a slicing sound was followed by six metal prongs breaking through his chest and his gut. As he turned, Joseph recognized immediately what had sliced most of his internal organs into thirds. A stair tread, the kind meant to pierce through solid rock had been weaponized.

.

As the man fell, the Tread Setter already had another tread weapon in zir hand. Standing beside zir, Dominguez took a photo of Joseph standing at the foot of the carnage.

"That'll be a good one." Dominguez noted as he slid the Rollei back in his pocket.

Joseph ran to hug Tread. He saw the burn marks from the ropes and was just glad zie was alive.

"How?" Joseph asked, wondering how zie escaped The Master's captivity.

"This fool cut me loose." Tread gestured to Dominguez.

"The Concierge asked me to take care of Tread." Dominguez said with fragile bravado.

"Don't push it, asshole!" Tread warned. "I could've got those ropes off myself."

"You were in the middle of that when I cut you down." Dominguez interrupted. As he said this, Tread beaned him with a piece of cobblestone, knocking him silent.

"Shut up!" Tread barked.

"Joseph, the scene is still active." The voice of The Concierge called over the loudspeaker.

"Bullshit. The goalpost has just been moved. The scene is over. The play is over." Joseph bellowed into the fog.

Some gasps from the audience were followed by silence as the fog was driven up and away by unseen blowing fans in the ground. For a moment, everything seemed crystalline clear as if the eyes were celebrating the ability to focus on anything. Then the image was projected on the ceiling.

The Concierge was held at knife point by The Ripper.

"The play will continue." The Ripper said to Joseph. To the audience, this looked like a strange new addition to scene III. They watched with rapt attention as Joseph's image was placed into a split screen.

"You were the one going off script!!" Joseph screamed at the projection. "What happened to the sacred words of The Playwright?"

"They went away the day you arrived." The Master said sullenly, poking the blade into The Concierge's neck just enough to draw blood.

"That's alright. I have a few script changes of my own." Joseph said darkly. The words visibly struck The Master with fear and disorientation. What did Joseph have up his sleeve?

Joseph dropped his blades and crossed his arms together. Everyone saw this on the huge projection. It was a signal. In a few seconds, the message was received. Suddenly a blast of sound. A train's whistle.

A steam train!

From a separate projector, the image of The Conductor, battered and bruised in the control box of his sacred machine filled the opposite end of the Gaslight ceiling.
"OY! Hold on to yer britches, you bastards!" The Conductor screamed as he blew the train whistle again and lurched forward.

Another projection appeared, showing the City of Stalingrad moving slowly from its dock at the station, gaining speed and pulling a huge chain behind it.

Only Joseph and The Conductor knew what was happening. Soon everyone, including The Master, understood the plan when then traced the chain all the way back to the Tower of London where the links were laced around the entirety of the building. A great gasp from across Gaslight filled the stage.

The Master's eyes said it all and the audience burst out with screams for Joseph.
"Get 'em! Get 'em!" One man shouted over the cheers.

"E-M, E-M, E-M, E-M!" One side of the crowd chanted for the Elephant Man.

An audible buildup of gasps from the audience as the slack in the chain ran out as the 4000-ton train gained speed.

Finally, it ran out and the chain made an earth-shattering "TWANGGG" sound that seemed to travel through the bodies of anyone near it. The locomotive's front wheels lifted off the track, making it resemble a rearing horse.

The force concentrated in that chain was brutal and swift. The Tower of London was no match for it. Constructed with a brick facade, the steel beams underneath buckled as the giant chain cut through it like butter. The level above the cut seemed to hover mid-air for a moment before crashing down across the stage, taking The Master's repaired control station along with it.

Applause turned to screams as the audience ran for their lives. The video projection flickered and stabilized, revealing the damage to the stage. Joseph, Tread and Tessa came out of fog of dust looking like warring angels.

Dominguez was covered in dust, but still managed to capture a photograph of this moment that would later go on to be iconic. Joseph and Tread standing with the dead attackers at his feet and the burning remains of the Tower of London in the distance. Joseph didn't notice Dominguez. His mind was focused on finding The Concierge in that rubble.

At the site of the ruins, they saw the bloody footprints of The Master leading to the Twelve Bells. Strewn all around them was the console used to run the multitude of systems on the stage. Everything, air supply included, ran on that system and without it, the automated systems that ran Gaslight would fail in a few hours. That was a worry for later as the problems now were a second-by-second affair.

"Joseph." The Concierge's weak voice called out for him from beneath a pile of broken drywall. Joseph, Tread and Tessa dug down until they saw his face beneath the debris.
Digging further, it was obvious that his leg was broken.

"Don't waste time with me, Joseph. Go get the bastard!" The Concierge commanded. "This place has two hours before the air is cut off along with the lights. It won't be possible to evacuate everyone in the dark."

"I'll be back for you." Joseph said, realizing that The Concierge was right. The Master had to be stopped NOW.

"Little Jackie lives." The Ripper raged over the sputtering speaker system. "No freak can stay Little Jackie's hand."

"Joseph, look!" Treat called to Joseph, pointing at the ceiling.

The camera mounted to the cab of the train was lifted from its placement. The Master had it in his hand, filming himself with a sardonic grin.

"Can you follow the script now, freak? Can you complete the story?" The Master said as he turned the camera around, revealing The Conductor lying on the steel floor of the control room, his coat and hair in flames from the nearby firebox, another friend lost.

Joseph knew that the next scene was a final battle that was set on the moving train. A battle that the Ripper was supposed to win. That was before things changed and the goalpost was moved.

The cameraman moved into Joseph's face and the audience seemed to regain their previous form, suspending disbelief even after everything they had seen. "Could this all be part of the act?" They thought, desperately trying to explain away the real danger that they all faced now.

There was no more discussion to be had. Joseph commandeered a passing taxi. He didn't need to tell the driver what to do. The Taxi Driver, snapped his whip and the horse drawn Taxi started off after the train.

Soon, they saw it. The City of Stalingrad, its throttle wide open with The Ripper riding on the roof, taunting Joseph to join him. The taxi driver drove the horse hard, running alongside the train, machine and animal running at maximum.

"You gotta jump now!" The Taxi Driver screamed at Joseph. He knew his horse and how far he could push her. The point of exhaustion was coming up fast and after that, the poor beast couldn't keep pace with the steam engine that was gaining speed.

Joseph positioned himself like a spring, ready to pounce. He leapt as hard as he could, then slipped, falling to the cattle guard at the front of the train.

Hanging on for his life, The Ripper laughed at Joseph's weakness. "Is that the best you can do?!" He screamed through the locomotive's raging steam.

Joseph looked up at him as he gained his foothold on the oily steel. As he climbed up to the train lantern, he planted his feet on the tiny crewman's walkway around the train's parameter. As he did, The Ripper retreated out of sight. At that moment, everything went dark.

THE TUNNEL

Inside the tunnel, there was no light but the train's headlamp and the LED on a drone camera that burst out of a compartment by Joseph's foot. It hovered just ahead of the moving train, feeding a signal to the audience.

Joseph didn't care about that. He only cared about the light illuminating his target, The Master.

Joseph climbed atop the train and felt the ceiling of the tunnel scrape against his head. The Master could've smashed his fingers, but he didn't. If he did that he couldn't finish the scene properly. He would be an actor alone with a climactic scene to complete. For The Master, there was nothing worse, even now.

"Aren't you going to kill me, freak?" The Ripper's bellowing voice penetrated the din of the train.

Joseph hesitated, pulling in the strength from the character he was playing. He needed The Elephant Man. Perhaps he had always needed him. That barrier between actor and character had been breached for him, perhaps for the last time.

"You lose your nerve, freak?" The Ripper's words went through him like radioactive waves.

The Ripper felt a chill as he watched Joseph's eyes. They were different now. Predatory with his complete immersion into madness. Whatever he had unleashed in him, The Master knew, was out of his control now. Out of anyone's control.

Joseph lunged at The Ripper, catching his cape as the drone camera whizzed around him. The Ripper countered with a slash with his surgical blade.
At first, Joseph felt nothing except coldness, then hot thick fluid poured into his eyes. He'd been cut across the forehead. The deepest part of the cut had engraved a channel into his skull.
The Ripper pointed at the wound and laughed, amused at the deep gouge in Joseph's head.

Rather unexpectedly, Joseph started to laugh too. It was that insanity that frightened The Master. Joseph didn't lunge, but moved slowly, forcing The Master to take a step back, then another.

The next line was supposed to be The Elephant Man's. Joseph remained silent, approaching The Ripper with those eyes. Those frightening eyes.

There was an awkward pause as The Master broke character.
"Say your fucking line!"
But no line came. Just the plodding forward motion of a predator fixed upon his prey.

The train lurched forward, sending Joseph hurtling forward like a black leopard through the smoke.

Joseph landed at The Ripper's feet. The Master realized that the train had just been seized by the simulation cradle. The Elephant Man at his feet didn't care about any of that as he sliced through The Ripper's Achilles tendon, rendering the man lame on the right side.

The Master screamed and drove his knife down as hard as he could between Joseph's ribs. A sudden loud sucking sound wasn't the train, but Joseph's left lung collapsing.

The pain was agonizing and immediate. A burst of red and white artifacts flooded Joseph's vision as he struggled to breathe with one lung. The Ripper's knife was lodged and as Joseph convulsed in pain, he turned hard, forcing the blade out of The Ripper's hand.

Through the miasma of pain, Joseph saw the opportunity and sliced at The Ripper's other tendon, sawing at it like a twig until it broke with a rubbery snap. The Ripper, The Master, Franco Valor, was down.

Joseph stood, the blade still sticking through his side. He took a deep, sick breath and finally said his line.

"Do you know my mother's real name?"

The Master couldn't reply, simply shook his head.

"It's better that way. Her real name was beautiful." Joseph said as blood from his sliced lung overcame his vocal chords. "I know it. I know it and I keep it a secret deep inside my heart." The Elephant Man started to weep. As he did, he tossed his blade away.
The Master watched, unable to make a decision. He had one last card to play.

With The Elephant Man still overcome with tears, The Ripper rose to his knees and shuffled to the edge of the train.

"Goodbye, Mr. Merrick. Goodbye sir." The Ripper said, omitting the slur "freak" for the first time. The Elephant Man looked through his bloody tears just in time to see The Ripper fall backwards into the darkness.

The train slowed and finally stopped, becoming silent enough for Joseph to hear his wheezing breaths. The train platform for Brighton activated to his right. Animatronic actors spoke pleasantries against a fake sunny backdrop.

"Good morning, I would like a ticket to London, please." A sunny faced female animatronic spoke into the ticket window.

"Very good, will you be traveling coach or first class?" The mechanical ticket taker asked, looking at the ledger as he spoke.

"Oh, first class. I've been saving up, you know." The female animatronic seemed almost giddy as Joseph limped past her. Several other robots went about their daily lives within the limitations of the train platform. Suddenly one of the old gentlemen animatronic turned 180 degrees and seemed to look right at Joseph.

"Joseph." The animatronic spoke in the voice of The Concierge. "Your blood pressure is dropping. Get on the shuttle car back to the stage!"

Joseph tried to speak, but another glob of blood came up from his lungs.

"Forget about The Master. Get your ass over here!" The animatronic surrogate for The Concierge commanded.

"OK." Joseph relented, realizing that he might not have the strength to get to the shuttle. If he couldn't do that, he would probably die. He realized that he might die anyway.

Joseph found the stairway leading to the shuttle and shuffled down it, pushing himself against the handrail and he descended. Suddenly, a rumbling sound followed by vibrations caused Joseph to lock his arm on the baluster. The giant rotating mechanism turned past two more station platforms until reaching one that was nothing but a blank space. A blank space with the symbol of the double oval. The hidden door to the secret tunnel slid open rudely. It was at this blank platform the simulation cradle that held the train fell away. A red light illuminated the tunnel followed by a jarring bell alarm.

Joseph watched as The City of Stalingrad hissed and slowly chugged forward into the unknown.

THE SPIRAL PATH

Joseph didn't remember how he got into the shuttle. He stared at the ceiling of the tunnel, resigned to the fact that he no longer had the strength to move.

There was a dull thud as part of his head prosthetic was ripped away as the tunnel tightened into a tight aperture.

When he woke, The Concierge was standing over him with a wheelchair. The Tread Setter was there too as were most of the audience, crammed into Whitechapel as far as he could see.

They spoke to him, but it sounded like noise. His ears thudded and drowned out the sounds.

Something seemed to be happening. Something involving him.

A nurse ran to him with a backpack. She kneeled before him and rifled through vials. She drew a dark medicine and injected him with it. (Joseph wondered why the knife was still in his lungs.

His hearing started to return. He got bits of it from the conversations around him. Something was going on involving The Master.

"We got the power back on. You're gonna be Ok." Tread told

him.

"Tessa?" He whispered.

"We went to fetch her. She's coming." It was the last thing he heard before everything went dark.

The Master piloted The City of Stalingrad onward through the darkness on a slightly sloping, spiral angle that the train struggled to navigate. He knew that the tunnel existed, but even he was unsure of what waited for him at the end.

He tore off his Ripper attire until he only had a t-shirt and pants.

Trying to shuffle on his knees had become intolerably painful as the tendons hung loose, bumping against nerves, sending bolts of agony through his lower extremities. Standing was out of the question.

"Joseph Merrick, The Elephant Man. Freak. Tool of Satan. Your revenge will never bring that whore back to you. Will never free you of that mangled visage that you call a body. Confucius said 'When planning revenge, first dig two graves.', but I go further. I want our graves combined so I can be with you, even in death. Goodbye, Mr. Merrick. Goodnight, my only worthy adversary."

An alarm sounded in the cabin of the train. The Master closed his eyes knowing that something was about to happen.

THE MOUNTAIN

The City of Stalingrad exploded out of the side of the mountain like a bullet. As its wheels came down, there was no track to take the train any farther. It was just the dark sandy soil that the wheels jammed into. The locomotive flipped on its side, leaving a huge scrape as it cut through the soil to its final stop, just shy of the cliff's edge leading to the ocean below.

For a moment, there was complete silence save for the hissing sound of leaking steam.

The drone shot out of a broken window and showed the audience in the stage below the fresh wreckage of The City of Stalingrad. The drone came closer to the train just as The Master reached to find a handhold.

Pulling himself through the shattered window, the man that had overcome Gaslight fell over the side with pitiful moans of despair. As he landed, he realized he had probably broken a rib. Inhaling was sharply painful now and the best he could do was to prop himself against the wreckage of the train. As the minutes passed, the drone grew closer to The Master until it was within his reach. It was now that he realized that there was one bit of performance remaining.

"To have dreams. To have dreams is to know pain. Have pity on those who try to live a dream. The dream itself becomes the addiction that blinds you. I never intended cross the boundaries into darkness, but I encountered, as dreamers will eventually encounter, a crossroads. It's at that crossroads that the darkness will come to you. You will be at that crossroads one day. That is where I will see you again. That is where I will see you again."

With that, the drone shattered, struck by a rock from a sling. Cut off from his audience, The Master, the man once called Franco Valor glanced up to see the people he tried to kill. Tessa approached him, sling still in her hand.

She kneeled down to The Master. With the hundreds of fellow Assets behind her, she spoke.

"The play is over. There is no one here who cares about your acting. They just wanted to know why their lives were worthless to you."

The Master had no response to this query.

THE BLACK ABSINTHE

Joseph woke in the hospital. He was naked. As he felt his face, he realized his makeup had been removed and he had been cleaned. A middle-aged nurse was injecting something into his right arm. She didn't seem surprised that he was awake.

He put his hand on the wound and didn't feel the knife. He took a deep breath and felt a sharp sting in his right lung, but was able to inhale again without that asymmetric sensation of breathing through a single lung.

The nurse brought in a pair of scrubs for him.

"Put these on. They're waiting for you." She said.

Where was he going? To his execution maybe? He dutifully put the prison-like clothes on and stood with some difficulty.

"Do you want a wheelchair?" The nurse asked. Joseph waved away the suggestion.

"Shoes would be good." Joseph said with a raspy voice.

"Be right back." The nurse returned later with a pair of slippers.

"That's all you have?" Joseph winced as the wound started aching again.

"Put them on. They're waiting for you." The nurse gestured to an open door.

Joseph put the slippers on and limped to the door, leaning on the jamb, trying to process what was ahead of him.

The hundreds of Gaslight customers that refused to follow The Master were there. Hundreds of others, some who Joseph recognized as the guards had their hands tied with rope and were being led to the elevator.

The crowd opened a hole for Joseph, A pathway that led to a single folding chair. Joseph felt a chill, still not understanding what was about to happen to him.

The Concierge appeared and gestured for Joseph to sit.
With accelerating dread, Joseph limped to the chair and sat, waiting to hear his fate. He glanced to his right and saw Tessa who had what Joseph read as a pained expression. Tread was next to her. Zie was watching The Concierge, only sneaking a quick glance at Joseph.

"Watch." The Concierge clicked on a remote control. The projection of rescue boats in the harbor loading the bound and unbound evacuees.
"No one will be kept here against their will again, except for one man." The Concierge clicked the remote again, revealing an infa-red image of The Master kneeling in the dim illumination of the basement. Joseph recognized the place immediately. It was the

basement dungeon. The Master was surrounded by the dead Assets, people that he had murdered.

"Say farewell to old Master. His reign has come to an end." With that, The Concierge clicked the remote control and the audience saw the last pitiful image of their old Master and his audience of his own making.

When Joseph looked down, the bartender from The Glass Paris approached him with a platter.
On it, a glass.
In it, Black Absinthe.
With every eye on him, Joseph froze. The Concierge whispered to him.
"Take it, you have nothing to fear. You are our new Master."

Made in the USA
Monee, IL
22 June 2023

36371204R00333